# PRIVILEGE

*Books by Leona Blair*


A WOMAN'S PLACE
WITH THIS RING
PRIVILEGE

# PRIVILEGE

*Leona Blair*

BANTAM BOOKS

TORONTO • NEW YORK • LONDON • SYDNEY • AUCKLAND

PRIVILEGE
*A Bantam Book / October 1986*

Grateful acknowledgment is made for permission to reprint the following:

Excerpt from "The Age of Anxiety" by W. H. Auden from *Collected Longer Poems* by W. H. Auden. Copyright 1934, 1937, 1941, 1942, 1943, 1944, 1946, 1947, © 1969 by W. H. Auden. Copyright renewed. Published by Random House. Reprinted by permission.

Verse 70, adapted, from "The Gospel of Thomas" in the *Nag Hammadi Library* in English translated by James M. Robinson. Copyright © 1978 by E. J. Brill. Reprinted by permission of E. J. Brill and Harper & Row, Publishers, Inc.

Excerpt from *Murder in the Cathedral* by T. S. Eliot. Copyright 1935 by Harcourt Brace Jovanovich, Inc.; renewed © 1963 by T. S. Eliot. Reprinted by permission of Harcourt Brace Jovanovich and Faber and Faber Publishers.

Excerpt from "Second Fig" by Edna St. Vincent Millay from *Collected Poems* by Edna St. Vincent Millay. Copyright 1922, 1950 by Edna St. Vincent Millay. Reprinted by permission.

**Library of Congress Cataloging-in-Publication Data**

Blair, Leona.
  Privilege.

  I. Title.
PS3552.L3463P74     1986     813'.54     85-48227
ISBN 0-553-05132-6

*Published simultaneously in the United States and Canada*

---

*Bantam Books are published by Bantam Books, Inc. Its trademark, consisting of the words "Bantam Books" and the portrayal of a rooster, is Registered in U.S. Patent and Trademark Office and in other countries. Marca Registrada. Bantam Books, Inc., 666 Fifth Avenue, New York, New York 10103.*

---

PRINTED IN THE UNITED STATES OF AMERICA

DH          0 9 8 7 6 5 4 3 2 1

*For Martha Friedman*

. . . and with special thanks to Jeanne Bernkopf, John Davy, Harvey McGregor, and John Addey

We would rather be ruined than changed.
We would rather die in our dread
Than climb the cross of the moment
And let our illusions die.

—W. H. AUDEN

# PRIVILEGE

# BOOK I

Safe upon the solid rock the ugly houses stand:
Come and see my shining palace built upon
the sand!

—EDNA ST. VINCENT MILLAY

# 1

"Emalie!" Her father's voice boomed up the stairs from the kitchen behind the store. "Wake up, I'm coming with your milk."

His voice erased her daydream of a handsome prince and a fairy castle. In her reverie her hair was spun gold, not dark chestnut, and her gray eyes azure blue the way a princess's eyes are supposed to be. Her father's voice pulled her back to her parents' bed in a section of Paris she did not yet know was a slum.

She felt very grand, lying in the big bed. This shabby room under its sloped ceiling was the best in the dark little house. In this room her mother had told stories of her girlhood on a farm in Alsace, speaking in an accent that echoed the province's German conquerors—"But now we're going to take it back!" her father bragged lately, eager for war. And here, in the patchy mirror of the battered old wardrobe, Emalie had watched herself grow up and had learned to retreat from her crowded, noisy world into fantasy.

"It's all your doing," Sylvie Bequier would complain loudly to her husband. "Calling her Princess! She has work to do!"

"Shut your mouth, woman," the father always replied with sullen authority. "This is my house, I'll call her what I please."

Today Emalie was feverish and her throat was so sore she could barely speak, but it was delicious to nurse her cold and spin her fantasies in the cozy warmth of the bedroom while her sisters were still at school. The voices of her father's customers, floating up to her from the dingy store downstairs, did not disturb her.

The only sound she had heard until her father roused her was the April rain drizzling on the roof. Maman had gone to see the curé and downstairs the store was empty. Even the raucous, turbulent Rue Momette, bisected by dark alleys where rats scuttled past the privies, was quiet. The street had settled down for its midday meal and the long siesta that followed it in France, no matter how poor the neighborhood. She heard her father roll down the wooden volets that protected his tiny grocery store. She heard him lock the door, then come through the kitchen and start up the stairs in his wooden clogs.

Jacques Bequier's head rose over the landing, and Emalie smiled at the big man with his red cheeks and his deep, rough voice. He carried a crock by its bamboo handle, and a steaming milk jug. He smiled back at her.

"Eh, bien, Princesse," he said, "are you any better?"

She nodded and stretched blissfully in the double bed. It was a lovely thing to be her father's favorite. His fierce temper was rarely turned on her, and he bragged about how clever the Sisters said she was, declaring that she would continue her lessons for as long as she liked, even until she was married.

"I have just the thing for you, ma beauté," he said, setting the jug and the crock down on the bedside table. "Some hot milk simmered with borage and honey and butter, and your mother fixed some white lard to rub on your chest."

He sat down on the bed, slid his hands under Emalie's arms and sat her up as if she were a feather. He untied the narrow strings that fastened her nightdress and pushed it down to her shoulders. Then he took two fingers of mixture from the crock. The strong odor of the camphorated oil and eucalyptus her mother had pounded into the lard was pleasant as her father's hands kneaded the grease into her flesh. She breathed in deeply to let the vapor ease the congestion in her chest.

Then she felt him push her gown farther down and knew that her round breasts were uncovered. She reddened and opened her eyes.

"Nice, eh?" he said, his hands stroking her breasts. "This will make you feel better. Sacré nom d'un nom, look at you! Fourteen and a woman already." His voice did not boom now, it was husky. His eyes looked strange.

She blushed painfully. "Papa, arrête, you mustn't," she said in her hoarse, cracked voice. She tried to pull her gown up over her breasts.

"I'm your father," he said, "sit still."

She was terrified of this stranger whose big, rough hands were pinching her nipples. She began to cry.

"Jésu," he muttered deep in his throat. Then he stood up abruptly and took off his belt. She cringed; he was going to beat her now—what had she done? But that was not why he had taken off his belt. His face told her why as he approached the bed.

She twisted away from him when he reached for her, but he pulled her down until she was flat on her back. One large forearm was pressed across her throat so that she could neither move nor speak, and his enormous hand grasped both her wrists. With his other hand he ripped the blankets from her, exposing her legs. His hand, still coated with grease, slid down over her. She was utterly helpless as he forced her thighs apart to invade her and she was maddened by her shame. She tried to kick him.

"Be still . . . let me . . ." he muttered, restraining her legs with his torso, touching her where no one had ever touched her. She could smell his sweat and the wine on his breath, could feel his hand and the sting of the camphorated grease on her secret flesh.

Then he hurt her, assaulting her with his turgid body. She was immobile under him, but something inside her barred his way and excited him to push harder against the barrier. When it broke she cried out from the pain, but it was a muffled cry that no one could hear, not even him because he was groaning. Then a last long growl came from him before he shuddered, panted, and lay still. It was over. She had seen dogs do this in the alleys of the Rue Momette, she had seen drunken men and women do it, and she knew it was over.

He pulled away from her and turned his back while he buttoned his trousers and replaced his belt. When he turned back, his eyes shifted, avoiding her face, her eyes.

*"Merde!"* he whispered. "You're bleeding on the sheet." He pulled her gown down and stuffed it between her legs just as her mother knocked on the back door of the shop. He leaned over her, his face inches from hers. "Keep your mouth shut, or I'll kill you," he said. He was menacing, all-powerful. "I warn you, not a word. You hear me?"

She nodded. Hastily he poured the milk, now tepid, into a tin cup and thrust it at her. The butter was bright yellow, congealed on the surface. "Drink that," he ordered as he started down the stairs. "Drink it!" Dominated by him, she obeyed, gagging on the coagulated butter. She heard her mother's voice and began to cry again, her sobs raucous and scratchy in her sore, congested chest, her face drenched with sweat and tears. She was frantic to get out of this place that had become a horror chamber to her, but there was nowhere for her to go.

"She had a nightmare from the fever," she heard her father say. "And she's got her *règles*, she's bleeding on the sheets. You ought to stay home and look after her instead of praying with that *sacré con de curé*."

In a few moments Sylvie Bequier came tiredly upstairs with a basin of warm water which she set behind a screen near the window. "Nightmares," she grumbled, "a great girl like you!" Then she saw Emalie's face and the rumpled bed and her eyes widened. For a brief, agonized moment mother and daughter looked at each other before Sylvie turned away to rummage in a cupboard. Her face was rigid when she handed Emalie a rag for the bleeding and a clean gown.

"Go and wash yourself," she said in a distant voice, jerking her head at the screen, "while I change the bed."

"Maman," Emalie sobbed, her voice so choked it was almost inaudible.

"Be still," Sylvie said, her mouth working as she stripped the bed, her hands trembling. Her next words were few but carried an unmistakable warning. "Don't say a word."

And Emalie knew she never would.

# 2

From the trolley Emalie heard the newsvendors shouting about a place called Ypres and watched as Parisians clustered around the kiosks on the quai. But the war made very little difference to Emalie—or to Paris, either, for that matter, since the Germans had been stopped at the Marne in September. Except for the uniforms of bright French red and blue or dull English khaki, there were no signs of war, no queues, no food shortages. The weather was mild and bright this fine autumn day, and people strolled and fished and sunned themselves on the cobbled walks along the Seine as if the capital had not been under siege a few weeks ago, as if the Germans were not still entrenched just sixty miles from Paris.

"*Bon Dieu*," the two drunken soldiers sitting behind her scoffed, "they were thirty miles closer before we made *le miracle de la Marne*."

Some of the passengers smiled at them indulgently—drunk or not, they were the poilus, the fighting infantry of France—but Emalie sat very quietly, clutching her reticule as the tram rattled and clanked along. She had to fight her own war and she no longer believed in miracles. She was aware of her father's constant appetite for her; he would force her again if he had the chance. She was careful not to smile, not to be alone in the house with him, or let him see her in her underthings. Her little sisters still climbed into the laundry tub behind the stove for a bath once a week, but Ema bathed in a basin in the dark after everyone was asleep, lest he see her when she was naked. She always felt dirty; she thought she would never feel clean again no matter how much she washed herself.

"Did you hear that, Mademoiselle?" one of the soldiers asked her with tipsy glee. "There's a great battle under way at Ypres, but what the hell, you're safe in Paris."

"And we're right here to protect you, *ma petite dame*," the other poilu said. He put his hand on Emalie's shoulder and leaned around the seat to look at her.

"Leave me alone, I'm not your little lady," she said, flinching away from his hand and the smell of his breath. *"Fichez-moi la paix."* It was street language, rather rough than dirty, and the two men laughed with the exaggeration of wine.

The tram came to a clanging halt at the next stop and Emalie got off hastily, even though she was quite a distance from her destination. Still, there was the lovely autumn sunshine on her face and she smiled faintly as she walked.

She was often called a pretty girl but she was, more accurately, a girl who never went unnoticed. Her erect posture and the economy of her movements were rare in the young, and her gray eyes seemed to hide whatever she felt behind a direct and often disconcerting gaze. Her burnished brown hair was held back by a black bow, and the slightly battered hat she wore shaded a wide forehead, an angular jaw that made her face less than perfectly oval, and a decided chin.

"You look so stern these days," Sister Marie Angélique had lamented only yesterday. "Where is that sweet little face I have so loved to teach?"

But Sister Marie Angélique knew nothing of what pain and shame it was to be a woman. She had never felt rigid male flesh thrusting savagely inside her, tearing her open. The Sisters came daily from their convent to teach the girls of the parish until their parents demanded that they stop doing lessons and earn their keep. Emalie's father no longer boasted that his favorite daughter could stay in school as long as she liked; now he wanted her to work in the store with him.

"I'll run away before I'll work in that store," Emalie had told the Sister passionately.

"But child, you must obey your father; he needs you to help with the household expenses."

"No! I'll run away, I swear by the Virgin, or I'll hang myself."

It was because of the nun, unsuspecting but alarmed by her pupil's vehemence, that Emalie was on her way to the great fashion house of Thiboux, where Sister Marie Angélique's niece managed the sewing room.

"Long hours," the nun had warned Emalie, "hard work. But you will learn something of the world, *ma petite* Emalie. You have never been far from the safety of your home, dear child. You must pray to the *Sainte Vierge* to keep you pure." The nun's hand had stroked Ema's hair. "You're such a bright child, I wish I might have gone on teaching you."

Lessons won't set me free, Emalie thought as she turned into a wide, clean avenue; money will. She looked in wonder at the great stone houses set in leafy parks behind iron gates, and she prayed, not for the purity she had already lost, but that one day she would escape from the Rue Momette to a house on a street like this and the clean scent of green trees everywhere.

She rang the bell at the number she had been given—there was no indication that this was not a private residence—and was severely reprimanded by a uniformed maid and sent around to the service entrance. Her carefully pressed black serge schooldress felt all the more shabby when she found Sister Marie Angélique's niece, whom she had been instructed to address as Mademoiselle Hortense. Mademoiselle Hortense, buxom and with arched brows that gave her a look of constant surprise, was very elegantly dressed in black taffeta and white organdy ruching.

"You may work today," she declared, doubtful but not unkind, "and we shall see if you get on. We are overwhelmed already by the spring collections. Who would think there was a war on?" And Mademoiselle Hortense rustled away.

Emalie's job was first to keep the floors clean and spread with fresh muslin so that the luscious silks and satins would stay pristine as the workers sewed upon them. Then she must collect every hook and button, every plume and pearl and bead and sequin that remained on the sewing tables or fell to the floor. She must do it quietly and unobtrusively, as directed by Mademoiselle Hortense, since "Madame Thiboux cannot abide noise." Next Ema must sort the trimmings she had collected and store them for reuse, putting the colored beads and buttons into appropriate compartments in the right boxes. Finally she must look through every scrap of fabric from all of the cutting rooms, fold away anything over one metre long, sort the rest according to size and carry the heavy bales down to the rag merchant's cart when he called. Madame Thiboux, it seemed, was fanatically opposed to waste of any kind. When required, Emalie must also carry refreshments to the clients in the dressing rooms, "but not today," Mademoiselle Hortense decreed. "If you are hired you will wear a uniform."

Emalie worked as quickly as she could until lunchtime. She ate the bread and cheese she had brought, and after a whispered consultation with a young seamstress named Clothilde, she was shown a water closet. It was the height of luxury to her; she was accustomed to a privy in the alley behind the store.

She was weary by the end of the day but reluctant to go back home. She crossed her fingers when she approached Mademoiselle Hortense to ask if she had been hired.

"Yes, yes, you'll do, Marie Angélique was right. You must be here by seven every morning. Now then." Mademoiselle Hortense took a shapeless black uniform from the rack where the seamstresses hung their smocks and held it up to Emalie. "You will wear this while you work, and a cap and apron when you serve in the dressing rooms. You must wash your uniform once a week—and yourself every day. And you must never eat garlic. Madame Thiboux will not allow malodorous persons to serve her clients. That is all, you may go. Well, what is it now?"

"I do wash every day," Emalie objected, blushing hotly. "I am not mal . . . what you said."

"Tut, tut, who said you were?" The eyebrows soared even higher. "Those are the instructions for everyone who works here. Madame Thiboux is most *exigeante* on the subject. Now, run away, girl, I have a million things to do."

Emalie went, tears of embarrassment in her eyes. She had been treated like a dirty, ignorant peasant just because she was poor, and she would not go back there! But by the time she reached the end of the clean, beautiful avenue, she knew she would be back tomorrow morning. Thiboux would keep her away from her father for six days a week, from early morning until suppertime, when her mother and sisters were always at home. And Sister Marie Angélique had promised to teach her English by reading the Bible with her on Sundays after mass.

She climbed onto the tram, calculating rapidly. She would earn seventy-five sous a day—the soldiers at the front were paid only five!— and after she had saved enough for a new pair of shoes she would buy some remnants from Thiboux and make herself a decent winter suit. She hated to sew, although she was good with a needle, but no one would ever again think she was smelly and stupid because she looked poor.

"Where were you all day?" her father growled when she got home, but she did not answer.

"Sister Marie Angélique found her a good place with her niece at a fashion house," her mother said. "Set the table, Emalie, I'll be right down."

"Sister Marie Angélique," he mumbled while his wife disappeared up the stairs. Even Jacques Bequier would not dare to challenge the wisdom of the church. "What does she know about it, your Sister Marie Angélique? You'll be working with a flock of loose women." His eyes, already heavy with wine, watched Emalie's body bend and straighten as she moved about setting the supper table, and inside herself she shook with fear.

# 3

In a week Emalie was able to do her job without thinking about it. The redoubtable Madame Thiboux never appeared, and soon Emalie felt comfortable with the women, who gossiped with relish as they pumped the treadles of their machines or placed the finishing stitches by hand, making the inside of each dress as beautiful as the outside. They gossiped about Thiboux's wealthy clients, with their husbands and lovers, their gorgeous houses and equipages, their travels and parties and assignations. It sounded wonderful to Emalie; only an innocent like Sister Marie Angélique would call such a life wicked. The world was an evil place, anyway; as well be rich in it as poor.

By the time the year turned she was reading the columns in *Le Gaulois* and the other gossip sheets. She knew who gave the best dinner parties and what lady had taken a new lover or gone to the country for a "cure"— which usually meant an abortion. All day long Emalie listened to the women tell scandalous stories about the wives and mistresses of the most powerful men in France, and she laughed, along with Clothilde and the others, at how easily a clever woman could manipulate men.

Emalie was awed by the beauty of Thiboux's pampered clientele, whether it sprang from a natural harmony of feature or from that chic, so particular to Frenchwomen, that contrived to make the world applaud glaring imperfections; only the French would describe a woman as *une belle laide*—a woman whose startling homeliness was beauty of a kind. She watched these pampered women lounging in their magnificent undergarments while she served them tisanes in the fitting rooms. The skin of their arms and breasts above pink broché corsets and handmade silk drawers and petticoats was as delicate as Madame Thiboux's Limoges teacups, and the scents of fine-milled soap and expensive perfume filled the air about them.

To Emalie these wives and mistresses were like goddesses, splendid and utterly careless of ordinary morality. They ignored the church's interdicts against fornication and adultery, but they had not been punished as far as Emalie could see—quite the contrary—nor did they seem any the worse for the sexual favors they bartered for all this privilege. She soon understood that sex was a game to them, that they used the power it gave them over men. It was the only weapon women had, Emalie concluded with disgust.

"It is a fact of life," one of the women said, catching sight of Ema's expression. "When it comes to a woman, a man thinks with his *zizi*." She rolled her eyes suggestively. "A woman who doesn't take advantage of that is a fool."

"It's not so bad, really," Clothilde added. "Sometimes it's quite pleasant—or you can just lie there and think of France, or your new spring costume."

It seemed that for most of *le gratin*—the upper crust—of French society, the maintenance of a fashionable wardrobe was the most time-consuming activity, with yachting, hunting, and gambling not far behind. But sex was their preferred pastime, and in Paris there were bodies aplenty to satisfy every variety of it.

"I don't see why men bother to marry at all," Emalie protested. She was accustomed by now to the laughter that greeted most of her remarks as she listened and swept and gathered in the sewing room.

"To have children, *petite ignorante*. Once they produce a few legitimate heirs to inherit their titles and their property, they can amuse themselves as they like. So can their wives, but far more discreetly, of course."

"You must understand, Emalie, that a Frenchman of fashion takes his mistress seriously. He installs her in a house and buys her a lavish wardrobe. He entertains his friends at her establishment rather than his wife's—the atmosphere is so much gayer in the demimonde."

To Emalie's further astonishment, it seemed that any girl could succeed as a mistress, no matter how poor she might be. All she needed was a pretty face and a willing body to be instantly, staggeringly rich.

"You would be a perfect mistress, Emalie." A roar of laughter greeted Ema's blush. "*Mais oui, mais oui*, you are *très coquette* in the new suit you made yourself. *Quelle jolie forme!*" She described Emalie's figure with her hands. "But you are too somber, *ma petite*. Here, try a red flower in your corsage. You could have a lover"—the woman snapped her fingers—"like that!"

Emalie retreated to where her boxes and sacks of cloth were kept and sorted her scraps briskly. She could not bring herself to follow the women's advice, although she believed everything they said. They were women with no illusions but they had been very kind to her; they had

helped her choose fabric and fit her black alpaca suit, praising her skill at
sewing. But they did not want the same things she did. They were willing
to work here for lower wages than they would have earned in a factory
because they could buy Thiboux remnants to make their clothes; they certainly preferred it to the lonely domestic drudgery of most women. But
what really made such loyal slaves of them, Emalie soon realized, was
their link, however tenuous, to the fashionable world. It dazzled them.
They would never have sumptuous clothes and houses or fine food and
wines, but the reflected glory of those who did made their drab lives bearable.

Reflected glory was not enough for Emalie, although she felt its allure.
She had already seen that the way to the top in the fashion industry was
an extraordinary talent for design—and even then a girl would need a
wealthy patron to provide the money. Emalie had discovered that she had
good taste but no talent for design, for the creation of a new fashion out of
thin air. What was more, she hated to sew, however well she did it, so why
should she labor for five years as a scrap girl only to graduate to the sewing rooms? If she stayed at Thiboux, she would never be able to leave the
Rue Momette—unless she married, and the thought of that was still revolting to her when she had been at Thiboux for over a year.

Men looked at her eagerly as she went back and forth from work, but
her demeanor was severe and forbidding. She was sixteen now. She had
grown to be a little taller than was fashionable, but she looked well in her
winter suit and her summer ensemble of ecru sacking. Her old school
shoes were too short and hurt her feet, but she refused to spend any of
her precious horde on new ones, not now. She finally had a plan for her
future that required every penny she did not spend on carfare and bare
necessities: she would be a secretary in an office!

She would wear her skirt and shirtwaist all day, not a shapeless black
uniform. She would sit at a neat desk and type important letters to men of
affairs while someone else cleaned the floors! Then, too, professional
men were serious citizens, not given to the brutality of the poor or the
vices of the nobility. Everyone at Thiboux ridiculed office work as dull and
bourgeois, but she confided her plan to Sister Marie Angélique.

"It is a sensible change, my child," the nun sighed. "With no men left to
marry, you girls must earn a living. But where will it end? What will become of all those women without husbands?"

Emalie had no time to worry about the future of French womanhood.
The war that had begun two years ago was still a distant calamity to her,
although in Paris there were more reminders of it. Women were driving
trucks and trams now, running railroad switchboxes, and delivering mail.
The network of muddy trenches that stretched from the Swiss border to

Nieuport on the Belgian coast was called the Western Front, but the soldiers who came to Paris on leave—dressed in horizon blue now because
their red caps and trousers had made them such easy targets—called it
"the mincer."

The mincer affected her in one very vital way; it was grinding up shop
assistants and law students and office clerks along with the farmers, con-
ductors, and factory workers, who had already perished by tens of thousands. The newspapers Emalie collected from the Thiboux fitting rooms
advertised every day for stenographers and typists: "Women are invited
to apply," they all said. Some of them even said "cordially." There were
schools that taught the skills she would need, and Emalie had already
selected one and begun saving rigorously for it. In another month she
would have enough for the registration fee; her salary would pay her
weekly tuition for night classes after that.

When she was given her wages at the end of July 1916, she went into the
water closet at Thiboux and put the coins into the leather purse she always wore tied around her waist, even when she slept. She had just
enough money to begin, and she walked to the tram hardly noticing the
pain in her feet, feeling closer to happiness than she had for over two
years.

She saw her father through the store windows when she got home and
she went in through the alley door, calling up to her mother to be sure she
was there. In the tiny back bedroom Emalie took off her suit and hung it
neatly inside a garment bag made of muslin scraps she had spirited out of
Thiboux and stitched painstakingly together. She hung the bag on a hook,
put on an old cotton dress and an apron and crossed the kitchen into the
store. Jacques Bequier insisted she help him whenever she could—"to
earn your keep," he growled, but it was because he wanted to look at her
in that sullen, nasty way he had.

He was weighing out onions and talking about the battle raging at the
Somme with one of the two customers in the store. Barely acknowledging
him, she measured out two hectos of grated cheese and wrapped two
eggs in a piece of newspaper for the second customer. When both had
gone she set about wiping the cutting board and counters. There was a
heavy silence until he spoke.

"What's wrong with your legs? You walk like a lame cow."

"My shoes are too short," Emalie said, not looking at him. She moved
farther down the counter, out of the overhead light into the shadows near
the herring barrels.

He took some money from the till. "Come here," he said, holding it out
to her, "here's money for new shoes." When she did not go to him he put
it on the counter and watched her hesitate before she came forward swiftly

into the light and picked it up. "You see?" he said cajolingly. "I give you everything you want. You're still my princess. Come and kiss your old papa."

He waited, but she had retreated into the shadows.

"I'm your father," he said, his deep voice soft and persuasive. "I didn't mean to hurt you. I only want to teach you about life." He took a step toward her. "Be kind to me, Ema," he whispered, "it doesn't hurt after the first time, you'll see."

She picked up a slicing knife from the counter. "Don't come near me," she whispered from the shadows. "If you touch me, I'll kill you."

The door to the store opened. She dropped the knife with a small clatter and went back to the kitchen.

# 4

## COURS DE STENODACTYLOGRAPHIE

The big letters made an arch on the second story window on the Boulevard St. Michel. MADAME DANIELLE LARCHET, GÉRANTE was painted beneath it.

Emalie went up a narrow flight of stairs and the same legend in smaller letters led her to a door. She could hear the clatter of writing machines in an adjoining room as soon as she opened it.

"Please take a seat," a gaunt woman said over her shoulder. She was standing behind the desk, talking into a wall telephone. A small plaque on the desk announced that she was the Danielle Larchet who ran the school.

Emalie did not sit down. She had been taught by Sister Marie Angélique to stand in the presence of her superiors. The woman was as neat and angular as the buff-colored room. Her hair was pulled so tightly into a chignon that it raised the skin at her neck and temples into a neat row of tiny protuberances. Jet earrings dangled inkily from her ears. A bunch of keys were visible at her waist, as if she were the keeper of a dungeon. When at last Madame Larchet replaced the receiver and turned to Emalie, she revealed an utterly homely face with downward lines around her mouth and chin. Her only other adornment was a gold-rimmed locket of black enamel pinned to the bodice of her starched and pleated blouse. Her small black eyes were chilly as she tilted her head to one side.

"What may I do for you, Mademoiselle . . . ?" The woman sat down at her desk and waited for some identification.

"Bequier, Emalie Anne. I would like to register for the shorthand-typing course, Madame Larchet."

Danielle Larchet studied her. This girl looked very young and too poor to buy a decent lunch, much less to pay for a course. Her gray suit was well cut and of excellent material, but by contrast her handbag had defied any attempts to polish it, and her gloves had been repeatedly darned as, Madame Larchet supposed, her black lisle hose and every stitch of her underwear had been. Still, the white collar and cuffs that frosted the suit were spotless and crisp with starch. The girl's shining hair was piled high under a small black boater trimmed with a black and white ribbon, and her shoes were new. Her face was intelligent, the features strong but finely drawn. Danielle was taken by her large gray eyes—although a man would certainly notice her mouth or her figure first.

Bewildered by the woman's silence, Emalie opened her worn black purse. "I have a note here from my teacher," she began, but Madame Larchet shook her head.

"This is not a *lycée*," she said gruffly. "It is open to anyone who wants to enroll."

"Oh, I do, Madame," Emalie assured her fervently. "I only waited until I could save enough." She stopped abruptly and clasped her gloved hands in embarrassment at having mentioned money. A real lady would not speak of money.

Where had she got the money—and that suit and the shoes, Madame Larchet wondered, and then thought again how lovely she was despite her slenderness and pallor. It occurred to her that perhaps . . . but she rejected that idea. This was not the sort of girl who would sell her body to the military. She had a luminous quality about her, like her eyes and her complexion, and, Danielle brought herself up sharply, all of that was worth precisely nothing in the school's till. "Please sit down, Mademoiselle," Danielle said, waving a hand. "There is the matter of tuition."

Emalie sat. "I am prepared to pay weekly," she said.

"And the registration fee," the woman pushed on relentlessly.

"I have it here," Emalie said proudly. "Twenty francs, just as it said in *Le Figaro*."

"Ah, but you see," Madame Larchet began, then stopped while the girl took a pile of change from a battered coin purse. The school's registration fee had just been increased, but the coin purse was obviously empty now. Madame Larchet reminded herself that she was a lone widow. "The registration fee has been increased," she said.

Emalie's lips went white. "But that can't be," she said, shaking her head.

"I assure you it is," Madame Larchet almost whispered, suddenly ashamed of herself.

The girl's head moved as if she had been struck. "I can't pay any more," she whispered. "This is all I have."

"Then—I regret—you must wait until you have saved more."

"No!" Emalie turned back, her gray eyes dark and brimming with tears. "I can't wait. I've waited too long already." Her voice broke. "You don't understand," she began, then shook her head again. "You don't understand."

The girl was desperate, not merely ambitious. Danielle Larchet understood desperation.

"Mademoiselle," she said, leaning across the desk and added, when the stricken girl did not respond, "Emalie, listen to me. I will accept this, it is enough for you to begin." She patted her prominent nose with a black-bordered handkerchief as the girl's gray eyes began to shine again, and said, "but you know it is not refundable and you must still pay for your classes by the week."

Emalie nodded, her smile radiant. It was a devastating smile, Danielle thought, it had her whole heart in it.

"Now you must fill in this form," Madame Larchet went on, replacing her handkerchief in the cuff of her blouse and trying to be formal again, "and report for your first class on Monday night at eight punctually." While the girl wrote her name and address on the card, Madame Larchet rustled her papers and wondered what had possessed her to break her one unbreakable rule. She had struggled long for the small security she had. Extending charity to lovely young girls was better left to women more blessed with life's bounties than Danielle Larchet had been. She had buried the loutish, pinchpenny Monsieur Larchet a year ago with gratitude for her deliverance, but Emalie Bequier, at once so determined and so vulnerable, moved her in a way she could not define and chose not to resist.

She read the card Emalie gave her. "*Très bien*, all is in order," she said, but she knew the Rue de la Pompe, knew this shabby girl had never lived there, except perhaps as a servant. "*Au revoir*, Mademoiselle," she said. "Until Monday."

Emalie walked to the door and opened it. "Thank you, Madame Larchet," she said with feeling to the woman watching her. "I will never forget your kindness."

"Pray do not speak of it." Danielle was embarrassed by sentiment.

"Very well, Madame," Emalie said, her smile flashing again. "But I'll always remember it." She stood for a moment, then closed the door behind her.

Danielle Larchet's hands smoothed her strained hair, touched her too-prominent nose and wide, thin mouth, then dropped to her flat, sturdy chest. What must it be like, she wondered, to look like that? Then she shook her head and went back to the papers on her desk.

# 5

"No," Emalie said firmly. "I won't." She kept her eyes on the untouched soup before her. Her sisters stopped eating, waiting to see how long it would take their father to punish this defiance. Emalie sat near him in the place he insisted she occupy.

"You'll do as you're told," he ordered, noisily spooning up soup. "You're past sixteen now. You had too much schooling in the first place. Look what you're turning into. I won't have you out on the streets until all hours. You'll work in the store."

"No," Emalie said clearly. She watched a cockroach inch along the rim of the table, and her disgust with it, and him, sustained her.

She felt him looking at her with the cruel smile that always preceded his explosions. "So *Mademoiselle la Princesse* expects to live here free while she does as she likes, is that it?" He reached out a hand and patted her head, as if in fatherly affection.

She moved away from his hand. "When I finish this course I'll be able to find a real job, in an office." The roach, brown and shining, had stopped its progress. Its feelers waved and her knotted stomach churned.

Her father's counterfeit laughter flooded the room. Then he shouted, "And the money for the course? How will you pay it?" He grasped her arm, shaking her.

She shouted back at him, furious herself. "I earned the registration fee and I'll earn the rest." She twisted her arm away from him.

His fist hit the scarred surface of the wooden kitchen table, making the plates dance, the soup slop, the roach skate down the leg of the table. "You should have been working here, for me! Every cent you earned is my money and you can hand it over right now."

"Go to the devil," Emalie said. "I've already paid the registration fee and they won't refund it. I start Monday night." She would not look at him.

He stood, his hands going threateningly to the buckle of his belt. "You little slut, you won't be able to walk when I finish with you," he said.

She raised her head and he stopped fumbling with the buckle. Her gaze went from his eyes to his crotch, then back to his face with contempt and undiluted hatred.

"You devil," he whispered, crossing himself.

She said nothing. Her gray eyes blazed at him.

"You're a devil!" He plunged through the curtain into the store. They heard the faint clink of glass and knew he had taken two bottles of red wine from the shelf. "I give the orders here and I say you work for me! Or from now on you'll pay room and board, d'you hear?" he shouted on his way through the kitchen to the back door. The door slammed behind him. *"Ici c'est moi qui commande,"* he shouted again, his voice dwindling away down the alley.

There was silence in the kitchen until the mother stirred. "Marie, Babette, finish!" she ordered the girls. "There's still the floor to wash and the ironing to do." She said nothing to Emalie, pretending not to notice her rigid body and her untouched supper. She poured some wine into a tumbler and set it in front of Emalie, but the sour smell of the *gros rouge* was revolting and Emalie shook her head.

Sylvie shooed the girls into the store with their brooms and cleared the table, stacking the dishes in a deep wooden tub. "Ema," she said, nodding her head toward the stove, and Emalie brought the heavy kettle of hot water and half-filled the dishtub, adding cold water from the pump near the sink.

"You'll have to pay him," Sylvie whispered, her eyes on the curtain between them and the two girls. She touched a graying dishmop to a cake of yellow soap and swilled the dishes indifferently.

"I need every cent I make, he knows that! He's trying to stop me, but if he keeps on, I'll tell the curé everything," Emalie said, her voice like steel. "I'll tell Sister Marie Angélique too."

Sylvie shook her head but said nothing, her lips white.

"Why do you live with him?" Emalie demanded, her voice dripping with scorn. "How can you sleep with him? With that pig?"

Sylvie leaned over the tub, her shoulders shaking. "He's my husband," she said. "It's my duty."

"Who says it is?"

"The curé."

"That old man in skirts? What does he know about rape?"

"I don't know what you're talking about," Sylvie said, her eyes darting to the curtain again. "For God's sake, be still!"

"I will not be still!" Emalie's whisper was cutting. "I despise you as much as I do him."

She stopped when Babette came into the kitchen to pour warm water from the kettle into a pail. The girl took a mop from behind the stove and then looked from her mother to Emalie curiously. "He'll beat you," she said to her sister without any particular feeling.

"Take the pail and get out," her mother said.

"He will, princess or not," Babette insisted.

"Get out of here, you little bitch," Emalie shouted, and the girl went, tossing her head. Emalie turned to her mother.

"You have money hidden upstairs. All I need is one gold piece," she said in a rush as Sylvie shook her head violently. "It'll pay for the course so I can pay him his rotten food and board. He'll never miss it."

Sylvie hesitated.

"When I get a job I'll pay it back. I have to get out of here or I'll kill him, I swear it. Then everyone will know." She grasped her mother's arm. "If you don't give it to me, I'll take it, I'll take it all, everything, and run away. I could have done that already!"

Sylvie dried her hands on her apron. "Come with me—but be quiet," she said, leading the way upstairs. She lit the lamp and, taking a pair of long, pointed scissors from her workbasket, rolled back the thin mattress of the double bed. Carefully she snipped at the stitches in one corner, making an opening just large enough for the small purse she pulled out of it. She opened it and Emalie gasped at the little cache of gold napoleons.

"How did you get so many?"

"We saved to buy them, sou by sou, since the day we were married."

"Holy Virgin, there's enough there to have got us all away from here! What's money for, if not that?"

"It's for war and sickness, not fancy clothes and houses." She held out one piece, and Ema took it, feeling the small gold coin like a benediction in her palm. Sylvie's mouth worked. "Now give me my needle."

Ema watched her mother's rough red hands sew up the corner, replace the mattress, and smooth the bedclothes. At the sight of those hands a wave of compassion swept over Emalie, a woman's anguish for the plight of another powerless woman, and with it a yearning for love that tore at her more than her ravished innocence.

"Maman, please," she began, an unbearable longing in her to be close, to be cherished; but her mother shook her head.

"That's all I can give you," Sylvie said, starting down the stairs. "Don't say another word."

"No, Maman," Emalie said, bitterness overwhelming her again. Her silence had been bought and paid for. The bargain was concluded.

# 6

---

Emalie rose at five o'clock every morning so that she could leave the house before her father awakened from his mercifully besotted sleep. She still avoided him, but she was no longer the helpless child she had been, or the timid scrap girl at Thiboux. For three months now she had been a secretary at Saxon, Vaillant, Merchant Bankers.

Saxon, Vaillant did not open its doors until eight o'clock, but Ema always had a café au lait and a roll at Cesar's on the Rue de Rivoli and then walked to the bank in the Place Vendôme, surely the best address in Paris.

She put water on the stove to heat and went out to the privy, mastering her distaste. When she came back to the dilapidated kitchen she washed with the warm water, listening intently for any sounds from upstairs. She dressed quickly in her freshly laundered underwear and her navy blue suit. Clothilde still bought fabric from Thiboux for her, and Ema had made herself a new suit and three shirtwaists. Today she chose the white cotton and a crisp cravat of navy and red striped taffeta from the precious box of trimmings she had taken piece by piece from Thiboux—in lieu of a decent salary, she told herself. She had black cotton gloves and stockings and she had found a decent handbag of real leather at a flea market. She swept her hair into a knot and tucked a scarlet feather into the band of her navy blue felt hat.

When she was dressed she went into the store and made a lunch of buttered bread and cheese, then wrapped her warmest black shawl around her and left quietly by the back door, walking along the Rue Momette to the dusty square, where a few trees struggled to survive the winter. She waited at the tram stop opposite the church.

A trickle of black-clad women, clasping rosaries, was entering the church for mass. Almost every family in France wore mourning in this third year of the war. It was not going well, and the poilus on leave from the front were no longer content merely to scratch their cropped heads in astonishment over the capital's insouciant joie de vivre. The butcher's son and the cobbler's nephew, home on leave, had whispered about mutiny.

Emalie thought they were right to complain, however much she hated to listen. The trenches might be on another planet for all the notice she took of the war—except that she owed her job to it. But *Sainte Vierge*, it was not her fault! She cringed when she heard about rotten food and no water to wash in for weeks on end. "Nothing except that *merde* they feed us," the nephew said, "about glory and honor."

Emalie shook her head. She had no time to ponder the honor of men. The escape from herself and a father whose lust for her was almost palpable was all she could think about when she wasn't working. She had studied hard at the *Cours Larchet*, and Danielle, unable to resist a girl so quick and so eager, had helped Emalie become an accomplished stenographer-typist in record time. "Before you waste away to a shadow," Danielle had said. "You can't go on forever, working all day and studying half the night."

Madame Larchet valued her own privacy and kept a certain distance between them, but she was Emalie's only friend. Sister Marie Angélique was everyone's friend, and the girls at Thiboux were no longer interested in her friendship, except for Clothilde. Ema listened attentively to Danielle's instructions on dress and table manners and office procedures and especially on how to succeed in a business world hostile to women.

"You must polish your business English," Madame Larchet counseled. "Here is a book on proper form for letters. Above all," she said when it was time to make this very blue suit for Ema's first interview, "you must look the part. Better two shirtwaists of good fabric than a dozen cheap ones. Never, never flirt! If you do, a man will immediately assume that because he hires you he can take you to bed. He will try anyway."

That warning came as no surprise to Emalie after what she had learned about men at Thiboux. She listened and studied, determined to work at one of the better offices in Paris. In December, just before Emalie and the century turned seventeen years old, she was hired by Saxon, Vaillant because of her skills and her fluent English—and because she looked soberly chic and smiled coquettishly at the young man she would assist. As a result he overlooked her lack of experience.

The bank was privately owned, the Paris Vaillants having been united by marriage to the London Saxons some eighty years before. Now, three months later, Emalie was still awed by the hushed grandeur of the place, but she was no longer nervous about her work or what kind of impression she made on the rest of the staff. Much to her delight, they called her a snob, although never to her face. She was the assistant, after all, to Henri Vaillant's private secretary.

The tram rumbled into the Square Momette. "I'll leave here for good someday," Emalie told one of the little trees before she climbed aboard. "And no one will ever know I had anything to do with this place."

At a few minutes before eight she was approaching the elegant little banking house along with its thirty-odd clerical employees. There were a few elderly men, but the rest were women. They were not like the gossips at Thiboux, ribald and warm-hearted. The younger girls were constantly nervous about their work, as Emalie had been at first, but they were incapable of hiding it. A few, who felt they should have had her job, were cool and sour. Emalie was distantly polite to everyone, but she went out to eat her lunch on a bench in the Tuileries whenever the weather permitted. Or she read an English novel while she ate in the cloakroom and then walked along the Rue de Rivoli, longing for the beautiful things in the shop windows, until she went into Cesar's for her coffee.

She had decided to make no friends at work; she had nothing to gain from people no better off than she was—and they might discover where she really lived. She gave Saxon, Vaillant the same address on the Rue de la Pompe she had given Danielle, that of a pretty apartment building she used to pass on her way to Thiboux. A flat in that building was her dream castle now. She had been brutally wrenched from her other castle years ago.

She went through the bank's marble foyer and up the broad stairway, hanging her hat and shawl in the cloakroom before proceeding to her desk. Walking to her desk was the favorite part of her day; it convinced her that she was really here, a part of this better world.

She went along a row of executive office doors, still marveling at the deep plush chairs and Turkish carpets, the polished woods and tasseled velvet draperies and the silk-shaded lamps. She had heard of this kind of luxury in the Thiboux sewing room, but she had never seen it or touched it before she entered Saxon, Vaillant.

Her desk stood between two windows at the end of the corridor. There was a door on either side; one led to Henri Vaillant's office, the other was François Martin's. He was private secretary to Vaillant and Emalie's immediate superior.

Martin emerged from his office almost immediately, carrying a sheaf of papers. He was a pale man in his early thirties with a small mustache, lank brown hair, and wire-rimmed spectacles. Martin was very conscious of his exalted position: Henri Vaillant was the director of the bank's Paris branch and his opposite number in London was Sir James Saxon, a baronet. François Martin took to heart this tenuous connection to a title.

"Monsieur Vaillant has written out the terms of this trust in English," François said, handing her the papers. "You can start with that."

"*Oui*, Monsieur Martin," Emalie said. Vaillant could have dictated directly to her, but it would accomplish nothing to say so to François; she must find the opportunity to tell Vaillant herself, as if inadvertently. She smiled demurely at François, and after a moment he smiled back, dropping his lordly manner.

What an ass you are, she thought.

He leaned over her desk. "Mademoiselle," he began, and paused. "Emalie?"

"Yes, Monsieur," she said, rolling paper into her typewriter and beginning to type rapidly. She was not going to acknowledge his advances, not until she wanted something from him.

He drew back, confused by the sudden change in her manner, and retired to his office. "Be as quick as you can with that," he ordered.

I would be better at your job than you are, Emalie thought, clattering away.

Maybe the army would take him, the generals must need secretaries to write their dispatches. She moved uncomfortably in her chair. Holy Mary, she didn't want him to get killed. A nice, safe billet behind the lines would be just the thing.

The army had taken her father but not, unfortunately, to the front. He worked for the army quartermaster corps in a depot on the outskirts of Paris, stealing almost as much as he shipped to the soldiers.

She looked up. An English lieutenant was coming along the corridor, his cap held formally under his arm. She guessed at once that he was Julian Saxon, the London baronet's son. The girls in the cloakroom had whispered that he had been married a few months ago, just before he came out to France for active service. They called him *le bel anglais*—and he was certainly the best-looking man, English or otherwise, Emalie had ever seen.

He was not unusually tall, but his stride and his bearing made him seem so. His uniform—wide-belted tunic, breeches, polished leather boots—was as elegant as any frock coat she had seen strolling around the Place Vendôme, but it was his face as well as the way he walked that made her sit so still as he came closer. His thick dark hair was parted on the side, not slicked straight back with pomade in the current fashion. He was clean-shaven, with a high forehead, a straight nose, and a well-defined mouth. His complexion was fair, without the high color of some English officers she had seen on leave in Paris.

His face was almost too perfect, like a painting, and its immobility convinced her that he was haughty as, she supposed, a baronet's son should be, until he was close enough for her to see his eyes. They were deepset and almost black, but there was a greater darkness behind them and she thought for the merest second that it was not haughtiness that made his face so still and distant, it was the control he exercised to mask whatever he felt, just as she did.

They looked at each other in silence for an instant. The darkness in his eyes flickered and changed and the split second of affinity vanished as if it had never been.

"Good morning, Mademoiselle, I'm Julian Saxon. Monsieur Vaillant is expecting me." His French was unaccented.

"Yes, sir, I'll tell him you're here."

She pressed the buzzer on her desk and spoke to Henri Vaillant through a cone-shaped mouthpiece. Saxon vanished into Vaillant's office and Emalie sat down again and resumed her typing.

Now, there's a man, she thought with a feeling that was new to her, a feeling of admiration rather than suspicion and disdain. But what kind of man did she mean? *Un beau mâle*, of course, but there was something about him that was as fine as his looks. It was breeding, she decided. He was an aristocrat to his fingertips, but totally unlike the effete dukes and counts and princes she had heard about at Thiboux, had seen right here at the bank.

She waited expectantly until he came out of Vaillant's office, but although his smile was charming when he wished her good day, his behavior was exactly that of a gentleman to one of his employees.

For weeks she dressed and did her hair each morning even more carefully than usual, hoping he would come back on leave. She looked up eagerly from her work whenever a figure appeared at the end of the corridor. On her bench in the Tuileries Gardens she felt a flare of anticipation every time she saw an English officer, and she wondered about him constantly, where he lived, what sort of man he really was, what his wife was like. Emalie envied Julian Saxon's wife her undoubtedly patrician background, her clothes, and her education.

It must not be torture to be married to a man like that. He was a gentleman, after all, not a brute like her father, or a musty little clerk like François Martin, or even a middle-aged banker with a wandering eye like Monsieur Vaillant.

She wondered if he had a mistress—or if he wanted one. At the bank it did not seem impossible that he might want her; other men did. But each night, when she returned to the Rue Momette, she knew she could never aspire to a man like him.

What she had accomplished seemed insignificant compared to Julian

Saxon and the life he led. Now there was a form to the grace and beauty she had always dreamed of, and she would never have it, not even if she worked hard all her life.

# 7

He came to the office at the end of March, as unexpectedly as before. His beautiful face looked much older, but they talked for a moment before she announced him to Monsieur Vaillant, and she was sure he would stop at her desk again when he came out.

But Vaillant came with him, avuncular and proprietary, sweeping him down the corridor and out of her sight again, probably to lunch at some marvelous restaurant. Disappointed, she took her copy of *A Tale of Two Cities* to the Tuileries Gardens to read over her solitary lunch, but she did not even take the book out of her bag. She wondered anew if he had a woman when he came to Paris, if he took some ardent *grande dame* or even a stunning girl from the Folies to his family's large house in the Avenue d'Iéna. He was newly married; that would not have stopped a Frenchman, but everyone knew the English didn't have any Latin *tempérament*. Perhaps, Ema thought hopefully, they were more chivalrous than passionate, like Ivanhoe and King Arthur and Sidney Carton.

She shook her head, impatient with herself again. She was spinning daydreams, just as she had when she was little. With all the beautiful women in Paris, what would Julian Saxon want with her? She was pitiful by comparison with him, a slum girl who worked hard for a living and had lost her virtue long ago. Clean underwear and decent clothes would never change that.

She was unaware that he had seen her leave the bank and had followed her into the park on an impulse. He was weighing it carefully as he leaned against a tree and smoked a cigarette. There was more to the girl than a lovely face and figure; he had thought so the first moment he saw her. Those clear gray eyes seemed to look right into him, to see the despair hidden deep within the once-eager officer. A foolish fancy, perhaps, but more foolish still that she had been on his mind constantly when he wasn't under assault by shell fire, gas, and the screams of dying men.

When he went up the line it helped to think of women; all the men did. He had kept himself sane through many weeks of appalling carnage by remembering the sweet voices of women, the softness of their breasts, and the silky warmth hidden between their thighs. Then why did he not think of Davina, his wife, to whom he had pledged himself, instead of this tall gray-eyed girl whose name he didn't even know? There were plenty of women in Paris if he wanted sex; he didn't need to seduce an office girl from Saxon, Vaillant like some medieval lord of the manor claiming maidenheads as his feudal right! She had made him want sex, but he hadn't spent the one night of this leave with a woman; he had driven to a country inn about thirty miles outside Paris, where he could hear only silence and smell only green fields and think of making love to this girl, now eating her lunch on a park bench.

He looked at his watch; in a little while he must go to the station for his train back to the front. He could do her no harm in an hour.

Emalie had almost finished eating when he approached. The bread in her hands mortified her, but he took no notice and asked if he might sit beside her. She nodded, munching as unobtrusively as she could.

"You have the advantage of me, Mademoiselle," he said. "I don't know your name."

She told him and refused the cigarette he offered her when, at last, she had swallowed the bread and replaced her gloves.

"Do you like working at the bank?"

"Yes, very much."

He smiled ruefully. "I'm not very good at banking myself," he said, looking less strained as he talked. "Heaven knows they've tried, I've had to go to about every branch we own—London, Paris, Germany, Venezuela."

"But it must be wonderful to travel!"

"Not for me, I'm too fond of Stridings—that's the name of our house in Kent. If I were lucky enough to get back there, I'd never leave it again." His voice hadn't changed, but a cold chill swept through her at the way he said it. "Have you ever been to England, Mademoiselle Bequier?" he asked.

She almost laughed—as if she had the choice! "No, I've never been out of Paris."

He looked around at the broad walks of the gardens and the trees about to burst into leaf. "It's a beautiful city." He drew deeply on his cigarette. He wore a signet ring on his right hand. His hands were beautiful, the fingers long and graceful and clean. His uniform was immaculate. It was hard for her to imagine him in those trenches, killing Germans.

They went to Cesar's for coffee. "Tell me about Stridings," she said, pleased that the proprietor had welcomed her as if she were a lady.

"I'll show you." He took out his billfold and gave her a photograph. It showed part of a handsome stone mansion with an oval drive and a shallow flight of steps leading to a massive carved door. The windows she could see were mullioned, and there was ivy on the walls. She had never been to the country, but she had read about it and she imagined the abundant trees and the sweet green tranquillity that surrounded that house. He gave her another picture, a rose garden in full bloom.

"It was my mother's," he said. "She grew the loveliest roses in England. There's an enormous flower garden, too, and greenhouses going down to the river."

She was hoping to see a picture of his wife, but he had put his billfold away and the clock in the corner of the café coughed twice. "I must go," she said.

They said good-bye in front of Cesar's. They had been speaking French, but for some reason she spoke in English now, looking up at him, hoping to see she knew not what. "Are you going back to the front now?"

He nodded.

"Be careful," she said softly, still searching those dark eyes while she held out her hand.

He took it for a moment, and she felt the warmth of his hand through her glove. She was convinced he wanted to say something more, but he released her and she went quickly back to the bank, disappointed, expectant, thinking furiously as she walked.

She did not know about men of his class. He was complex and enigmatic and not in the least obvious about what, if anything, he wanted of her. Yet her instinct told her that he wanted something, and sex was what every man wanted, that was a given. He had sought her out in the park, he had spent a precious hour of his leave with her, but he had not been suggestive in the least. Perhaps the English aristocracy really were more civilized. She would have to wait until his next leave to know if he meant to see her alone, if he wanted more from her than friendly conversation.

She remembered Clothilde saying, "It's not so terrible; sometimes it's even nice." If she could be his mistress, her future at Saxon, Vaillant would be assured. She would have François Martin's job for the asking, and after the war . . . Her mind raced ahead to the flat he would rent and furnish for her in the Rue de la Pompe, to the elegant clothes she would wear when he came to see her and when they dined at Fouquet or Maxim's together. He wouldn't be able to come often. Her body and her life would be her own most of the time.

*Idiote!* she told herself when she got back to her desk. He doesn't want you.

"Emalie." It was François Martin calling her through the open door of his office. She went in, prepared to be scolded for being late, but he was sitting at his desk and his normally pale face was chalk-white.

"What is it, are you ill?"

He shook his head. "I've been called up," he said.

"But you told me you've been called up before and Monsieur Vaillant fixed it."

"He can't fix it this time. I have to go." He looked like a frightened child. "In two weeks."

She went around the desk and took his hand in hers. She must get him to recommend her for his job. Papa Vaillant knew she was efficient, and he was obviously aware that she was pretty too.

"*Allons*, François," she said briskly, "they aren't going to put a secretary with bad eyesight in the front lines! You'll be some sort of clerk."

He brightened at that, and his grip on her hand tightened. "You're very kind to me, Emalie. I'll miss you."

"I'll miss you too."

His hand was beginning to sweat. "Will you write to me?"

"Of course I will. And I'll keep all your files in order until you come back."

She agreed to have a drink with him after work and she was back at her desk, typing briskly, when Henri Vaillant came back from lunch, mellow with good wine. She put on a troubled expression and followed him into his office.

# 8

In the deserted, darkened offices Emalie let François kiss her again.
They were pallid, forgettable kisses, just like François, but in exchange
for the promise of more, he had helped convince Vaillant that Emalie
could do his job until he came back.

"*Soyez sage*, François," she insisted when his hand brushed her breasts.

"How can I be good," he murmured, "when you're so beautiful?" But
he complied and kissed her again.

"*Emalie, chérie*," François breathed, his hand closing insistently over her
right breast, his lips now glued over hers. His breath smelled of garlic and
his suit of several years' wear on a body too rarely bathed. She felt him
getting hard against her thigh and pulled away before his tongue invaded
her mouth. He disgusted her. He was utterly without finesse, as all men
were when their senses were inflamed. Then all they wanted was to
thrust themselves inside a woman. But if the man were Lieutenant Saxon,
it could be borne. That was probably what women meant when they said
they were in love.

"Let me," François said through his busy lips, trying to undo the buttons of her blouse. "There's no one here. I love you, Emalie." How men
used love! But it meant only this frantic fumbling to them, not the myste-
rious ecstasy Emalie read about in novels. François was kind, he was not
a bad man, but she could never let him—or Henri Vaillant, either, unless
her father drove her to that. She took his hand away from her blouse.

"I'll marry you, Emalie," he panted. His hand darted up her leg and his
fingers wriggled under the edge of her corset and touched her through
the thin cotton of her drawers. He gasped at the feel of her, and his fingers
tweaked frantically. "I'll marry you on my first permission, I swear it," he
said breathlessly. "The war will be over soon anyway, now that the Americans have come in. Please let me, Emalie."

She moved away from him. "That's enough, François. Now stop it," she said, more bored than angry with him. He would never be anything but a glorified clerk, and even her body was worth more than he could offer in exchange for it.

Finally she waved him off to his home and family with promises to write and to wait for him. She wiped her mouth with a handkerchief, smoothed her hair, and began to put her desk in order for the morning. She wanted to call Danielle to tell her she had the job, but Danielle would be teaching night classes at the school. There was no way to put it off; she had to go home.

Her new salary was not as much as François's had been and nowhere near what she needed to move out of her father's house. She had to pay her mother back for the gold piece and pay her father every week for her room and board. She might manage to save a little after buying what she absolutely needed and paying her carfare, but it would not be enough to escape the Rue Momette. She would need a man to take her away from it.

She locked her desk drawer, put on her hat and jacket, and went down the darkened stairs to the marble lobby of the building. She stopped when she saw Julian Saxon get out of a taxi and talk to the porter.

"Here is Mademoiselle Bequier now," the porter said. "Perhaps she will know."

The lieutenant was hatless and the lamplight glistened on his dark hair, on his gleaming leather belt and boots. It turned the April mist into an aureole around him. Illumined, he bowed gracefully and shook her hand.

"I was to meet Monsieur Vaillant here, but my train was late. Do you know where he's dining tonight?"

"Yes, at Maxim's." She wished mightily that she had not known.

He hesitated. His eyes were in shadow; she could not even guess what he was thinking. Then he thanked her politely and disappeared into the waiting taxi.

"*Le bel Anglais,*" the porter said, clicking his tongue in approbation. "And now, *vive les Américains,* eh?"

Emalie said good night to the old man and walked quickly out of the Place Vendôme in the direction of her tram stop. She ran to board a car as it pulled away, her earlier elation about her new job completely gone.

He was in Paris on leave and he had made no attempt to see her! And she had been so sure, so sure he would. Her schemes of seduction and wealth mocked her, and she sat in silent desolation until the tram stopped in front of the little church and she got off and walked wearily to the place she had to call home.

# 9

"Emalie!" her father roared, and his lusty voice crashed along the Rue Momette to the square. It was after supper and she had gone to watch the neighborhood celebrate because the Americans had declared war on Germany.

She ignored her father and stayed on in the square, but she thought the celebration was premature. The Americans might not come in time to save France—or Julian Saxon.

Her father called again, and this time she flinched at the sound and her eyes moved as if searching for a way out. Then he bellowed like an angry bull, and she pushed through the jubilant crowd on the street, back to the dingy store that proclaimed itself an *épicerie fine* although nothing of quality had ever adorned its shelves.

Her father loomed, an angry Goliath. "Get inside," he ordered. "It's bad enough that old man you work for has you on his desk for breakfast every morning, but you won't shame me in my own house."

Emalie blushed painfully, aware of the men snickering in the street.

His voice dropped to a persuasive purr for a moment. "Stay near me, my little beauty," he said, first with a tipsy smile, then with a sudden frown. "And keep away from those Americans when they come, you hear? They're supposed to fight the Germans, *les salauds*, not make whores of our daughters."

He followed Ema into the store, where Marie and Babette mopped disconsolately, and appraised all three of his daughters, but his gaze came back to Emalie. She avoided his eyes. "Mind what I say, all of you!" he warned, then waved them to their chairs in the cramped little kitchen, where their mother sat sewing.

Sylvie Bequier and two of her daughters sat like statues while he gargled down a bottle of wine and sang "Madelon" at the top of his lungs— and at his insistence they sang weakly with him. Only Emalie was silent. She sewed on a pale yellow linen shirtwaist for the spring.

"Bequier!" a neighbor yelled from the noisy street. "Come on out here with us!"

He stood to go to the door, waving a beefy hand to steady himself, then fell back on the chair that was too small for his bulk. After a moment of confusion he laughed stupidly and let himself be led upstairs by his wife, cupping her buttocks with one hand, her breasts with the other, while he shouted to his daughters to lock up the store and go to bed.

Undressing in their small bedroom, Babette and Marie giggled at the sounds from above stairs.

"*Ils font l'amour,*" Babette said.

"Making love?" Emalie said it with contempt, thinking about the English soldier in the lamplight. "What's going on up there is not love!"

"*Toujours la grande dame,*" Marie sniffed. "What do you know about it, sewing shrouds for your fancy clothes?"

Emalie brushed her hair savagely and did not reply.

"Maybe Papa is right," Marie persisted slyly. "Maybe you have a beau in that snooty office of yours."

"Shut up, *petite salope,*" Emalie hissed, reverting to the language of this place. She slipped her nightdress over her head, and snatching a shawl from under her pillow, she walked past the curtains into the store. The springs were creaking upstairs, the headboard beginning to bump against the wall.

Emalie covered her ears against that sound, but she could never keep out the smells of the store—clotted milk and strong cheese, onions and sour wine and age-old dirt. They permeated her hair and her clothes, her very pores. Work was a joy because it got her away from here. Work was all she had.

To think she had once loved the pungent gloom of this place—had once been her father's princess! She could not forget the feel of his hands, meaty and thick, with coarse black hair. The memory made her sick. Now that the Americans had come into the war, the army would never send him to the front, and he would never be killed. He would go on watching her, wanting her to have swinish sex with him.

"But that isn't love," she whispered in the grubby little store. Love could not be what her father was. Love had another face, spoke in a different voice. Love was the man she had been dreaming about for weeks in the dark of the night, in the incense and shadow of the church. His hands were clean and graceful; he smelled of soap and bay rum cologne. He was nothing like the boys of this slum, nor any of the men she had ever seen before.

Emalie clutched at her shawl, pacing back and forth on the far side of the counter. She had no time for love; she must think of her future! To get away from here she had to be either a wife or a mistress, and love had nothing to do with either condition.

In the dark her mouth twisted suddenly at her impossible hopes. She would have to settle for a repulsive creature like François, marry him and let him use her body anyway he liked. She shuddered.

The headboard stopped its drumming and her father subsided from grunts to snores. Emalie went back to the dark little kitchen. There was no sound from the back bedroom and she filled a basin with water at the pump and washed her underthings with her own lemon-scented soap.

Outside there were still sounds of revelry, and Emalie wondered how soon the Americans would come to Paris and what they would be like. Monsieur Vaillant said they were nice, the Americans, and kind, like big children. Hanging her laundry on a cord behind the stove, she wondered what it would be like to live in America.

She went to the bedroom and got into her narrow bed, forgetting the Americans, not caring if they ever came. She was acutely conscious of her woman's body. She imagined that Julian's hands caressed her, his mouth was urgent on her lips, his flesh was joined to hers. She felt a thrill of anticipation perversely heightened by fear, and she realized that she had been corrupted by her father's lust into wanting what terrified her most.

# 10

"Come to the station with me," he said, holding her hands in his.

From the start it had been more than a chance encounter.

For the second time that week Emalie had allowed herself the luxury of coffee at Cesar's before she went home. She sat at her favorite corner table thinking about the day they had come here from the park and talked. That was months ago, and she had supposed they would never talk like that again. Yet there he was, obviously looking for her through the smoke and noise of the café. His face was very drawn, more so than the leg wound he had suffered at Passchendaele warranted. He relaxed when he saw her and limped across the room to put his hand on the chair opposite.

"*Bonsoir*, Mademoiselle Bequier. May I?"

She nodded and he sat down, ordering iced champagne from the waiter for both of them. The collar of his tunic stood away from his neck.

"I'm glad I found you," he said.

She did not even ask why he had been looking for her. His need and hers were there between them, different but equally powerful. She had planned to be charming and gay if she ever saw him again, but all she could say, after the champagne had been poured, was "You're a captain now."

"Only because all of the officers senior to me were killed at Passchendaele." The lines deepened at the corners of his mouth. "I'm really not the sort to shout 'Charge!' and lead men gallantly into battle."

"Forgive me, you don't want to talk about the war."

He looked down at the checked tablecloth while he took a cigarette from the pocket of his tunic. His manner was calm, but his voice had an edge. "It doesn't matter. It's just that I shouldn't be commanding these men, you see. My sort keeps them in their place in England. I have no right ordering them to die out here." He lit the cigarette. "I never thought about class until we were being shot at together. Death makes no distinction at all."

For a second she saw that privilege did not confer immunity from doubt or pain, but she dismissed it. It was only because of the war he seemed so vulnerable. She watched his lips close around the cigarette and felt an impulse to protect him, to comfort him, but that kind of womanish sentimentality was not the real point of this meeting.

"I beg your pardon," he smiled, looking up and pouring more champagne. "I don't know why I went on like that."

His smile made him look even younger than his twenty-seven years and, like his doubts, made him less godlike. "I wish you had stayed in England," Emalie said impetuously. "They need you there to run the farms in Devon."

He eyed her curiously; this was a side of her he had sensed but never seen, the lack of pretense that attracted him so much. "How did you know that?"

"Monsieur Vaillant. He said you did a fine job of it until your father recovered." Her cheeks flushed and she leaned toward him impulsively. "Everyone's not meant to kill people; you said so yourself. You'd have been safe there."

His dark brows arched. "My safety isn't the issue—although I suppose that's how it sounded."

"No, please, I didn't mean that." She leaned back, defeated. It was all wrong. She had planned to be flirtatious, even seductive, and she had ended by seeming to question his courage. "I worry about you all the time," she whispered.

He took her hand and raised it to his lips for a second. "Emalie, I had to see you, no matter how I tried not to. I had to find you tonight before I went back to the front."

She averted her eyes, confused and crestfallen. "I thought you'd just arrived on leave."

"No, I've been in the country for three days, trying to stay away from you."

"But why?"

"Because it was the honorable thing to do."

Their eyes met again. "I know very little about honor," she said.

He sat gazing at her. She was dressed in a gray summer suit that matched her eyes, eyes abrim with an invitation she could not bring herself to utter—how could she, she was only a girl! He saw the burnished coil of hair he wanted to take down and the wide-bowed mouth he had already kissed so many times in his imagination. He wanted her as he wanted peace and the sweet green fields of England, to lie down upon and sleep. He made another attempt to fight a passion he had never felt before.

"I must go . . . the last train . . ." He lost the thread of it. The noises of the café receded and all he heard was the message in her eyes. In the place where he had been and to which he would return tonight there were no visions such as she, no beauty, no warmth, whiteness, paradise. She was all of that and indefinably more. He wanted all of her, even as something warned him not to take it. Just a few more moments, he promised himself, just a few more and then I'll never see her again.

"Come to the station with me," he pleaded, taking both her hands in his. She nodded eagerly, and he was filled with tenderness for her.

But the acts of rising, leaving, getting into a taxi broke the spell of that wordless communion in the café. In the taxi caution and conscience sat rigidly between them and they did not seem the polite acquaintances they were supposed to be, but rather strangers on the brink of the same abyss.

The taxi stopped at the Gare du Nord and she went with him into the muted roar and confusion, the agonized farewells of a railway terminal in wartime. They walked toward the quai in their own bubble of silence, aware of the distance between them.

The clasping of their gloved hands when they said good-bye was a mere amenity now, and he was halfway down the ramp to the waiting train when he turned to wave politely to her. He saw her face, and his arm dropped; without thinking he ran back up the ramp, struggling against a tide of entraining soldiers to get to her, his hands reaching out for hers. She walked into his arms and he kissed her as if he had been longing for her not for mere months but all his life.

"Next time," he said. "Will you come away with me next time?"

"Yes," she whispered, "yes."

And he was gone, not turning back this time, leaving her there to wait, perhaps for months, perhaps forever.

# 11

―――――

"It's incredible," Emalie said, entranced by the life-size statue of a man and a woman seated side by side. Julian Saxon, naked, would look like that.

Danielle tilted her head and walked slowly around the stone lovers in the museum. "Precisely, my dear, incredible because it is so unrealistic."

To Emalie the sculpture was astoundingly real. The marble figures had the glow and warmth of living lovers. The man had just turned to the ardent woman at his side, a woman who craved his embrace too much to wait for it. Her arm encircled his majestic head and urged his mouth down to hers. Her nipples grazed his chest, her body implored him to possess her.

One of his hands, strong and graceful, rested for a chaste second on her hip, but if he were freed from that stone, Emalie knew, he would turn the whole of his Olympian body to hers and take her with colossal force and tenderness.

Julian would be like that.

"Come along," Danielle said, returning from her circuit, "there are other sculptures to see."

"Not like that one," Emalie murmured with a backward look at the couple, eternally imprisoned in that prelude to their passion.

It was a misty September morning and the Sunday crowds had not yet invaded the museum. Emalie had spent the evening with Danielle and stayed the night on her divan. Even her father could not object to that. Danielle's apartment was on the Left Bank, a small but comfortable two rooms, with a hip tub in the kitchen that was utter bliss to Emalie. The late Monsieur Larchet had brought his wife here as a bride, but there was not a sign of him to be found anywhere, not even, Emalie suspected, in the black enamel locket Danielle always wore. But she never pried into Danielle's life, any more than Danielle pried into hers. Emalie was in the habit of keeping secrets by now; it came as naturally to her as breathing.

"Why do you say it's not real?" she persisted, looking back at the statue again. "They're ready to leap into life."

"But only to make love, yes? With none of the problems of life and in the perfection of their consummate grace and beauty." Danielle raised her eyebrows, and her homely face seemed even longer than usual. "*Ma chère* Emalie, romantic fiction to the contrary, all mortals are not beautiful. The music of the spheres does not play when ordinary people make love. There are other sounds, other details not so pleasant. And there are always consequences."

"You are such a cynic, Danielle!" Emalie laughed.

"I am a realist. I thought you were too."

Emalie nodded. "I don't believe in love either."

Danielle shook her head, her black eyes bright. "I know nothing of what is called love—if, indeed, it exists outside the imagination—and given the tendency of women to be enslaved by it, I consider myself fortunate." She looked back at the soaring statue. "Maybe it moves you because you and she are both beautiful. But I doubt there is a man alive who is anything like him."

"Physically?"

"No. He has integrity. He is sexual but not obscene. I never met a man like that."

When Emalie made no answer, Danielle eyed her curiously. "Is there something troubling you, *ma chère*?"

Ema shook her head. She was ill-accustomed to talk about herself, even to her only friend, and she was ashamed of some of the thoughts that troubled her lately.

"It is a man," Danielle said with woeful certainty after another moment's scrutiny. "And he is married. Am I right?"

"Yes." She felt both foolish and relieved to say it.

"*Grand Dieu*, Ema, don't do anything stupid!" Danielle's long face shone with consternation under her iron-gray hair.

"He's not like most men. He's far above me."

Danielle made an impatient sound. "I thought you were more intelligent."

"Nothing has happened."

"Not yet—but it will, won't it?"

"I don't know. I hope so. He could do a lot for me."

"He could ruin your life," Danielle said.

"How? I don't want a shabby little house and a baby every year, and that's what I'll have if I marry the kind of man who wants to marry me. I don't have my own business like you, and I've gone as far as I can go at the bank. So I'd rather be a rich man's mistress than a perpetual office worker or a poor man's wife." She said it quietly, what she had thought out so carefully. "But I don't mean to worry you about it. Now I've had enough of the museum, let's walk in the Luxembourg."

The Luxembourg Gardens were filling with children, nursemaids, and older folk sunning themselves on benches. The only young men were soldiers with their girls, smiling the secret smiles of lovers. The autumn sunshine soothed both women as they walked along. There was a similarity between them, despite the difference in their ages; it was in their air of purpose.

They were both dressed in loose skirts and boxy tunics cut in mock-military fashion, Danielle in black, Emalie in deep garnet. Their skirts revealed more ankle than had been seen outside a boudoir in a few thousand years—but there was no choice if women were to do men's work. Neither of them wore the long, laced corsets of prewar days; Ema had never owned one, and Danielle had donated her iron stays to the war effort three years ago with sighs of relief. A short girdle with whalebone stays was enough for them, but some women still clung to their pink carapaces, fearful that men could not control their carnal lusts if womanflesh were so accessible. "But it's how we've always been," Danielle said disdainfully, "accessible, corsets or not."

The two friends said no more about Emalie's revelation, but speaking about it had reinforced her decision. She managed to stay calm and efficient at work, but she was in a perpetual state of anticipation.

"Mademoiselle, you are as quick as a firefly," Monsieur Vaillant said one day, mistaking nervousness for the ardor of youth.

She told him it was worry that made her so energetic.

"Ah?" He sat back in his chair. "You have someone at the front?" When she nodded he appraised her somewhat differently. She was very efficient, but she was very pretty, too, he had noticed that from the start. He often imagined her naked. "Well, we at home must give each other what comfort we can, *n'est-ce pas?*" he invited. "Take our minds off our worries." He was mildly annoyed when she did not respond and wondered briefly if she was pregnant by her soldier. Then he continued his dictation, hoping he would not have to find another secretary before François came back.

Her father noticed her nervousness too. "What ails you?" he demanded in the store. "Are you sitting on the nest?"

Careless by now of what he said or who heard him, she went on weighing out butter for a customer. "The whole country's ailing," she told him sharply. "Haven't you noticed we're losing the war?"

"*Sacré nom de Dieu,* never! I'll fight the Boches in the streets before I let them beat us!" He looked at her with the mixture of lechery and awe her success evoked in him, even though she had already changed to her old clothes and swathed herself in a huge apron. He appealed to a gray-bearded man waiting impatiently for a piece of blood sausage. "Women! They don't know how to fight, eh? Back in 'seventy . . ."

"*Merde* on your 'seventy. Is that all the sausage I get?"

"You're not supposed to get any today—two meatless days a week, remember?"

When they were alone he returned to his probing, trying to discern her figure under the apron. "Don't think you can whelp any bastards here," he said, at once lubricious and fierce.

"I wouldn't let you near a child of mine," she said. "If you're so brave, why don't you go fight the Germans yourself? Maybe they'll kill you; I wish someone would." They glared at each other before she left the shop.

In November, as Monsieur Vaillant dictated a letter to Sir James, she learned that Julian had been wounded again.

"It is not serious," Vaillant concluded. "There is no sign of sepsis, and the lad is recovering in a field hospital behind the lines. I am assured by the general that he will soon be fit to fight again, so you must not worry overmuch."

You old fool, Emalie thought, not worry when he might be killed as soon as he goes back to the front? With a mighty effort she took the letter calmly, typed it out, and mailed it to Sir James Andrew Saxon, Bart., at number 9 Frederick's Place in London. She said nothing to Danielle—how could she without revealing who her lover was? When she was alone she yielded to Julian Saxon as an opium addict yields to the pipe, her visions of wealth sometimes obscured by erotic fantasies, both irresistible and terrifying, when she remembered that kiss.

# 12

The snow fell in France and the country's morale with it, and Julian Saxon came back to Paris.

She wondered if he would recognize her.

The station was quiet, but tension radiated from the knot of women with anxious eyes who waited behind the arrival gate on the quai. Emalie joined them just before eight, her face carefully calm, as if this were any other evening in December and she were accustomed to assignations with men she hardly knew.

Shame assailed her, as it had so often since she had received his brief note. Did he suppose she had done this before? She had no idea what opinion men of his class had about easy women; the same as other men, she decided, and it was not flattering.

But what did he know of her except that she was pretty enough to take to bed and all too ready to go there?

She shook her head, mocking herself. This was just another of life's bargains, like the one she had made with her mother. She was no worse than many a woman, or many a wife, from what she had heard. Women married for security if they weren't fools. She had lost her claim to vestal modesty long ago.

His note, discreetly worded, had asked if she could come to Neuilly for the weekend, and the small valise she carried had been hidden at the office for a week, packed with the prettiest lingerie she could afford, a ruffled blouse, new stockings. Sylvie, careless of what Ema did now, believed she was spending the weekend with Madame Larchet. Emalie had said nothing at all to her father.

The tense quiet was shattered by the chuff of the engine, the shouts of the men, the eager cries of the women.

"*Enfin,*" someone said, and the little group of women surged forward, watching the great engine heave into view with ten mud-splattered carriages in its wake. Heads bobbed from the rolled-down windows like ball fringe trimming on a valance; eyes strained to meet familiar eyes, to find a special face in that sea of faces.

Then the train stopped and a uniformed mass swarmed up the ramp toward the gate, officers from the front carriages overtaken and swamped by the troops who followed them, eager to get to the women.

Emalie saw Julian and smiled, although he could not see her yet in that crowd behind the gate. She watched the thrust of his legs in their breeches, and that unfamiliar excitement suffused her again. She had folded her gloved hands in an effort to be more dignified, more ladylike, when she saw his lips move and realized that he was talking to the officers on either side of him. They were obviously his friends, and if she stayed where she was, they would see her and know why she was here—did they know already, had he told them? Or was he planning to pass her by with no acknowledgment at all until his friends were safely out of the station?

She ducked behind a cart piled high with luggage, her hands grazing her hot cheeks, her hair, her clothes. The deep garnet suit of which she had been so proud seemed shabby now, and her hand-knit shawl was a mean substitute for a fur. She looked pathetic in the only jewelry she possessed, her first-communion earrings and a locket that had been her grandmother's. The cheap cardboard valise in her hand was like a flaming lantern, advertising her availability for dirty weekends, and she saw herself through his friends' eyes, her body spread on a bed in some seedy hotel, naked and common.

But it isn't like that, she cried piteously to herself, hardly knowing what she meant. She wished she had never come at all as Captain Saxon and his friends advanced relentlessly.

They passed the gate just a few yards from her hiding place and all three stopped a moment. From behind the cart she saw Julian's eyes searching the crowd. The other two officers swept off their caps in a gesture of gallantry to the women who hurried by them onto the quai, and she noticed that one of Julian's friends had the brightest golden hair she had ever seen.

She turned away from them again, crouched against the sharp edges of the baggage, breathing hard in her degradation. She could not show herself to these lords of creation—they would know her for what she was. She would have to be other, better, different even to approach their charmed circle. "Damn them all," she whispered, "someday I'll laugh at all of them."

She watched him, hating him for his superiority. She watched him when his friends had gone, his air of anticipation fading like twilight as the minutes passed. Then he shook his head dejectedly and made for one of the exit doors, carrying his leather case. She saw him go, his stride hesitant from the old wound, but still graceful, the set of his shoulders heavy with disappointment.

Why shouldn't he be disappointed, she thought, must he have everything he wants?

But she was here for something *she* wanted. She could not give it up without even trying!

She went quickly through another exit door and approached him just as he took some keys from an agent of Wagon Lits Cook.

"Captain Saxon?"

"Emalie! I was afraid you weren't coming." She had never seen him smile like that before. It dazzled her.

"I'm sorry to be late."

He took her valise, his eyes searching her face. "It doesn't matter, as long as you're here." He waited a moment, studying her. "What is it?" he asked, as if he sensed her confusion.

She could not meet his eyes and only shook her head briefly.

"Never mind, we needn't go to Neuilly," he said gently after a moment. "We'll just dine in Paris and I'll take you home. Would you like that better?"

She blushed, her eyes still fixed on the second button of his tunic. Then she looked up at him. "But I want to go to Neuilly with you."

After a moment he touched her cheek and nodded. He took her arm and a wave of feeling for him rose in her. No one had ever asked how she felt, no one had ever cared what she wanted.

The car parked in front of the station was a half-open cabriolet, and the whistling wind made too much noise for conversation as they headed for the outskirts of Paris. Emalie was grateful for that—and for the December dark that veiled her eyes whenever she looked at him.

His face was even stronger in profile, almost stern, until he glanced at her and smiled again as he had before. Feeling for him billowed up again, and she warned herself to keep her head. There were more important things to think about.

What must she do in bed to please him? She knew nothing of the little tricks the girls at Thiboux hinted at, yet she must please him or he would never make her his mistress.

He took her hand and kissed its palm, and she was aware of her body, as she had been so often in her bed at night. Her breasts tingled, the nipples pushed against her camisole.

When they arrived at the Auberge du Père Monsatte they sat in front of the fire in the little salon to drink an apéritif. Their host, a chubby little man with squeaking shoes and the ribbons of a former soldier of France, bustled in with the glasses.

"*Mon Capitaine, Madame*. It's a good omen to have you with us for the new year. Perhaps it means the war will end soon."

Emalie smiled graciously. *Madame*. Over dinner she made him laugh with tales of Saxon, Vaillant's more eccentric clients, trying to be what Davina Saxon must be—serene and charming. She imagined she was wearing a silk eau de Nile evening dress instead of a skirt and jersey. She could feel a string of perfect pearls around her neck and a wedding ring on her finger. She pretended she had grown up in an English manor house like Stridings and was on her honeymoon in France.

They went back to the fire for brandy after dinner and finally Monsieur Monsatte squeaked away to his rest and left them alone. Julian looked at her again as he had done at the station, as if to read her thoughts, and his face changed. "I think I should take you back to Paris, Emalie," he said. His dark eyes were unfathomable and his hand stroked her hair gently.

She took the stroking hand and held it to her cheek. "But I want to stay." She moved toward him and touched her lips to his, her hands framing his face.

His arms went around her and he kissed her, not hesitantly, as she had done, but in a way she had not imagined. "I've thought of this," he whispered. "Lord, how I've dreamed of you. But you're so young, Ema. What will happen to you after the war?"

"Hush, Julian, it's bad luck to talk about the war." She stood and held out her hand to him.

They climbed the stairs to a room that smelled of applewood and beeswax. It was almost completely filled by a canopied bed and a plump chair covered in flowered cretonne. Starched white muslin curtained the bed and the windows. There was an unlit lamp on the mantelpiece and a candle lantern on the nightstand, but he didn't light either; the fireglow was enough.

He kissed her for many minutes, undressing her, then himself. Her eyes were closed when he put her on the bed, and he let down her hair, burying his face in the scented softness of it. His lips lingered again on her mouth and her breasts until, amazed, she was eager for that deeper touch of his hands she had imagined, for the feel of him over her and the rise of his body to enter hers. He moved inside her, calling up a pleasure that rose and fell then rose again, each time more than the last.

She had gone stoically, purposefully to his arms, but now she was carried away by him. She took him to her with a voluptuous ardor that gave and demanded more than comfort, more even than erotic satisfaction. In a life until this moment totally devoid of beauty, she knew, for the first time, bliss.

She woke before he did in the morning and watched him as he slept, profoundly moved by his face, so beautiful, so young, so trusting. Again she felt an irresistible impulse to comfort him, a woman's impulse, age-old but new to her.

She touched her lips to his smooth shoulder before she slipped out of bed, took her nightdress from her valise, and put on her shawl. The maid ran her bath in the *salle de bains* down the hall, and as she lay back in the warm water she knew she could never hurt him.

But how could it hurt him to give her the little she wanted so desperately? He was rich and a man of the world; he would have a mistress eventually. Why not now, why not her? She would delight in it; she would be faithful. But she must go slowly, slowly. He must never suspect she wanted anything from him.

He was still sleeping when she came back from her bath. She wanted him to make love to her again, but she would shock him if she woke him to tell him so, and he needed rest. She dressed and went down to a breakfast of buttered brioches and café au lait and then out into the crisp air of the country. How clean it was and how quiet! She could hear the river gurgling just out of sight, and smiled as a fat goose and a dainty hen trailed across the yard of the inn toward the water. Suddenly she threw her arms over her head and laughed aloud, whirling around to see him standing in the doorway, watching her.

"I never heard you laugh before," he said, delighted.

"And I never saw you look so well."

He drew her arm through his and they set off for a walk in the woods. "You're usually so serious," he said.

"I wouldn't have my job if I weren't." She winked at him, feeling happy, feeling good.

"And it's important to you?"

She nodded. "It's all I have."

"Surely not. You have a family."

"It was different before my father died. My mother needs what I earn now if we're to live as we always have." She hesitated, then decided to chance it. "But I want more than my mother had."

"Tell me."

She bent to pick up a fallen branch. "An apartment of my own, a car, a box at the opera. I want to travel, all over the world—and have thousands of books and the time to read them."

"Where did you learn English?"

"Sister Marie Angélique," she said, knowing he would assume she went to a convent school. "Do I speak it well?"

"Very well, with a charming accent." He stopped and turned to her. "Everything you do charms me, Ema."

She colored slightly and tossed the branch aside. "Is it—am I—what you wanted?"

He put his arms around her. "Oh, yes," he said. "More than all my dreams of you." He kissed her gently. "Emalie, you mustn't be hurt because of me. Do you understand?"

She nodded and then hesitated before she said, "Julian, show me a picture of your wife."

After a moment he nodded and took a tinted photograph out of the billfold she had seen before. Davina Saxon was a glorious blonde with tilted blue eyes and a heart-shaped face. Her features were small and fine, even feline, and she was aristocratic from the proud angle of her chin to the assured smile on her dainty lips. My fairy princess, Emalie thought, envious and worshipful.

She handed it back with a little nod that acknowledged the strict limitations of the affair that had just begun between them. But she had him now; he was here with her. He had said nothing about giving her all the things she wanted, but it was too soon. Desire overwhelmed her, and she kissed him with the new abandon she had shown last night.

"Come back to the inn, to our room," she said. "Make love to me again."

They walked back in the breathless ecstasy of anticipation, and when she was finally in his arms again she was amazed at how well her body knew the language of love without ever having learned it.

# 13

---

"Shoot him," Captain Saxon said.

Lieutenant William Poyndexter looked up from the revolver in his hand, light from the oil lamp glinting on his blond hair. "Come off it, Julian, we'll have the whole sector in an uproar if I fire a shot in here."

"Then beat him to death—I don't care how you kill him, but kill him."

The two men, who had been friends since their schooldays, were alone in their quarters. Tony Holland, the other man Emalie had seen with them at the station, was out playing bridge with the colonel. Near the lamp at one end of the rough table was an opened bottle of wine, two mess cups, and a chunk of cheese. At the other end was a two-day-old copy of *The Times* of London under a tin of sweet biscuits from Fortnum's. A burlap curtain separated them from the troops in the trench outside, and glaring at the two men from the wall opposite was an enormous trench rat, its eyes glittering in the light.

"He's a bloody great devil, isn't he?" William said, putting down the revolver he had been cleaning and looking around for a quieter weapon. "As big as Alice's Cheshire cat."

"Why shouldn't he be; he's been feasting on British corpses for three years."

William took a shovel and advanced on the sleek creature, so partial to the scent and flavor of human flesh that it stood its ground, its nose and whiskers twitching, its red eyes fixed.

"Bastard!" William shouted when the shovel hit only the duckboard flooring and the rat streaked out past the curtain. They heard the shouts and curses on the other side of it and a muted scuffle as the rat ran a gauntlet of angry men and fled over the side of the trench.

William threw down the shovel, poured some wine into a cup, and looked at his friend apologetically. His hair and his blue eyes made Julian think of a painted cherub, although William's exploits with women belied his angelic looks. "Probably just as well," William said with his irresistible grin. "It would have made a mess of this place."

Julian shrugged and glanced around the bunker eloquently. He stood up. "I'm going out to get some air. I can't breathe in here." He didn't ask William to join him, and the omission resounded between the two friends.

"I say, old man, are you all right?" William was carefully casual, but his blue eyes studied Julian anxiously.

"No, how could I be, out here?"

William hesitated. "I mean about that girl. You've been seeing her rather a lot, haven't you?"

Julian's expression closed. "Leave it alone, William. It's not your concern."

"I'm sorry, but it is. I've had a letter from Davina asking why you haven't once come home on leave."

Julian sat down abruptly. "Oh, God," he said. "I wish she hadn't."

William poured more wine. "You can't blame her, poor old girl. She doesn't know what's wrong."

"No, and she mustn't."

"You could spend one leave there," William urged. "You'll be going home to live with her someday."

"Don't be a fool, William, none of us will make it through this war. We ought to have died months ago." Julian shook his head. "I can't waste what little time I have left."

They sat in silence for a minute, William making no objection to Julian's assertion about their prospects. Statistically six weeks was as long as most men survived on the Western Front. "What'll I tell Davina?" he asked.

Julian rubbed his eyes. "Tell her I have to spend my leaves at the American hospital in Neuilly for special treatments on my leg. It's what I've told her, but she'll believe it from you." He looked up at his friend. "You'll be out of it, then. I'm sorry you were ever involved."

William nodded silently and Julian got up and went out, careful not to disturb men too weary even to stir at the flares and sporadic rifle fire from the German lines. In the distance the work of the night went on. Repair parties mended the wire to keep the Germans beyond grenade distance of the forward observation posts. Digging parties extended the "saps," the shallow trenches that led toward no-man's-land. Sometimes he felt like walking out there and disappearing.

He clambered out on the rear side of the line and walked along for a while, through mud so chill and slick it sucked at his boots like viscous offal. It was cold enough tonight to make all of them miserable, but not cold enough to freeze over, as hell was eventually supposed to do.

He came to a shattered tree and sat down on its charred trunk. The heavy six-pound box respirator and helmet they'd been ordered to wear constantly, even to sleep, hung on his neck like one of the corpses he saw every day, always there to bear the warriors company. One is never alone in hell, he thought, or in paradise.

A flare illuminated the blackness and he bent to blend the lines of his body into the tree trunk. When the light faded, Emalie's face came before him.

He rested his head in his hands, skewered by remorse and conscience for both her and his wife. Deliberately he thought of Davina. They had gone to their first parties together; he had shared her first kiss. There had been other women while he was at Oxford and abroad for the bank, but almost since their childhood everyone had assumed he would marry Davina. And then when her parents had perished with the *Titanic*, he had felt obliged to look after her. A year ago he had gladly vowed to be faithful to her for as long as they both should live, but that last phrase had a different significance now.

He had no doubt at all that he would die out here tomorrow, or the next day. Soon, at any rate. Until that happened he would not surrender the one thing he had to keep him sane.

He no longer believed what he had been taught about honor, duty, and the essential benevolence of the ruling class. He wanted no part of a code that sacrificed life with such prodigious indifference and called it honor. It was of no mortal use to think of Davina; she led him inevitably back to what his father called his duty and his sacred honor; she led him back to war. He would have no respite from it if he crossed the Channel to England; Emalie was his respite.

He had seen her three times since that weekend in December, brief hours of more intensity than all the years of his life. Out here he felt exposed, terrified, unmanned; with her he was a man again. He covered her and she surrounded him. They never spoke about death; it was bad luck. They both believed he would be safe as long as they stayed together.

A machine-gun clattered from the German lines, and he flattened himself on the trunk again, clinging to it. The rough dead bark bit into his cheek, and he winced from the old wounds in his leg. He became aware of the dampness that mortified his bones. He got up stiffly and crouched, simian in the darkness, to move slowly back to his quarters.

Tony Holland had come in and now slept, rolled up in a blanket on the third bunk, nothing visible but the tip of his nose and the swirling waxed mustache of which he was so proud. William was sleeping flat on his back, his respirator askew and his golden curls rumpled. The wine bottle stood on the table, honorably left half-full.

"Sweet Jesus, don't let them be killed," Julian whispered, unexpected moisture filling his eyes as he covered William and stood looking from him to Tony. "Not before me."

He mopped his eyes with his handkerchief, took writing paper from his portfolio, and sat down at the table. He opened the new fountain pen his father had sent him, dropped an ink pellet into the water cartridge, shook it, and began to write.

He wrote three condolence letters to the families of dead subalterns in his command. In the morning he would inspect their personal effects to make sure that no evidence of random sin with the ladies of Paris remained to add embarrassment to a family's grief. It was curious and touching, what men saved as mementos of wartime copulation—a handkerchief, a ribbon, a passionate note.

He put his portfolio away, then sat staring at the corrugated iron walls for a long time, as if he could find instruction there.

Once he had loved her as a young man who is daily kissed by death loves life. Now he could not let her go, even though he must.

Just once more, he thought, I'll see her just once more and then I'll give her up, I swear it.

He lay down on his bunk and shut himself away with her as into a warm, perfumed room. In an ocean of blood he held fast to her until he slept.

# 14

JULY 1918

"It's madness," Danielle said, "the things women do for love." She handed Emalie a towel.

Ema stood and stepped out of the bath. Her hair was already done, piled high on her head. "It's a woman's lot to hail a hero," she said, "that's what we're here for." She laughed, although whether in desperate irony or high spirits Danielle could not tell.

Danielle snorted—that was certainly not her view of woman's lot—and moved about tidying her kitchen while Emalie dried herself and dressed. Danielle had watched Emalie tumble into love. She had seen her prepare with trepidation for that first weekend, with a scented bath and a lemon rinse for her hair, and return from it with a vivid glow of sensuality on her, like a lily in the sun, to wait for the next rendezvous as if it were all in life that mattered. Danielle accepted Ema's physical passion for this man, whoever he was; some women enjoyed sex even if she herself never had. It was Ema's failed purpose that worried her. She was in love with the man she was going to meet today, whether she admitted it or not, and it had changed her.

"Sometimes I think you've lost sight of the future entirely," Danielle ventured now.

"No, Danielle, but how much farther can I go at Saxon, Vaillant?"

"At least secure what you have! If there are any men left alive when this war is over, they'll be back to claim jobs like yours. Remember how hard you worked to get it!"

Julian could have secured her position at Saxon, Vaillant easily, but she would not cheapen their relationship by asking favors. "There's nothing I can do about it," Ema said.

"You might show more interest in your work," Danielle countered.

Emalie knew that was true. Her mind was always on her next meeting with Julian. Besides that, she now spent every penny she earned on clothes; the sheer cambric underwear she had just put on cost a small fortune. Her meager savings were entirely gone, and with them any hope she had of moving out of her father's house. Danielle's apartment was much too small to share. But none of that seemed important.

She finished dressing in a white tarlatan summer suit trimmed in navy blue. Her hat, lying ready on the table, was white straw with a band and pouf of navy silk ribbon. A silk parasol, ruffled with white, was on the table with her new dressing case and a pair of soft white kid gloves.

"*Très chic*," Danielle said when the suit was buttoned. "Did he buy it for you?"

Emalie said nothing, pinning on her hat.

"*Bon Dieu*, Ema, you've never had a real gift from him! A clever woman doesn't give herself for nothing."

"Danielle, he can hardly shop for diamonds on the Western Front," Emalie said, then with a smile and a shake of her head she kissed Danielle good-bye, gathered her things, and went out into the streets of a Paris saved again from invasion. Paris had been bombarded since March by a monster field howitzer seventy-five miles away, but that only made the citizens of Paris more determined. They made vulgar jokes about the gun's size, calling it *La Grande Berthe* after Bertha von Bohlen of Krupp munitions. They vowed they would never surrender Paris to *la grosse connasse*.

Today the jubilant atmosphere in the streets heightened Emalie's anticipation. She had waited months for these few moments with him. She and Julian lived in the moment. It was all they had—that and the way it was to be together.

She walked through the celebrants, thinking of that. Passion blurred all the differences between them when she was in his arms, yet he had a sense of his place in the world and she had none. She was always eager to hear him talk about his life in England; it sounded like a fairy tale to her, but he was convinced that people like him—"our sort," he called them— were a vanishing breed, a casualty of war.

"My father and men of his generation refuse to see it," he told her during one of their long walks in the woods, "but the ruling class can't rule alone anymore, not after this war. There won't be enough old boys left— bullets are very democratic." He had stopped to light a cigarette and then leaned against a tree, turning her to rest against him, his arms around her. She felt his breath stir her hair, and nestled closer to him.

"Old boys?"

"Men with the right family connections and the right school ties. Like me." There was a black note in his voice. She knew he blamed his sort for letting the war go on so long. "War was a sport before this, something gentlemen directed and a paid army fought. It stopped for the winter, like other outdoor sports, and everyone went home, the soldiers to repair their farmhouses and the officers to waltz until spring came again. There were rules for everything, even war, but it's going to be a different world now. I don't think anyone who survives will ever be the same—and I liked it the way it was. I liked knowing who I was, how to behave, and how the other chap would behave."

"But there'll always be an England," Emalie said, "and an English monarchy." She had read that in Mr. Trollope's novels and in Henri Vaillant's *Times* of London.

"Not the same England, Emalie. The British Empire is based on class and the assumption that every man knows his place and wants to stay in it. But the men who share those trenches with me don't want to be the lower orders anymore. The class system is dying, and the England I knew with it."

"Will you miss that part of it? The class system?"

"Oh, yes, very much. It was a lovely way of life for people like the Saxons."

Since then there had been many hours to think about that. Her ambition to join the ranks of the privileged had made her even more class conscious than he was.

And now she knew—and was desolated by the knowledge—that there was more than a wife between them, there was that vast social chasm that could never be bridged. It took generations to produce men like Julian Saxon, William and Tony—and their women.

Julian's friends were unfailingly polite to her when they met at the station, even gallant when they all dined one evening at Fouquet, but they knew she did not belong, however elegantly she dressed, however carefully she behaved. Their perceptions were not blurred by desire, and she could tell they knew.

When the war is over I'll let him go, like a lady, without a fuss, she promised herself again. She stopped walking and looked for a taxi to take her to the station, but suddenly she felt a chill, even though the sun was hot, even though she was on her way to meet him.

But how can I let him go, how can I? she thought, shuddering. I love him so.

But for him she would have been like an unlit lamp; she would have lived her whole life in terms of that mother, that father, harsh and grasping, unloving and unloved. How could she let him go who had brought love and a glimpse of honor into her life? Who had never lied to her, never degraded her?

I hope the war never ends, she wished fervently, forgetting the taxi, walking on. I hope it goes on forever.

She passed a church and, on an impulse, walked into the cool gloom and sat down, still trembling. She had gone to church often during the desperate weeks of the German advance, when rumors reached the city of whole British battalions decimated in the onslaught, with the living wandering like ghosts among the mangled dead.

Blessed Jesus, not him, she had prayed desperately, not him. I don't care if the whole world dies, but not him. I promise I'll never see him again if You let him live.

Soon after, it seemed to her that God had accepted the bargain, abandoning her and Paris, too, as the battle raged southward to the Marne, with no word from Julian.

It had been 1914 all over again, children evacuating, the government prepared to flee, even the menacing rumble of guns on the Marne. Emalie did not hear them or the German Gotha planes that bombed Paris; all she heard was her promise to God never to see Julian again if he lived through the German advance.

And then, miraculously, the advance lost impetus, slowed, and was stopped in a salient that bulged across the Marne to within thirty miles of Paris. Emalie, careless of whatever punishment awaited her for it, had renounced her vow and surrendered to life when at last a letter came from Julian.

Why not? she thought now, standing up in the pew, what has God ever done for me?

She left the church and went to the station to meet his train.

# 15

"You'll have to battle your way through that mob," William said. "Better wait, it'll be easier to find her."

Julian nodded and they hung out of the window of the railway car with Tony Holland, watching the troops from the rear carriages bulge up from the quai and erupt into the station's vast hall.

William thought he was probably worrying needlessly over Julian. Tony wasn't worried about Julian's affair. "It's the war," Tony said, "he'll be right as rain when the war's over."

At length Tony went to meet his girl and the other two got off the train and made their way up the ramp toward the gate.

"There she is!" Julian said, and at the sound of his voice and the sight of the girl Poyndexter's concern returned. Office girl or not, she was very pretty and he had never been able to resist a pretty woman. When he greeted her his charm bubbled up like champagne because she looked so delicious and so French, but almost at once he was impatient to get away from her and Julian. They were totally absorbed in each other, the attraction between them so intense that for a second William saw them making colossal love, never mind poor old Davina waiting back in Blighty. He left them.

Emalie searched Julian's face to see what the last fearsome battles had done to him; he was a major now, but she said nothing about that. She thought his eyes had a curious brilliance that could have come as much from exhaustion as from joy at seeing her. He never relaxed completely until they were alone together, but William could usually make him laugh, and he needed to laugh. "Maybe we should have asked William to dine with us," she said absently.

"No," he said, gazing at her. "Sweet William has a pressing engagement with a girl at the Folies—and I want you to myself." He kissed her then, his hands still resting on her waist. A fresh scent of lemon verbena came from her, warmed by her body, intoxicating to him. He wanted to rest his head between her breasts. He wanted to keep her with him always.

"I thought you'd never come," Emalie said. "I thought I'd never see you again." She touched his cheek.

"Ah," he said, "you thought I'd gone mad out there, with the rest of them."

She shook her head. A broken promise to God was insignificant compared to what he had just come through. "No, it was foolishness."

"Of course it was!" His dark eyes swept over her face, lingered on her mouth. "Let's go where there are lights and music and dancing. I've never danced with you."


The Place du Tertre in Montmartre was always lively, the more so now that the Americans were finally fighting in force and the German advance had been stopped. The many small restaurants around the square spilled over onto it, tables and bright parasols blooming on the cobblestones like giant flowers.

They took a table outside and watched a souvenir peddler, an accordionist, a mime, and an acrobat. There was a man who cut silhouettes out of black paper with lightning speed, and another who did inept portraits in charcoal.

Emalie turned to Julian, her eyes sparkling. "Could we?" she said, pointing to the artists.

Julian beckoned to the men, and they posed with mock seriousness, trying not to smile at each other, to laugh with the sheer joy of being together, until the artists had finished. That nervous glitter had faded from his eyes.

"They almost look like you," she said, treasuring them already.

"But no artist can do justice to you," he said. "It's impossible to capture you with charcoal and paper."

They leaned toward each other. "But you have," she said softly.

His eyes took her in again in that intimate way that made her heart and her body come alive. Her lips parted and she sighed aloud the way she did when they were in bed together. Then she blushed because everyone would surely see their passion for each other. She looked down, rolling the likenesses up carefully. "How long do you have?" she said.

"Two nights this time. Can you stay with me through tomorrow night without any trouble?"

She looked up again and nodded. "I'll call the office in the morning and say I'm sick."

"Will they believe you?"

She laughed. "Why shouldn't they? I've never missed a day."

"You were a different sort of girl before you knew me, weren't you?"

"I hated that girl," she said quickly, wondering exactly what he meant. "I was no one at all before I met you."

"No dreams for the future? No young men to beau you about to parties?"

"Not a single one. François said he wanted to marry me, but all I wanted was his job. He helped me get it too. It was a bad bargain for him." François Martin had been killed in June. "Poor François. I was determined to take his job away from him, but not that way." She made a motion with her hand. "Let's not talk about the bank tonight."

"No, not tonight. Tonight is ours." He took a small box from his pocket. "I have something for you." The ring was an opal set in gold filigree. He put it on her finger. "Do you like it?"

"Oh, Julian, yes, it's beautiful." Her eyes were as wide as a child's. "But how . . . ?"

"How did I find it on the Western Front? I asked a friend to bring it back from a leave in London." He kissed her hand.

There were shouts of approval from the next table, where a quartet of young American officers had raised glasses to drink a toast to them. "To love," the Americans cheered, "and lovers."

"They all look like William," Julian said, acknowledging the toast.

"Is he in love with the girl from the Folies?" The ring glowed on her hand, the first thing other than flowers and perfume he had given her. It's just a trinket to him, she reminded herself, it doesn't mean anything.

He was amused. "Hardly—our William isn't interested in love. All he wants is a little comfort, just as they do." He watched the Americans flirt with some French girls.

"They're in luck, but their men will find precious little comfort in Paris," Ema said. Comfort was all he really wanted of her; the ring was payment for it.

"Why not?"

She smiled, determined to be lighthearted. "You know that President Clemenceau offered American troops freedom of *les maisons de passe*?"

"Quite right," he chuckled. "It was the courteous thing to do."

"Ah, yes, but Daddy Pershing turned him down and put all the bordellos off limits to American troops. Papa Vaillant heard it from Monsieur le Président."

"What was General Pershing's point?" He loved her even more when she was like this, not so proper, discreetly naughty. He had never told her he loved her; it was better not said. He had let things go too far as it was.

"He wants Americans to be not only the best fighting troops in the world, but the most moral as well," Emalie finished. "That's a burden we French will never have to bear." She was glad to see him laugh.

"I pity them all the same," he said, glancing at the American officers again.

"Pity them? Why?"

"Because all they have is a little comfort and I have you." He touched her hand. "Ema, you fill my heart when you look at me like that," he said softly.

"Oh, Julian, *j'ai le coeur joie, moi aussi.*" It was true. Because of him she had a joyous heart.

He ordered cognac after dinner and smoked lazily while they drank it until, as if at some unspoken signal, the square cleared, a snare drum joined the accordion, and people began to dance.

"Dance with me," he said, holding out his hand, and in a moment his arms went around her. She could feel his uniform through the thin fabric of her dress, and she memorized the sensation, knowing she would relive every moment of this night for the rest of her life, wanting this to be the rest of her life, his arms around her, his face so close that she could see the hint of dark beard shadowing his clear smooth skin. She put her cheek close to his so she could feel that roughness on her face. Her eyes closed and she whirled around to the reedy music, possessed by love.

He could hear her soft, even breathing over the night sounds outside the inn, the swinging of the sign on its rusty chains, the soughing of the summer wind through the trees. He lay awake, looking at the dancing patterns of moonlight on the ceiling, and was overcome by the magnitude of what he felt for her. No other woman in his young life had ever made him feel this. Before he met her he had thought himself inured to death, but because of her he wanted desperately to live just a little longer.

Just once more, he thought again, just once more. But each time he went back to the charnel house that was eroding his soul, there was only Emalie to cling to, not only her body but Emalie, the way she was. How could he leave her, whether it was death or duty that called him away?

He turned, rising on his arm to look at her. There had been some kind of tragedy in her life already; it was in her gray eyes that were sometimes so clear they reflected colors, sometimes stormy and dark as slate. They were brilliant, intelligent eyes, always intent and appraising and sometimes so wary he wanted to shelter her from whatever threatened her.

He knew she came from poorer people than she pretended; her bearing and her clothes were too careful and correct to be those of someone to the manner born. But it meant nothing to him ana he never alluded to it; she had the same right to wear a public mask as had he, adorned with medals for gallantry he did not feel, fighting for king and country no matter how he despised the enormities they asked him to commit.

She was naked in the warmth of the night. There was surcease in her round breasts, the curve of her hips, her welcoming thighs. The touch of her mouth was paradise.

He was kissing her when she woke. She was languorous with sleep, as if she were underwater, alive because he breathed for her. Her arms came up to enfold him, and he made love to her this time with a poignance that was as sad and sweet as love itself.

"I love you, Emalie, I love you, I love you," he whispered to her in the tumultuous swell of ecstasy, as if he had just discovered the words. "I can't live without you."

"My darling, you *will* live. I'll keep you safe, I love you." She was filled with him; they were omnipotent.

But that declaration of love opened a door that had been closed to her, and the next morning, lying next to him, she made herself walk through it.

"Did you love her too—Davina?"

She felt him shake his head.

"Then why did you marry her?"

"I thought I loved her—and our families expected it. Everyone called it a perfect match. We know the same people, we do the same things, we were even taught by the same dancing master when we were small. And we *liked* each other. I thought that was love; I thought it was enough." He moved so he could see her face. "I didn't know what love was until I met you—but Davina was my mistake, Ema, and she's my responsibility."

"I know, I know," she said, clinging to him. "It's all right, don't look like that." She was stricken by his anguish and furious with herself for asking what she already knew. He loved her, only her, even if these random moments were all she could have of him now. She did not ask him what would happen when the war was over. She was sure she already knew. She would have him for a lifetime of random moments—all she had wanted once, before she loved him. But she had always loved him, from the first moment and long before she knew him.

Yet the spoken truth, rare and always unexpected, had cast a spell upon them both, like the arcane words of a magician. From that night on he wrote to her whenever he could, telling her things he had never told her before about his friends, his favorite books and music, his memories of the two of them as if they had lived a lifetime together. The spell was still upon them when he managed an overnight leave in September.

They stayed in Paris at the Crillon—they were beyond caring who might see them, but no one did—because there was not time enough to go to Neuilly. In the morning she poured tea for him while he dressed, added milk, and looked up to find him watching her with an expression of the most profound longing on his face, like an artist trying to capture a fleeting moment forever.

"What is it?" she said.

"I wish there were a lifetime of tea trays for us."

There was nothing she could say.

"I love you so much, Ema. I will always love you."

It broke her heart; there was so little left of always for them.


On the train back to the front Julian sat next to William, rapt in thought. Tony slept, as usual, his thin body curled on the seat. The troops in the rear carriages sang lustily, and the sound floated up to the officers' car.

> Oh, they've called them up from Weschurch,
> And they've called them up from Wen,
> And they'll call up all the women,
> When they've fucked up all the men.

They sang spiritedly about Tipperary and packing up their troubles, then movingly about a long, long trail a-winding. They sang about the home fires and the roses of Picardy, where so many men had died, and that new song from America about smiles that love alone can see.

Julian was silent, seeing more clearly with the eyes of love than he had ever seen before, and still there was nothing he could do because of Davina, his wife, whom he had never loved like this. He sighed deeply. His head dropped to his hands.

"Julian?" William was tapping him lightly. "Julian, are you all right?"

Julian nodded, infinitely grateful that William cared. "I was only thinking of the things we do so carelessly. Then we discover they're like this war; there's no way to stop them."

# 16

Just a month later Emalie, with a dark premonition, went to Cesar's to meet him after work. He had never risked calling her at the bank before.

He was sitting on a banquette across from the bar, so withdrawn that he did not see her until she was standing near him. There was a bottle of brandy and two filled glasses on the table.

"Julian, what happened?" She took the chair across from him.

"I've been ordered home," he said. His voice was as hollow as his eyes.

"For good?" She could hardly say it.

"No, for a short leave."

She breathed again. "Is anything wrong? Your father?" There was influenza everywhere, as deadly as the war.

"It's William and Tony. They're dead." His hands shook, holding the glass.

Her eyes blurred with tears. "Oh, Julian, no! When? How?"

"Two days ago. They'd gone out with a wire-repair party." He drank off the brandy. "Tony was quiet after the shell hit, but William kept calling for me. It seemed like hours before he stopped, but they say it was only a few minutes. The firing was very heavy, we had to wait until dawn to go out for them."

She refilled his glass, waiting for him to go on.

"We found them in a crater puddle. Tony'd got a piece of metal through his head, he died instantly. William . . ." He took a ragged breath. "William's shoulders and legs were broken by the blast, he couldn't pull himself out of the water. He kept his head up as long as he could, then he drowned." Julian shook his head. "He called to me and they wouldn't let me go to him."

She gasped, weeping for his friends, for him. "I'm so sorry, darling, I'm so sorry." After a while she said, "And you were ordered to take them home?"

He nodded wearily. "The colonel seems to think I need a break. Ema . . ." He stopped, then spoke again, tonelessly. "I was going to mail this from the station before I left." He took an envelope from inside his tunic and gave it to her.

She hesitated before she took it. "What does it say?"

"That we can't see each other again."

"No," Emalie said in a desperate, pleading whisper. "No." The letter scorched her fingers.

"Ema, we can't go on forever," he said, his hands still trembling as he lit a cigarette. "We always knew that, no matter what we wanted to believe. There's been too much grief; I can't inflict more on the people who trust me, and certainly not on you."

"But not yet, Julian, not now! The war'll be over soon, everyone says so, wait until the war is over, until you're safe."

He shook his head and took her hand for a moment. "That was a beautiful fiction we wanted to believe, a lovely excuse for doing as we liked. But it's impossible for all of us, especially for you. You're everything to me, you know that, but Davina is my wife." He took his hand away. "It's for your sake as well as hers. There's no future for you with me. You'd have to stay hidden away somewhere until I could steal time from my real life to see you."

"I won't care, Julian, whatever we have will be enough."

"No, Ema, no! You should have infinitely more. You should have everything." His face was white. "I should never have let it begin, but I loved you so even before I knew it, long before I said it. I never stopped to think how you would feel when this moment came. I know now." He stopped speaking abruptly and took his hat from the banquette. "I must go, I'll miss my train."

"Let me come with you."

"No," he said with anguish. "I couldn't bear it." He stood. "I can't bear this."

She put her hand on his arm. "Julian, I know you must go to England," she pleaded. "But come back to me, give us the little time we have left, that's all I ask. I'll never ask for more, trust me."

He looked down at her. She thought he hesitated and her hopes soared, but then he shook his head again. "It's myself I can't trust. If I held you in my arms again, I'd never let you go. I'd desert Davina and break my father's heart."

"And me? How can you leave me before you must?"

"My darling, will it matter when we say good-bye? Will it ever be easy?" He touched her cheek and she shook her head. "Then let me do it now. I love you, Ema. I never meant to hurt you. That's the only thing I regret, your hurt, not mine." His hand rested for a last brief moment on her shoulder, then he walked quickly to the door of the café and let himself out, taking with him everything she had ever wanted.

She sat for a long time, looking at the empty place. He had left the packet of cigarettes on the table and she put down the letter to light one. The unaccustomed bite of the smoke in her throat made her cough, but she smoked it down to the end. Her desolation was an old feeling, well-remembered. The years stretched long before her now, stark and lonely.

She put the letter into her bag and went to the telephone on the bar to call Danielle at the school. "May I stay with you tonight?"

"Yes, of course, I'll be home in an hour," Danielle said quickly, obviously busy; then she stopped. "Ema? Are you all right, what is it?"

"I must see you," Ema said. "I need you." She hung up and left the café.

In the apartment Danielle listened, her expression grim. It worried her that Emalie refused herself the luxury of tears, but this girl had learned to hide her deepest feelings long ago. At least she had stopped shaking. Danielle refilled the ceramic *bouillotte* with boiling water, corked it, wrapped it in flannel, and replaced it at Ema's feet.

"He may not have deceived you, Ema, but he seduced you." Danielle poured more tea, loyal to Emalie, furious with the man who had deserted her.

"That isn't true, I love him—and he loves me, Danielle, right from the start, before either of us knew it. You can't make a choice about love."

"He left you!" Danielle said. "He had a choice about that."

"No, we're too different. If we'd ever spent more than a few days together, he'd have been ashamed of me." Emalie's head dropped into her hands. "*Mon Dieu, mon Dieu,* what will become of him now?"

Danielle came to her and they sat in silence until it was time for bed.

# 17

"What will you do?" Danielle asked anxiously the next morning, pouring coffee for them both.

"Do?" Ema said dully. "Go to work." She shrugged. "That bank was all I cared about once."

"Oh, Ema, I'm so sorry," Danielle quavered, undone at last by the girl's lusterless eyes, her still, white face. Then she regained command of herself. "Go and finish dressing now, it's getting late."

She cleared away the breakfast things with a clatter. She still had no idea who the man was. She had not asked about the letter Emalie had read and reread a dozen times the night before, holding it as if it were the Grail before she placed it in a drawer with the other letters she had brought here for safekeeping.

"At least he didn't just mail it," Danielle muttered, drying the cups, "as if she were a servant to be dismissed with a character reference." Whatever else he had done, the man cared for her, Danielle was certain of it. Emalie couldn't love a man who wanted only her body. "I wish he *were* a scoundrel," Danielle said through her teeth. "I wish he'd thrown her over for someone else before she fell in love with him."

The doorbell rang, and with a snort of annoyance at an interruption so early in the day Danielle went into the hall, closing the door thriftily behind her to keep the heat inside the living room.

A burly man stood there, his beret planted flat on his head, a cigarette dangling from his lips. The broken veins of a drinker stained his nose and cheeks an unhealthy red. "Who are you?" Danielle said, disliking him immediately.

"Jacques Bequier," he said, his brows lowering. "Ema's father."

More than revulsion, Danielle felt shock that a brute like this had begotten Emalie.

"This is an odd hour for visitors, Monsieur," Danielle said. "What do you want?"

"I've come for my girl," he said doggedly. "She says she stays here all the time. I want to see for myself."

The door opened behind Danielle.

"How dare you come here?" Emalie said. It was rough, a voice and manner Danielle had never heard her use before.

He balked, more surly than ever. "You're my daughter," he said. "I have a right to know what you do."

"You have no rights over me at all," Emalie said viciously. "Get out of here or I'll call the gendarmes."

He backed out of the doorway. "I'll teach you manners when you get home," he said. With a threatening look over his shoulder he went heavily down the stairs, leaving the two women rigid in the hall until they heard the street door slam shut below.

Danielle closed the door to the apartment and locked it. "Mother of God," she said, shaken by the colossal hatred of the girl for her father.

"I'm sorry, I'm so sorry," Emalie said almost inaudibly, her voice shaking now. "I never told him where you lived. I don't know how he found out."

Danielle nodded shortly and put her arm around Emalie. "It's all right, don't speak of it, you must not go home, you must stay here until you are . . . better." She released the girl. "Now we must go to work, it's late." *Sainte Marie*, she thought, that man must never know the truth, he would kill her.


A week later Julian was in Flanders again, just forward of the old Ypres salient. It was a terrible place to be, rank with the smell of death and still festering from three pitiless battles in as many years. Now they were preparing to advance again across this open graveyard in a surprise attack.

Julian was moving forward of the line with two men; they were going to deal with a German machine-gun nest that dominated the field from a ridge and sprayed gunfire on the British below. Whether or not the Germans were aware of the impending attack, the nest must be taken out before the attack began. The small patrol worked its way up the slope under cover of the debris that fringed the field, planning to cross the ridge, move to the gun emplacement, and take it from behind.

Julian came parallel with the crest of the ridge before the others did and looked through his field glasses. He drew in his breath sharply. The noisy nest at the far end was only a decoy! There were four more between him and it, deeply dug in well forward of the German line and sitting silently just under the ridge. When the British advanced as scheduled, they would be cut to ribbons.

He looked at his watch. There was very little time before the British attack began, but one man, if he were quick and quiet, could do what had to be done.

He sent the other men back to warn the colonel and tell him to order continuous fire from below to cover the sound his own shots would make. Then he passed over the crest and inched along the soggy back slope, the wet leaves muffling his progress, until he was behind the first nest. There were two soldiers in field gray, hunched quietly over their gun.

Julian waited for the covering bursts of British fire to begin and shot the two Germans in the back with his revolver. He was a very good shot and he killed them quickly and neatly and without letting himself think. He removed the feed block from the gun and threw it as far as he could. He checked his revolver before he climbed out of the hole and moved on to the second nest.

He had killed seven more men before he got to the last post. He covered its two occupants from behind and ordered them, in German, to remove the feed block and throw it. When they refused, he killed them too.

The colonel, who had watched his progress through field glasses, now looked at the time and shook his head. "You haven't got a chance, Saxon!" he urged in an agonized whisper. "For the love of God, run the other way, surrender!"

As if Saxon had heard him, the colonel saw him remove the last feed block and throw it. He saw him drop his revolver, take off his tunic, and walk toward the German lines, his hands high over his head, his white shirt gleaming in the sun, just as the British artillery barrage began. The colonel couldn't see him after the first shell hit.


On the other side of the hill the major lay like a rag doll, with only the tattered remnants of his trousers left to say who he had been.

After the battle had veered sharply west and come to an end, a mule and wagon plodded up the far side of the hill and set about collecting bodies. The two Germans driving it were very young, but their faces were dark with dirt and the one who climbed down from the wagon moved like an old man. He approached the body and bent over it.

"*Ist er tot?*" his companion called from the cart.

"Not yet, but he won't live long." He brushed dirt from the trousers with the care of a valet. "Looks British to me. He's theirs, not ours."

The other snarled. "Theirs, ours! What difference does it make when they're dead?" He got down and came to look, shaking his head at the white bones protruding through the man's flesh. "Poor bastard, he'll be better off dead." He tore the trousers from the broken body. "Now he's ours. To hell with their rules, I'm not going to leave him here. No man should die all alone in the dirt."

The first man nodded and together they gathered up the limp and silent body, put it on top of the ones already dead, and headed back to the German lines.

# 18

"Oh, it's you, dearie," the woman at the British Leave Club said. It was the same one, dumpy in her Woman's Auxiliary uniform and with an accent difficult to understand, who greeted Emalie every evening. "Here's your *Times*; come and sit yourself down all comfy like."

She shepherded Ema to a corner table past the admiring glances of the tommies in the club. "You look done in; would you like a cuppa?"

"Thank you, no."

The woman went back to her tea urn and Emalie sat down. She had been coming here every day for weeks to read the war news, trying to discover where Julian's unit was. She had plenty of time today; it was Sunday.

She hid behind the paper and began with the short lists on page one. KILLED IN ACTION. DIED OF WOUNDS. Then she turned to the headline on page two: FALLEN OFFICERS—ROLL OF HONOUR. She read the list under each subhead—Killed, Wounded, Missing, Missing Believed Killed—and stopped because he was there.

Saxon, Maj. J. A., DSO, son of Sir James Saxon, Bart., of Stridings, Kent.

She lowered the paper to the table and sat staring at it. It took a while for her to grasp that his name was really there, that this was not part of her perpetual nightmare.

Then she felt someone shaking her, holding a cup of water to her lips. "Here now, luv, have a sip of this, then get up, that's it, and come into the office."

In the little office the woman swept papers off an old divan and made Emalie lie down, still clutching the *Times*. "Killed?" she asked brusquely, her face sympathetic.

Ema looked up. "Missing believed killed. What does that mean?"

The woman shrugged. "It means you can hope if you have the heart for it. You must try to find out more. Your husband?"

Ema shook her head.

"Oh. The authorities won't give information to anyone but his family." She met Ema's pleading eyes. "All right, then, I'll try. What's his name?"

Emalie showed her the listing, then lay absolutely still. It seemed a long time before the woman put the telephone receiver back into its hook. "I'm sorry," she said, "they won't tell me anything more." They looked at each other. "You might try his army headquarters." She scribbled an address and handed it to Ema.

"You've been very kind all these weeks," Emalie said, sitting up.

"Here, you're white as a sheet. You want to rest a bit."

"No, I'm all right," Emalie said.

The woman went with her to the street. "You'll be better off at home, luv, with your family. Do you want a taxi?"

"No, I need some air. Thank you for everything, thank you." She set out for the address the woman had given her, past the Place de la Concorde, where captured enemy guns and planes sat on sullen display. The great Place was empty, and there was a hush, strange in a city on the verge of victory, but the influenza epidemic had made people fearful of crowds. She thought how many ways there were for people to die without a war to kill them. Why had they believed he would survive just because they loved each other?

There was a crowd inside the headquarters when she finally got there, her legs trembling with fatigue. She was shunted aside in the mounting excitement of continued Allied victories and rumors of an armistice.

They want it to end now, she thought, now that they've killed him.

"I regret, Mademoiselle," a suspicious captain told her impatiently when she finally got his attention, "but we do not supply information to persons unrelated to British officers. We may not know anything final about the missing for weeks." His opinion of her was clearly conveyed by his expression. "Bloody camp followers," he said when finally she turned away, but she hardly heard him.

Missing believed killed. It was a cruel phrase, the uncertainty of it agonizing.

His father will be the first to know what happened to him! she thought suddenly. Sir James would tell Monsieur Vaillant and eventually it would be announced to the bank's staff. Until then she must wait, no matter how terrible the wait would be. Even Danielle could not be expected to share this night's vigil. There was nowhere to go but home.

She felt dizzy. There was a pool of nausea in her stomach, and the exhaustion that had plagued her in the past few weeks deepened. She wondered idly if she was coming down with influenza—it was killing over a thousand people a week in Paris—but she did not really care what happened to her anymore. She had always known he might be killed, but she could not believe he was dead.

The slatted wooden volets of the *épicerie* were closed when Emalie walked along the alleyway to the back door. The smells from the privy made her sick, and she vomited outside the door. When the spasms stopped she went inside and pumped some cool water to rinse her mouth and her face. Then she sat down at the table, shuddering.

She had no idea how long she had been sitting in the kitchen, when she heard footsteps and looked up to see her father coming down the stairs, yawning and scratching himself through his woolen winter undershirt.

"What are you doing here?" she said, confused.

"I'm off this Sunday."

She said nothing and he peered at her.

"You're sick," he said. "Maybe you have *la grippe*."

She did not reply.

"I'll make you a grog," he said after a moment.

He lit the stove, put tea leaves in the pot, set out the sugar he had cadged from the supply depot, then sat down at the table with her.

"Emalie," he said with the old fondness in his rough voice. "Can't you forget what happened? It was so long ago." He waited. "Ema?"

She looked at him, her gray eyes blank. She hadn't really heard him.

"It doesn't matter," she said. "Nothing matters anymore."

A smile spanned his wide face. "That's my Ema," he said with gruff pleasure. He would have said more, but the water boiled over and he went to pour it over the leaves in the pot. He swilled the tea leaves around, humming a little, and took a bottle of cognac from his store of stolen delicacies in the cupboard, sniffing it appreciatively. He strained the tea into a heavy cup and added four lumps of sugar and a dollop of cognac, pouring a large measure of the liquor into a glass for himself. Still smiling, he pushed the steaming cup over to her. "Let it cool a little, *ma petite fille*. It'll do you good."

It was when he called her his little girl that she began to cry. She wished she were still his little girl, the one who sat on his knee while he sang at the top of his huge voice, the one who watched him play at *boules* in the dusty square. She had loved him then; he had protected her from the terrors of life and kissed away her hurts.

He patted her hand awkwardly. "There now, you're crying because you're sick. You need some medicine. I'll go fetch the doctor."

She shook her head, still sobbing. "I'm not sick."

"Then what's the trouble? Tell your old father."

"He's dead," Emalie Anne said to her papa. "He was killed."

His fond air vanished. "Who was he?"

"A man I loved."

"Who was he?" he demanded again, and in the depths of her misery she did not take warning from his face.

"It doesn't matter, Papa, he's dead now."

He poured another glass of cognac, drank it down, and sat looking at her through hooded eyes while she wept. "You're pregnant by him, aren't you?" he said at last. His voice was soft, but his eyes were sly and slitted.

She looked up, startled by the idea. Her astonishment grew as she mentally catalogued her symptoms and finally, with another sob that was half anguish, half joy, she nodded, amazed that it was so. He gave a muffled roar when he hit her, and she came back to reality and pain and danger. "*Putain!*" he growled through his teeth. "Whore!"

She stared at him, paralyzed by new grief and old terror.

He stood, red with fury, and dragged her up with him. "A filthy whore, that's what you've always been. You tempted me!" he shouted. He slapped her repeatedly while his fury mounted—and suddenly shifted. "I'll show you what you are," he said, and jerked her against him, insane with years of lust and jealousy. He smelled of bad teeth and stale sweat, and she felt sick again.

He pushed her back toward the table, pulling up her skirt. He pressed her down to the wooden surface, tearing at her underwear. She found the hot tea and hurled it at him and his hands flew to his eyes long enough for her to dart out the back door and flee down the alleyway. She heard him calling "Emalie, Ema," and she ran faster along the Rue Momette until she got to the church. She waited inside, clinging to the back of a pew, fighting the nausea until a tram came. All she had when she boarded it were the clothes she wore and a few francs in the pocket of her jacket.

# 19

She was wearing the same suit when she boarded the train for England ten days after the armistice. Influenza had left her pale and unsteady. Her hat and shawl were Danielle's, as was the extra blouse packed in her carpetbag with a change of underwear, a nightdress, and Julian's letters. The rest of her clothes were still in her father's house; she would not go back to that place or allow Danielle to go for her. Danielle, remembering the bruises on Ema's face that Sunday when she arrived in a state of collapse, remembering Jacques Bequier, did not press her. She went only to the bank to collect the things in Ema's desk and tell them she was very sick.

"Emalie," Danielle pleaded one last time as they stood together now on the platform, "don't go yet. You can stay with me as long as you like. You're not well enough to travel."

Emalie shook her head. "I'll never get well until I know what really happened to him. His father can tell me." She had not returned to the bank; she had made up her mind to go to England before she did anything else. She had not even called Henri Vaillant to ask about Julian; more than ever she had to keep their secret.

"Then write to his father," Danielle pleaded.

Emalie shook her head again. She knew what the fate of such a letter to Sir James would be. She expected no better welcome from the man himself, but she did not care. Her business with him was all that mattered.

"I can't bear to think of you alone in a foreign country! You must come directly back."

Emalie touched the woman's long face and kissed her cheek. "You mustn't worry. I'll be all right. And I'll write to you, Danielle, I promise."

"*En voiture!*" the conductor shouted, impatient with the lingering women.

"Here," Danielle said, "take this, for good luck." She thrust a small tissue-wrapped packet into Emalie's hand, hugged her, and watched her mount the steps. Emalie hurried along the corridor until she found a seat near the window of a third class compartment. She rolled the window down and leaned out to clasp Danielle's hand. "I can never make it all up to you, my Dani, but I'll try, I swear I will, no matter what."

"I'll miss you, Emalie." The train began to move, and their hands parted but Danielle still strode along beside the open window of the carriage. "If you need more money . . ." Her black eyes were wet.

"No, my dear friend, no. You've given me far too much as it is. *Au revoir, Danielle chérie, au revoir.*" She was calling out the words now as the train put distance between them, Danielle dwindling away to doll-size on the platform.

"*Nom de Dieu, fermez la fenêtre,*" a man's voice said. "It's freezing in here."

Emalie closed the window and sat gratefully in her seat. She still had spells of vertigo, but the influenza had hidden her pregnancy from both the overworked doctor and Danielle, who had nursed her through it. She still wondered why her father had not come after her, and the thought of him made her put a protective hand over her stomach. She was not going to London solely to hear what had happened to Julian; she was going because of his child.

In those long, empty days of illness and recuperation while Danielle was at work, she had thought constantly about what she would do if Julian were dead, trying to accept that he must be. The child, unanticipated, never even considered, she thought of as Julian's, not hers. If he had lived, he would have cared for her and his baby. But if he were dead . . .

She had asked herself if the baby should be born at all if he were dead, but the idea of aborting his child was repugnant to her. Yet one thing she did know: a bastard born in France would carry the brand of illegitimacy throughout its life in the *carnet de famille*, that little book of civil particulars that followed every French citizen from cradle to grave.

In England such matters could be arranged more discreetly; she had heard about things like that at Thiboux. No matter what she had told Danielle about her immediate return to Paris, Julian's child would be born in England.

She could work for a while in England until the baby was born; the loose fashions would hide her pregnancy. She could work afterward, too, but what sort of life could she hope to provide for Julian's child on a secretary's salary? Julian's child had every right to a fine home, an upper-class education, a good life. And Julian's father must provide it.

She tried to recall everything Julian had ever said about his father, all the letters the baronet had written to Henri Vaillant, even the few times

William and Tony had mentioned him. He was an English aristocrat of the old school, staunch in his traditional beliefs; he had not fully appreciated how much the war had changed his son in that regard. But Julian had loved him very much; he could not be the sort of man who would abandon his son's only child, no matter who its mother was.

Julian's father personified wealth, privilege, and power—the very things she wanted for her child. She was awed by his position, but she was not afraid of him.

She did not think she would ever be afraid again. There are worse things, she reminded herself. Most of them had already happened to her.

She turned the opal ring on her finger and the tissue paper packet from Danielle crackled. She undid the paper and opened the flat little box inside. Danielle's gold-rimmed black enamel locket lay there, the one she always wore pinned to her shirtwaists. Emalie opened it and a brown-tinted photograph of Danielle, younger but not much different, looked back at her. To Ema it was the saddest and the wisest woman's face she had ever seen and the most beautiful, too, because it was the face of a friend.

She knew the message it carried. You're not alone, Ema, I'm your family now. That long, homely face, that shrewd mouth, those black eyes harbored no illusions. Danielle was securely insulated from the follies women commit for love, and from now on Emalie must be as well.

She pinned the locket to her jacket, then suddenly covered her face with her hands and began to cry for the first time since that terrifying afternoon in her father's kitchen. The other passengers in the compartment glanced at her only briefly, at her hollow cheeks and her black suit. They looked away, embarrassed by such naked grief, threatened by emotions that rack the body and bestir the soul.

Emalie leaned against the window and sobbed, careless that Paris was fading from sight.

# 20

Sir James Saxon's expression changed when he heard the light tap on his office door. He had always frowned on displays of personal grief, and did all the more so now, when England mourned an entire generation of young men.

"There is a woman to see you," his secretary said from the doorway, and added, "a Frenchwoman who speaks English." He seemed confused about a proper social category for the caller who, whatever she might be, was clearly not an English lady. "She says she was a . . . friend of Major Saxon."

"Indeed?" Sir James bristled at this last, his dark eyes glinting under the arches of his silver brows. London was overrun with foreign girls making preposterous claims on British officers and men. "You know better than to trouble me with a woman of that sort!"

His secretary persisted. "She is a secretary at the Paris branch, Sir James."

"Good heavens, man, why didn't you say so? Go and bring her up at once."

He had received no message from Henri Vaillant regarding the visitor, but the mails from the Continent were slow now that the Western Front had closed over its hosts of dead. He hungered to talk to anyone who had known Julian, even casually, but he rarely indulged himself; talking about sorrow only prolonged it.

He sighed deeply and sat looking out as dusk fell over Frederick's Place. Once, the warm comfort of his office—walls lined with leather document cases and richly bound books, deep carpets soft underfoot, a cheerful fire crackling in the grate—had made it pleasant to contemplate winter through the windows. Now the cold had invaded his soul. At fifty he felt even older than the white hair that had fallen like ashes over the last of his youth when his son went away to war. A man should not out-live his child; it was unnatural. How he and Margaret had waited for that child—and how well worth the wait Julian had been!

His eyes returned to the portrait of Julian in uniform on the wall opposite his desk. The boy resembled him strongly, but Julian's face was more than handsome. He had been an exceptional young man, casting the same spell over men and women alike with no conscious attempt to do so.

Sir James took a small leather box from the top drawer of his desk and looked down at England's supreme award for a member of her armed services. The ribbon was claret, the Cross was bronze. He turned it over. There was a lion passant guardant on the Royal Crown, and beneath it, in a scroll, the words FOR VALOUR. The Victoria Cross. But it was his son he wanted, the heir to his name and his fortune, the last of the Saxons. No matter how proud he was of the VC, he would never see Julian's face again, except in oil on canvas, and there would never be another Saxon baronet.

There was a knock at the door. He put the medal away and composed himself before he said, "Come in." His eyes met those of the woman who approached his desk. She was very young, a girl really, but she had a certain flair characteristic of Parisiennes, whatever their age or class. She was comely, even pretty, but the unadorned black suit and hat she wore accentuated her thinness and an unnatural pallor. Sir James got to his feet, and the secretary presented her as Mademoiselle Bequier before leaving the room.

"Please sit down, Mademoiselle," Sir James said, doing so himself. "This is a surprise. Monsieur Vaillant did not advise me of your visit."

She remained standing beside the chair and a warning bell sounded in his mind when she said, in good English, "Monsieur Vaillant does not know I am here. I left his employ over a month ago." She had a low-pitched voice that pleased him—the French tended to be raucous—but her manner, unexpected in a secretary, was too direct and very unsettling. Her gray eyes were fixed on him. "I came to ask you about Julian," she said abruptly, and her eyes moved briefly to the black band on his arm. A faint tremor shook her.

He felt another stab of suspicion at her familiar use of his son's name and said nothing.

"He's dead," she said, leaning forward as if imploring him to deny it, and her urgency made him nod. A low moan escaped her, and she covered her face with her hands, swaying slightly. He went quickly to help her into the chair, then poured water from a carafe on his desk and handed her the glass.

"Where? When?" she asked, piteous and insistent.

Again he felt constrained to answer. "Flanders, in October. It was not made official until last week, when the search was concluded." He went back to his desk, talking more to himself than to her. "There was no trace of him in the hospitals on either side. His colonel expected none, but for a while we hoped."

"I know," she said. "I too."

She wept quietly, almost lost inside the big leather chair. Her presumption that she could share his grief offended him. He waited for her to regain control of herself so he could ring for his clerk and send her away.

"Mademoiselle," he said after several moments. "I am a busy man. I don't know why you came here, but this interview is at an end."

"I had to know what happened to Julian. No one would tell me in Paris."

"You saw Major Saxon at the bank?"

Her gray eyes darkened and he realized with astonishment that she was angry with him. "Why did you let him go to war? He stayed out there only for something he called honor—but it was someone else's honor, not his." Her look said it was certainly his father's. "He thought the war was cruel and stupid and need never have been fought."

Sir James was not totally ignorant of his son's opinions. "Did he tell you that?"

"Yes, but there was no need. Anyone who really knew Julian would know that. I loved him."

His silver eyebrows rose. "Mademoiselle, your feelings for my son do not concern me."

She raised her head, still angry but very proud. "He loved me too."

He looked at her with cold disgust. Could this office girl be the reason Julian hadn't come home on leave until last September? "If there is nothing more, Mademoiselle . . ." She did not move. "I'll have a cab called to take you to your hotel."

"I came directly from the station. I have no hotel." She flushed painfully, the color hectic in her white face. "I have very little money."

"That is not my concern, either."

"I am pregnant with Julian's child, Sir James. That is certainly your concern."

He was furious. "How dare you come here and attempt to blackmail me? The police know how to deal with creatures like you." His hand reached for the telephone.

She remained where she was, apparently indifferent to his threat, and for the first time he was truly alarmed about this business. She could never prove what she claimed, but she was the sort who would not hesitate to make a scandal. There was no softness about her now. She was without shame, even ruthless.

"This is not blackmail. I loved Julian," she said. "I never wanted his child. I only wanted him. They are unpleasant, are they not, the facts of life."

"This is outrageous!"

"But still true. Why shouldn't I tell you the truth?" Her voice was unsteady. "There was never any future for us, we knew that. We never thought of a child. I have nothing more to lose now that I've lost him—I have nothing at all except his child."

"What proof is there that it is Julian's child?" he said coldly.

"Why won't you believe I loved him?" she demanded. "You believe I went to bed with him. It's because of who I am, isn't it? You think 'creatures' like me are capable only of lust."

When he did not reply she opened her bag and took out a packet of letters. She handed one to him.

Julian's familiar script leapt at him, and he sat down again abruptly. With another furious glance at her he read the letter, his alarm mounting as he did so. This was a son he did not know, a man of infinite despair and soaring passion, whose love for this girl, by his own description, was the one true joy of his life and whose guilt for having ruined hers the one abiding shame.

No man wrote words of such power and intimacy to a woman unless he loved her. But was Julian the only one? How many men had slept with her? How on earth was he to know the truth about the child? The letter trembled in his grasp and she held out her hand for it. He thought for a moment of destroying the letter, but it would have served no purpose. She had more in that packet and had undoubtedly hidden others; and the letter was no longer the point, the child was, if it were really Julian's. "What do you want?" he asked.

"Enough money to have the baby safely and raise it the way Julian's child must be raised." She was very precise. "A good home, the best education."

"And a substantial stipend for yourself," he said with contempt.

She did not reply.

He folded his hands tightly on the desk. "I need time to think about this. I shall pay for a hotel, where you can wait for a day or two. Your things are at the station?"

She indicated the carpetbag. "This is all I own."

He flushed, appalled that Julian should have fathered a child on a woman like this. Then his secretary opened the door in answer to his signal. "Book a room for Mademoiselle Bequier at White's and call a cab to take her there. She will need some sterling."

A silence fell upon them when the door closed again, each absorbed in thought until his secretary rang and she rose to go. Turning, she saw the portrait. She stood gazing at it for a long moment. Then her gray eyes, dark with tears, looked at him hauntingly before the door closed behind her, and he sat down heavily, utterly shaken and wondering what he must do.

He was desperate for the child to be Julian's, desperate for his son and his name and his line to live on—but he knew he must keep his head. After some moments his hand went to the telephone to call Henri Vaillant in Paris and inquire about the girl, but he drew it back. At this point it was wiser not to let anyone know he was even aware of her existence.

Too nervous to sit still, he walked to the window and looked out, not seeing the darkness or the reflection of his lean, handsome face, so like his son's, in the windowpane. He stood for a long time, thinking intently.

Suppose the child were a boy! A bastard could inherit his property, if not his title. But he shook his head. Suspicions would arise, the truth would get out, it always did, and there had never been a bend sinister in the Saxon coat of arms. He would create the very scandal he sought to avoid.

He sighed. The title would die for want of a legitimate male heir and the property revert to his sisters' children, who were not true Saxons in his view.

But there must be a way out, there must be! He needed time to think it through. He went back to his desk and this time put through a call to Davina.

"Something's come up, my dear. I shall have to stay in London tonight. Will you be all right alone?"

Her voice, soft and feminine, assured him that she would be. "I've been walking all day and I'm tired. I'll have an early night. Will you come down tomorrow?"

"Yes, in time for dinner."

"Good night, then, Uncle James." She had always called him that, ever since she was a little girl escaping her nanny in her haste to find Julian.

He sighed in pity for her as he left the office, and was driven to the twenty-room house in Regent's Park. He kept a full staff there—butler, housekeeper, cook, two housemaids, and a footman—but it felt empty to him.

My God, he thought, to have Julian's son running through the halls here and at Stridings! To have it all come alive again!

His breath caught in his throat, and he knew he would not sleep tonight. He had to find a solution and quickly, too, before the pregnancy advanced any further.

Long before midnight, while he paced in front of the fireplace in his bedroom, he had accepted that the child was Julian's. Julian was not a fool; he would not have felt such guilt over a harlot; he would not have loved a woman who consorted with other men. And he would not have put such a letter in her hands unless he trusted her.

"Oh, Julian, that *was* foolish of you," he murmured once again, but without rancor, forgiving his dead son even as he chastized him. The child was the only consideration now, Julian's child, whether or not it was a bastard.

He paused in his pacing when the idea struck him. What if this child were a boy and *believed* to be Julian's legitimate son? The baronetcy would not have to die with Sir James! Stridings and the rest of his property would not pass to strangers. Julian's son would have his birthright, not ignominy as the bastard son of such a mother. It was not Julian's fault; it was the war: but for the war, Davina would have been the child's mother—and so she would be!

He breathed quickly, his fatigue completely gone. The plan was forming in his mind, but without Davina's collusion—there was no other word for it—it would be impossible to accomplish. Turn the thing around as he would, he could see no other way. It would be a monstrous risk, but there was more at stake than the title. There was Julian and Julian's child.

He was not a sentimental man, but he knew he could never cast that child adrift; Saxon blood prevailed over everything, even the girl's inferior social status. French! And probably a papist in the bargain, like all the French! But the girl herself did not interest him. She was just a cunning female who had profited from the unbridled emotions of war to bewitch his only son when he needed that kind of comfort. With any luck she would die in childbirth; if she survived, he would know how to deal with her.

He slept only a few hours, rising early to pursue his plan, to refine it. He would arrange it all himself, he would overlook no detail, and, above all, he would ensure its absolute secrecy. He did not go to his office at all that day. He stayed in his study, making notes, making telephone calls, consulting the books of civil law statutes on his shelves from time to time.

By late afternoon he was ready. He ordered the car brought around to take him to Farningham, to Stridings, thinking, as the Bentley rolled homeward, how he might best put the thing to Davina. He must make her agree to it, whether he hurt her or not. Only the child mattered now.

# 21

When he had dressed for dinner Sir James went down, through corridors of painted Saxons, baronets for nearly three centuries, to join Davina. He loved Stridings, every softly weathered stone of it, every mullioned window and gracious room. His son had loved it, too, had known each blade of green grass on its spacious acres, each tree and stream and copse that cradled the broad and welcoming house.

He went to the end of the gallery and stood for a moment looking over the grounds. The gardens and greenhouses stretched over twelve acres; they had been Margaret's special province, and fresh flowers for the London house in Regent's Park and the bank in Frederick's Place were still sent up weekly in the second Bentley. He sighed, missing his wife. Margaret would have approved of what he planned to do, he was certain of it.

The house itself, square and solid, rose from two drawing rooms, a morning room, a library, and the large and small dining rooms on the ground floor. There were twelve bedrooms on its two upper stories, with servants' quarters in attic and basement. He preferred it, as Julian always had, to the London house or the estate in Scotland.

He stopped before the portrait of Mademoiselle de Roth Vaillant, who had brought the French branch into the family in the early nineteenth century, along with the Scottish holdings and the mansion in the Avenue d'Iéna in Paris as her marriage portion. Davina had brought the broad farmlands in Devon.

"None of it shall be lost," he promised the high-nosed Mademoiselle Vaillant before he made for the stairs. "Not while there's a real Saxon alive to inherit."

He found Davina in the small drawing room curled up on a sofa near the fire and lost in her own impenetrable reflections. It came to him that he had no idea what Davina thought about most things. There had never been any reason for him to know; she was the right match for his son and had always done to perfection whatever young ladies should do. She belonged here, a welcome presence since her childhood and a special comfort to him now. Poor girl, he thought. First orphaned, now widowed. She was his responsibility now.

"Hello, Uncle James." He bent to kiss her smooth cheek, admiring, as always, the rosy blush of her perfect complexion, the smooth gilt of her hair, the scent of the soap and talcum she used. After Margaret, she was the prettiest girl he had ever seen, and the severe black gown she wore made her blondness breathtaking. He could not help comparing her to the woman who had come to the bank yesterday.

"Shall I fix you a drink?" Davina offered, returning his kiss.

He nodded his thanks and sat down on the sofa while she poured a whisky for him and took a sherry for herself. It was a pleasure to watch her. She was a gentlewoman, whether she wore a gown or a Red Cross uniform or a riding costume. She had redecorated this room after Julian went off to war, and the blue damask walls and silk draperies, the delicate Aubusson rugs and pastel brocade chairs and sofas, were a perfect setting for her chiseled beauty. He was grateful to find her waiting for him each evening in a house that had once rung with the noise and laughter of Julian's flock of school friends clumping about the place. They were all gone now—Tony, William, Julian. What would England do without them?

He roused himself to take the glass from her. "Did you go to your meeting today?" He had urged her to resume her clubs and committees and not to shut herself away as she did—but now he hoped she had not gone out. Her long seclusion since Julian's last leave would serve his purpose.

"No, it all seems so stupid now. I don't really care how they decorate the hunt ball. Or whether they have one."

"Nor I. We have something more important to think about now," he said heavily, and she turned to look at him. "I want you to hear me out to the end and, above all, to remember that we have no choice."

He chose his words carefully. He did not describe the woman—he felt it was inappropriate, nor could he have easily conveyed his impression of Mademoiselle Bequier, whose threatening quality lay in her character, not in her appearance.

He described the child as an accident of war, not the issue of Julian's profound love for that impossible woman. It would be very cold comfort to Davina to hear that Julian's fall from grace had been with such a woman as that.

"But all that matters," he finished, appealing to her womanly sentiment as he had already appealed to her sense of duty, "is that it is Julian's child and must be raised as such. We must ignore in what unfortunate circumstances it came to be."

He saw when he looked at her that the delicate features of her face were twisted by fury. "It belongs with you," he added hastily. "But for that hellish war it would have been yours."

She turned her contorted face away. "How could he?" she whispered, her fingers so tight around the stem of the sherry glass that he thought it would snap. "A child! How could he humiliate me as much as that?"

"He hadn't been himself for a long time. We knew that from his letters, and his colonel confirmed it." He patted her shoulder awkwardly, wondering if the colonel had known about the girl.

Davina looked at him with an arctic gleam in her eyes he had never seen before. "So, Uncle James, you want me to raise this creature's bastard as my own. But she's a whore; the child might be anyone's." With a crisp move of her wrist she drank off the sherry.

"The child is Julian's, Davina; my inquiries have determined that beyond any doubt." He kept his voice steady; the only proof he had was a letter that Davina must not see under any circumstances. The brittle, furious woman sitting there would never agree if she knew Julian's adultery had become passionate love for another woman.

He went on. "Do you think I would suggest such a thing if I weren't certain, if there weren't more at stake than your pride or mine?" His voice trembled as he rose from the sofa and leaned against the mantelpiece, looking down at the fire, bracing himself on his outstretched arms. "The whole situation is as repugnant to me as it is to you. I cannot bear that you should have to pay for an indiscretion my son committed when he was not himself, but how can we let his only child go, now that he's gone forever? I promise you, Davina, that the entire responsibility will be mine. I will arrange everything—and once the child is born I will see to it that the woman never returns to England. I do not expect you to love the child, only to play the role of its mother." He turned back to her to see an expression of disgust cross her face.

"And its *mother*?" She fairly spat the word at him. "What is *she* like?"

"No one. A little French girl he turned to in a lonely moment, not one of us."

"Is she pretty?"

He waved a hand, disliking the turn of the conversation. Davina herself was not pretty to see at this moment. "She is not in your class, Davina. She is—irrelevant." He waited for her consent, but when she made no answer, his words became deliberate.

"Davina, I am determined that my property shall go to a Saxon, if not my title. I shall recognize this child as Julian's, legitimate or not, and damn the scandal. What I am suggesting would cause no scandal to add to your pain. Julian was home on leave. It might have been your child."

She flashed him a look of pure malevolence, and for another interval sat in silence, her bosom rising and falling until she had regained control of herself. At length she looked up at him, her expression blank, and he knew he had won. "Very well," she said. "But I want to meet the woman." She was once more as patrician as her shining hair. Her graceful fingers rested lightly now on the stem of her empty glass.

The prospect alarmed him. "For what earthly reason? Only the child matters!"

Her eyes met his briefly, guardedly, and returned to her glass. "I want to see the woman whose child I'm to mother; that is my one condition."

He was apprehensive about what was hidden in Davina's cerulean eyes, however calm her manner, but there was no other way. "I will arrange it as soon as possible, in London."

"No," Davina said. "Here, at Stridings."

He was not surprised at the ransom her jealousy demanded; the Frenchwoman must come as a suppliant to the place Julian loved most, where only Davina had a right to be. "Be careful, Davina," he warned. "I mean what I say."

She nodded, silent but implacable, and he gave his reluctant consent.

# 22

"Such a lovely costume, Madam," the little maid said, and Emalie only nodded, as unaccustomed to the form of address as she was to having her meals served to her in bed, or to the luxury of soaking in a full-size bathtub for as long as she liked, or to deep, soft towels and linen sheets. She had slept for most of the past three days and felt stronger.

She would need her strength today. She was dressing for a meeting with Sir James so that he might tell her his decision. One of the gods handing down an order from Olympus, she thought.

Her mouth was grim as she thought of Sir James. How contemptuous of her he was! She had expected anger and indignation—she was pregnant with an illegitimate child, after all—but not such towering contempt, as if she alone had done this thing and Julian had no part in it. It was worse because he was so like Julian! His features were not as finely etched, but his eyes were Julian's and the way he held his head—and his voice, his voice! If she closed her eyes, it was Julian speaking to her again. But not like that, not with such cold disdain.

Well, no matter. Whatever he thought of her, she was convinced that he had decided to give her the help she needed. He had telephoned each day to ask how she was, briefly and distantly, but he had asked, and that could be only for the child's sake. For the same reason he had provided her with warm winter clothing. The costume the maid admired—a slate-gray wool trimmed in dove-gray velvet—had been chosen from an assortment he had ordered brought to her hotel room. The shop's proprietress had arrived with three assistants, a fitter and a pile of boxes, chattering and fussing over Ema as if she were a client at Thiboux. There was a selection of lingerie as expensive as the suits and dresses she brought.

"Everything can be run up in one day and finished in another,

Madam," she had assured Emalie, whose natural reticence stood her in good stead; it was taken by the woman for ladylike hauteur, and Ema made a mental note of that.

"This russet melton," the woman had chirped, "trimmed with red fox, is you, Madam. It brings out the color of your hair."

With a mental shrug—knowing she could not possibly sink lower in his estimation—Emalie had taken it as well as the gray suit and cape and two pleated silk shirtwaists, wondering where on earth she could wash and iron them. In the bureau drawers were extra stockings, some petti-slips and knickers of lace-edged nainsook, and a nightdress and peignoir of pale apricot batiste that was more appropriate to this grand hotel than Ema's shawl over Danielle's plain cotton gown.

A gray velvet hat and gray leather gloves and shoes completed the ensemble she had chosen for this meeting. She wore Danielle's locket and Julian's ring. She pinned on her hat, took up her cape, and went downstairs. She was bowed into a black Bentley by a liveried chauffeur, and in that plush and insulated sedan she was driven out of London toward Stridings.

It was the first time she had been out of doors in three days, the first time she had seen a city other than Paris, and for seconds at a time she was diverted by places Julian had described to her. But it was when the car left London and traveled through the English countryside that she knew why Julian had so loved it and why he had sought the quiet of Neuilly whenever he could.

She wondered why his father had arranged this meeting at Stridings. It was certainly not out of consideration for her; he had none. The telephone calls and the clothes were to keep her quiet and out of his sight until he had made known how much he was prepared to do for his grandchild and, unavoidably, for the child's mother.

She looked out at the gentle landscape and saw a neatly lettered sign. Farningham. They were approaching Stridings, and for an agonizing moment she let herself think of Julian, but only for a moment. She could not mourn Julian until she had assured his child's future.

It took her breath away when she saw it at the end of a long driveway, set like a gem amid reaches of moist, velvety grass more lushly green even in winter than any Emalie had ever seen. Stridings accomplished what Sir James had failed to do; it made her feel insignificant, powerless, without even the reckless courage of despair.

No wonder Julian had not come back to her, as she had so stupidly hoped he might through all those terrible days after his leave! No wonder he had chosen this. Had he been free, he would not have married her and brought her here to raise his children because she simply did not belong.

Not even the child could change what she had come to realize, that to be of this place and these people one must be born to it.

She needed all the courage she had to leave the haven of the car and wait until the massive oaken door, black-wreathed, swung open and she was permitted to go in.

# 23

Sir James watched the car approach and saw her alight. Far better, he had concluded, despite his apprehensions about a meeting between the two women, to let her see what he was offering her child before putting his proposition to her. She would covet Stridings for her child. He had been clever, too, to lavish gifts upon her; she wanted money for herself.

She came into the small drawing room clearly overwhelmed by its opulence, precisely as he had intended. This was not the brazen hussy who had stormed into his office. He greeted her with the suggestion of a nod. "I hope you have recovered from your journey," he said, and rang for tea, indicating that she should sit on the sofa near the fire.

The lines of exhaustion and the pallor had almost vanished, and he was relieved for the child's sake. But she was more than pretty, he saw to his surprise, she was beautiful in an earthy sort of way. The sobriety of the gray costume was a disturbing contrast to her vivid sensuality.

Her appearance revived his misgivings over this meeting with Davina, but he had Davina's solemn assurance that she would say nothing to make this girl reject, out of female spite, the offer he was determined she should accept. In any case, this woman had never wanted the child, only Julian. She had said so herself.

"I must thank you . . ." Emalie said, struggling under the weight of her gratitude to this hostile man. She was unable to say more, and her hand touched the collar of her jacket.

He shook his head and moved to stand near the great stone surround of the fireplace. At its center was the same insignia she had seen on Julian's seal ring. "English winters are colder than you could have known," he said.

She almost laughed at the way he fobbed off her destitution as an error of selection, a mere oversight while she was packing for her journey, leaving the sable out, putting the flannel in. He must want something of her, probably Julian's letters. Ah, they were masters of hypocrisy, these Britons; Julian had said so.

Tea was brought and poured by the butler—for an anxious moment she thought Sir James would ask her to preside over that magnificent tray— and then they were alone with the silver tea service and the translucent Royal Doulton cups and saucers and the Saxon child growing within her.

"You cannot deny to Julian's child all that it deserves by nature's law, if not England's," he said when he had told her what he proposed to do.

It was very quiet in the large room. Streaks of the setting sun slanted through the broad, high west windows, suffusing the room with a glow that neither of its occupants noticed. He had put forth his case, and now he waited, watching as she sat with her hands over her body in that protective way pregnant women have, the way Margaret used to sit when she was carrying Julian.

He felt a vague sense of apprehension about the dangerous masquerade he was planning—heaven help them all if it were ever discovered!— but he would not change his course. There was no other way to take Julian's son—for he was convinced the baby was a boy—away from her permanently. He was determined to rear his grandson as the next baronet, no matter what he had to do.

Emalie, under the spell of that voice at once so familiar and so strange to her, had listened closely, her heart racing as his intent became clear. It was so much more than what she had asked, but it meant the total surrender of the child.

What he had proposed was a simple arrangement: he would raise her baby as his legitimate grandchild and in return he would care for her until it was born and afterward provide her with enough money—a fortune, it seemed to her—to make a very comfortable start for herself in any country she might choose, excepting only England. Her daughter, for she was convinced it was a girl, would have everything she had a right to—fine clothes, this splendid house, the best schools, marriage to a man like Julian.

But what of herself, Emalie? She was to be banished, paid off, and cast away like the whore he thought she was, as if Julian had been nothing to her, nor his child, either, the one thing she had left of him!

"Why should I?" she demanded, her eyes flashing as they had in his office. "I didn't come here to give Julian's baby away. I came for money to raise her."

The shift in her demeanor affronted him. He had supposed her thoroughly chastized by her surroundings, and he was not accustomed to disdain from women like her. His face mirrored his implacable intent. "You will either accept my offer or you will have nothing—not a farthing. You can starve in the streets for all I care, and your bastard with you. The child will be a legitimate Saxon or it can go to the devil."

She flinched, suffused by anger and choked by her impotence. If he had literally torn the baby from her arms, she could not have hated him more. "Damn you," she whispered, "damn you."

They gazed at each other, yards apart but locked in a combat of will. Then he said softly, with the unerring instinct of a man who must win at all costs, "Do you think Julian would want his child brought up as you were?"

She gave a little cry at that and rose from the sofa. Her hands moved for a moment over her face and shoulders as if to drive some unseen pest away. She looked around the beautiful room and saw again her mother's rough red hands, smelled the store and the alleyway, heard the head-board thumping against the wall upstairs, felt the bed move under her father's weight, and knew she was beaten again as surely as she had been then, humiliated, violated, forced to act against her will.

With a strength born of years of practice she buried what she felt and made a mighty effort to think clearly. She would promise this man any-thing to secure her child's rights, but the promise would be good only for as long as she kept it—and someday she would have more from Sir James Saxon than money. Someday she would pay him back.

She nodded quickly, not looking at him. "All right," she said. "You win. How will it be done?"

"You must leave that to me. I have already put the thing in motion." He paused. "Julian was home in October. There is no reason why the child should not be Davina's."

"And she agrees to say it is?" She was first amazed, then curious.

He nodded. "For Julian's sake, yes, she will. The child must be legiti-mate to inherit the title, and there is only one way to accomplish that."

"It will be obvious to everyone that she hates this child!"

"She hates you, not the child," he said, believing it absolutely. It was how he felt himself.

Deep within her a protective instinct ruffled its wings, but she would not let it take flight. These were civilized people. "Go on," she said, pur-suing the heart of the matter, the baby's legitimacy.

"You will both go away—separately," he added quickly, "and Mrs. Saxon will come back with the baby."

"And the baby's birth certificate will say that Julian is the father?"

He nodded. He would not tell her to what lengths he would have to go to arrange all that. "And that Davina Fitzross Saxon is its mother."

She did not even flinch, but went on resolutely to the end. "And in exchange for my promise to leave England you will raise my child as you did Julian? The best of everything?"

He nodded, and there was silence between them again until she said, speaking to herself, "He would have wanted his child to grow up here." She looked around the room again, then her eyes met his, and he could almost believe that she had loved his son. Then he dismissed the thought. She was without womanly emotion. Even her concern over Davina's feelings for her child had to do with hiding its illegitimacy, not with assuring it any mother love. He was glad of that; it meant she would never make a public scandal no matter what she might be planning for the future. She was too eager to make her child a Saxon; she would never compromise its rights.

He poured some sherry from a decanter on the end table and handed her a glass. "My daughter-in-law wants to meet you."

She looked up. "Yes," she said with cutting irony, "I'm sure she does."

His brows curled with apprehension. "If she is . . . difficult, I hope you will understand?"

"And if I am, will she?" Then she shook her head. "It doesn't matter, Sir James, there are worse things. Is it to be now?"

He pulled the bell cord and she stood waiting silently until the doors opened and Davina Saxon came into the room. She wore a long-sleeved black wool dress relieved only by a string of pearls at the high neckline. Her hair made a flaxen frame around her face. She was composed except for the electric blue eyes that did not once leave Emalie's face as she walked across the room. She stopped at the other end of the sofa, and her gaze moved over Emalie, missing nothing of her figure, her clothes, or her reaction to this ruthless, hostile inspection.

"So you have agreed to it," she said to Emalie. Her voice was expressionless; it was all in her eyes.

She has just walked over my grave, Emalie thought. "On condition the child won't suspect you're not the mother."

Sir James moved a step nearer the two women.

Davina waved an imperious hand. "It is not for you to set conditions. For me this child has only one parent, my husband. You simply do not exist." With a small movement of her head she dismissed Emalie and left as silently as she had entered.

The two in the drawing room avoided each other's eyes. Emalie felt naked and clumsy, seeing herself through Davina's eyes as she had been through William Poyndexter's, common, promiscuous, and coarse. "When must I leave?"

"In two days, if you are up to it? Good. You will go by rail to a village in Scotland, where a car and chauffeur will be provided for you. A midwife will accompany you and stay with you until the child is born, then a nurse will replace her until you are ready to leave. You will be known as Mrs. Seaton, I as your uncle." He hesitated. "I trust you will communicate with no one? Your family?"

Emalie stirred. "I have no family. But there is one friend in Paris."

He frowned. "I'm afraid I must insist . . ."

"So must I," Emalie said. "She is my only friend. She knows nothing about the baby; she doesn't even know Julian's name. I will tell her nothing, but I must let her know I'm all right."

"Then she must write to you in care of a post box in London. I will collect the letters and send them on to you."

"Yes, yes, whatever you like." Her hands rolled and unrolled her gloves. "I would like to go back to London now."

He went with her to the waiting Bentley, his face showing the strain as much as hers. He got in and sat beside her, talking quietly so the chauffeur would not hear. "I shall ring through to you tomorrow with more details. The woman will see to all the proper clothing and supplies and will bring them with her."

She nodded again, eager to be gone, and the door clicked shut. She leaned back in the car and closed her eyes as it pulled away. She heard the crunch of gravel under the wheels from inside a maelstrom of emotions—anger, made impotent by the shame of that woman's punishing contempt; amazement that Julian could have married anyone as cold as that; and above all, piercing envy.

"If I could have been like any woman in the world, it would have been Davina Saxon," she whispered against the cushion of the car.

In her hotel room she paced for a long time before she sat down to write to Danielle. What she wrote contained only one truth, that her anonymous lover was dead, as she had expected. The rest was a lie about a position as governess she had found that would start in Scotland and take her traveling far afield, a wonderful opportunity at a very good salary "so that when I come back to Paris it will be in style!" She would send a mailing address as soon as she had one.

She wrote nothing about Stridings or Sir James. She did not say that she would not allow herself to imagine Julian and his wife in bed together. And the letter said nothing about the child inside her and the incredible bargain she had just struck.

But was it so incredible? It was only in the world of fantasy that the prince married Cinderella, and for Emalie that kingdom was forever sealed. She must seize life as it really was and make of it what she could so that someday, somehow, she could pay these people back.

# 24

It has all been too easy, Sir James thought as the door to his office closed behind his secretary on a wet Monday morning some three months later. Easy or not, he was constantly weary from the weight of the secrets he was committed to keep for the rest of his life.

He had been in Scotland for another long weekend, ostensibly to visit his pregnant daughter-in-law. He had, of course, lodged at Davina's discreet rented house just outside Edinburgh, but he had also driven to Silvermoor Cottage in Glengowrie for his monthly call on Emalie Bequier and the midwife. There was nothing amiss there—or anywhere. It was all too easy.

His friends and colleagues agreed without exception that Davina needed rest and absolute seclusion if she were to carry Julian's posthumous child to term and bear it safely. Where once Sir James had rigidly masked his grief for his son, now he let it show. People, thank heaven, didn't expect him to socialize until the birth of his grandchild and had left off trying to bring him out of himself.

The girl herself, Emalie, was quiet, if not serene. She would never be serene, Sir James had decided. It was not in her nature, but at least she played her role perfectly. She was in glowing health, the midwife told him, although she spoke little. She was always absorbed in the books she requested at such an astonishing rate.

It was not lost on Sir James that most of them were Julian's favorites. So Julian had told her those things too. The relationship, no matter what Sir James wanted to believe, had obviously been more than carnal.

She was intelligent; from the few remarks they exchanged for the sake of conversation he knew she understood what she read. She had asked only for English history and fiction at first, arousing his suspicion that she meant to break her word and stay on in England; lately, to his relief, she was studying the United States.

He took a cigarette from the carved box on his desk and was lighting it when the telephone rang.

"Yes?"

"A call from Munich, Sir James, a Dr. Herzog, who will speak only to you."

"Put him through," Sir James said. Business with Germany, admittedly clandestine, was resuming at an astonishing pace, for there were great pickings to be had in a country as totally beaten—economically, militarily, and morally—as Germany had been. This was probably another director of a German chemical firm seeking financing from abroad.

"Sir James Saxon?" a deep voice asked, and proceeded almost immediately. "I am chief surgeon at the military hospital in Munich, and I call you on a most urgent matter."

Mystified, Sir James waited.

"I do not wish to shock you," the doctor went on, and it was then that Sir James felt his heart lurch and begin to race. "And you must reserve your judgment, but there is a man here who claims he is your son."

"Dear God," the father murmured, clutching the receiver. He shook his head. "But it can't be true."

"It may not be. But he gave his name as Julian Saxon and his home as . . . ah, here it is, Stridings, Kent. A servant there just told me where I would find you."

"Julian?" Sir James pleaded. "Is it Julian?"

The doctor's voice took on medical authority. "My dear sir, I have told you all we know. He still sleeps most of the time. He has been slipping in and out of consciousness for many, many months. He might have given the name of a friend; they sometimes do that."

Was it William? Or Tony? Sir James thought in his confusion. No, they were both dead. Julian had brought them home. Some other poor young fellow Sir James had never even met? He steadied himself and spoke firmly. "Please tell me the truth, Doctor," he said. "How badly hurt is he?"

"Very badly," the doctor said, "but mercifully he has lost no limbs. He was naked when they found him. We thought he was one of ours." The doctor sighed. "A wounded soldier belongs to all of us."

"Yes," Sir James said. "And a dead one." He wiped his face with his handkerchief, trying not to believe what he had just heard until he could see the wounded man for himself. "Will he recover?"

The doctor hesitated. "He is very weak, of course. And there is much infection that is stubborn to heal. He has a fair chance, much better now that he is semi-conscious. It would help him to see someone he loves."

"I shall come at once," Sir James said. "But, Doctor, has anyone else been told?"

"No, we keep these things very quiet until final identification has been made."

Sir James nodded. "No one must know. We could not bear the publicity."

"Neither could he." The doctor gave him the location of the hospital before the connection was broken, and Sir James, after a moment's anguished communion with Julian's portrait and a surge of hope he could not deny, hurriedly left his office to pack a small bag and board the afternoon train at Victoria Station that would start him on his way to Munich.

His elation alternated with despair as the long journey ground on. It can't be true, Margaret, he told his dead wife—and then, Be alive, my Julian. Only live and I swear I won't ever let anything hurt you again.


The hospital room in Munich was dim when Sir James entered it with the German doctor and went immediately to the bedside. He bent to look closely at the man lying there. The face was painfully thin and waxen, but unmistakably Julian's face as it would be when he was an old man. Sir James took one emaciated hand and raised it to his lips.

"Is it your son?" the doctor asked.

Sir James nodded, too moved to speak.

The nurse, who had been sitting near a towel-shaded lamp, approached. *"Guten abend, Herr Doktor,"* she whispered.

*"Er shlaft?"* the doctor asked.

She nodded and whispered a few more words. The patient had drifted off again just a few moments ago, but he had been awake and aware before that. The doctor peered at Sir James. "It will be very hard for you to wait like this for one moment that might not come again for hours. Come and be comfortable in my office. The nurse will call us."

"No," Sir James said, "thank you, I want to be here when he wakes again."

Doctor and nurse stepped outside so the father could be alone with his son. A few moments passed in the quiet room, then the sleeper stirred and his eyelids fluttered.

"Julian," his father said. "Can you hear me, son?"

"Father?" It was the merest whisper.

"Yes, it's Father. Don't talk, my dear boy, I'll tell you everything. You're in an army hospital near Munich. It's April now; you were brought here last November after the armistice, from a German field hospital. You were unconscious when they found you and too sick since then to identify yourself." He paused. "Can you hear me, Julian?"

"Armistice?" The word was formed by the pale lips rather than spoken.

"Yes, the war ended soon after you were wounded."

A faint nod of the head acknowledged that deliverance.

"You've been barely conscious for a long time. You were badly hurt, but you're whole, Julian, you needn't worry about that. When you regain your strength you'll be good as new, do you understand?"

There was no response from his son, and Sir James waited to see if he slept again. But the paper-thin lids opened with great effort and Julian's dark eyes looked up at him with love. It was a sight Sir James had not expected to see again on earth, and tears rolled down his cheeks.

"My boy," the father whispered, stroking his son's face tenderly, "my beloved boy."

After a moment he wiped his eyes with his handkerchief. "You must sleep now, Julian. You must eat and sleep as much as you can."

He spoke as if to a child, although the man lying there was a hero. Still, this was his boy, his flesh and blood. He had taught Julian to fish and shoot and ride, to tell the truth and be kind to inferiors and keep his word and honor women, especially the ones whose bodies he enjoyed. He had taught him that last too well; the worry in the father's face took on another cast when he thought of the pregnant woman at Silvermoor Cottage in Scotland.

One of Sir James's bitterest regrets had been that he had not really known the man Emalie Bequier knew. Now he had another chance and he vowed, standing over the sleeping form, that he would not make the same mistake again. He would penetrate the hidden reaches of his child's heart, the better to protect Julian from himself.

He went to sit in the nurse's chair. Now he must tell Davina that her husband had been found.

But first he would enlist the help of his friend, Lord Broadhurst, to keep this story out of the press. A resurrected hero would be meat and drink to the newspapers, but he would make it a point of honor with Broadhurst to keep it a secret. Sir James could not risk having the girl discover the truth.

The child would be born in about two months, and Sir James must make sure she left England before Julian was brought home.

Julian would come back to his wife and child, the war and its madness behind him. He would recover, God willing, and resume the life he had always loved. And there would be no bastardy for the child, no humiliation for Davina, and no scandal for the Saxons. Julian himself would agree even if he knew the truth about the baby, but Sir James had no intention of telling him. And Sir James would make sure there was no trace of Emalie in Paris if ever Julian tried to find her.

But that was for the future. His son's life was the primary issue now.

The returning nurse roused him, and after waiting some moments more at Julian's bedside he put one worry aside and went down the hall to see the doctor about another.

"He looks very ill," the father said.

"He is," the doctor returned. "It's amazing he's alive at all, that we were able to put all those shattered bones together and sew them back inside his body. It will take a long time for him to heal. Weak as he is, the wounds keep reinfecting." He shook his head. "His body will be badly scarred; you must be prepared for that. He is married?"

Sir James nodded.

"I thought so," the doctor said. "He called always for his Emma. It broke my heart to hear him, but I believe it was his longing for her that pulled him through."

Sir James nodded again, his expression impassive.

"You must warn her about the scars," the doctor continued. Then he paused and glanced at the exhausted man opposite. "He has children?"

"One expected in two months. Why?"

"He sustained several injuries to the groin." The doctor put up a hand as Sir James paled. "I am almost certain that he will not be impotent once he regains his strength, but whether the passages are too much damaged to sire children is another matter. Time alone will tell, a very long time I regret to say." He paused again. "I think it is better that he is not told about this even when he recovers; fear can be as paralyzing as a wound. Home and a loving wife are probably all he needs—and time. You must all be very patient."

Sir James nodded, then hesitated.

"Yes?" the doctor said kindly.

"How long was he unconscious?"

"He suffered a severe concussion when the shell hit. It exploded very near him, to judge from his other injuries. And then"—the doctor shrugged—"he might not have wanted to wake up. Some of these cases never do. A man who served in the front lines as long as your son did might very well choose not to wake up to that nightmare. The miracle is that he clung to life at all. But," he finished, "I have seen no signs that his mind is affected. He is perfectly lucid when there is no fever and he has the strength to speak." He turned to a cabinet in the corner and took out a bottle and two glasses. "A drink?"

Sir James returned to his hotel room at ten o'clock that night, too weary to eat, but before he slept he telephoned Davina.

# 25

She held the telephone receiver, her eyes closed and her lips parted in a tremulous smile. Then she remembered where she was and why. She replaced the receiver and paced nervously around the bedroom of the rented house in Edinburgh, her expression changing again as she resurrected Julian, the boy she had known all her life, the man she had sworn to marry.

She remembered the first time he ever kissed her, the two of them leaning against a tree near the river, and the craving at the core of her, as sharp as the bark of the tree, to have him to herself. She had considered urging him to make love to her that night, but men like Julian did not seduce the women they would marry.

She remembered the night of their engagement, a night of green summer sweetness and the scent of roses in the garden, the ardent pressure of his mouth and the pent-up desire in him that made her smile triumphantly and call him "John Anderson my jo" from the Robbie Burns poem they had read together as children.

She had whispered it again on their wedding night when he made love to her at last. "My jo," she called him when at last his long man's legs were stretched the length of hers, his breath deep in her throat, his body buried in hers. She remembered his hands, first on her breasts, then under her hips, turning her up to receive him. She could still feel the shudders of him inside her, proof that he was really hers, then and now, for always.

He had been her "jo" since they were children, her darling, her prize, her husband, hers.

"And he'll always be mine," she swore vehemently in the quiet room, no matter what price she had to pay and no matter what he had been driven to tell her on their last night together, he tormented, she hysterical, after she persuaded him to make love to her.

\*     \*     \*

"I hate you for telling me, I hate you and your disgusting truth. Why did you make love to me, then?"

A silence, brief and eloquent. It was she who had made love to him. Then he said, "I wanted to make a go of it; I never dreamed it would be like this."

"Like what, damn you?"

"I love her, Davina, I can't change that."

"You love *me*! I'm your *wife*, Julian. You promised to love *me*!"

"But that's impossible now; it isn't fair to either of us."

"Shut up, shut up! I won't listen to you. I won't listen!"

But there was more. He was proposing divorce as the only solution, divorce after the war. He would take all the blame, he would go away forever because he loved another woman more than he loved Davina, his wife of eighteen months, his bride of only a few nights.

"Is that why you finally came home, to tell me this?"

"I came home determined to tell you nothing, to do my duty."

"You bastard, you bastard! I despise you, I wish you were dead. I hope they shoot you, I hope you die!"

And she thought he had.

\*     \*     \*

"Little fool." She smiled at the mirror now. "You should have been more dignified, more understanding. He would never have left England and Stridings and his father, not for any woman."

Then she thought of how this particular woman had made her beautiful drawing room seem pallid, without vibrance. "She's coarse," she whispered, resuming her pacing, "and that appeals to men in bed. Very well, I can be coarse too." She clutched her robe closer to her, recalling the strong beauty of the French girl's face, the penetrating gray eyes that never faltered, her sensual mouth and her figure. There was an earthiness about her that would arouse any man, and she was certainly clever—all those French girls were—even if she was a slut. Davina was far too clever herself to underestimate a rival. Julian must never see her again, or he might still believe he loved her. Love! He lusted after her, that was all.

"I'll make him lust after me," Davina said. "I'll find someone to show me how."

She pressed her lips together. She would adhere to that woman's condition, indeed she would: no one would ever suspect that Davina Saxon was not the baby's mother. She would have to live with the evidence of Julian's betrayal for the rest of her life, but there were two sides to every coin; the child would prove to everyone that Julian loved his wife, the child would bring Julian to his senses.

God alone knew what her friends had really thought when he hadn't come home on leave in all that time! She was sure their sweet sympathy masked a suspicion of the truth, that they whispered behind her back when month followed month and she waited for him, fallow.

They had always laughed at her single-minded pursuit of him. They had hinted archly, with the salaciousness of virgins, that she would stop at nothing to get him, and she had smiled archly, as if, indeed, she had not stopped.

"Davina's done it!" they crowed enviously on her wedding day; they were flushed and ignorant, palpitating with visions of ecstatic defloration—and jealous because every debutante in her year was in love with Julian. Then he had gone away to France and had not come home on leave. Had they guessed why? Had they laughed because she was barely married before he wanted to desert her for a French whore?

"But I'm having his child now. Now they'll have nothing to say." Her clenched hands relaxed and she went to her dressing table and lit a cigarette. He would never leave his child—or his child's mother—not even for that woman. And he was too badly hurt to look for his mistress before time and the child had done their work. It was right that Davina should have him; she loved him more, enough to take him back in spite of what he had done, enough to make that woman's child her own even if Julian could never know the full extent of her sacrifice in so many words.

She sat at her dressing table and smiled into the mirror again, Davina's sweet, serene smile. She had nothing to hide from anyone. Then she leaned forward to examine her face. She put the cigarette down in an ashtray and fluffed out her hair, the golden hair Julian loved to bury his face in. She opened her robe and pushed it and the satin nightdress from her shoulders. Her graceful hands cupped her breasts and stroked them until the nipples were pink and rigid. She rose and stepped out of the robe and the gown and stood naked, touching her thighs as he would touch them, sliding her fingers past the darker golden hair between them to find, with satisfaction, that she was warm and wet with desire.

"My jo," she whispered. "I'll never let you go, I swear it." She went to the bed and lay down, coaxing desire to its peak, and for once her lonely satisfaction did not end in sobs because she had lost him long before he died. No one would ever say that now, least of all Julian, whose conscience had made him a husband again just long enough to make her a mother.

She prayed with all her might that the baby she had wished dead along with its mother would live and thrive and save her marriage for her.

# 26

"Teatime, Mrs. Seaton." Mrs. Atherton's voice chirped through the open window.

Emalie left the garden and went up the path to Silvermoor Cottage. She would not have believed anyone could be as consistently cheerful as the midwife, but the woman's determined good humor never failed her. They were very cordial to each other when they spoke at all, but they never discussed anything more personal than childbirth and the weather.

Silvermoor Cottage was a charming place, some three miles from the village of Glengowrie. It belied its modest stone and thatch exterior, furnished as it was with fine fruitwood tables and chintz-covered chairs and sofas. There was a fireplace in the kitchen and lounge and in each of the two bedrooms upstairs.

A comfortable aroma of toasted scones and hot oatcakes filled the house when Emalie went inside, and Mrs. Atherton, ruddy of face and spare of figure save for her astonishing bosom, bustled in from the kitchen with a cozy-covered teapot on a tray.

"I'm dying for some real coffee," Emalie said, backing up to the wing chair and letting her bulk drop into it.

"Come now, coffee is bad for the baby," Mrs. Atherton said, presiding over the teacups, "and for us. We won't sleep and we need our strength for the delivery." She passed Emalie a cup of milky tea.

Emalie balanced the saucer on her belly. She was due next month and her girth dismayed her, although Mrs. Atherton assured her she was no bigger than most and smaller than some. Ema was impatient for the confinement to be over and at the same time reluctant to have it end. For the first time in her life she was coddled, protected, secure. She had been weary enough when she arrived here to go to bed and stay there for several weeks, but it was her melancholy more than her fatigue that had concerned the midwife then.

Mrs. Atherton, however, thought she understood the situation perfectly. Young Mrs. Seaton, even though she was foreign, was obviously well bred. A widow, she had got herself in the family way and her uncle, Mr. Jerrold Seaton, had stepped in to conceal the scandal when her lover was killed. He had been distant with his niece at first, an understandable reaction from a gentleman of the old school—such a handsome man, he was, too—but he had changed toward her of late. He was very fond of her, Mrs. Atherton could tell.

The midwife was to leave immediately after the birth—obviously, then, the child was to be given over for adoption to persons who wished to remain anonymous. It was all the same to the midwife; she had been well paid to keep her own counsel, and she intended to do so. Mrs. Seaton was not happy—what young woman in her position would be?—and was inclined to be difficult and taciturn, but the deep melancholy of the first month had passed.

"Have a little rest now, until your uncle comes," Mrs. Atherton said to her charge. "It's warm enough to nap outdoors."

With unaccustomed docility Emalie submitted to being pillowed and shawled in a chair under the oak tree. A great contentment had settled upon her in the quiet isolation of Silvermoor. She had always lived in a place pululating with shouting people and dark-brown smells, but now she could breathe, now she could smell the earth and watch the wonder of approaching spring.

She had plenty of time to read, too, and Sir James sent her all the books she wanted. After she had finished Julian's favorite classics, she wanted to read as much as she could about the country her child would live in, its history, its empire, its traditions. For herself, she had decided on America because it was new and it was far. It would be easier at that distance to hold her vengeance in check until she was ready to take it.

She walked a great deal and wrote Danielle happy fictions about the small girl who was supposedly in her charge while her own child moved vigorously within her. She wrote about the child's magnificent clothes, her curls, her pony.

Danielle's replies to the post office box in London were just like Danielle, affectionate but terse—until one arrived with unexpected news.

"Your mother came looking for you yesterday. Your father had a stroke on the Sunday that you came to me. He never recovered and died a few weeks ago. I thought you should know, although there is nothing you can do about it."

So he was stilled at last, that great monster of a man, his deep voice and his revolting body powerless now to hurt her! She did not stoop to the hypocrisy of sorrow; she had wished him dead often enough. But was that why he had called her back? And by not going, had she killed him? She was more withdrawn than usual for a day or so, but soon resumed her reading, to Mrs. Atherton's relief.

Emalie dozed under the tree now, wondering why Sir James had missed coming last month to check on his property. She smiled wryly. She was perversely amused by her relationship with "Uncle Jerrold." He played his role expertly. He had let Mrs. Atherton see his disapproval, but he kept his disdain and suspicion to himself. Their dislike for each other was mutual, but she knew she could trust him with her child and that was all that mattered. He had never seen the silhouettes and drawings from Montmartre. She kept them hidden with Julian's letters. They were for her own comfort and for some future purpose that was not yet clear to her.

An uncle was expected to be fond, apparently, and his lips grazed her cheek when he arrived and when he left. She wondered how he would behave on this, his last visit before Julian's baby was born, and so wondering drifted off to sleep. She did not hear his car when it arrived. She slept on when Sir James Saxon walked across the garden and stood looking down at her.

Her hair was loose and soft around her face, her cheeks flushed, her lips slightly parted in sleep. Her face was young and gentle and very sweet. The shawls hid her condition, but there was a ripeness about her that was overpoweringly female.

A beautiful woman, he thought, and stood very still, watching her.

He wanted her. For some time he had privately acknowledged his grudging respect for her quick mind and the unfailing courage she had in her convictions, no matter that she despised him for his. But today, vividly, he saw Julian making love to her and he wanted her himself.

In all of his life he had never known a woman as sensual as this woman, his son's mistress. He felt a painful hunger to possess her and a searing envy of Julian, and he was ashamed of his lust and his jealousy. But he could not deny the stirring of his body. His desire for her had grown along with his respect, even in the shadow of his shame. It was no wonder that Julian, who had kissed that mouth and possessed that body, had fallen in love with her.

He tried again to tell himself that only one kind of woman in her present condition could dazzle a man, but he knew she was no prostitute. Still, he reminded himself sternly, she was not of their sort and therefore not to be trusted. He intended to keep track of her when she left here, to know where she lived and how. Soon she would be gone and he would be safe from her; they would all be safe.

She stirred and her eyes fluttered half open. The sun was at his back and all she saw was his silhouette, the familiar tilt of his head. He said, "Emalie," and she smiled at the sound of his voice, a radiant smile that took his breath away. She stretched, arching her back, so languorously seductive that he began again to tremble.

"My darling," she said, and then came fully awake and realized where she was and with whom, just as he leaned over to kiss her, mercifully, at the last moment, resisting her mouth. Their eyes met. She stilled her body and her face closed like the covers on a book of erotica; she was once more the calculating girl he knew.

He straightened and went into the cottage and she lay there, stunned by what had just happened, not even sure it had. How dared he watch her as she slept and let her think he was Julian? How dared he kiss her . . . but he had kissed her before. She shook her head, denying her instinctive certainty that this time was different; she had surely imagined it.

She was composed when he returned to her after having tea and a consultation with Mrs. Atherton. "There are matters we must discuss now that the time is drawing near," he said. His manner was distantly polite, but he was more preoccupied than usual. She wondered again why he had not come last month.

"Yes, of course." She waited. If she could learn to behave like a lady, she might be taken for one—never by him, of course, but by the people she would meet when her new life began. Much as she despised Davina, she still wanted to be like her, not like Emalie, gauche and unpolished, the prey of unruly passions.

"Would you like to walk before dark?" he asked.

She nodded; he had something important to say that Mrs. Atherton must not hear. He helped her up from the chair and put a shawl around her shoulders as they set off through the garden. They walked slowly, mindful of her bulk.

She took a deep breath. "*Ça sent le printemps*—it smells like spring."

"You have chosen to go to America," he said, unmoved by spring, "rather than back to France, a very wise decision. Since you are embarking on a new life, I think it would be as well to have a different name."

"I never thought of that," she said quietly, "but yes, it would." She had no great love for Emalie Bequier. She had been struggling to escape her since she was fourteen years old.

"And what name will you choose? There are papers to be prepared."

She thought a moment, then a name she had once admired in a French novel popped into her head. "Emanuelle Beranger," she said. She pronounced it in the French fashion—Bay-rahn-jhay—although it would be Ber-in-jer in England. She stood looking up at him through the gathering dusk, hoping in this unguarded moment for some sign of approval—for her name, herself.

"Very well," he said, and resumed walking in the gathering twilight. He took her arm lest she trip on the darkening path. He was aware of the fresh verbena scent she used and the pressure of her breast against his arm. "Mrs. Atherton will notify me when your travail begins," he said more brusquely than he had intended.

She stopped and looked up at him again, studying each feature of his face. At length a faint smile curved her lips, appraising, unlike that earlier, dazzling smile, and he had the appalling conviction that she knew he wanted her.

"Is this the last time we'll see each other?" she asked.

"That was part of our agreement," he returned. "Everything you need will be given to you when you are ready to sail. Shall we go back?"

He took her into the cottage, said good-bye to Mrs. Atherton, and turned for a last time to her. His hands on her shoulders, he bent for the ritual kiss. He felt her smooth skin against his mouth and the soft warmth of her body under his hands.

"Such a charming man, your uncle," Mrs. Atherton said when he had gone. "And so fond of you."

"Yes," Emalie said, "I know."

# 27

In the early hours of labor the swelling contractions left her time to recover, to rest, even to think. Emalie lay decorously under the honeycomb counterpane in her bedroom and feigned a stoic calm while she watched the sun's progress across the garden, from jonquils to daisies to irises, wanting desperately to talk to someone who knew all about her and how she had come to be lying here frightened like this.

But no one knew all about her, and she must make certain no one ever did.

"We're doing very nicely," Mrs. Atherton said at noon while Emalie shrank from the inspection. The midwife replaced the light cover and wiped the perspiration from Ema's face. Then she continued her preparations on a table near the bed while Emalie watched. She laid out freshly boiled strips of muslin to wipe the baby's eyes, olive oil to be warmed for its body, Vaseline, scissors, a needle and thread to sew the binder closed. "First babies," she said cheerfully, "often take their time coming."

By dusk Emalie had thrown aside the cover. She cared nothing for modesty now, only surcease from the punishing pain.

"Now, now, Mrs. Seaton," the midwife kept saying, "you must not bear down; it is still too soon for that."

And Emalie, nodding, would fall into a few moments of exhausted sleep, only to waken to that massive viselike grip and a visceral grunting that she realized came from her.

"Take short breaths," Mrs. Atherton ordered, her voice sharp but her hands gentle as once more she inspected her laboring patient.

"How long?" Emalie pleaded, panting.

"All in the fullness of time, my dear, all in the fullness of time."

Dusk lengthened into night and Emalie heard voices downstairs.

"Has he come?" she asked in a whisper.

"Yes, my dear," Mrs. Atherton said, sponging Emalie's forehead, then her arms and legs. "Your uncle is here."

And is she here, too, Emalie thought, the fairy princess with the basi-lisk eyes, waiting to snatch Julian's baby away?

It was the last coherent thought she had, crushed by that savage em-brace that hardly stopped before it began again. Now she was told to bear down with each contraction, and Mrs. Atherton gave her no quarter even when she moaned that she was too tired. "Nonsense, you're a fine, strong girl," came the answer. "Bear down."

*"Je n'en puis plus, je t'en prie."*

"All right, relax now, Mrs. Seaton. You must speak English, I cannot understand you." A cool cloth wiped Emalie's face. "Never mind, dear, push again, push as hard as you can."

Pushing, Emalie called as loudly as she could.

"Hush, Mrs. Seaton. She isn't here."

"Who?"

"You called for your mother."

"No!"

"Why not? A woman wants her mother."

"No, not mine," Emalie began to cry.

"Hush then, we won't have her."

"Who came in?"

"Only the wet nurse, Mrs. Seaton."

"Danielle, I want Danielle."

"Bear down, it's almost here."

"Keep him away from me, don't let him touch me."

"He shan't hurt you, I promise."

The woman's reassuring voice, her steady hands, made Emalie go on with the rending struggle until, in a gush of hot blood, the knot of exqui-site pain passed from her body and she lay in a half faint while the infant cried. She heard the wet nurse say, "There, 'tis bonny it is, the dear wee thing," and in a gesture that she remembered only later and could never forget, Ema reached for the baby.

There was a moment of silence from the women, then whispers, then she heard the door open and close and the mewing cries faded away. Her arms fell back and she felt Mrs. Atherton's pressing, tending hands for a few moments more while she lay empty-armed, her body hollow, until exhaustion overcame her and she slept.

When she awoke she was, as she had been told she would be, in the care of a nursing sister, a dour and taciturn Scotswoman with a heavy burr who had been well paid, Emalie was sure, to ask no questions. The silence of the house, like the quiescence of her body, oppressed Ema, and she languished for two weeks, eating little, weeping silently, longing for a friend.

"I'll fetch Doctor if ye dinna give over weeping," the nurse said. "Ye'll never be oop and aboot if ye go on so."

"Leave me alone," Emalie mourned, her gray eyes huge and dark in her thin face. "How can you possibly know what I feel?"

The stern face gazed down at her for a moment, and then the woman sat down on the bed and put a large capable arm around her. "There now, lassie, any woman knows what it's like to lose a bairn. You must have a last cry now, then ye must get on wi' it."

"What was it, a boy or a girl?" Emalie wept against the woman's shoulder.

"I know not, but there now, it's dead, what difference should that be?"

Rocked in a stranger's embrace, Emalie sobbed for Julian's baby wrenched out of her body and never touched, never held in her arms for a farewell embrace before they took it away and told this woman it was dead. She cried for Julian, who was really dead, and vowed she would never risk loving again, no matter how great her loneliness, no matter how urgent her need.

She stood in the bath that afternoon while the nurse sponged her almost-familiar body, washed her hair, and helped her dry it in the warm June sun.

That evening she ate a hearty supper downstairs in the lounge for the first time in two weeks and then looked through the documents Sir James had sent her. They attested to the world that she was nineteen years old, born and orphaned in Lyon, British by marriage to a Welsh lieutenant in the fusiliers who had been killed in action in France. Her name was Emanuelle Beranger.

Sir James had sent, along with the proofs of her birth and marriage and a soldier's death, a first-class passage ticket on a steamer from Plymouth to New York, a substantial amount of sterling for the trip, and a letter of credit on a New York bank for one thousand pounds on which she could draw two hundred a year for five years. That was to keep her out of England; he had told her at Stridings that the money would be stopped if she ever came back. She had no idea how much it was in American money, but it was a comfortable sum in England and more than she had ever seen in France.

Sitting in her wing chair, Emanuelle Beranger began to think about New York.

# BOOK II

First say to yourself who you would be and
then do what you have to do.

—EPICTETUS

# 28

Emanuelle turned off Fifth Avenue onto East 32nd Street. She saw immediately that her destination was in the middle of the block: a long line of chauffeured cars was parked at the curb, and girls in dark blue uniforms and broad-brimmed felt hats streamed out of the doors. Ema smiled as she approached the Treadwell Female Academy, four brownstones united behind a single façade. It was pleasant to be among rich girls and she watched some of the smaller ones as she went up the steps and rang the bell.

She was admitted by a uniformed maid and shown to a seat in the parlor to wait for Miss Treadwell, the school's owner and headmistress. It was a dark parlor, crowded with ponderous furniture on clawed feet and aspidistras in crackled China pots. Its windows were heavily draped and its colors murky in the gloom, but it was clean and comfortable. The school was well-established, to judge from photographs hung about the walls of the many classes it had graduated.

A schoolmistress, Ema thought, of all things!

She had been in New York for three weeks now, longer than she had planned to be here without work, but she had changed her first-class passage to third class—she was not yet ready to move in high society—and the refund, added to her travel money, could have seen her through another month or more in New York. But she had no intention of staying idle longer than she had to. Born in poverty and trained to thrift, she was determined to increase her nest egg, not squander it.

As soon as she had arrived and was installed in a drab hotel for ladies, she looked through all the London papers she had missed in transit. There had been no birth announcement from Stridings, and she realized now there would be none, Sir James was too cautious. He would keep it a private announcement, using Davina's grief as an excuse. She stopped buying the London *Times* and turned instead to the New York papers. At first inspection she thought she had been wrong to let him pay her over five years; she might easily have bought a business of her own with the whole of her five thousand dollars.

Still, she reflected, this city was totally strange to her, even to the color of its lights and the sound of its taxis. She explored it for a few days and decided she must know a lot more about America and Americans before she parted with a penny. For the moment she was fascinated by New York, despite the absence of broad esplanades like the Place de la Concorde and wide, rolling boulevards. It was an indoor city, not like Paris, where so much living went on in the gardens, on the Seine, in the sidewalk cafés.

On one of her walks she had bought some fabric, and she spent her evenings at the hotel manager's machine, making the few things she needed for the autumn. She had recovered all of her strength on the ocean voyage, but memories could still make her feel helpless, and she concentrated on all she had to learn about America once she understood the money, things like the bus fares and the price of stamps, and how the telephone worked. And she thought about clothes. For the winter she had the gray ensemble and the russet melton Sir James had bought for her in London and the dowdy summer dresses she had bought in Edinburgh for the crossing. She made a lightweight suit in navy blue flannel for the balmy autumn weather, *l'été de la Saint-Martin*—they called it Indian summer here.

With the instinct of the city-bred she soon knew which were the fashionable parts of New York and asked for work in those areas when she applied to the most prestigious female placement agencies she could find. She gathered that the only jobs available to Frenchwomen in New York were as governesses, saleswomen, and ladies' maids.

The Treadwell Female Academy, however, was just starting its fall term and urgently required a French teacher. That intrigued Emanuelle; she could study American history at such a school, perfect her English, and learn how upper-class young ladies behaved in this country. The interview had been arranged and Emanuelle, appropriately dressed in her blue suit, waited now for it to begin.

She stood when the door to the parlor opened and a woman some years older than she came in. The woman had a plain round face, round spectacles, and a solid figure. Her hair was pulled back into a bun, but unruly little tendrils curled around her face, softening the severity she had set out to achieve. She was wearing a dark skirt—in the gloom it was difficult to tell whether it was blue or black—and a loose tweed jacket buttoned over a white silk blouse. Her laced boots made no sound on the carpet as she crossed the room, speaking with an anxious air.

"Miss Beranger? I'm so sorry to have kept you waiting, I'm Katharine Treadwell." She sat down opposite Ema. "Would you like some coffee?"

Emanuelle refused politely; the coffee in America was almost as bad as in England. She already knew she wanted the job, but she sat quietly through the conventional exchange of information. The salary, though, was lower than the agency had told her.

"Oh, dear," Miss Treadwell said, flustered by the mention of money, "they sometimes do that when they send someone they know I'll want, but I truly can't afford more, the bookkeeper would resign." She smiled, a sweet, worried smile that made Emanuelle feel like patting her. "Perhaps," Miss Treadwell suggested shyly, "perhaps if you live here, that would even things out."

"Live here?"

"You'd have your own room and bath, of course. This is a very big place, especially at night and on weekends when the girls aren't here. I rattle around in it since my parents died. I'd like company, but the other mistresses are very grim." Her smile was mischievous now, like a schoolgirl caught drawing caricatures of her teachers; then she looked at Emanuelle's clothes again, at her face and her hair. "But I suppose you already have a place of your own."

"No, Miss Treadwell, and I would like very much to live here." It would be a great saving for her—even a tiny apartment in this part of town would cost a lot. Besides, she liked Miss Treadwell. They went upstairs to see the room.

That weekend she moved her few belongings into the comfortable bedroom on the second floor. It was the first time she had ever had a room and bathroom of her own; Silvermoor did not signify, it wasn't hers. This room was spacious and furnished in the same solid style as the parlor, with a comfortable easy chair and a desk, bookcases, a wardrobe, and a large bureau in addition to a four-poster.

She settled in, grateful to have found a safe harbor. She had been more nervous about coming to New York than she had let herself admit. This was certainly an odd place for a woman with her past and the future she wanted, but she could be only one thing at a time, after all, and for now she was Frenchmistress at a fashionable girls' school in New York.

# 29

"*Il y a peu de femmes*," Emanuelle wrote on the blackboard, "*dont le mérite dure plus que la beauté.*" She put down the chalk and turned to the class. "Translation, please. Miss Blessing?"

The young girl stood awkwardly, looking like an unfinished piece of pottery. "There are few women whose merit outlasts their beauty."

"Very good—but I think 'worth' or 'value' is closer to La Rochefoucauld's intent than 'merit.'" Miss Blessing sat down and Ema continued. "Your weekend assignment, girls, is to write an essay on that *maxime*, what you think it means and whether or not you agree with it."

The bell rang and she dismissed the class. The Blessing girl's mother, a slight but daunting female and one of New York's social lionesses, came into the room to collect her daughter, the eldest of three enrolled at the Treadwell Academy. She read the sentence on the blackboard.

"Is that your opinion, Mademoiselle?" She had a voice like brass and amazing style, but she was not in the least beautiful.

Emanuelle shook her head. "Most emphatically not. I want to see what the girls think of it."

"Are you teaching French or philosophy?" Mrs. Blessing inquired, a shade too sweetly.

"One seems to involve the other," Emanuelle said with a conciliatory smile.

Mrs. Blessing bore her intimidated daughter off with a last appraising glance at the French teacher whom she had never addressed, although Emanuelle had been teaching for over a year.

It was the last class of the week and Emanuelle looked forward to the weekend. Katharine Treadwell, true to Ema's first impression of her, was one of the most endearing women Ema had ever known, despite her compulsion to do what people expected of her. She was actually eight years Ema's senior and had never had money. Her socially prominent parents had lost everything just before Kate was born and had been reduced to running a school for the daughters of their rich friends. Kate was by nature warm, affectionate, and utterly charming, but apologetic, as if her arrival had precipitated her parents' bad luck and she must excuse herself to the world for it.

Before Emanuelle's first month was out, the two young women had slipped into the habit of spending their evenings together. They sat in Kate's cozy little study while Emanuelle did the lessons assigned to the senior girls and Kate corrected papers. On weekends they went to museums or to Central Park together or window-shopped the big department stores. Occasionally they went to the opera, sitting high up in the family circle; Emanuelle was as much dazzled by the opera as by the spectacle of New York society in the tier of boxes aptly called the diamond horseshoe. Someday, she promised herself, I'll own a box in the diamond horseshoe.

This weekend the weather held fair on Saturday and they decided to drive to Long Island in the venerable Treadwell touring car. "I never have to look at the calendar," Ema told Kate over breakfast. "I can tell what day of the week it is by what you're eating for breakfast—oatmeal, eggs, or pancakes—and which color you're wearing—black, brown, or gray."

The self-imposed rigidity of Kate's life had first startled Emanuelle, then amused her, but as the first year passed and the friendship formed and deepened she was determined to rescue Kate from the loveless future she had accepted as her lot. That was partly because her parents had convinced her that without looks or money single blessedness was all she could expect, partly because of her apprehensions about sex. She kept her only suitor at arm's length, reluctant to face the intimacies of marriage.

"I've always dressed like this, come to think of it," Katharine said after some reflection, savoring the strong coffee Ema had introduced her to. "The mothers expect it of a headmistress—as it was they thought I was too young to take over when Father died."

"But I don't dress that way," Emanuelle said, "and they've accepted me. I swear I saw a glint of approval in Mrs. Blessing's eye yesterday."

"That's different, you're French, you're a Mademoiselle." Ema had chosen to be Mademoiselle to the girls; there had been a doleful finality about widowhood, even at twenty.

"Well, here's something to brighten your life." She gave Katharine a flat box and watched her delighted smile as she opened it.

"Oh, Ema, thank you, it's lovely!" Kate tied the red silk scarf around her neck. "You shouldn't have."

"I couldn't resist. If you really like it, wear it, even to class. I don't think the mothers will object in the slightest. They won't even suspect you're in love with Spencer."

Blushing, Katharine got up to get more coffee. Spencer Atwood was an accountant who kept the books for the Treadwell Academy in his free time. Katharine had inherited him along with the school, the furniture, and the Treadwell name, but loving him was her own idea.

He was a tall soft-spoken man of thirty-odd who was not at all social and far from rich. He loved Kate, that was obvious to Ema, but he hesitated to propose marriage to a Treadwell, even an impoverished one. The land and the buildings belonged to Katharine—"but you can't pay bills with bricks and mortar," she had told Emanuelle when they first began exchanging confidences.

She was still blushing when she came back to the table with her coffee and sat down again. "I hope Spencer doesn't suspect!"

"Kate, *chérie*, it's not enough for him to suspect! He'll never propose until he's sure you'll say yes; he's as shy as you are."

"I'm not sure I want to get married," Kate said in a low voice. "Now, finish your breakfast, Ema, it's a long trip."

Ema said nothing more, but she had never been able to sit by and let things just happen, it was her nature to act. She knew Kate really wanted to marry Spencer and what Kate wanted, Ema was determined she should have. This love story could have a happy ending; it needn't be a catastrophe like her own.

The story she had told Kate in those first confidential exchanges was the one Sir James Saxon had provided for her. She was beginning to believe it herself, even to having lived on the Rue de la Pompe when she moved to Paris from Lyon to be nearer her husband when he got leave.


"What was your husband really like?" Katharine ventured one night at the start of Ema's second year on 32nd Street.

"Beautiful," Ema said. "People called him *le bel anglais*, but not only because he was handsome—there was a special luster about him, everyone was aware of it, his friends, his business associates. I could never love anyone else."

"Ema, dear, you're so young and so lovely." Kate's brown eyes filled with tears. "You mustn't talk as though your life is over."

"Not my life, just a part of it."

They were drinking hot chocolate in the kitchen, their hair rolled up in rag curlers for a drive to Coney Island tomorrow with Spencer and one of his friends, who was certain to be overwhelmed by Mademoiselle.

Emanuelle was not impressed by the American men she had met so far, but they had all been ordinary, not the upper-class men she intended to meet, somehow, when she was ready.

"I think," Kate offered after a moment, as if trying to convince herself, "that every woman needs a husband."

"Maybe, but it won't much matter to me who mine is." Provided he's very, very rich, she thought.

"Ema! How can you say that about a man you have to . . . you know."

"Sleep with?" Emanuelle smiled. "I knew a girl once, her name was Clothilde, who said she could close her eyes and think of France while it was going on."

"Did you do that with your husband?" Kate asked, her romantic visions crumbling.

"No, of course not. I never thought of anything but him. I loved him. Besides," she went on, seizing the opportunity to reassure Kate, "it's wonderful to make love, it's nothing to be afraid of. Everything was designed to fit together, you know. Men aren't made like the fig leaves in your silly American museums!"

Aside from American puritanism, it was her pupils' preoccupation with beauty that amazed her as the months passed. Neither charm nor intelligence nor wit counted for anything. The most popular girl at Treadwell was invariably the prettiest.

"*La beauté, la beauté!*" Ema exclaimed impatiently, fitting a new dress on Kate. "A woman is more than that! The most remarkable woman I know looks like the back of a tram, but she has character and verve and panache. Turn a little, Kate." The new dress was a clear red silk for the holidays, the second Christmas Ema would be spending at the school. The dress set off Katharine's creamy skin and the warmth in her nearsighted brown eyes. Ema had absolutely refused to make anything in black, brown, or gray.

"She sounds like Mrs. Blessing," Kate said, turning.

"Ah, that one, *une force de la nature*. She sits in my last class every Friday since that first time, observing me. Actually I was thinking of Danielle, but Mrs. Blessing certainly has panache. There, you can look, what do you think?"

"Oh, Ema!" Kate marveled. "Is that really me?"

Kate wore the red dress to go out with Spencer on New Year's Eve and Ema waved them off, feeling like a mother hen. They would soon marry, she was sure of it, but in any case, over two years had gone by and it was time for Ema to move on. She couldn't spend her life teaching school no matter how comfortable she was here, no matter how much she cared for Kate. She had scores to settle, put aside but by no means forgotten. There was not a day she didn't think of Stridings and how she could turn what had happened there to her advantage without ruining her child. One thing was certain—she could do nothing until she had acquired some money and status.

She took a bath and washed her hair and while it dried she tried to read *This Side of Paradise,* but her mind would not stay on the page. It was the winter recess and with no lessons to prepare and no essays to correct she was aware, as she had not been for a long time, of how very much alone in the world she was: twenty-two years old tomorrow and a stranger in a strange land still.

Suddenly she missed Paris achingly, the way one misses a gracious home. She longed for the wide avenues and the Seine and the cafés. There were no cafés in New York, only bars, where a woman alone could be arrested for soliciting! They were so foolish about sex, these Americans; when they did not ignore it, they made it obscene.

I'm homesick, Ema thought, but I don't know where home is. There was Danielle, of course; they wrote to each other faithfully—the new name Ema explained as "a whim"—but Danielle's apartment was not home. Nor, certainly, was the store on the Rue Momette. Her sisters had married and gone to live in the south; her mother eked out a living in the store and would not have survived without the money Ema sent Danielle every month to be given to Sylvie through the curé.

So, where was home? Would she ever have her own home, not just a corner of someone else's?

Finally she put the book down and went to the bottom drawer of her bureau. She took out the silhouettes and the charcoal sketches from Montmartre, protected by cardboard and wrapped in muslin. She carried them back to her chair and sat down, looking at them, waiting until she heard the music and the laughter of the Place du Tertre, until she felt Julian's arms around her.

# 30

APRIL 1922

"Mademoiselle Beranger!" A strident voice cut through the polite buzz of the Waldorf-Astoria's Peacock Alley.

"*Nom de Dieu*," Emanuelle whispered to Kate. "It's Mrs. Blessing." The two friends watched the sleekly fashionable woman advance along the wide corridor, past potted palms and armchairs plushly supporting New York's most elegant derrieres. Matilda Blessing was needle-thin in a calf-length black silk dress and a black velvet cocoon coat frothed with black fox. One large spray of diamonds was pinned to her shoulder and another to the draped black satin hat that set off two cascades of diamond earrings. She was smiling, her wide mouth accentuated by bright scarlet lip rouge.

"Well, well," she said. "This is a surprise." She acknowledged Katharine with a nod, then examined Emanuelle with care, missing no detail of her low-waisted red jersey dress and hip-length jacket or the veiled felt hat set atilt on Emanuelle's shingled russet hair. "*À la mode*, as usual, Mademoiselle. I had no idea this was where teachers came to play after school."

"Good evening, Mrs. Blessing," Ema said. She made no move to rise and Katharine, checked, kept her seat as well.

"I hope you haven't forgotten our talk," Matilda said. "I can't wait forever."

"I promise I'll give you my answer next week."

The woman made a brisk birdlike movement with her head, spread her encarmined mouth in another carnivorous smile, and made a progress from the gallery on the arm of a tall attractive man.

Katharine sighed with relief. "I was ready to stand up and curtsy."

"Why should you? You own the best girls' school in New York." Ema put a cigarette into a holder and lit it. She sucked in the cigarette smoke appreciatively; it was a new habit she enjoyed.

"Maybe so," Katharine said, "but I have a full roster of students mainly because of Tillie Blessing. Everyone in New York follows her lead." Katharine's face wore a worried frown. "I can't imagine why she hasn't sent her girls to Foxcroft yet. It's catching on like wildfire."

"She wants them where she can bully them, poor things. Was that her husband?"

"Yes, Thomas Blessing, shipping and banks."

"I keep my savings in one of his banks, but I didn't know he was such a handsome man."

"Don't let Tillie hear you say that! She's as jealous as a queen bee. Everyone knows he plays around, but they say she does all sorts of things to keep him coming back to her." Katharine shifted her hips in her chair and recrossed her rayon-clad legs.

"What kinds of things?"

Katharine looked uncomfortable. "Sex things."

Emanuelle raised her eyebrows but did not pursue it.

"What did you two talk about, Ema?" Kate asked.

"She needs a secretary and she wants someone French for effect. She's offered me the job. I was going to tell you tonight over dinner."

Kate looked anxious. "Will you accept?"

"Yes. It's time I got on with my life—and it'll be fun."

"To work for Matilda Blessing?" Kate shivered.

Ema leaned forward. "I agree, she is *une femme terrible,* but it's a good opportunity, Kate, the best I'm likely to get. I've learned most of what I need to know—English grammar and literature, etiquette, enough art and history and music to get by. But I can't go on doing lessons for the rest of my life—and you knew from the first day, I didn't plan to teach French forever."

Katharine nodded gloomily.

"Kate, please don't look like that," Ema said.

"I'll miss you."

"You'll have Spencer soon, I'm sure of it, and I'm not going to the end of the world, darling, only to Fifty-second Street. Terrible Tillie has agreed to at least two evenings and one day off—more if she doesn't need me."

"She'll need you. She gives more parties than anyone else in the Social Register. She'll keep you hopping."

"And pay well for it too. I have to think about the future. I'm not an American Treadwell. I didn't inherit your name and your school."

"And my mountain of debts. But you have a face and a figure. That's all a woman needs."

Ema shook her head. "That'll get me to about thirty—and then what? No, a woman needs money. She can acquire position, but even that's no good unless she has pots of money. Your rich Treadwell relations wouldn't ignore you if you didn't have to work for a living."

"If I looked like you," Katharine insisted, "they'd have got me married off long ago." She hesitated a moment. "You'll marry again someday, Ema. I'm sure you will."

"So will you." Emanuelle put out her cigarette. She wouldn't say so to Kate, but she planned to marry the kind of man who frequented the Blessing mansion, a man who belonged to clubs like Brook's, the Metropolitan, the Knickerbocker. "Who knows, I might make a killing on the stock market, then I won't have to marry anyone!" She stood. "Let's walk to the restaurant."

They gathered their things and walked the length of Peacock Alley. The Waldorf-Astoria was the only hotel de luxe in New York to admit unescorted females—and allow them to smoke in the public rooms. New York's working girls came to watch the parade of wealthy women—"and see their Paris clothes," Ema exulted, glad she could copy the latest styles for herself and Kate. She was strict about living on her salary and banking each thousand dollars from Sir James as she received it. There were only two payments left to come and then she must do something with all that money. Her days at Saxon, Vaillant had taught her that. After a year or two with the Blessings she intended to know how to invest it, husband or not.

It would be hard to leave Kate, but teaching was not the way to become a woman of wealth and position, like the people she read about in Cholly Knickerbocker's column. Ema wanted to eradicate her past and at the same time—she never really stopped to consider that it was a contradiction—make herself worthy of the child who linked her to that past.

She thought about her daughter as she and Kate emerged onto 34th Street and crossed Fifth Avenue to look at clothes in Best & Company's window, then linger, bedazzled, before Tiffany's display.

"Someday," Ema said, admiring the gorgeous gemstones, the heavy gold rings and bracelets. She wore Danielle's locket and Julian's ring, but the only precious metals Ema owned were the narrow wedding band she had worn in Scotland, the silver frames she had bought for the likenesses from Montmartre—and the gold pieces she bought from the bank with some of her savings and kept hidden in her mattress. "Like a French peasant," she always muttered when she sewed them in, but she needed the security the gold coins represented, accessible if she needed them, under her own control.

"At least while I'm waiting," she finished with another sigh at Tiffany's, "I have New York. I'm beginning to love this city."

"More than Paris?"

"Differently. It's more exciting than Paris. It's young—and new—and unexpected! It's always changing."

"Someday you'll be dripping in more diamonds than Tillie," Kate said, her arm linked through Ema's.

"But not all at once; it's vulgar unless you're as old as she is," Ema said.

"Tillie *is* vulgar," Kate said. "The Blessings aren't very old money."

"Who is—except the *Mayflower* Treadwells?" Emanuelle ticked off on her fingers the people she had been reading about. "Andrew Carnegie was a bobbin boy in a cloth mill less than a hundred years ago. Rockefeller was a fifteen-dollar-a-week bookkeeper on the Cleveland docks. John Jacob Astor was a German butcher's son before he was a fur trader and up to his elbows in smelly fur pelts in a store on Vesey Street. And Vanderbilt was a poor Staten Island ferry-boy before he was a shipping magnate."

Kate laughed. "Well, someone did say that four generations of gentlemen were enough to admit anyone to society. Of course the Old Guard in Boston and the south still think the Astors are parvenus."

Emanuelle shook her head. "Maybe, but it seems to me that all you really need to belong to the ruling class in America is money."

That must be why, she was thinking as they left Tiffany's window, she had an enormous affection for America; here there was an honest chance of attaining what she wanted, not only wealth, but position too. Emanuelle could be part of America's aristocracy of wealth; her daughter belonged to an aristocracy of blood.

# 31

Davina Saxon rinsed her mouth and came out of the bathroom naked, patting her face with a towel. The towel was acceptably clean, but it was cold and scratchy, not like the towels in the new bathrooms she'd had put in at Stridings.

"Well?" she said to the man on the bed.

He propped himself up on his elbows. "You're the damnedest woman," he said. "You can shoot a man over the moon and stay cold as mutton doing it. You won't even let me fuck you proper anymore; you'll only do the fancy stuff."

"I didn't hire you to fuck me," Davina said coldly. "I hired you to show me how to fuck you. And I think by now I've learned all I need to know."

"You wouldn't be trying to say bye-bye, now, would you, luv?"

Davina put on her blue silk knickers and a binder that flattened her breasts, then sat down to pull on her white silk stockings. "I don't propose to tell you anything," she said, snapping her lacy round garters into place.

He sat up. "I don't want to stop."

Davina got into her white wool dress, put on a matching helmet hat with gold leaves appliquéd on one side, and picked up her sable coat. "Nevertheless," she said. She took a considerable amount of money from her purse and dropped it on the bedside table, then started for the door.

"Lady Bountiful," he said, looking at the money, then at her. "But suppose I want more—of it and you."

She turned back. "Suppose you do." She smiled with crushing contempt. "Just how do you propose to get it?"

"I could find you easy enough; I know who you really are. Rich crumpet's always in the papers, drinking tea and doing flower shows. I'd find you, never fear, and then you'd give me anything I wanted to keep my lip buttoned." His voice turned cajoling. "Here, I don't want to make trouble for you, luv. I just want to fuck you. You used to love it. You used to wail like a banshee when I made you come."

She walked to the bed and looked down at him. Her face was calm and her voice expressionless. "I needed it. I never loved it, not from you. If you ever come near me, I'll kill you. I'll say you tried to rape me and I'll blow your head off with my husband's hunting rifle. Do you understand?" Her eyes glittered like blue ice.

He stared up at her, transfixed. "Jesus, Mary," he said. Then he shivered and pulled the covers over him while she left the small flat.

Davina walked back to Harrods, where the Bentley had dropped her and would come to collect her in a little while. She picked up the purchases she had made earlier—a floating blue chiffon dinner dress she would wear tonight, deerstalker caps for Julian and Uncle James, and a set of toy soldiers for the boy.

On the drive to Stridings she looked out at the countryside without seeing it. Four years had passed since Julian had been brought home more dead than alive, years of doctors and nurses, infections and fevers and wounds that would not heal. It was only a year ago that he was able to leave his wheelchair. That was when Davina, because he did not come to her, went to someone else.

"I had to," she murmured to herself yet again. "I had to."

But that was finished now. Soon Julian would be back in her arms, it would be Julian who made her body sing. She was sure that when that happened, the ugly memory of his last leave would be blotted out and things would be as they once were before the war changed him. On the surface things were fine: Julian was tender and caring toward her, but it was affection, not desire; it was remorse for his infidelity, not love. His love was for his son, Andrew James Julian Saxon.

Drew, thank heaven, was the image of his father, with nothing of the Frenchwoman about him. Had it been otherwise, Davina could not have held him in her arms minutes after his birth and mothered him—distantly, as was the custom of her class, through a nurse and a nanny—ever since. But Julian adored him and that, too, was bearable because she profited from Julian's feelings for his son. She cherished Drew in Julian's presence, so that Julian's eyes would fall on both of them, mother and son, with the same loyalty and love.

She demanded nothing of Julian, but in the way of a woman with a man she let him know she wanted him. She waited. She had prepared herself for the time when he would come to her, when, gradually, she would enthrall him sexually as that woman had done. He was as fully recovered as he would ever be and soon, soon, he would come to her.

When she arrived at Stridings she heard laughter from the small drawing room and the piping voice of the boy. She frowned briefly before she went in to join them; the boy's smudgy hands would ruin the pale satin upholstery. Then a smile lit her face and she came in upon them like sunshine.

"How are my three men?" she asked, and held out her arms to Drew. It was something she never did when she was alone with him and the four-year-old child hesitated before he went to her to be hugged and kissed. She felt Julian's eyes on her and she held on to the boy's hand while she kissed her husband and her father-in-law. "Mummy has a lovely surprise for you, darling," she said to Drew. "I have presents for all of you."

The butler came in with the Harrods boxes and she released Drew and distributed the gifts. The men were pleased—until Julian saw the soldiers.

"I don't want him playing with soldiers," Julian said, controlling his anger with difficulty. "They're not toys and war is not a game."

"Oh, darling, I'm so sorry, I didn't think." That was certainly true, damn it! "All the other children have them and he wanted them so." That was a flagrant falsehood, but a safe one. "Come, darling, give the soldiers back to Mummy, they're nasty. We'll buy something nice tomorrow."

The little boy obeyed, less anxious about his father's anger than his mother's annoyance, for which he somehow knew he was responsible. He never knew how she felt about him, sometimes he thought she liked him and sometimes he knew she didn't. He didn't much care about toy soldiers anyway; he wanted a pony and his father wouldn't let him have one until he was five. Maybe Grandfather would help persuade him; Grandfather was always ready to help Drew.

"I think I have time for a drink before the dressing bell," Davina said when Nanny had taken Drew up to the nursery. She looked beseechingly at Julian. "Forgive me, darling. There were crowds of children going mad for those soldiers at Harrods and I wanted Drew to have the same fun as the others." She went to kiss him.

"I'm sorry I lost my temper," he said. "I can't be reasonable on that subject."

His arm around her waist was bliss. She leaned against him, feeling his arm against her breast. "Have you decided about standing for a seat in Parliament, Julian? I think you must—there's no better man than you." She was convinced that if Julian had an interest, no matter which, his life would be more normal in other ways.

"If he doesn't stand voluntarily," Sir James said, "he may be drafted."

Julian shook his head. "Not yet. Someone has to do something to get our veterans all that was promised them. They didn't go through that inferno to sell pencils on the streets." He poured two more drinks for himself and his father. "As for the government," he said with disgust, "they do nothing—nor have they stopped playing their deadly games. Marching into the Ruhr to extract reparations from a country too poor to feed its people—it's just the opportunity the generals need to start waving flags again."

Sir James looked dubious. "Even so, Julian, German reparations are part of the Treaty of Versailles. Shouldn't nations honor their obligations?"

"With what, Father? It's wringing blood from a stone. Desperation always leads to political upheaval."

"You mean the communists?" Davina put in.

He nodded. "Or fascists, like the ones who just gained control in Italy. In my opinion they ought to abrogate that bloody treaty."

Sir James and Davina looked at each other. "Perhaps you'd better not suggest that in public just yet, Julian," his father said. "That treaty was hard won, as no one knows better than you."

"I won't sail under false colors, Father." He shook his head. "I'm not the sort of candidate they want."

There was a short silence, then the subject was changed until finally they went up to dress for dinner. Davina could hear Julian in his dressing room, where he had been sleeping ever since he came home. A special bed had been installed until his wounds stopped draining and healed completely, but for a year now there had been no reason for them to sleep apart.

Sometimes she wondered if he was impotent from his wounds, but her intuition told her otherwise. He kept away because of what they had said to each other on that humiliating night so long ago.

Davina left the bedroom door ajar every night when she got into the double bed, straining to hear any sound that might mean he was coming to her. She left it open when she dressed tonight, so he might catch a glimpse of her naked. She wanted him so violently it was painful. Her "lessons" had eased her hunger, but they had not satisfied it; no one but Julian could do that.

Midway through dinner she was sure that tonight he would come to her. It was the way he looked at her, with a physical edge to his customary affection. She knew she was beautiful tonight. The blue chiffon dress deepened her eyes and made her hair look like spun gold. Her creamy arms and shoulders glowed through the sheer capelet.

They avoided politics at dinner and Davina made them laugh with her talk about the new books and plays and the latest gossip. She felt something stirring between her and Julian, a ripple of excitement when they looked at each other, an anticipation of pleasures already proved together. Her face flushed and her eyes sparkled, but she went quietly upstairs at bedtime as if this were any other night, leaving him in the corridor. She went into the bedroom of their suite and he into his dressing room.

She undressed, her fingers clumsy with excitement, her heart pounding. She put on a sheer silk nightdress that barely covered her breasts and was wide enough to make the rest of her easily accessible. Then she got into bed, put out the light, and lay still, listening tensely, until she heard what she had been waiting for so long. He came into the room and stood beside the bed.

"Davina?"

She stirred. "Yes, darling?"

"I must talk to you. I've waited too long already." He sat down on the bed and took her hand.

Don't talk about her, she pleaded silently. Make love to me. "What about?" she said quietly.

"About our life together. I've been selfishly preoccupied with my own problems. I want you to know that I'm . . . grateful to you for so much. For Drew, of course, but for so much more, too, for your patience and your kindness."

"Please, Julian, it isn't gratitude I want." Love me, she begged him, love me.

He stroked her hair the way he used to. "No, of course not, you deserve much more. Davina, I want to talk about what happened that last night. I want you to understand."

"But I do understand now, better than you think," she said passionately, putting her arms around him. "Don't talk about it, Julian, please don't bring it back; it's over, like the war. I acted like a child, I was a child, but I'm a woman now. If you care for me and Drew, don't talk about it again. We have each other, that's all that matters."

She kissed his mouth lingeringly. "There can be more sons, my jo, as many as you want." She unbuttoned his silk pajama top and kissed the scars on his chest and, briefly, as if she had wandered there innocently, his belly. "Stay with me, darling, sleep here with me so I can hold you. We need each other."

He kissed her tenderly; it was to her craving as a raindrop is to a desert, but at least he was aroused by her. He lay down beside her and made love to her in the same gentle way, kissing her breasts, parting her thighs—and he was hers again, his hands and mouth and body touching, caressing, penetrating.

But after Davina's body arched and shuddered under his and was satisfied, her hunger for him was not, no matter how contentedly she seemed to nestle in his arms. She knew with anguish that he was not all hers. She had his affection, even his dutiful love, but not his passion. The woman had that; she was still there, in the bed with them.

Davina did not sleep. She listened to his even breathing and knew she would never possess him entirely until his passion for her equaled hers for him and his dreams of that slut were replaced by a more seductive reality. She would go slowly—it would be a mistake to offend him with too-avid sexuality—but now, at last, she could fight fire with fire.

# 32

---

"Good morning, Emanuelle," Thomas Blessing said.

Ema, surprised, stopped halfway down the staircase and returned the greeting. She tried not to come downstairs until his Rolls-Royce took him off to Wall Street each morning.

"I understand your naturalization is in progress," he said. "I can have it hurried along. All it takes is a word in the right place." He smiled a secret little smile and observed the rope of pearls—a Christmas gift to Emanuelle from the Blessings—that had slipped over to frame one of her breasts. "It would be my pleasure to do that small favor for you."

Ema smiled and shook her head. He was the kind of man who would demand favors in return. "That's very kind of you, but it will be coming through in a few months."

He examined her hips and legs while the butler helped him into his coat. "Let me know if you change your mind," he said in almost comic disappointment.

She waited until the door closed behind him, then descended the broad staircase and walked across the silky Oriental rugs of the vast entrance hall into her office. It was draped and carpeted in moss green, with a Chippendale desk, several comfortable armchairs bracketed by small tables, and a battery of mahogany filing cabinets. There were fresh yellow roses in a Daum vase on her desk, several lamps of Sèvres porcelain, and a profusion of crystal ashtrays and cigarette boxes.

Ema sat down, consulted her calendar, and opened the first file on her desk. She worked quietly for a while and had just completed three of the telephone calls on her list when Matilda came in carrying a crossword puzzle. She was never without one; she said they settled her nerves.

"What was Susan Pace-Abercrombie whispering to you last night?"

Matilda demanded without preamble. "Is she trying to hire you away
from me again?"

Ema nodded, suppressing a smile. Tillie was violently possessive, even
of her hired help. "I refused, of course," she assured Matilda, turning
back to the open folder on her desk. "Is there anything else for the jazz
party next Saturday?" Through the smoke of Matilda's cigarette she admired her employer's mauve satin morning pajamas. Matilda was very
slim; her hip bones jutted through the silk.

"I don't think so, you know what to do. Just be sure the champagne is
very dry and the musicians very black."

"Do the dark ones play better jazz?"

"Probably not," said Tillie, "but I want the best effect in my white ballroom, without any artfully artless comments from you."

Emanuelle inclined her head by way of apology. After eighteen months
in Matilda's employ she knew that this woman had only contempt for
people who were afraid of her. But she was a virago, deadly to anyone
who stood up to her too brazenly. Her rebukes were immediate and violent, or sly and delivered some time after the fact. Now she held out her
hand for the guest list and sat down to read it. Ema, apparently, had escaped easily this time.

Matilda's moods apart, it was a wonderful job. Emanuelle lived in a
suite on the third floor of the Blessing mansion, modest by comparison
with the rest of the house but still luxurious. She traveled in the Blessing
style to palatial establishments in Newport and Palm Beach; she accompanied Matilda in the long Packard limousine to mah-jongg parties and the
board meetings of Blessing charities and teas, taking notes. Once she was
invited to Matilda's box at the opera; she wore a nearly new castoff of
Matilda's she had skillfully altered herself. There were a half-dozen such
French imports in her closet upstairs; Matilda preferred to give Emanuelle
clothes and an occasional evening at the opera rather than to raise her
salary. The lap of luxury, Ema soon discovered, was her natural habitat.

Matilda was forty and terrified of getting old. She tried every new nos-
trum and regimen that promised eternal youth. She dieted rigorously,
had massages and facials and high colonic enemas, did daily calisthenics
and spent two weeks each winter at a spa in Arizona. She longed to try
Europe, but that was too far away from Thomas.

The gossips were right about Thomas. He was a notorious womanizer
and Matilda was insanely jealous. But since no one, man or woman,
dared refer to it in Matilda's presence, the fiction prevailed that Thomas
Blessing was faithful. Ema, not in the least interested and aware of Tillie's
scrutiny, kept him at a very cool distance.

Once she had passed that test, her position was secure, especially when women like Mrs. Pace-Abercrombie began to pursue her: Matilda's other raison d'être, after her husband, was to be envied, and New York's social hostesses envied her the elegant, well-educated Parisienne who had such original ideas at her fingertips for party decors and favors. Actually Ema read tabloid reports of turn-of-the-century excesses at the library and the current French press for the latest Parisian extravagance. She sometimes bought the British papers as well, but there was never any mention of the Saxons in the court calendar or the society pages.

"You were widowed by the war, weren't you?" Matilda said now, handing back the list and regarding Ema speculatively.

"Yes, Mrs. Blessing." Ema flushed, wondering how she knew. Kate was the only person she had told. Then she realized that Matilda had simply made a lucky guess.

"How long were you married?"

"Not long, about a year and a half—but he couldn't come to Paris very often."

"Don't you miss it?"

"Paris? No, not very much."

"Paris be damned. I mean sex, my girl. A woman like you must want a man, at least once in a while. You've discouraged all the married men—and a good thing too. You wouldn't be working for me otherwise; but you discourage the bachelors as well. Why?"

Ema shrugged. "Their interest in me is too limited."

Matilda nodded, her eyes glittering with satisfaction. "I thought so. You won't surrender your fair white body except for a wedding ring! Well, it won't work. You'll have to be a little more accessible to the bachelors if you're out to marry one of them, Madame Beranger. A woman in your position must allow the bees to sample the honey pot, at least, even if you don't let them dive into it."

Ema's face was rigid. "Thank you for the advice, Mrs. Blessing."

"You won't take it, I'm sure. You're too intent on being a lady, but with no family and no money you'll never get to the salon except via the bedroom." She rose from the desk and went to the door. "Make sure the flowers are all exactly the same red for the jazz party and send an azalea plant—pink—to Mrs. Pace-Abercrombie with my compliments."

Emanuelle sat at her desk waiting for her temper to calm, as calm it must. For the moment she was trapped here. A job with another New York dowager was easy to find but would be short-lived, Matilda would see to that with any malicious story she chose to tell. Without a lot more money behind her, Emanuelle was Mrs. Blessing's for as long as Mrs. Blessing chose to keep her.

Yet in one way Tillie had come very close to the mark this morning.

Ema's body was coming to life again, desire stirring in her flesh. She would never love another man, she was absolutely sure of that; but sex, to her astonishment, was something over which her mind and her heart had no control. For the past five years most of her energy had been spent in learning how to cope, especially after she came to work for Matilda.

Now she had her job under control and she felt almost completely at home in America. She had even begun to dream in the American version of English, but her dreams lately were vividly erotic. Her lover never assumed Julian's face and body; she went to sleep hoping to dream of him and awoke, either from sex with a stranger or with a hunger she thought had vanished with Julian.

She put her head down on her folded arms and her need for Julian flooded up and spilled over. It was always there, overwhelming her in unguarded moments, like a thief stealing away her makeshift felicity. And each time the moment passed she knew she needed someone.

But she had not seen one man at the Blessings with the grace and charm and polish of Julian Saxon, and she knew she never would. If she could not govern her body's craving, she might soon satisfy it with a lesser man.

The men who came to the Blessings' house had been born to wealth and worked diligently to increase it. They indulged themselves like sultans. Their mansions and motor cars and yachts were many and sumptuous, their wives and daughters sheltered and indulged. Their sons and mistresses were respectively encouraged to sow and satisfy every manner of wild oat. Rarely conversant with any language or culture but their own, they fawned over French food and fashion, English literature and tailoring, Greek architecture, Italian opera, and German symphonies. To Emanuelle it seemed they had cultivated nothing of their own but money. That was something she understood, but she wanted position with it.

Ema stirred at a tap on her office door. She dried her eyes and hastily lit a cigarette before she said, "Come in." She spoke in French to the small man who entered. "Good morning, Monsieur Denis, please sit down."

"I am grateful to you, Madame," the visitor replied, clutching his beret and seating himself carefully. "And croyez-moi, you will not regret giving me the business. I am better than Schultz. What do the Boches know about flowers?"

"I must warn you, Monsieur Denis, that Mrs. Blessing is very difficult. As for me"—she smiled—"I prefer to deal with a Frenchman."

She told him what was wanted: fresh flowers daily for the twenty-room mansion and Mr. Blessing's offices on Wall Street. This week she would require centerpieces for two dinner parties. "And I must have enough red flowers next Saturday to fill the ballroom, which I shall show you before you leave. Geraniums, roses, carnations, and anthurium. Mrs. Blessing insists they all be exactly the same color red."

The florist sucked in his cheeks and rocked his head from side to side. "It will cost a fortune to match them."

"Cost is not a factor."

"In that case . . ." He smiled, clasped his hands, and winked at her. "Of course the usual arrangement will apply *entre nous.*"

Emanuelle looked at him inquiringly.

"Five percent of the total price for you, Madame."

She said nothing, stunned. It was the first such offer she had received.

"*Eh bien,* ten percent. One does not haggle with a countrywoman."

She took him to see the ballroom, and when she was alone again in her office she began to laugh, muffling the sound with her hands. What a fool she had been! Ten percent of what the Blessings spent on their lavish entertainments was a healthy sum indeed. With her salary she might have enough money in a year or two to start a business of her own! What sneaks the caterers and suppliers had been, to take advantage of her ignorance. She had lost a fortune!

"They took me for a tinhorn," she told Kate while they shopped for Kate's trousseau the following week.

"A greenhorn," Kate corrected. "But Ema, those are kickbacks, they're unethical."

"Of course, but I don't care about ethics. I'm going to do what everyone else does."

Before the week was out Ema's "arrangement" with each of her suppliers had been established at ten percent—and she made it retroactive. Not one of them complained; the Blessing account was a plum.

# 33

OCTOBER 1923

Danielle's wire arrived a month before Kate's wedding. Sylvie Bequier was dying; the doctors gave her a few weeks, no more.

Kate was astonished. "You told me your parents were dead."

"My father is, not my mother—but we never got along."

"That couldn't have been your fault," Kate said loyally. She put an arm around Ema, worried by her pallor. "Will you go?"

"Oh, Kate, I don't want to," Ema said, shaking her head. "But I can't let her die alone."

"Of course you can't, darling," Kate said. "Shall I call Tillie for you?"

"No, I'll tell her tomorrow. I have to go up there to pack some things."

"She won't like it," Kate predicted, but what infuriated Matilda most was Ema's refusal to say why she wanted a leave of absence. "I demand an explanation," Matilda said while Ema packed.

"I regret, Mrs. Blessing, but this is a completely private matter." Ema closed her suitcase and snapped the locks shut. She looked at Matilda, her gray eyes dark. "You don't need me in Arizona, and nothing's scheduled until two weeks after you come back. I'll see that everything else is in hand before I leave."

Matilda capitulated. "When do you sail?"

"Tomorrow, on the *Lafayette*."

She traveled third class—it seemed the appropriate way to go back to the Rue Momette—but even the dismal journey could not prepare her for this return. The compartment on the boat train from Le Havre was crowded and noisy, and she was covered with soot from the coal engine by the time the train stopped at the Gare St. Lazare.

Trains and stations, she thought, I've lived some of the best and worst moments of my life in trains and stations.

Then she saw Danielle on the platform, tall and spare and still black-clad. Her skirt was short, as fashion dictated, and her gray hair was shingled like Ema's.

"I never expected you to meet me here," Ema said, putting her arms around the gaunt woman. "Oh, Danielle, I've missed you so."

The two women looked at each other, trying to bridge the years since they had said good-bye. The web of wrinkles on Danielle's face had deepened. "I've grown older," she said.

"So have I. But we both look prosperous," Ema said, kissing her cheek.

"We can't talk now, Ema. There isn't much time." She signaled the porter to follow them with Ema's suitcase. "We'll take a taxi."

"Danielle, you haven't been there, to the store?" Emanuelle was alarmed, not merely curious.

"No, the curé has always come to me. But I can't let you go alone!"

"Don't come with me, please, Danielle," Ema pleaded.

Danielle's shrewd black eyes turned briefly on Ema. "It's nothing to be ashamed of, Ema. You didn't choose to be born there. I know that's why you changed your name, but what difference has it made? You've still come back." Danielle sighed. "Go then, I'll take your valise home. Come to me after you've seen her."

The Rue Momette looked even meaner and shabbier than Ema remembered, and she shivered after she had paid the taxi driver and walked into the store, redolent with the smells that would always call back memories of her girlhood. Someone was behind the curtain in the kitchen, and for an irrational second fear prickled her scalp, as if Jacques Bequier still lay in wait for her. It was the curé, drinking tea, and he rose in surprise at the sight of Ema standing in the doorway.

"Emalie?" the old man quavered.

"*Oui, Monsieur le Curé*, it's Emalie."

"Thank God you have come, my child. Your sisters . . ." He shook his head, clucking softly in his throat. "They refuse to come; they have never been back since they married. She's been all alone, except for what you send."

"How is she?" She could not bear to hear how wretched her mother had been.

"She will soon be at peace," the curé said. "Go up to her, *mon enfant*, there is not much time. Send the nurse down to me."

Ema sat upstairs with her mother, beside the same bed where Emalie Anne had dreamed and been destroyed. Her mother's face was sunken, the skin around her eyes a dusty charcoal, like the cinders in Ema's hair.

Sylvie stirred and her shadowed eyes opened, gray eyes like Ema's. "*C'est toi?*" she murmured, and touched the silk of Ema's blouse. "*Tu as bien réussi.*"

"*Oui*, Maman, I've succeeded," Ema said, crying quietly. "But no one knows it's I who have done it; only you know who I really am."

Sylvie gestured to the foot of her bed. *"Le matelas."*

Gold pieces, she was telling Ema to look for the gold pieces in the mattress. But Ema needed more from her mother than gold.

Tearful and angry, she smoothed the rough hand. "We could have thrown him out, we could have been free of him all those years. Why wouldn't you believe me, Maman?" she pleaded piteously.

"Liar," her mother muttered, trying feebly to pull her hand away. "*Va-t-en,* go away."

Ema released her, and straightening up, sat in silence, the tears turning chill upon her cheeks. So be it, then, the only person left in the world who knew what had happened here was dying. It was what she had always wanted, to keep that secret safe, but suddenly it seemed too big a burden to carry alone.

Sylvie abandoned her forever an hour later, without waking. Ema went to the closet behind the screen for the scissors and took the purse from the mattress. It contained enough gold napoleons to pay for a decent funeral, buy some new things at Thiboux, and travel to America in first class. She did not even question why her mother had lived in such misery with that much money hidden away; some people loved to clutch their fetters. She paid the nurse and made arrangements with the curé for the funeral before she lowered the volets for the last time.

"It's over?" Danielle asked at the flat, taking Ema's coat. *"Eh bien, c'est la vie,* at least you were in time to say good-bye. Go and have a bath—it's a full-size tub now, look—a hot bath always made you feel better. We'll talk later."

Danielle and her school had indeed prospered. She now rented a whole floor of the building in the Boul'Mich to teach the army of young women who wanted secretarial jobs. "They'll never marry, most of them," Danielle said. "The men of their generation never came back. I suppose they will be pitied, but not by me. The women of France will have to be different now, more independent. And you?"

"For the moment I'm still in thrall to my female dragon, but I've thought of a way to escape as soon as I have enough money. I'm going to start a party service of my own. I can do as much for any hostess in New York as I do for Mrs. Blessing." Her smile was cold. "She's told everyone I'm a war widow, and now she hints that my father was a nobleman who disinherited me for marrying beneath him. *C'est ridicule, non?* Who could be beneath my father?"

After Sylvie's funeral Ema went to a notary and arranged to have him sell the store for whatever pittance it would fetch. She had taken nothing from it except memory, the one thing she did not want. She booked a first-class passage on the *Paris* and in the few days before she sailed she went to Thiboux and bought some samples from the last collections that would still be six months ahead of New York. Most of the women she had known at Thiboux were gone; those who remained were pleasant, but distant; she was no longer one of them.

"I have to look and act the part if I'm to succeed," Emanuelle told Danielle, displaying her purchases the night before she sailed. "I have to wear the right clothes and travel in style to meet the right people. I want to attract the women who need help when they first get into high society—not everyone's born there, after all."

"That's very democratic, coming from you," Danielle said. "I thought one had to be born to the purple to belong."

"In Europe," Ema said. "Not in America."

"Will you ever come back to live in Paris?"

"No. I miss it, but I don't belong here anymore. America is new and brash and young. I was never really young, Dani, but America makes me feel that way. America is the future." She looked appealingly at Danielle. "Would you consider coming to New York to work with me once I'm established? You'd make more money in New York."

Danielle shook her head. "I'm too old a tree to be transplanted, whatever the attractions of the new world. Perhaps I'll come for a visit one day, when you've made your fortune. But Ema . . ."

"Yes?"

"You're a person of quality, just as you are. Be yourself."

Too moved to reply, Ema busied herself with the last two boxes from Thiboux. "These are for you, Danielle."

In one box was an ensemble of silk gabardine in deep garnet. The jacket was lined in the same heavy ivory silk as the pin-tucked blouse that went with it. The second box contained a beige linen nightgown with inserts of ecru lace.

"To replace the things you gave me." Ema tried to say it lightly but finished with, "As if I ever could."

"There was no need!" Danielle began reproachfully. Then Ema's watchful wait for her approval made Danielle put her arms around the younger woman and hold her close. "They are beautiful things, *ma chérie*, but I shall treasure them all the more because you gave them to me."


A person of quality, Ema thought when she was standing on the Promenade Deck of the *Paris*. The ship had steamed from Le Havre across the English Channel to take on passengers at Plymouth, and Ema stood looking at the pier where she had embarked, undertaking never to enter England again. "Someday," she murmured softly to herself, "someday."

But she certainly could not be herself. If she were, she would not be one of only three-hundred-odd people traveling first class, with flowers in her cabin and three new ensembles and two evening dresses hanging in the wardrobe beside Matilda Blessing's cast-off Patous. This trip had cost her almost all the gold in the mattress, but she had spent it gladly, with a strange emotion that still persisted. It was a sense of freedom, she realized now; she was free of an immense and early burden. She felt light enough to fly. She would be home in plenty of time for Kate's wedding, with the exquisite lace veil she had bought in Paris.

"It's Emanuelle Beranger, isn't it?" a man's voice said, and she turned.

He was tall and very blond, like William Poyndexter, she thought with a pang, although the resemblance ended there; he was older than sweet William had been and very American. "I didn't mean to frighten you," he went on. He smiled and his teeth were even and brilliantly white, like the collar of his silk shirt. "I'm Rupert McAllister, I met you at the Blessings'."

"Oh, yes, hello," she said, holding out her hand. "Did you just come aboard?" He was very much the kind of man she wanted to know.

"Yes, I was in London on business—for Mr. Blessing, as it happens. I'm working for him, so you and I have something in common."

She thought wryly that they had precious little in common: Rupert McAllister's blood was as rich and his pockets as well-lined as the Blessings'. His "work" would be the leisurely apprenticeship wealthy men provided for each other's sons. But she smiled, aware that his blue eyes were frankly admiring her and that she liked it.

"Will you have cocktails with me?" he asked. "And dinner?"

"I'd like that." Something stirred inside her. She knew she would go to bed with this man before the voyage was over, probably even tonight, and that, by the look of him, he would know how to play as evocatively upon her body as a virtuoso on a violin.

"Look," he said, "they're casting off. We'll be under way soon. This looks like it will be a marvelous crossing." He moved closer to her, and she could smell the expensive scent of his cologne. Together they watched the liner begin to pull away.

Ema had no reason to notice the nondescript little man in a bunchy suit who watched her from the pier until the last line was singled up. He had been instructed to do so by a colleague in Paris who, in his turn, had been notified the moment Emanuelle Beranger sailed from New York.

When the ship was well away, the little man went to the telegraph office on the pier and sent a wire to Sir James Saxon at number 9 Frederick's Place in London.

# 34

Sir James tore the wire into pieces and watched them drift into the wastebasket under his desk with a profound sense of relief. This was the first time Emanuelle Beranger had ventured out of America, and he had been unable to rest until she was on her way back. The report from Paris made it clear she had gone there for her mother's funeral and had seen no one but her friend, the Larchet woman.

He had just taken a cup of tea from the serving tray near his desk when Julian came in with a sheaf of papers in his hand. Sir James glanced down at the shredded wire before giving his son his whole attention. Julian looked ill again.

"Have you seen these figures, Father? If the expansion in America continues, she'll be a financial force to reckon with."

He doesn't look feverish, Sir James thought, it's something else. "That's a bit premature, isn't it?" he said, glancing from the young lieutenant's portrait to the man before him. The canvas had more life. The only time Julian came alive was with Drew—or when he was demanding better treatment for the veterans of the Great War. It was a noble cause, of course, but the public tired quickly of noble causes.

"Not at all," Julian was saying. "The way things are in Europe, an American branch bank could be turning our biggest profit in a few years. We must think seriously about establishing Saxon, Vaillant in New York."

Sir James nodded, privately determined to block the project somehow, or at the very least to keep Julian away from America. It would be safer if Julian devoted himself to interests outside the bank. "Very well, I'll put the matter in hand and have a thorough study made of it. Sit down and have a cup of tea with me, Julian, you look like you need a few moments' quiet."

To his surprise, Julian complied. "I do."

"Have you seen the doctor lately?"

"No, I'm perfectly fit."

"You look strained. Perhaps you've been working too hard." But the father knew it wasn't strain or fatigue; it was something deep inside his son. Sir James handed him a cup of tea. "I never thought you would take to banking."

Julian agreed that he hadn't. "I'm interested in the money to be derived from it though. I need it for my troops, as Davina calls them. And a poor, benighted lot they still are in a nation that promised to care for them if, by some miracle, they survived." He shrugged. He had said it all before.

"You ought to take Davina away on a holiday somewhere, just the two of you," his father suggested. Sir James could have sworn things had settled down in that marriage at last. Julian had moved back into his wife's bedroom and Davina had the sleek and saucy look of a cat who feasts regularly on Devon cream and kippers. It was obvious to everyone that she was passionately in love with her husband. If her hands could not caress him in public, her eyes did.

"I don't need a holiday," Julian said at length. "Besides, there's too much to be done."

"But you can't do it all alone, Julian! You can't change the world by yourself. You have to do it through existing institutions, through the establishment, whatever its imperfections. Any other way is anarchy." Sir James nodded his aristocratic head vigorously. "I'm convinced you should accept Broadhurst's offer of support and stand for a Conservative seat in Parliament. They can find you a constituency without the slightest trouble—and you'll win, Julian, you'd win anywhere."

Julian's anger was apparent. "And why would I win anywhere? Because I'm a hero of their catastrophe! How can I make political capital of something I despise, for men I don't respect?" His brief show of feeling subsided as suddenly as it had come, and he spoke quietly. "They want to use me, Father, surely you can see that. They need the veterans' votes and they think I can deliver them."

"But you aren't seeking political capital!" Sir James stood, offered his son a cigarette, and lit one for himself. "You have a cause, to make sure England never fights another war. Your opinions will carry more weight precisely because you know what war really is."

Julian sat in somber silence for some moments while his father paced. Then he shrugged. "Perhaps you're right, Father. I might talk to Lord Broadhurst about it again. We're going to him in Devon for the weekend, and I understand a large party of Conservative MPs will be there."

"Good, good," Sir James said. "This is something you can put your heart into." He sat down again at his desk, pleased for a moment until he looked at Julian and knew that his son had no real heart for politics or his marriage or anything else, except young Drew.

Damn that woman! Once she wound herself around a man's heart she was there to stay. His eyes went again to the bits of yellow paper in the waste bin. "My boy, why are you so unhappy?" he asked gently. "Can't you tell me?"

Julian closed his eyes and drew deeply on his cigarette once, then again. "I feel as I did when I was out there, Father, as if I were drowning in madness. I look about me and I see—no, I sense—more danger, more insanity. The world is not a peaceful place; men are not by nature peaceful. I hear reports of rabble-rousing in Italy and Germany and I hear the cannon roar again and smell that stench of death and I think, but of course, of course, we're made of such crooked stuff, how could it be otherwise?"

"But so it has ever been," Sir James argued. "And still we have managed to curb the beast a little, to build a civilization. There are monuments to our better side—Mozart, Magna Charta, St. Paul's Cathedral. We can go on building those." He stopped his pacing and when he spoke again his voice was tender. "Julian, you've suffered so much. Can't you enjoy what good there is in life with a joyful heart?"

Julian's eyes were still closed by that weariness that seemed to emanate more from his spirit than from his body. "I had a joyful heart once, in Paris. I never dreamed I could know joy like that."

Sir James waited, his body tense, while Julian crushed out his cigarette. "I was in love, Father, with a girl I met in Paris." He smiled bleakly. "You remember Browning's *Confessions*—'We loved, Sir—used to meet; How sad and bad and mad it was—but then, how it was sweet!'" He fell silent for another moment, and when he spoke again the smile was gone. "At first I thought I wanted her for the usual reasons, because she was lovely, because I was sick of the sight and smell of men and I wanted the touch and scent of a woman. Then I knew she was the only woman I wanted, to share the air I breathed, the food I ate, my passion, and my life. There was something so . . . I can't find the words to tell you what she was like, but her face took my breath away and, yes, she filled my heart with joy."

He stopped a moment before he went on. "I was never a hero, Father. Sometimes I could feel my mind slipping away from that inferno and I wanted to let it go. When no one could see me, I shook until my eyes rattled in their sockets—from fear and disgust and the monumental insanity around me. But with her I was sane again. I knew I wouldn't let down the side or disgrace you. I even believed I'd be safe as long as we stayed together. She never talked about what would happen after the war. She was not a scheming woman, but it was a hopeless situation that was hurting us both."

The father listened, condemned to hear it all, and Julian's head dropped into his hands. "When William and Tony were killed, I wasn't sure I could go on—but I couldn't face any more pain of my own making. So I said good-bye to her and came home to my wife." He shook his head. "I tried, Father, I truly tried, but it was no good. I had to tell Davina the truth."

"You told Davina?" In a flash James Saxon understood his daughter-in-law's reaction when he first told her about Emalie. "But why, Julian, if it was over?"

"Because it wasn't over, Father. I knew I had been too much with death to accept half a life—or offer half a life to Davina. But how could anyone understand that who hadn't been there with me? How could Davina? She said she would never divorce me. I couldn't see any other way. I was going to stay in France after the armistice." His head came up and his dark eyes looked hopelessly into his father's. "Except for Drew, I would have gone back as soon as I recovered. I still love her, Father. I will always love her. I miss her all the time; she's the part of me that isn't there."

"But Davina? Davina and you? She loves you."

"She doesn't love me, Father. She wants to own me! She does own me. I owe her a penance I can never pay in full. Once I thought it was love, too, her hunger to possess me totally, but love has open hands."

"I had hoped things were better between you," Sir James said. "That you had found some happiness since you were . . . together again."

Julian looked at his father and abandoned the gentleman's code of silence on such matters. "Davina is an exciting woman. Her appetite for sex is contagious and *l'appétit vient en mangeant*, the French say, appetite grows as you feed it." He shrugged. "I'm no more immune to her special talents than any other man would be. And I'm her husband, she has a right to expect sex from me. If marriages were made in bed, ours would be an unqualified success." He said it remotely, disclosing the intimacies of his marriage as if he were describing a star.

His father persisted. "Have you ever tried to find the girl?"

"And ruin her life a second time? No, I have too little to offer her. Davina is the mother of my son; I would never desert her or Drew." Julian pushed himself out of the chair. "I must go; we're expected to dine with the Broadhursts. Good-bye, Father, thank you for listening. Tell Drew I'll spend next weekend with him."

"I will," Sir James said, waiting until Julian was safely out of the door before he sat down in his chair. It was in his power to put the light back in Julian's eyes, the joy in his life. He looked from Julian's portrait to the door, from the charismatic likeness to that shell of a man his son was now.

But he could not do it! He could not ruin his grandson or betray Davina, his partner in crime. He chose, instead, to betray himself.

# 35

Emanuelle yielded to pure sensation, her sole perception that of erotic pleasure. Even after she passed its peak she drifted on the edge of it, only opening her eyes when Rupert McAllister's golden head rose like the sun from between her thighs. He traveled slowly up the length of her body until he lay beside her, erect and expectant.

"I love you, Ema," he said, and, reluctantly tonight, she bent and complied with his silent demand. "Oh, Ema, that's wonderful," he groaned, his hand guiding her head until he reached down and pulled her body over his. He rolled over her with the guttural sound of possession he always made at this moment, slid up inside her, and began the deep glide in and out that he could maintain for as long as he chose. Again Emanuelle let herself go and her hips circled slowly, rhythmically, until she erupted with him and he lay over her panting.

In the darkened bedroom of Rupert's bachelor apartment Ema opened her eyes again.

When his breathing was regular again, Rupert lifted himself off and went into the bathroom for his ablutions. Emanuelle made a faint grimace. He always did that almost immediately after sex, as if the main event of the evening were over, like a polo match. She had seen him once, soaping himself, his eyes closed and a beatific look on his face. He had a magnificent body and he took excellent care of it, but he was overly fond of his penis and the small mole on its shaft to which he liked special attention paid.

Ema lay still, satisfied but not content. She had been sleeping with Rupert for months and he hadn't once mentioned marriage—except to lament his family's preoccupation with it.

"You don't know those McAllisters," Kate had warned her darkly. "They'll choose Rupert's bride for him out of the Social Register."

"They've been trying to do that for five years," Ema insisted. "Maybe he wants to choose his own wife. He says the girls in the Social Register bore him to death. He says he loves me."

"Only in the throes of ecstasy. McAllisters don't marry for love, Emanuelle, they marry for mergers. Love may mean marriage to you, but to him all it means is sex."

What of it, Ema thought, lying in Rupert's bed. The same is true of me. She would never love any man but Julian, but she was eager to marry this man. Her body enjoyed him even if her secret heart did not.

But when they parted this time, nothing had been said and she sat in her office at the Blessing house the next morning trying to talk sense to herself. No matter how high her hopes might climb after a spectacular night with him, she of all people should know better than to trust a man.

She had not been careful enough with money, overspending to dress the part of a McAllister fiancée. She seemed further from her goal than ever. She would have to double her capital before she had enough to hold out against Matilda's certain vengeance when she left her. Since meeting Rupert, she had even lost sight of her ambition to start a business of her own; it would have been so much easier to escape Matilda as Rupert's wife.

"You're looking a bit frazzled," Matilda said when she came down. Her body was still slim and hard, but her face was beginning to show the effects of stringent diet, cigarettes, and coffee. "Better stop these late nights, my girl, we have a full schedule from Thanksgiving right into 1925."

Emanuelle made the right suggestions as they discussed the middle Blessing daughter's birthday party and began to plan Tillie's annual Christmas ball, but by now she knew Tillie's moods, and something nasty was coming. Matilda saved it for a parting shot.

"Have you heard about Rupert McAllister?" she inquired when she was leaving, as if she knew nothing of Ema's liaison with him. "He's engaged."

"Really?" Emanuelle said, always in complete control of her voice and her face in this house. "I must have missed the announcement."

"There hasn't been any yet, but it's coming." Matilda studied Emanuelle gleefully for a moment. "Well, she's a lucky girl, don't you agree?" she concluded. "I hear Rupert's one of our better cocksmen."

Ema repeated it to Rupert that evening at a speakeasy on 45th Street. "I hope you didn't tell her you know I am for a fact," he said, smiling fatuously.

"Why confirm what she only suspects? Anyway, your parents are always trotting out the dullest girls in the country for you to marry, you've said so yourself. I knew it wasn't true."

His blond brows rose. "But it is true. This time I've capitulated."

"You can't be serious!"

"Very. The announcement will be in the *Times* tomorrow. That's why I wanted to see you tonight, to tell you."

"How considerate. Why didn't you tell me last night—or on any of the other nights you said you were in love with me?"

"They were much too exciting to interrupt." His even white teeth flashed again. "I hope we'll have many more."

"What a swine you are," Ema said viciously.

"Oh, come off it, Emanuelle," he said, "you didn't suppose I'd marry you!"

Her silence was answer enough.

He was languidly amused. "Emanuelle, you're a beautiful woman and great in bed, but we don't belong together except there. I have to marry someone from the same kind of family as mine; you know the sort of thing."

"Yes, I know the sort of thing very well. Tell me, Rupert, have you found out yet whether you and your bride are well matched in bed?"

His handsome face hardened. "No. McAllister men marry virgins."

"And sleep around before and after the wedding! There's logic for you. Why don't McAllister brides demand virgins too?"

"That's different."

"Why, because your equipment is different? *Mon Dieu*, you think with your plumbing!"

"Don't be vulgar," he said loftily.

"*Con*," Ema said clearly. "*Salaud.*"

"I don't speak French," he said, the cold gleam in his eye belying what he said.

"I'll translate. You're a prick, Rupert, and a rotten bastard." She got up from the table.

"You didn't think so last night."

"Considering where your brains are, thinking is something no woman can risk in your company."

She left him and walked rapidly out of the place, turning down Fifth Avenue toward the Treadwell Academy without even thinking. She was grateful for the crisp air that stung her eyes, but she knew she must do something! Still another door had been slammed in her face because of who she was. She had come far, but it was never far enough.

Stop crying, she told herself as she turned into 32nd Street. No one's ever going to love you for who you are, only for what you can do for them.

"Ema! What's wrong?" Kate said in alarm when she opened the door.

"I've come to cry on your shoulder. Is Spencer here?"

"No, he's working at a client's tonight. Your teeth are chattering; come in and sit down, there's a fire in the living room and some hot coffee."

Kate, her hard-won figure thickened by pregnancy, pressed Ema into a chair and brought her the coffee. "Now drink that, and when you stop shaking, tell me what happened."

Ema sipped the hot coffee gratefully. "It's so stupid," she said. "Rupert's engaged."

"Who told you?"

"Tillie—with exquisite relish, of course—and then the great man himself, tonight. Last night he was too busy saying he loved me."

Kate's face flushed with anger. "Well, to hell with him! He's not good enough for you anyway."

"I know that. I'm not in love with him. I just wanted to marry him and be . . . safe."

"Because he has money—and social position," Kate said despairingly. "Ema, you need to marry someone you love. Then you'll feel safe. You couldn't stand to live with a man you didn't love."

"I won't live like this, either," Ema said, her cheeks wet. "Always trying, always on the outside looking in, always the one who steps aside."

"But once you were inside, where you belonged. It can be like that again with the right man."

Ema's hands came up to cover her face. "I never belonged."

"With your husband, you did."

"I had no husband, it's all a story that was made up for me."

Kate made herself sit quietly until, in short bursts of speech, Ema told it all—except for her father, she would never tell anyone about that. She could see Kate's hands rest protectively on her unborn infant when she heard about Ema's baby.

"But you had no choice, darling," Kate said, tears in her eyes.

"Hadn't I?"

"No, not at the time. Ema, you can't judge what you did then by the way things are now. It isn't fair! You couldn't know what life would be like for you; you were all alone."

Ema nodded. "Sometimes I forget that."

Kate hesitated. "Do you know anything about the baby?"

"No, but I'm sure she's a girl and at least I know she has all she had a right to have. I think her grandfather loves her, even if her so-called mother doesn't."

"It wasn't the baby's fault. Any woman would be kind to a helpless child."

"Not that woman." Ema shivered slightly again. Then she said, "It's getting late, I don't want Spencer to see me like this. You won't tell him anything, Katharine?"

"Of course not, darling. But stay here tonight, you can go up to bed before he comes home."

Ema sighed and shook her head. "You ought to see my desk—I have to start early in the morning."

"Then I'll call you a cab—but I don't like your sleeping under the same roof with that Blessing bitch." She put her arms around Ema. "You don't need a toad like Rupert, honey, and you ought to get away from Tillie. She's no friend to you."

I have to get away from Tillie, Emanuelle thought in the taxi. I have to get out of that house.

# 36

DECEMBER 1924

Even before the guests arrived, Emanuelle knew this would be the most brilliant Christmas ball Matilda had ever given. It was certainly the most expensive. Even the invitations—silver on white vellum—were works of art.

"A white tree?" Matilda had exclaimed when the huge sprayed spruce was brought into the entrance hall, newly tiled in white marble for the occasion.

"You must wait to see it with the ornaments you approved," Emanuelle answered. "Sterling silver and crystal."

"Are you trying to ruin me?" Thomas had demanded genially of his wife and her secretary, smiling indulgently at Emanuelle.

But there had been no objections once the tree was trimmed. It shimmered like an ice palace and its tiny crystal bells tinkled whenever the front door was opened.

On the Saturday after Christmas the white ballroom and all of the rooms on the first and second floors were banked with pure white blossoms of every kind; the scent of Monsieur Denis's gardenias, roses, and lilacs perfumed the air; orchids and camellias seemed to blossom on silvered trees. The buffet tables were draped in white velvet and set with the Blessing silver-rimmed white china service and Waterford crystal. The party favors were dazzling: silver watchchains and fobs for the men and slim bangles of white gold for the women.

"It's spectacular," Matilda said to Emanuelle, making a last survey of the rooms just before ten o'clock on the night of the ball. Matilda was dressed in silver tissue faille, white fox, and diamonds. "I hope you'll be able to top it next year."

Ema smiled, thinking of the fortune she could have made on this party if she'd been paid a fee, not a salary. Her experience had increased considerably. She had already decided which suppliers and caterers and florists and jewelers she would use for her own business when she had it, and she had copies of Tillie's most recent lists—the families, the weddings, the births, the debutantes, the bachelors, the menus of bygone dinners, the decors of bygone parties. It was invaluable information.

But only if she had the courage to use it! It had been a dreary year, but she still did not think she had saved enough to weather Matilda Blessing's certain attempts to sabotage her if she left.

"That's not one of my dresses," Tillie said suddenly, her heavily shadowed eyes examining Emanuelle.

"No," Ema said, consulting the leatherbound checklist she carried. The dress, made to her measurements by Thiboux, was of white silk fringe cascading in tiers from a low-cut bodice to the floor. Its only decorations were the bugle-beaded straps on Ema's creamy shoulders. She wore a beaded band around her forehead, the pearl bracelet and pendant earrings Rupert had given her at the start of their affair, and Julian's opal ring.

"Very simple," Matilda decided, "until you move. Then it's positively obscene." She would have to keep a closer eye on the girl, Matilda decided. Tillie had to put up with her husband's myriad affairs, but Emanuelle was precisely the kind of woman to make Thomas lose his head. He was at the dangerous age, when men divorce their wives and marry girls thirty years younger than they are.

"There's the bell," Matilda said, and swept down to receive in front of the Christmas tree, her red lips gleaming with hospitality.

By midnight the mansion was brimful of the most important people in New York and Ema knew the party was a success. She took her first glass of chilled champagne and went to the library to relax for a moment before she made another tour of the rooms.

"Good evening," a man's voice said.

Ema returned the greeting without looking up and sank gratefully into a chair, kicking off her shoes.

"Tired?"

She raised her eyes. He was standing near the window smoking a pipe. He was a good-looking man, with a face that was strong rather than handsome. He was fairly tall, with an impressive head and a compact, muscular body, like a boxer's. His brown hair was a little unruly, and he was youthful, but not young—in his mid-thirties, she guessed.

"My feet hurt," she said.

"I always wonder why women wear those things." He gestured at her shoes with the stem of his pipe.

"Fashion," Emanuelle said.

"Clothes make the woman?"

"No, they make the impression, and that's all that matters." She took a cigarette from an alabaster box on the table and he came over to light it for her, then relit his pipe with the same match. He had nice eyes, dark and friendly.

"I don't think so," he said, sitting in the chair next to hers. "The woman is what matters."

Emanuelle looked skeptical. "You'll never convince them," she said, nodding toward the guests in the next room.

"I know," he agreed ruefully. They smiled at each other and sat smoking in comfortable silence for a while. Then he said, "I should introduce myself. I'm Harding Ellis."

"Emanuelle Beranger," she said, holding out her hand.

His expression changed as he took her hand. "Ah, yes," he said. "I've heard of you from Tom Blessing. You're his wife's social secretary."

"And I've heard of you; you're the new owner of the *Star-Tribune*. I'm surprised I haven't seen you here before, Mr. Ellis."

"I was here once, for a private dinner with Tom. I'm not much of a party-goer. I don't have the time."

She smiled. "That's not very kind. Where would I be if no one came to Mrs. Blessing's parties?"

They lapsed into a friendly silence again while she finished her cigarette and her champagne. "I must go back to work," she said.

"May I see you again?"

"I'll be back soon for another sitdown."

He shook his head. "I don't mean here. Will you have dinner with me?"

She looked at him more attentively for a moment. "Yes, I'd like that."

"Tuesday night?"

She nodded. "You can call me here and tell me where to meet you."

"I'll come for you."

"No, Mr. Ellis. I prefer to keep my private life private."

He watched her go, her body fluid and supple under the swaying white fringes of her dress. He left the party soon after.

Ema saw him leave and wondered about him. She knew he was a bachelor, but not "social" and therefore not considered eligible by most of the society mothers of New York. They still refused to let new money pollute their pedigrees. They had reservations about a man like Ellis, who had started on the wrong side of Chicago and made a tidy fortune all by himself—but too recently, even by their standards.

Emanuelle made an inelegant sound. Damn them all, anyway; they ought to admire Ellis's success—anyone's success, hers, too, but would even Harding Ellis have looked at her so admiringly had he known where she came from? Or about her private performances for Rupert McAllister before he threw her over?

She put on her shoes. She was going to dinner with Ellis, not to bed. She had lived without sex for five years before Rupert and for many months since. She had abandoned the idea of using it to marry for money. The kind of man she wanted to marry—very rich and very social—wouldn't want to marry her unless he were old enough to be seduced into marriage by youth and sex. Ema didn't think she had the stomach for it.

Anyway, it was money she really wanted—not a husband to dole it out, not a man to control her and use her and tell her what to do—and soon she would take the risk and start making money for herself. But it would be nice to have dinner with Harding Ellis. She liked his eyes and his wide smile and the way his hands held the bowl of his pipe.

*Idiote*, she thought, standing, why must you think of sex just because a man asks you to dinner?

With a little grimace of pain from her tight shoe she went up to the ballroom to check on the champagne.

# 37

She realized how much she was enjoying herself midway through dinner at the lively restaurant he took her to. "A journalists' hangout," he said, "I hope you like it."

She was glad she hadn't dressed. Most men in his position would have worn a dinner jacket; he wore a business suit, but she was sure he would have been more comfortable in an old sweater and slacks.

The steaks were perfect, but it was the atmosphere of the restaurant she liked. Some of the men and women were engaged in earnest argument, some had come to relax and laughed uproariously over their private jokes. There were a few talking at top speed into the five telephones at the end of the bar. The rest listened raptly to a jazz pianist at the other end of the room, sometimes singing with him.

"You can tell these people like what they do," Ema said. "So do you, I think."

He nodded, pleased that she knew that. "If I'd had the choice, I'd have been a journalist from the start. I'll be the *Star*'s managing editor as soon as I find the right people to run my other interests. I own some other papers, but I waited a long time for a New York daily." His eyes were bright with the kind of enthusiasm Ema never saw in the Blessing set.

"What will you do with it?"

"Make it the best paper in the country," he said confidently. "Print both sides of every issue as honestly as I can and keep my opinions on the editorial page." He put down his knife and fork and spoke earnestly. "It's unethical to influence the public by slanting the news—you'd be surprised how easy it is to do that, just by the way the story is written. I won't have that in the *Star*."

"The rumor is that you can't be bought," Ema said, wondering how he would take that.

Ellis laughed. "I'm sure you heard it from Blessing, but he wasn't above trying. That was why he invited me to dinner that once. He wanted to know where I'd stand on things like income tax and the Bolsheviks."

"And you wouldn't play," Ema said with obvious satisfaction.

"No, I wouldn't."

"He can't have been pleased with you." She smiled broadly.

He was indifferent to Thomas Blessing's pleasure. "Tell me, Miss Beranger, do you read the *Star*?"

"I haven't the time—except for the society page, of course."

"And what do you think of that?"

She hesitated.

"Tell me," he said. "I want to know what you really think."

"I think it's dull, *voilà tout*." Ema forgot her dignity and talked with French brio. "All those names and dates—it's dull. The only pictures are of engaged girls and brides. It doesn't tell enough about dances and balls, things ordinary women want to know about *le gratin*—the upper crust. And I'll bet anything the upper crust would love being talked about, no matter how much they pretend to want privacy."

He was attentive. "What do ordinary women want to know?"

She laughed. "The important things, of course! In France the social gazettes tell you what kind of pastries were served on what kind of plates, how many maids it took to dust the chandeliers, what kind of sheets Madame has on her bed, and what kind of lace trims the leading courtesans' knickers." Her gray eyes sparkled with fun.

He smiled. "It might create quite a stir."

"No more than your love magazines, Mr. Ellis."

"You've read them?"

"A few, *Real Love* and *Hidden Passions*." She shook her head. "Life is not like that, either moral redemption or eternal bliss."

He made no answer, merely looking at her quietly for a minute. "Coffee now?" he asked.

She nodded. He had ordered coffee with his dinner, a barbarous American habit Ema hadn't yet adopted, but his manners, as his clothes and his speech, were polished. "You're not a New Yorker, are you?" she asked.

"No, I was born in Chicago."

"Was your father a newspaperman?"

He shook his head. "My father was a drunk," he said sadly. "He was a happy drunk, a really sweet-tempered man. I loved him, but he couldn't hold a job. It was hard on my mother, but she got me through high school after he died." The coffee came and he added cream and sugar to his before he went on. "I went to work at the power company after that. I learned a lot about utilities that way. Now I own a few myself—unfortunately too late to help my parents."

She was amazed that he would talk so openly about such a childhood.

"Tom Blessing says I have the common touch," he went on. "That's certainly true."

Ema felt a surge of anger. This man was worth ten of Thomas Blessing! "I wouldn't listen to anything he said."

"I don't." Blessing had also told Harding about Emanuelle's affair with Rupert McAllister; he had been grossly explicit about his own desire to get Emanuelle into bed as soon as he could escape his wife's gimlet eye. Why the old goat thought he had a chance with a girl like this, Harding didn't know.

He kept his eyes on his pipe, glad of something to do. Now that he knew her, he was surprised she'd have had an affair with that fool McAllister, but physical attraction was inexplicable, and despite the purity of her face she was undeniably a sensual woman. He hardly knew what else to say to her. She was more than beautiful and bright, she had a quality that moved him. He was dazzled by her eyes; he noticed that they didn't always laugh when she did.

"I'm told you're a Parisian," he said. "It must be wonderful to live in a city as beautiful as that."

"Do you know it?"

"Briefly, toward the end of the war. I was lucky; I came too late for the fighting." He stopped. "I'm sorry, your husband was killed in the war, wasn't he?" He looked uncomfortable. "Tell me what it's like to grow up in France."

She let him light her cigarette before she told him the fable of a modest but respectable bourgeois childhood in Lyon, her marriage, her move to Paris. She talked about a girl dressed in a school uniform with black stockings and a straw hat, rolling her hoop in the park, a young woman convent-educated until she married.

They went to a speakeasy after dinner to listen to jazz and he took her back to the Blessings' shortly after eleven.

"Sunday?" he asked her in front of the imposing door of the mansion. "The Central Park skating rink at noon?"

"But I don't know how to skate!"

"I'll teach you. I'll even bring the skates."

He shook her hand and went off up Fifth Avenue, whistling one of the songs they'd heard that night. She was humming it herself while she got ready for bed.

# 38

"He's beautiful," Ema said. She held out a rattle for the baby to grasp, then bent to kiss him and got up from the blanket on Katharine's living room floor. Katharine was watching her with concern.

"My darling Kate, you mustn't look like that," Ema said, coming to sit next to her on the couch. "I love my godson and I'm happy for you, really, truly happy. I've put the past behind me."

Katharine smiled. "I'm sure the dashing Harding Ellis has something to do with that."

"Something," Ema said, smiling too. "He has such ambition, Kate! Someone's always trying to stop him, but he won't let anything stand in his way. You saw that when you met him."

"I saw that. He's a lot like you."

"Thanks, but even if that's true, what can a woman do with her ambition? Can I run a newspaper or open a bank? Be governor or president? That's where the power is."

"They say," Kate observed, picking up her son, "that the hand that rocks the cradle rules the world."

"Some man said it, to keep us in our place." But Ema didn't really want to argue the point. Kate was supremely happy with Spencer and her baby; it was all she had ever wanted. That would never be enough for Ema, not without Julian.

"Aren't you even a little bit in love with Harding?" Kate said.

"In love? No, but I admire him very much." Ema was thoughtful. "And he fought his way up, too, from a start not much better than mine, although I haven't told him how bad mine was." She glanced at Katharine, renewing her friend's pledge of secrecy. "So I understand him a lot better than men like Rupert—or even Julian. I loved Julian from inside, the way you love your son."

"You said you had put the past behind you."

"The past, but not Julian, not ever."

"But you've been seeing Harding for months now. Suppose he asks you to marry him?"

"He has no time for marriage."

"He'd make time for you, Ema, if you'd let him."

"I'm not so sure. He wants me, Kate, I could swear it, even if he's never so much as kissed my cheek, but marriage . . . I don't think he wants that. It's just as well right now. I don't want to get married. I'm close to being my own boss for the first time in my life. I will be as soon as I can get away from Tillie."

Kate sighed. "You could be Harding's wife and start a business too. It's because he's not social! Sometimes I despair of you, Ema."

On her way to meet Harding Ema thought about that, but marrying Harding—supposing he ever asked her—would be exchanging one kind of dependence for another. And Kate was right, he was not social.

Yet whenever she decided to leave Matilda the old fear overwhelmed her, fear that she might not succeed before she had lost every cent she possessed, fear that she would be penniless again. Change had been the rule of her life, but now any change felt life-threatening to her. So she had stayed on with Tillie, enduring her in exchange for the luxury, the salary, and that comforting ten percent the suppliers politely called her "commission." It seemed to even the score a little, and the swelling of her bank account was a comfort.

Before she met Harding she was beginning to think it was time to contact Sir James again, to demand more than the pittance he had given her. She knew that much as he hated himself for it, he wanted her. An older man could be very generous when he wanted a young woman.

But now there was Harding, a far more attractive solution. She was a peasant to Sir James, a harlot; she was Harding's equal.

She reached Harding's favorite French restaurant and caught sight of him through the sheer-curtained window, waiting for her in the booth that was always reserved for him. It was unusual for him to be still, although he was not a nervous man. His activity always had a purpose. He had holdings in steel, automobiles, and real estate, as well as utilities, and he watched over all of them.

He was leaning back against the deep red plush of the booth with his hands clasped on the tablecloth and an expression on his upturned face that touched her, as if he saw something he could never have. Yet she knew his wide-set dark eyes, his firm mouth, the virile strength of his face, made him a man women looked at.

Her physical attraction to him was very strong and she wondered why he never did more than shake her hand when he brought her home. But she had fun with him, enough to realize how little fun there had been in her life before. Casually dressed, they went to baseball games and the circus, to noisy informal dinners with bright, witty people and to Harlem to listen to jazz.

He liked informal clothes, but when they went out for a formal evening he was always impeccably dressed. Everything he wore with his well-tailored suits—ties, cuff links, shoes, and handkerchiefs—was in the best taste. "That's because my valet does all my shopping," he told her once. The valet also chauffeured his Rolls, but in Harding's leisure hours he preferred a nervous little Stutz. He taught her to drive it and liked to watch her at the wheel.

His apartment on 60th Street—where he had never invited her alone—was soberly elegant and large enough for *Star-Tribune* staff parties and the small business dinners he had begun to give. She liked newspaper people; they were a dedicated, friendly lot, witty and often bawdy, as the girls at Thiboux had been, as Harding was himself—as Ema would have been if she had ever let down her guard.

But—the thought came upon her unaware now—his dark eyes were not Julian's eyes, his mouth was not Julian's mouth. In a room with Julian he would have been eclipsed by heritage, gallantry, and grace.

She was ashamed for thinking it. It was not fair to compare any man to Julian. Harding was someone of value. She resented anyone who looked down on him because he had come up on his own.

He seemed to sense her presence and looked up. For a moment he did not move and his eyes stayed fixed on hers with that same yearning. An unaccustomed feeling filled her. She wanted to make him happy.

I don't love him in the way he deserves, she thought. I'll never love anyone that way again. She smiled brightly at him. But I could make him happy.

Harding gestured to her to come into the restaurant and went toward the entrance to meet her. He had seen the bright smile, but it was her too-bright, social smile that never reached her eyes. When she looked like that, it was hard for him not to take her in his arms and comfort her, protect her. The nature of his love for her surprised him—he had never felt this tenderness for any woman, or this passion—but he was not sure she loved him in the same way and he would not accept anything less from her unless he had to. He cared too much.

Sooner or later he would marry her and keep that look out of her eyes for the rest of her life.

# 39

"You look beautiful," he said, taking both her hands before he walked with her to their table. "How's Spencer Treadwell Atwood?"

"Thriving, thank you. Kate says hello."

They ordered dinner—a steak for Harding, as usual, and poulet chasseur for Emanuelle. They exchanged news of their latest projects: Matilda was having ten Pullman cars redecorated to train a large house party, most of them politicians and their wives, down to the Palm Beach house, there to choose a Republican candidate for the next presidential election. Harding had a business trip to Canada coming up, but he was still looking for ways to increase the *Star*'s circulation. It had been a dull, conservative paper, almost defunct when he bought it, but it was picking up slowly.

"Any publication has to be prepared to run in the red for at least two years, but with a little effort the *Star* might not have to."

"Is it a real worry?" Perhaps that was what preoccupied him tonight. Even millionaires could lose all their money, as the Treadwells had.

He shook his head. "I wouldn't have gone into this venture without the capital to get me through an extended loss period."

"I know what you mean. I have the same problem myself." She picked at her food before she raised her eyes to his. "It's a deep, dark secret, of course, but I want to start a party service of my own."

After a moment he nodded. "I think that's a good idea. After all this time with Matilda—how long is it, three years now?—you certainly have the experience."

"Oh, yes. I know who's who and who isn't. I know who's received and who's not—and why. I know the preferred foods and wines and where to get them. I know the places people go and what they do when they get there. But I don't have enough of a cushion yet. I'd have to make a very quick success of it, and I could, except for Tillie. She doesn't like to be crossed and she'd make trouble—for a while, anyway." She hesitated, not certain if she should say any more tonight. But damn it, she thought, I have to know if he's going to help me. "That would mean a considerable loss period, too long for me." She sighed. "*C'est la guerre*, I suppose. I want to get out of Tillie's clutches, but I can't take the chance."

Harding chewed a piece of steak to restrain himself from offering her all the money she needed there and then, but he didn't want a financial relationship with her. "Emanuelle, I think there's a way around Matilda Blessing. Will you hear me out before you decide?"

"Of course, Harding, what is it?" She was prepared to become his mistress tonight, if that was what he wanted.

"I would like you to edit the women's page at the *Star*, I mean plan the page, decide which stories to run and assign reporters to cover them, decide which pictures to use—that sort of thing."

She was glad she could always hide what she felt. Surprised and disappointed, she still listened attentively to what he was saying.

"I want to run an entire page twice a week, in addition to daily engagement and wedding announcements, with additional layouts whenever we need them—you'd know when that was better than I do, horse shows and the rest. I'm convinced you're right about what women want to read—and you certainly know enough about the social scene in New York to do a column."

He held up his hand when she started to speak. "Let me finish. I know what it means to want your own business—I sure as hell did—but I think you'll be in a better position to start yours once you're established on the *Star*. New York is publicity-crazy; people want to be in the papers, even the blue bloods who used to shrink from it. You'd be able to put them there." He leaned back, watching her. "In time you'll have a kind of power, you know, and power is what everyone wants."

She nodded then. Her astonishment had passed and her gray eyes were intent on him, although she did not really see him. Oh, yes, she thought, power is what I want. Finally she said, "There might be some problems."

"Tell me."

"I can't possibly compete with a columnist like Maury Paul."

"Why not? Anyway, it's not only a column I want, it's an entire women's page. That will carry us until the column catches on. Next?"

"Matilda will make trouble."

"She could possibly make a lot of trouble for her ex-secretary—but none at all for the society editor of the *Star-Tribune*. Anything else?"

"Money. I make a lot working for Tillie."

"I'll better your salary."

"You'd have to better it by a lot! If I leave the Blessings, I'll need an apartment of my own." He nodded his agreement, but she shook her head, tempted but not certain about such an arrangement with him. "I'm not even sure I could do it. The *Star* people would laugh at me. What do I know about newspapers?"

"Emanuelle, the world is starving for competent people. You're a very competent woman and you work hard. That's all it takes to do most jobs, but you do have the experience for this one. I want to expand fashion coverage—send you to the Paris collections. Who could do a better job of that than you?"

"The Paris collections?" she said, warming to the idea. "I'd love that!"

He looked at her quizzically. "You'll probably get all of your clothes free, too, not to mention other things. That ought to equal some of the kickbacks you're getting at the Blessings'." He took her hand. "Come on, Emanuelle, take a chance."

She studied him. "Why are you doing this, Harding?"

"Because I need someone good—and you're good." He colored slightly. "Of course that's not the only reason. You know how much I admire you."

"I know, and it means a lot to me, but I can't base my future on a man's admiration, not even yours. I'd want a contract, one that would make it very difficult for you to fire me."

He almost said, then marry me, that's an airtight contract—but he would not demean her or the job he was offering her—above all not his love for her—by linking a business deal to a proposal of marriage.

"Agreed," he said. "We'll make it impossible for me to fire you for five years—and impossible for you to resign unless we both agree to it. Fair enough?" When she nodded he said seriously, "Emanuelle, I really do need you for the *Star*. I have to put some life into my newspaper. This is no game."

"I know, Harding, I just want things to be clear from the start."

His dark eyes sparkled. He refused to be daunted by the total lack of trust in him implied by her condition; why should she trust any man after knowing such cold-blooded bastards as Blessing and McAllister? "Then you'll do it?"

"Yes, I'll do it!" Her enthusiasm broke through her caution like the sun through a cloud. She gave him that wonderful radiant smile he had seen only once or twice.

Soon, he thought, I'll hold her in my arms and she'll smile at me like that, only at me. I'll make her love me.

He gestured for the check. "Let's go to Louie's for some champagne. We'll sign the contract tomorrow, but we can start the celebration tonight."

She laughed, a hearty laugh, warm with pleasure. He loved the earthy side of her that she usually kept under such sophisticated restraint, the woman in her who had as much passion as intelligence and ambition. If a woman like Ema really loved a man, it would be with her mind and her heart as well as her body, and there was no better love than that.

"When will you tell Tillie?" he asked, and was delighted when she laughed again, this time with relish. "As soon as we sign the contract—and I can hardly wait!"

# 40

Ema dressed very carefully for her first day at the *Star-Tribune*. She wanted to look businesslike when she met her staff but not too severe, prosperous but not as if she didn't have to work for a living as much as they did. She chose a skirt and hip-length jersey in copper wool, a black coat with a monkey fur collar and a copper felt hat with a feather.

"They're going to hate me," she told Harding when they walked into the *Star-Tribune* building on 42nd Street.

He rang for the elevator. "After the way Tillie Blessing blew up, you won't even notice it."

"*Mon Dieu*, but she was angry!" Emanuelle said. "I thought she'd have *une crise cardiaque*. Then she threatened to ruin me if it took her forever."

"I wouldn't lose any sleep over her," Harding said. "You're not her property. As for your staff, I wouldn't worry about them, either. They're just nice young people trying to make it on a newspaper." He smiled. "Like us."

"However little experience they have as journalists, it's a lot more than mine." She went into the elevator with him. "They'll wonder why you chose me and draw the obvious conclusion."

"At first, maybe, but not when they see how good you are." He glanced at her. "Would you mind?"

"I can't very well, it's what everyone thinks already."

They said nothing more until the elevator doors opened on a vast room with rows of desks under green-shaded lights. She heard an energetic clatter of typewriters and telephones and felt a tension that was very exciting. She had been here before, but it was different now, she was a part of it. She waved hello to the people she knew as they approached an office with her name on the door. He held it for her and closed it behind them.

There were four people waiting in the little office, two young women and two men, one young, one middle-aged. Harding, who had already given her a list of their names, ages, and experience on the paper, made the introductions and left them, and Emanuelle hung her hat and coat on a stand in the corner and went to sit behind her desk.

"I hope you'll all stay with me and do what you've been doing. It'll take a while for me to get the hang of it. I have some ideas for a different kind of page and I'd like to know if you think I'm divinely inspired or just plain crazy."

They smiled at that and relaxed a little, settling down to listen.

"I've been to the library," Ema went on. "It seems to me that the society pages are what they've always been—it's the society column that's changed, especially since Café Society started mixing blue bloods with people in show business and the arts. I think we can mix the two on the women's page as well. The society column will be part of it, but only a part. We can't hope to outdo Maury Paul—he's a Biddle, anyway. It gives him a very wide entree."

"I heard you were a duke's daughter," Doris Birnham said. She was pert and stylish.

Emanuelle smiled. "I think aiming at a wider audience is bound to increase circulation," she said.

"As far as I'm concerned, the more cuts we use, the better," Kenneth Conan said with pleasure. He was the younger man, a photographer.

"We can start doing that right now," Ema said. "Photos will break up all that type people hate to plow through."

Kenneth nodded admiringly. He was just twenty-six, Ema's age, but he looked more a boy than a grown man. He had pale red hair, freckles, and a thin body that seemed held together at the joints with paper clips.

The other two were a plain girl named Sheila McCarthy—she probably does all the work, Ema thought—and Henry Styles, a veteran reporter-photographer who seemed content to take a back seat to Kenneth.

Ema took a list of upcoming parties from her handbag. "I've already called these hostesses and they'll let us in—provided we behave ourselves. We'll have to wear evening clothes—Mr. Ellis has authorized one set of evening clothes for each of us."

"Marvelous!" Doris said.

"How did you get them to let us in?" Kenneth asked.

"I've met them. I used to work for a very social lady."

"Yes, Mr. Ellis told me." It was Doris, bursting with curiosity about Matilda Blessing.

"I'll tell you all about it sometime." Ema smiled. "It was a rare experience—but now let's plan a few pages. I understand the page is—how do you say it, put to sleep?—two days in advance."

"Put to bed, Miss Beranger, most features are. It's the news stories that run at the last possible minute."

"Call me Emanuelle, please," she said, amused by her mistake. "Put to bed, then." In moments they agreed on a debut and a charity tea as two events certain to please female readers and set the new tone of the page.

"High jinks and good works," Doris commented. "Very neat."

"And we'll follow the money raised at the charity tea to its destination, show who gets it and how it's spent," Sheila said enthusiastically.

The cool politeness of the first few minutes was gone. For the first time since Ema had agreed to take on the job she began to feel she could do it.

"It looks sensational," Harding said when the first page proof came up a few weeks later. "Of course, we don't mix ital heads with roman type anywhere else in the paper."

"Why not, it makes a page less forbidding," Ema said carefully. "Great wads of gray copy under uniform headlines are hard to wade through."

"How long have you thought that?" Harding asked her.

She made a typically French moue, her lips pursed, her head tilted to the side. "Ever since I took a good look at it. The *Star* looks as gray as the London *Times*—and who but the English could read that?"

"Well, don't keep your opinions such a secret. I may not agree, but I'd like to hear them. Now, let's go out to dinner to celebrate."

They had many dinners together in the months that followed. Harding traveled a lot, to Europe and California, and she began to miss seeing him at the end of the day, whether they spent the evening alone or with *Star* people. She did not miss her travels with Tillie. She was happy to stay in New York.

She had found an apartment on Park Avenue, and as soon as the bare essentials of furniture were delivered she would move out of her hotel room. The apartment was expensive—she would need part of her savings to cover the rent—but exactly what she wanted. She preferred less space in that location to more anywhere else. The living room and dining alcove were in a corner overlooking Park Avenue. The kitchen, her bedroom, and the bathroom faced the quiet courtyard of the building.

Every time she rushed over to leave more purchases there she stood quietly in the sunny silence of the empty rooms for a few minutes, smelling the fresh paint as if it were perfume, touching the kitchen and bathroom appliances with the intense pleasure most women reserve for men or babies. But this was the first home Ema had ever had, the first place she could call her own. She was in love with it.

# 41

FEBRUARY 1926

"That's settled, then," Emanuelle said to her staff. She sat behind her desk, her felt cloche hat pushed high up on her head, and checked off the assignments on her schedule. "Two weddings, a hospital benefit, and the league tea. I'll do a story on Coco Chanel with the sketches from the Paris opening. We're all thinking up something original for the Kentucky Derby, and we have to set up interviews with Gertrude Ederle and Helen Wills." The interviews were for a new column called "Star Gazers."

"They're not high society," Doris remarked, still reluctant to give up total glamour.

"They're women and they're in the news. Even high society is interested in them—and fortunately you don't have to be in the Social Register to swim the Channel or win at Wimbledon." She stood up and stretched. "I think that's it."

"Miss Beranger, you forgot the Charleston party at the Blessings'," Kenneth Conan said.

Ema smiled. "No, I'm covering that one—with you to photograph, Ken, all right?"

He never called her Ema or Emanuelle as the others did. He had fallen in love with her on the day she walked into this office. It left him virtually inarticulate, but it never interfered with his talent as a photographer.

Ema worked well with Kenny and she liked having him around. She thought she would take him to Paris with her the first time she went to cover the collections. She had really earned this plum and she vowed she would never cover fashions by using press handouts alone.

When they had filed out of her office, Ema looked at her watch. It was four o'clock, time to go home to bathe and dress. Harding was taking her out to celebrate her six-month anniversary on the *Star*. She pulled her deep cloche hat down to her brows, put on a Chanel jacket lined with silk and edged with braid, and left her office, waving good-bye to the people she passed in the City Room on her way to the elevators.

She was exhilarated and not the least bit tired. Every moment she spent at the *Star* was challenging and, *grâce à Dieu*, she breathed every night in her delicious new bed, successful. And it had happened so quickly! After the first nervous months it seemed she had always run the women's page of a big New York newspaper; by now she was not surprised when restaurant captains greeted her by name and New York hostesses sent her advance notices of debuts and weddings. It wasn't the kind of entree into society she had wanted, but it was very satisfying. The *Star* gave her a special kind of power over influential people. And power was a habit she did not want to break.

Her page was popular, to judge from the mail. She had a special knack for spotting the details that ordinary women—who would never sit in the Metropolitan Opera's diamond horseshoe or go to a debutante ball—wanted to read. She loved the gaudy glamour of this explosive decade, wild with freedom and feverish with change. Her enthusiasm for it showed in what she wrote.

And—wonder of wonders—Matilda Blessing had finally sent Emanuelle an invitation to her Charleston party. It was addressed to the society editor of the *Star*. If Ema wanted any proof that her page was beginning to carry some weight, that was it.

When she opened her front door she stopped, as usual, to admire her apartment. It was still not complete, but it was very effective. Everything was in beige and white, a departure from the style that decreed a different color scheme for each room. Light colors were impractical in New York, people said, but Ema wanted the luxury of light and space. Harding had thought it would be cold at first, but now he appreciated the uncluttered serenity of the place. The embroidered Japanese triptych hanging over the white credenza in the living room was his housewarming gift and the only piece of art as yet; she had not put out her silver-framed mementos of Montmartre; she wanted everything perfect before she did that. They were still carefully wrapped, with Julian's letters, on the top shelf of her closet.

Two deep, soft armchairs to go with her beige velvet couch had just arrived, and she walked around each one to be sure it was in the best possible place. The walls seemed bare now that all the furniture was in place, but Ema had decided to add the finishing touches very slowly. She was over her budget, anyway.

"I'll imagine the paintings and the bibelots," she had told Harding, "until I find exactly the things I want."

Now she went through to her bathroom and turned on the bath taps while she undressed. She looked through her closet for something special and chose an amber chiffon model's sample she had ordered from a sketch of the last Patou collection—wouldn't it be *sensationnel* to attend the next one herself? She was not known in Paris yet, but once she presented her press credentials she would be, at least to the haute couture.

The dress had spaghetti straps and a precariously low-cut back. Its skirt was a shocking eighteen inches from the floor, with floating overpanels that barely reached her calves. From a drawer of exquisite French-made underthings she took a pair of amber crêpe de Chine step-ins, sheer silk flesh-colored stockings, and satin garters, all she could wear under this dress. She still loved beautiful underwear as much as she loved clothes.

She perfumed the bath water, stepped into its delicious warmth, and leaned back to think about Harding. He still kept a physical distance between them, but he was in love with her, she was sure of it. He was waiting for the right moment, and she thought that was touching in a man. She cared for him, for the man he was and the way he encouraged her to do things independently.

"You have to fly with your own wings," he told her. "You're that kind of person."

They had seen less of each other lately; Emanuelle, with Kenneth Conan in tow, went to the best of the social functions she reported, and Harding, aside from the other investments that took him out of town, was making the *Star* a popular political forum. He was criticized for fence-sitting, but he always pointed to the *Star*'s editorial page, where his personal views on an issue were very clear.

She was at ease with him as she had never been with a man before, not even Julian. The enormous social gulf between Julian Saxon and Emalie Bequier had darkened the very ecstasy it deepened. And the affair with Rupert McAllister had been mechanical, an exchange of purely physical services.

But with Harding, she thought, feeling with delight the silken lather of imported soap on her skin, there was more than strong physical attraction; there was friendship and the kind of camaraderie she had never had with a man before. Sex would probably spoil that, but she wanted him. She had reached no conclusion when she got out of the tub to finish dressing for the evening.

"Tell me the truth, Harding," she said after dinner when she was flushed with champagne and well-being. "Is my page really helping circulation?"

"Very definitely," he asserted. "You read the mail as well as I do. But let's not talk shop anymore tonight. Dance with me—at least until they play a Charleston." They exchanged greetings with several diners on their way to the floor and Ema's mood expanded even more.

He was a good dancer, smooth and easy to follow, and he looked distinguished in his evening clothes. His body was broad-shouldered and solid. She could feel his hand on her bare back and she leaned against him, her cheek close to his, wondering if a man could feel a woman's breasts through the heavy fabric of a jacket. He smelled of soap and pipe tobacco and a scent she had come to recognize, whenever they danced together, as uniquely his. They did not speak and she kept her eyes closed, happy with the rhythm of the music, with him, with herself.

When they left the restaurant they took a cab through Central Park and it was then that she turned to him expectantly and he kissed her. With a little sigh of delight she kissed him back, feeling his hand touch the bare skin of her back under her cape and move down to slide under her hips. He lifted her onto his lap and she lay back in his arms, delighting in the touch of his hand stroking the inside of her thigh.

She heard him change the address he had given the driver from hers to his and a delicious excitement suffused her languor. She went silently with him up to his apartment, and when he had closed the door he took off her cape and lifted her into his arms to kiss her again.

He carried her into the bedroom, talking softly between kisses, sliding her wispy dress and panties from her when they were lying on his bed. "I won't put on the light; I just want to touch you. I've been looking at you for so long, I only want to feel you."

They lay naked in the dark, like blind lovers discovering each other only with their fingertips—the line of her neck, the slope of his back, the softness of her breasts, the hard muscles of his thighs. She wanted him to prolong this voyage of discovery, and he seemed to know that and touched her lightly, slowly, intimately. In the long dark silence he adored her, he told her so with his body and his hands and the secret sighs of loving that escaped him whether it was his to summon or hers to offer back. There were tears in her eyes when finally they were quiet, but she was not in the least sad. She had been profoundly moved by him, not only to passion but to a genuine affection she had never thought to feel for a man again.

He went to get two glasses of champagne, and they lay in the dark sipping it.

"I'm in love with you," he said. "But you know that, don't you?"

"Yes, I know that. I'm glad of it."

"And you, Ema?"

She couldn't lie to him, not now, and the darkness made it easier to be honest. "I'm afraid of love, Harding, I have been for a long time. But I've never felt quite this way with anyone else."

He put his glass down and took hers from her. "What way?"

"I'm not sure," she said, "but I think it's as if I can just—be . . . me."

His arms went around her. "You're mine," he said, "you're mine now."

She would never be anyone's, but this was not the moment to tell him so, not while he was making love to her like this. It was not the same as the first time. This time he was less schooled, more passionate. He wanted more from her than reciprocal arousal. She was not to know until many years later exactly what it was.

# 42

"In the mattress?" Harding said, astonished.

Ema laughed. "In the mattress or down the well. It's where all French peasants keep their gold pieces. As this apartment has no well . . ." She patted the mattress of her bed where they lay reading the Sunday papers and drinking coffee. There was a fire blazing in the grate and the snow falling outside hushed the sounds of the city.

"But you weren't a farmgirl."

"Peasant is just another word for poor." It was not so hard to say it here in the warm bed with him beside her.

He looked at her, put down the papers, and drew her close to him. "Then it wasn't the way you told me."

"No, it was much worse." Her tone was one of disgust. "My father had a grocery store, but it was in a slum—dirty and noisy and ugly—older than any slum in this country. There was nothing beautiful in it, except for a few trees in the square. I hated it—and them, my family." Her eyes moved around her lovely bedroom, from the white silk window curtains under beige moiré drapes to the skirted dressing table and the fluffy white pillows and blankets of the bed. "It wasn't anything like this—and it wasn't mine. This is the first home I've ever had, the first place that's mine, that's why I love it so." She glanced up at him. "But you know what poverty is like; we don't have to talk about it."

He was grateful that he could remember love along with his poverty. All she felt was bitterness. Yet he knew she trusted him now. "Ema," he said, "tell me about your husband." It was not a description of the man he wanted, but something far more vital.

"Oh, Harding, not here, not now."

"Yes, now, if what there is between us has touched you at all."

It seemed a long time before she said it. "He was the only good thing that ever happened to me—and I loved him the way you love only once, when you're young. I took him into my soul and he'll always be there; he's part of me."

He understood what she was telling him, that she could never love another man in that total way he so longed for, and his heart sank, even if he loved her all the more for her honesty and her loss.

She looked up at him. "I think you *are* the people you've loved and they are you."

He couldn't stop himself. "Marry me, Ema, I know we'd be happy."

"No, Harding. It's perfect just as it is; don't ruin it. I don't want anyone else, you know that. I just want to be free to do as I like."

It took a mighty effort not to insist. "At least you'll never be poor again," he said after a while, stroking her hair. "You've arrived, my darling. You could go to any paper in New York if you wanted to. You don't need the *Star* and you don't need me."

"Harding! I have no intention of leaving the *Star*—or you."

He would wait and try again; it had been a mistake to talk about marriage while Emanuelle was still riding the first crest of her success, while she was still intoxicated by the novelty of answering to no one but herself. He would wait until that was not the only thing in life that mattered to her. Until she loved him as much as she loved money and influence and freedom. He didn't want her to be free; he wanted her to be his.

He had formidable rivals, but none so insidious as her husband. It was seven years since his death and nothing had changed for her, she would not even let herself forget. It seemed morbid to Harding, but he understood her thralldom. There had been no other man worthy of her trust, so she clung to a dead one.

But I'm here now, Harding thought, holding her closer, and a dead rival is better than a live one.

At least the phantom vanished when they made love. He could not have gone on otherwise; there would have been no hope then. She relished sex as she did good food and fine wine, but the most compelling thing about her was how completely she gave herself and the pleasure she took in pleasing him.

She was not deceiving him. If Ema thought of Julian now, it was only when she was alone. And if, with Harding, there was not that poignant, breathless bliss so well remembered, there was still a deep, uncalculating passion and an ever-growing trust.

"Then why not marry him?" Katharine demanded when Ema confided her feelings as they walked the baby in the park. Katharine was pregnant again and looked, behind her spectacles, loving and beautiful.

"We're happy as we are," was Ema's answer. "And Harding wants a kind of love I'll never feel for anyone again. He certainly deserves it. It wouldn't be fair."

"You're such a romantic!" Katharine remonstrated. "You think nothing will do but that first fine rapture. It wouldn't have lasted, you know, even with Julian. Ema, there are so many kinds of love. You'd be happy with Harding."

But Emanuelle was superlatively happy with her life exactly as it was. Through her own efforts she had a home of her own, a couture wardrobe, a little Marmon roadster, and an exciting career that was making her famous. If she was in love at all, it was with her total independence. She had not abandoned her plans for a business, only suspended them temporarily, to do the best she could at the *Star*. Harding was right, any business she started would benefit enormously from her present position.

There were enormous benefits already. After the caterers and florists had come couturiers, milliners, decorators, and restaurateurs, all eager to show their gratitude for the free publicity she created merely by mentioning their names anywhere on the women's page.

"It's incredible," she told Danielle when she was in Paris for the collections. "I hardly spend a penny. Harding says it's all right provided I don't solicit them and don't favor anyone to the exclusion of the others. I think it's bloody marvelous. I bank most of my salary."

Her confidences had a point: Danielle's financial situation had become precarious almost overnight. Europe, after a postwar spurt, had not recovered steadily, and now it was sliding into recession. France was not riding a wave of economic expansion like America. Quite the contrary, and Danielle had drastically lowered her fees to keep her expanded school going. "But I manage," Danielle said stoutly, as they drank herb tea in front of the fire. "I've always known how to fit my pattern to my cloth."

Danielle was too proud to accept an outright loan, and Ema did not insist. She offered to become a partner in the school, and was gently but firmly refused.

Danielle changed the subject. "Tell me about your Harding Ellis?"

"He's a diamond in the rough, Danielle, although he has more than enough polish for America. He wants me to marry him, but even though I'd miss having him, I don't want to marry him—or anyone. You, surely, can understand that."

"I'm not like you, *ma chère* Emalie. I was never fond of sex. Women who are ought to be courtesans or wives."

On her way to the boat train Ema asked the taxi driver to go past Saxon, Vaillant, Merchant Bankers, in the Place Vendôme. Impulse overwhelmed her, and she told the driver to stop and wait while she went past the bow-ing doorman and into the building. The same air of quiet luxury prevailed in the reception room of the *rez-de-chaussée*, and she stood for a moment looking at the small part of the world she had occupied during the most chaotic and exalting time of her life, when every second had a special intensity. She could still hear the rumble of the guns on the Marne and see herself rushing out of the bank after work to meet Julian at the station.

She went back to her taxi, parked where Julian's had been when he spoke to her under the lamplight that April night. That a voice and a presence could leave such an indelible mark on a woman's life! And at Stridings Julian's child looked at the world with Julian's eyes and smiled as he had. That, at least, was as it should be.

The taxi drove on and she saw Cesar's through a blur of tears. The parasols seemed to be the same ones she had sat under so often, but they looked as weary and dispirited now as Paris did, a city still beautiful but fallen on hard times.

She had not fallen. She would never be an English lady, but she could be an American one. So be it. The more satisfying her life became, the more her need to punish the Saxons faded. Let go of it, she told herself, the child is better off where she is and so are you.

When she reached Le Havre she went directly to her cabin on the *Carmania* and stayed there with her thoughts until the next morning, until the ship was on the high Atlantic and the ache inside her had receded along with the continent of Europe. She was Emanuelle Beranger again when she left her cabin, and she passed the voyage pleasantly enough in the company of several people she knew.

She unpacked happily in the quiet comfort of her apartment, eager to get back to work. Harding was in California on business for a few days, but there were masses of white roses from him and he called before she had finished unpacking. It was good to hear his voice, but it was good, too, to take a long bath, then sit on the couch in her robe, sipping a glass of champagne and smoking a cigarette while she planned the spread on the Paris collections.

Her life resumed its pace in New York and the summer of '26 sped by at gorgeous parties and weekends in Newport and the Hamptons. She felt she had her future firmly in her grasp—including the business she was ready to launch.

It was in mid-August that she came to the *Star* very early one morning and waited impatiently for Kenneth Conan to come in. She called him into her office.

"I need a favor, Ken, a very confidential favor."

"Of course, Miss Beranger, anything." He closed her office door and came to her desk, proud that she trusted him.

"If you got a girl into trouble, where would you take her for an abortion?"

He blushed crimson. "I never have, Miss Beranger."

"But you'd know where to go if you had to," she insisted. "Newspapermen know things like that. It can't be one of the society abortionists everyone knows; that always gets around."

He shook his head. "The others are too dangerous; sometimes they do those things in awful places, anywhere they can find. The girl might die, whoever she is."

She sat down behind her desk. "I'm the girl, Ken, and I don't want to die. You're the only one I can trust. Help me find someone safe, please."

He shook his head again, his face sullen with anger now.

Emanuelle looked up at him, her gray eyes dark. "Someone gave me a name yesterday, never mind who. I met the man this morning in a coffee shop downtown. He was a big man with stains on the lapels of his suit and big hands with dirty fingernails." She took a deep breath. "I asked him what he would do and he said for three hundred dollars he would put his fingers inside me and manipulate my womb. He said that usually did the trick the first time, but if it didn't work, he'd do it again, no extra charge for me." She stopped for a moment. "Help me, Kenneth."

"Jesus," Kenneth said, revolted. "Don't let him touch you! Why won't Ellis marry you?"

"There are reasons," she said, turning her head away from him. "They're not your concern." He could tell her anger was not directed at him.

She was furious that Harding's precautions had failed; her own method had seen her safely through the entire affair with Rupert, but sometimes she left it to Harding. *Harding.* The immediate cause of misfortune in her life was, once again, a man. She suspected Harding of planning this "accident" to make her marry him; he had asked her several times again. But she would not marry him. Her life was finally her own and she would never again surrender it to any man.

She looked up at Kenneth again. "I simply cannot have this child," she said.

And Kenneth, adoring her as a young man adores the distant moon, gave in.

# 43

Emanuelle got out of the taxi at the corner of 12th Street as Ken had told her to do. She walked three blocks to the address she had memorized and shivered as she climbed the steps of the building, although the night was warm. At the top of the second flight of grimy stairs she found Apartment G and knocked lightly three times.

The thin, balding man who opened the door looked harried, but not sinister. He had loosened his tie and rolled up his shirt sleeves. "Come in quickly," he said. He locked the door and preceded her through the empty apartment into a shabby kitchen. A bare bulb was suspended from the ceiling over a table covered with oilcloth. There was only one chair. A kitchen pail stood on the floor under the table. There was a wicked gleam from the kitchen sink, and she realized it came from a set of instruments laid out on a towel.

"You have the money?" he demanded.

She nodded and handed him an envelope from her bag, watching while he counted out five hundred dollars in small bills.

He rolled the money up and put it into his trousers pocket. "Take off your dress," he instructed her, "and whatever you wear under your slip—and the shoes—you can leave the stockings—then get up on the table." He took a bottle of whisky from the counter and drank deeply from it. "Want some?"

She shook her head.

"You won't feel it so much if you do," he advised. "I can't give you anything, you know. You have to get out of here fast, on your own steam, as soon as I'm finished. And you can't make a lot of noise, either, or I'll stop right where I am and get the hell out of here." Again he offered her the bottle, and this time she drank from it. "All right, get ready," he said, and drank again before turning to the sink.

She took off her dress, her shoes, and her step-ins and put them on the floor, then sat on the table. She heard the water running at the sink.

He turned to glance at her. "Pull your slip up higher and move your hips down to the edge." She complied. He dried his hands at the sink and sat down in the chair. "Lie back," he said, "put your feet on the table, bend your knees, and grab hold of your ankles." His fingers opened her and she stiffened with revulsion.

"Relax," he said impatiently. "I can't tell anything otherwise." He inserted a finger and made his examination, muttering to himself. "Almost three months," he said, pressing hard inside and out. "Uterus slightly prolapsed, but nothing to worry about." He withdrew his finger and wiped his hands on a towel. He looked at her, as careless of her position as if he were a mechanic and she a car up on a rack. "There's nothing unusual," he said, "you'll be okay." He took another drink from the bottle. "I do clean work." There was a note of pride in his voice. He put a towel under her hips. "Let's get started."


Harding replaced the receiver on its cradle and shook his head, mystified. He crossed the City Room to Emanuelle's darkened office. It was nine o'clock and the huge room with its rows of desks, telephones, and typewriters was in a clatter of preparation for the morning edition, its green ceiling lights ablaze. Feature pages like Ema's were locked up well in advance, and he didn't really expect to find any of her staff, but Kenneth Conan was there, sitting at her desk in the dark. In the light from the City Room Harding could see that he was the worse for the bottle of bootleg gin that slopped dark stains on Emanuelle's pristine blotter every time he took a swig of it.

Harding smiled to himself and put on the light. He and Ema were aware of the photographer's adoration of her and both of them behaved very discreetly around him. "Ken?" Harding said. "What are you doing here?"

"As you see," Kenneth said, taking another drink.

"What's wrong?"

The scorn in Kenneth's eyes was clear—and unexpected. He had always been an eager and contented kind of fellow. "You have a fucking nerve to ask that, Mr. Harding fucking Ellis, you know better than anyone what's wrong."

Harding closed the door. "What in hell do you mean by talking to me like that?" he demanded.

"I can't talk to you," Kenneth said sullenly. "She made me swear I wouldn't."

"You swore? To whom?" Suddenly Harding was very anxious. He came around the desk. "To Emanuelle?"

Kenneth put his head down on the desk and began to sob.

"For God's sake, man, tell me what happened? Where's Emanuelle?"

The words were broken, but Harding heard them. "Having an abortion."

"Jesus!" Harding leaned over the man, shaking him. "Where? And why, for the love of God, why?"

Kenneth raised his head. "You mean you didn't know she was pregnant?"

"No, for Christ's sake, no! Do you think I'd ever let her . . . Where is she, Conan? You've got to tell me."

"What's the use? It's too late now," the younger man sobbed. "She wouldn't even let me go with her; she said she didn't want me to get into trouble in case something went wrong."

"Conan, goddamnit! Tell me where she went!"

In seconds Harding was out the door and running for the stairs, not stopping to wait for the elevator. He hailed a cab and gave the address. "I'll give you twenty bucks if you get me there in five minutes," he said, and was jerked back against the seat as the cab shot forward.

Let me get there in time, Harding pleaded silently. Please let me get there before anyone hurts her.


The doctor—for so he had been—had reseated himself in the chair with an instrument in his hand when the sound of feet pounding up the stairs made him stop and look around warily.

"Ema!" Harding's voice shouted. "Emanuelle?"

"Is that you?" the doctor asked angrily, turning back to her.

"Yes," Ema said, dazed.

"Shit," the man said. "Goddamnit." Swiftly he rolled up his instruments in the towel, grabbed his jacket, and disappeared into another room. Ema pushed herself up and got off the table. She heard a window open and the sound of feet scurrying down a fire escape ladder and Harding's voice still calling her from the hall. Then she crossed the empty living room and opened the door and Harding stopped his pounding.

He winced at the sight of her rigid white face and her body, so vulnerable in its short slip. He closed the door behind him. "Emanuelle, what have you done?"

She turned and went back to the kitchen, and he followed, angry, fearful, insistent. He swore softly at the sight of the table and the open bottle of whisky and the panties lying on top of her dress on the floor. "Damn it, answer me," he said.

"There wasn't time to do anything," Ema said. She got into her dress and her shoes, rolling up the step-ins and stuffing them into her handbag. "And don't talk to me like that. I don't belong to you."

"Ema, why didn't you tell me about the baby?"

"Why? So you could stop me? That's what you want, to take over my life."

"I love you," he said frantically. "I don't want to take over your life. I want you to be happy."

"Yes, of course, provided I marry you. Isn't that why you arranged this little accident?"

He was angry. "I don't deserve that from you. It wasn't a child I wanted, I want you."

She took her bag and crumpled into the doctor's chair, searching for a cigarette with shaking hands. "Then you don't want it either." She tried to light the cigarette.

"That's not what I said. Of course I want our child, but I wouldn't trick you into having it. If you don't know that, you don't know me." He took the cigarette, lit it for her, and handed it back.

She looked up at him, moved by the anger and hurt pride she saw in his face. "I shouldn't have said that, Harding, but I don't want to get married, I don't want a baby. I don't know what to do."

They were like two strangers in their separate needs.

"Do whatever you want—except this." He looked around the kitchen with a shudder. "Ema, I'll recognize the child. I'll adopt it, whether you marry me or not. But don't risk your life; you have too much to live for, quite apart from me." His eyes moved down to her stomach. "Apart from us. It's my baby too."

She shook her head hopelessly. "*Mon Dieu, mon Dieu,* you don't understand."

"Then tell me," he pleaded, longing to lift her physically out of that harsh light and her unhappiness, but aware that he must keep his distance.

"I can't tell you," she whispered, "I can't—I'm not sure I know myself." Her eyes, huge and dark-shadowed by the light above her, met his. "I'm glad you got here in time, but I'm still not glad to be pregnant. It has nothing to do with you, but how can I give up everything I've worked for because of a stupid accident? I wasn't careless; we did everything we could to prevent it. But it's growing inside me anyway, and I can't stop it! It isn't fair! I had such plans, I was going to . . . but what difference does it make now?"

"You can go on working for months! As far as I'm concerned, you can work right up to the end—from home or the office, whatever you want— and come back right after you give birth to the baby."

"It's easy for you, Harding! You won't have a big belly when you make speeches supporting an Army Air Corps; you won't have to stop traveling. And you won't have to give birth, either," she said. "It's not the most pleasant experience in the world."

They looked at each other in silence for a moment before he spoke again. "All right, Ema, have an abortion if it's what you really want, but at least go to Switzerland or somewhere safe." Then he shook his head. "But it isn't only having a baby or a temporary halt in your career that brought you to a place like this. There's something else, something you haven't told me. Why don't you want to marry me?"

Confronted with it directly, she wondered why herself. He was an exceptional man. He represented everything she loved about America, the best of it. His power was based on wealth, yes, but wealth attained by merit. She herself had achieved a measure of status in this society, none of it thanks to aristocratic ancestors.

And she cared for him more than she had ever expected to care for a man again. She was eight long years away from Julian, so did it matter whose arms held her if Julian's could not, whose voice said he loved her if Julian's did not? Harding loved her, but the supreme moments of *her* life had already been lived. What could she fairly give to this man and this man's child?

"Harding, I don't love you in the way you deserve." She said it quickly, then she turned her back to him. "I admire you and respect you, I'm happy when I'm with you. It's all I can feel for anyone, but you want so much more."

His pride denied that he wanted more. His pride argued that she had just described love as any rational person would perceive it; she simply hadn't yet realized that love was what she felt for him. He knew he could make her love him, not that heroic shadow from her past. He went to her and put his hands on her shoulders. "Ema," he said, driven to lie to himself and to her, "that's enough for me." He turned her to him and took her into his arms. "We're going to be great together, you'll see."

She leaned against him gratefully. She had a fleeting sense that he had saved her from a loss beyond that of the child.

# 44

They were married at sunset three weeks later on the rolling lawn of a hotel in upstate New York. They reserved all the rooms for the occasion so their guests could stay overnight after the newlyweds left for a honeymoon cruise aboard Harding's new yacht.

"Fancy booking an entire hotel for a wedding!" Ema said, dressing with Kate in one of the upstairs bedrooms. "How lovely it is to be *rich* rich."

Katharine finished fastening the hooks of Ema's silver-gray organza gown, with its broad fichu and floating skirt. "You're not marrying Harding for his money!"

"Is that a statement or a question?" Ema reached for a wide leghorn straw hat; a cloud of matching organza encircling its crown was fastened with a fresh white camellia. The only jewelry she wore were earrings, and Julian's opal ring on a chain inside her dress.

"A statement. I know you love him, even if you never actually say so."

"He's a lovable man," Ema agreed.

"That doesn't mean quite the same thing."

Ema looked at Kate's reflection in the long pier glass. "No, it doesn't. I'm pregnant, Kate."

"Oh, Ema, that's wonderful!" Kate beamed into the mirror. After a moment she added, "You're happy about it, aren't you?"

"Yes—no—I don't know. It was an accident."

"And you detest anything you haven't scheduled well in advance! But you'd have married him sooner or later, you said so yourself!"

Ema nodded. "Yes, I'd have married him eventually."

"Darling, it's what you need—a husband who adores you." Kate hesitated. "A child too. Nothing can ever replace what you've lost, but this is a new life, Ema, with its own lonely places to fill."

"I know, Kate. I just have to get used to the idea." Ema reached for her bouquet of white calla lilies and camellias. "Ready? It's time."

The two women, Ema in gray and Katharine in apricot, went down the stairs of the colonial hotel and waited just inside the French windows of the salon for a signal from the judge who was to perform the ceremony.

Through the windows Ema could see Danielle in amber chiffon, waiting like a queen mother to give the bride away.

"It's a bit unconventional," Harding had said, smiling broadly when they met Danielle's ship at the pier. "But a bride ought to be given in marriage by someone who loves her."

"Provided she's given to someone who loves her as much," was Danielle's reply. After a moment's close scrutiny Danielle had made her decision. "I'm sure you do."

"Then I'm doubly glad you've come," Harding had returned sincerely, "for my sake as well as Ema's."

Danielle, stylish and gaunt as ever, her iron-gray hair still cropped, had sailed hastily in response to Ema's plea, cabled along with money and a first-class passage for the voyage.

"You always said husbands were an overrated commodity," Ema reminded her in private while Danielle tried on the dress Ema had ordered made for her in New York.

"*Bien sûr*, for me. Not for you. And particularly not for an expectant mother."

"That's a perfect fit!" Ema had exulted over the dress. Then she regarded Danielle carefully. "You don't seem surprised about the baby."

"*Mais non*. In your letters you sounded very happy as you were, so why else would you suddenly decide to marry within three weeks?" Danielle had nodded slowly at Ema. "Yes, my dear, I entirely approve of your marriage, including the baby."

I'll name the baby after her, Ema thought now. She'll like that. She'll have a family, she'll be Tante Danielle.

The other guests sat in rows of small gilt chairs on the lawn. They were almost all people from the *Star*; the wedding had been scheduled late on a Saturday afternoon so that they could be there. Significantly none of Emanuelle's society "friends" had been invited, although she was always at their weddings—and their teas, balls, and luncheons too.

This was a small wedding, with Danielle, Kate, and Spencer as attendants and Ken Conan to take the pictures, but while Ema was planning it, a fact almost obscured by her pregnancy had resurfaced: she was marrying a millionaire.

In the past two weeks she had received a flood of gifts Harding had been reluctant to give her when she was his mistress. There were two Manets and a Seurat, an ermine coat, a gleaming red sports car and an enormous marquise-cut diamond engagement ring. "It's longer than the engagement," Ema said. She knew if she never worked another day in her life, she would still have all she had ever wanted of worldly goods.

It was a comforting thought, yet her comfort was not complete. What she still wanted most—she knew it now—was the unalloyed respect of Sir James and the child he had taken from her. Harding could not buy that for her. She had to earn it for herself.

A vagrant breeze stirred her dress as she stood waiting and carried, from some vault of memory, her own voice reciting a translation from the Bible for Sister Marie Angélique.

For where your treasure is, there will your heart be also.

Then Kate's hand urged her gently onto the broad portico where Harding and Danielle waited. Walking toward him, Ema knew she cared as much for him as she could for any man alive, but he was not her treasure, and he did not have her heart.

Harding saw her come through the door, her eyes shaded by the broad-brimmed hat, and he sensed her reservations. Much as he welcomed the child, he wished they had both come unburdened to this day, that he had met her long ago when the girl Ema was yet to be won.

But I'll find that girl yet, he swore fervently, and I'll win her, no matter what it takes.

They were married as the sun bathed them both in the russet glow of a September sunset. It was a good omen, everyone said, but Kate, uneasy, hid her misgivings and hoped.


Harding sat at Emanuelle's left in their box at the Metropolitan Opera and watched her enchantment with infinite pleasure. The way her face reflected the passions of the story moved him far more than the action on the stage. Kate and Spencer Atwood, their guests, were on Emanuelle's right.

Ema was almost always lost in the music, yet tonight she found part of her mind turning away from the proud father on the stage, rejecting his son's unworthy mistress, and toward her own marriage. The aching sadness of her wedding was beginning to fade. She had come to terms with her life and she liked living with Harding more each day. The panic that had driven her to that kitchen table on 15th Street seemed exaggerated now, and lately—perhaps it was the euphoria of pregnancy—she was curious about the coming child. She hoped it would be a boy, for Harding's sake. She wanted him to be happy.

She was in her sixth month, but her empire gown of royal blue peau de soie disguised her condition. In the early months she had relied on large shawls and scarves for camouflage during daytime social events, but she stayed in her office now and let her staff cover for her. She was busy at home too; they had rented a much larger apartment in her building on Park Avenue, and she wanted it to be ready before the baby came. The apartment had five bedrooms and baths and servants' quarters for a housekeeper, her own maid, Harding's valet/chauffeur, and a baby nurse. Downstairs there was a big kitchen, a living room, a dining room, a library, and a private study for each of them.

The baby stirred inside Emanuelle again, but she was intent on the importunate tenor on the stage. He was slim for a tenor, dark and mustachioed, and he reminded her of François Martin, Henri Vaillant's *secrétaire particulier*, that poor dull young man who had been savaged to death like nine million others, like Julian, all passing into memory while life went inexorably on. The tears she shed at the end of the act were not only for Julian, as they had always been in the past, but in part for the luckless heroine on the stage and for her own lost innocence.

"That was so lovely," Kate said when the applause died away and the house lights came up. Kate beamed through her glasses. As round as Spencer was spare—Kate called him Jack Sprat—she was supremely happy with her marriage and her two sons and it showed in her radiant face.

"Beautiful," Harding agreed, helping Emanuelle with her ermine wrap. She loved beautiful things and he could lavish on his wife all that would have seemed a form of barter when she was his mistress. His wife! His child! He was overwhelmed by his good fortune.

Don't let anything change, he wished fervently. I swear I won't ask for more, just let things stay as they are.

"There really was a lady of the camellias," Spencer was saying as they left the box and approached the grand staircase. "She was famous for her temperament, in the French sense."

"Paff!" Emanuelle said with a Gallic grimace. "Americans have such a distorted view of Frenchwomen and their sexuality. We don't all dance the can-can and indulge in amorous dalliance by the Seine! The middle class still guards its virgins. Only the rich and the poor—and men, of course— are free to enjoy sin in France, like anywhere else."

Matilda Blessing's familiar bray sounded from the throng of operagoers behind them. "How are all the lovebirds?" she inquired. "Katharine, are you pregnant again? No? What a mercy. Emanuelle, you are ravishing, as usual. How goes the great gestation?"

"Swimmingly, thank you," Ema said, wondering how this woman had ever seemed threatening to her. "Where's Thomas?"

Tillie made a vague answer, her smile growing more fixed, but it was the one question that invariably annoyed her. Where Thomas was didn't bear thinking about.

They had reached the street. A long line of black limousines, lightly powdered with snow, approached the entrance, yawned open to admit their respective owners, and rolled ponderously away. Emanuelle pulled the soft ermine cape around her, relishing the fresh November air and the falling snow and the bustle of New Yorkers enjoying one of the wonders of their wonderful city. She felt a rush of well-being that was becoming familiar to her. Harding was on her right, Kate and Spencer on her left. She felt surrounded by loving friends.

She recognized Davina Saxon even before that bright blond head turned to say something to the man who stood at her side as their car approached the curb. Ema's heart lurched and her eyes swept the area around Davina to see if the child was there—no, that was stupid, Davina wouldn't bring a seven-year-old to the opera. But Davina was alone except for the man at her side in an opera cape and top hat. It was when he turned to hand her into the car that Ema saw his face.

Julian! *It was Julian!*

Ema shook off Harding's hand. She was unaware of his voice as she rushed down the shallow steps to the curb and ran after the car that was pulling away from the opera house. She saw Julian's face again, without his hat, through the window. It was thin and somber and very much older, and the hair was streaked with gray. But it was unmistakably Julian.

She called to him as she ran, but the car had picked up speed and the sound that came from her throat was only a whisper. Harding was at her side before she came to a halt, breathless and restricted by her long gown, feeling the full weight of her pregnancy for the first time, aware again of where she was.

"Ema, what are you doing, who was that?"

She did not reply, standing in rigid shock while little knives of snow stabbed her face and an unbearable cold spread from the center of her stomach.

"Ema, darling, what is it?" It was Kate's voice now. "You're so white."

"Take me back inside to the lounge, Kate, I must lie down. I think I'm going to faint."

"I'll call a doctor," she heard Harding say, and then she was in the ladies' lounge lying on a tufted garnet couch and letting Kate give her small sips of water to ease her dry throat.

"It was Julian," she told Kate when the lounge was empty.

"Oh, darling, you know that can't be." Kate stroked her hair.

"It was, it was, I'd know him anywhere. Davina was with him—his wife. Holy Mother, he wasn't killed, he's alive. I have to find him. I have to see him."

"Ema, what good would it do?"

"Good? What do you mean, good?"

"He's married, the same as he was when you met him—and so are you now, and expecting Harding's baby too."

"But *my* baby? I want to know about *my* baby. I want to tell him about her!"

"Hush, darling." Kate glanced around nervously. "You know he must think it's his wife's child."

Harding knocked at the door. "There's a doctor backstage, Ema. He'll be with you in a moment."

"It's all right, Harding," Kate called. "She only needs something to calm her." She turned back to Ema. "Are you going to tell him?"

Ema's mind came back to Harding with difficulty. "No, no, I can't do that, he wouldn't understand. I'll tell him—I'll tell him I thought I saw my husband, it's closest to the truth." She clutched Kate's hands in a mixture of joy and bewilderment. "Oh, Kate, he's alive, he's alive!"

Then Harding came in with the doctor and she was grateful for the mild sedative he administered while Kate whispered the explanation to Harding. The medicine was a good excuse to say nothing in the car, to retire immediately and alone as soon as they got home. She dozed fitfully through the night, pretending to sleep each time Harding came in from the guest room to see how she was.

Julian was here in New York, that was all she could think about. She must see him. She must hear his voice again and feel him close to her.

She did not forget that he had chosen to return to Davina. She did not forget that he must believe Davina was the mother of his child. The world must believe it, for the child's sake, but did the lie need to be perpetuated between the two of them?

Why hadn't they told her he was alive, Davina and Sir James? She had been easy to find—and surely they knew that for her child's sake she would keep the secret.

Had Julian tried to find her after the war? Did he even remember her?

At dawn she slept, but she knew what she must do as soon as Harding left for his office.

# 45

Emanuelle had to call only three of the best hotels in New York to find the Saxons. She waited in the Plaza lobby for an hour before she saw Davina come in alone. Davina collected her key from the desk and was halfway across the lobby before Ema approached her.

"I want to talk to you," Ema said abruptly.

Davina, startled, glanced around the lobby to be sure there was no one there who knew her, then seemed to regain her composure. Her eyes swept over Ema, noting her pregnancy. "How did you know we were here?"

"I saw you at the opera last night. You weren't hard to find."

Davina, with the air of a woman who had long been expecting a disaster and was almost relieved to confront it, nodded. "Yes," she said, raising an eyebrow. "I've heard about your *new* profession. You're a society reporter." Her tone ridiculed the incongruity of social connections for a woman of Emanuelle's class. "I have nothing to say to you," she finished.

"Where is Julian?"

"Out." Davina's blue eyes widened. "But you can't talk to him!"

"I will most assuredly talk to him unless I talk to you."

"Yes, all right, we'll talk, but not here." Davina's eyes darted around the lobby again. "We can take a taxi through the park."

In the taxi Davina lit a cigarette. "We came to New York because Saxon, Vaillant is opening a branch here."

"I'm not here for a chat. I don't give a damn about the bank; I want to know what happened to Julian."

Davina pressed her lips together for a moment before she began. "He wasn't found until well after you were gone," she said, her roving eyes now fixed on the cigarette between her gloved fingers. "He was still half dead when they brought him home; he barely spoke for months." She paused a moment when Emanuelle hugged herself and leaned forward as if she could not bear what she was hearing. "He had no strength and the wounds wouldn't heal," Davina went on, "they were always draining, there was always new infection. He was in terrible pain. For weeks he was delirious from fever, then he would mend a little and relapse again. When he was well enough we showed him his child. We thought it would cheer him up. When he finally recovered there was nothing to tell him that would not have given him more pain."

Emanuelle had no reply to that. Julian had chosen Davina when he left Ema in Paris. It was in the light of Julian's choice that she spoke now.

"But why did no one tell *me* he was alive?" she said. "What possible harm could it have done to tell me that?" She did not see the fear in Davina's eyes.

"But we had agreed to have no contact with each other—for the child's sake. It was better to leave it that way for Julian's sake too. Surely you can see that?"

"No, I don't see it," Ema said. "It was cruel to let me go on thinking he was dead. It would have changed nothing to tell me."

"You know now—and it only makes things harder for you, for all of us." Davina put out an imploring hand, not quite touching Ema's arm. "You must leave him alone; he's suffered enough. Leave him in peace at Stridings, with Drew. Drew is his whole life, he would sacrifice all of us for Drew." She said it bitterly, but Ema's astonishment was too great for her to notice.

"Drew?" she asked. "Drew?"

Davina nodded. "We named him Andrew James Julian, but we call him Drew."

Ema's eyes widened. "A son," she whispered. "I had a son?" For so many years the infant, the growing child, had been a little Emalie with all that she herself had been denied and none of what she had endured. Now she was thinking of a future baronet! Ema had never thought she longed for children; it was one hunger with which the gods had not cursed her, but as she listened to Davina talk about the heir to Stridings she hated this woman who was mothering her son.

Silence had fallen in the taxi and once more Davina's veiled glance strayed to the woman who was still a threat to her and did not seem to know it.

"I'm pregnant too," Davina said. She saw Emanuelle move as if she had been struck, and something inside Davina, long festering, was soothed by the poetic justice of it, by this special punishment for a special kind of treason. But her voice remained soft and pleading. "It isn't for me. I know Julian will never make a bastard of Drew, but the truth would still tear him to pieces. What would he think of his father and me—and of you? You can't destroy what little he has left to believe in. The war very nearly did that."

"Stop here," Emanuelle ordered the driver. She left the cab without a word, unable to breathe the same air as this woman, who already had everything and had taken Julian and her son as well.

Her mind darted, whipping her heavy body along the snow-coated walks of the park, careless that her shoes were soon wet through. His chosen wife was pregnant. He must still think that leaving Emalie was the best thing he could have done. But had he forgotten the love that had come upon them both, a love much deeper than his need and her ambition? Did he lie in other arms and take pleasure in them?

*I* do, a ruthless inner voice insisted, *I* do!

"Maybe we're both well rid of love," Ema muttered. "All it does is clutter up a life."

Again she reminded herself that love was not the reason for his ultimate decision. Even had he come back to find her after the war he could never have brought Emalie Anne Bequier and her bastard into his world; it was as simple as that. And if he ever knew what she had done with his son, his choice would be vindicated. A man like Julian would despise her for that, no matter that it was for the child's benefit.

But as she walked unseeing through a park as white-draped as a morgue, she knew her son could never have been taken from her unless she had chosen to give him up.

Exhausted, she sat for a while on a bench, and the stirring inside her reminded her that she had a husband now to whom she owed—what? loyalty and respect, certainly—and a child she did not really want. She had never deluded herself that this child would replace Julian's; no mortal being could replace another. There had been Julian's child, now there was Harding's, but never hers. Her only child would be her own achievement.

Her contentment with Harding had begun to sap her resolve to attain a place of her own in the world, independent of Harding's, and money of her own, too, and as much power as the Saxons had. She should have remembered that contentment is ever the foe of ambition. There was much for her to do. She had accounts to settle.

She would wait until the time was right for her to see Julian again, but see him she would. She could not exist in the same world with him and not see him again.

Shivering, she got up and walked out of the park. She was already living that moment of meeting, seeing it from the heights of some inner landscape, not thinking that between her anticipation and the consummation of it she would give birth to another man's child.

# 46

"I don't think you ever do one thing at a time," Kate said. Emanuelle jiggled the telephone hook and placed another call before she answered.

"Too much to do. Just this call to my broker and then I'll tell you my big surprise." Emanuelle, at the desk in her study on Park Avenue, gave the broker some buy and sell instructions, speaking with the telephone receiver propped on her shoulder. With one hand she made notes on a pad; the other held a cigarette.

She smokes too much, Kate thought, and she never stops rushing around. Ema was eight months pregnant, but since that night at the opera she was more active than ever. She hasn't said another word about Julian or her son, either, Kate worried, watching her friend, not another word since the day she came home half frozen from the park.

There was an anger in her Kate had never seen before. Heaven knew Ema had good reason to be angry, but her determination to even the score with Sir James and Davina—although she would not tell Kate how—was frightening in its implacability.

"There," Ema said, pushing the phone away. "I'll make another fat profit as soon as that stock goes up and I sell it."

"What if it goes down?"

"Radio? It's the hottest thing on the Street! Harding's got hundreds of thousands in it and he knows everything about stocks."

"He still doesn't know how much you've made on the market, does he?"

"It's *my* money," Emanuelle said. "There's no reason to bother him about it. Want some tea?" She pressed a brass bell set in the oak paneling before she sat down near Kate.

Kate nodded. "I suppose you're right, it just seems odd not to tell him. Now, what's the big surprise?"

"Well, I have to be absolutely honest, Kate."

"You're always absolutely honest," Kate said, smiling. "Never mind, go ahead."

"I know you and Spencer are having money troubles, so don't deny it."

"I won't deny it." Kate's smile faded. "Boarding schools like Foxcroft are taking most of our enrollments these days. There aren't enough wealthy girls left in New York to fill all the private day schools in this city."

Ema nodded. "Then why not get rid of the school and go into the party business with me?" Her eyes sparkled. "I don't have time to run one, but I'm in the perfect position to feed it clients from my page at the *Star*."

"What would Spence and I know about running a party service?" Kate protested.

"It's no different from running a school! Spencer would do the books and the budgets; you'd see that things got ordered and delivered on time. The parties take care of themselves; the crazier you make them, the better. As for the weddings and debuts and funerals, you're Social Register, you know the protocol."

"The Register dropped me when I married Spence, but I do know the protocol. Still, designing parties . . . I wouldn't know where to begin."

"But the suppliers do that. They dream up all kinds of ways to use what they sell. We'll buy or hire everything we need—waiters, musicians, booze, favors. Every supplier in New York will be crazy to work with us!"

Kate looked as if she had just opened a sensational Christmas present. "Oh, Ema, do you think we could?"

"There's no way we can miss! We'll charge the clients staggering fees— they won't think we're any good otherwise—and collect enormous commissions from the suppliers as well. Now, don't look moral, Kate. It's standard practice; ask Spencer. Anyway, I'm not Jeanne d'Arc, I'm a businesswoman."

The maid came in with tea and scones. Ema poured the tea from a silver pot into delicate Royal Doulton cups. "Think of it, Katharine darling, you won't have to listen to a lot of *merde* from those girls and their Gorgon mothers! And I won't bother you; I'm much too busy anyway. I'll just send you clients and give priority space to the parties that use our service. We'll make tons of money!"

"But where would Spence and I get the money to invest with you? No one wants to buy a moribund school."

"Sell the house—you own four houses, actually. You'd get a great price for the land no matter what the condition of the property."

"Sell my house? But Ema . . ."

"I know, the Treadwells have lived there since the flood. So what? It's a white elephant; it eats money. If you can't sell a moribund school, sell the land. Then you'd have enough to move to a gorgeous apartment like this one—or buy another house if you must, but a new one that won't need repairs every two minutes. *Allons*, Katharine, say you will, it makes sense."

Kate left after tea, promising to talk to Spencer that night and persuade him to discuss it with Ema as soon as possible. "Spencer's very conservative, you know," Kate reminded her just before she left.

Emanuelle sat down again in the chair near the fire and lit a cigarette, wishing it could have been settled between her and Kate alone. Husbands always got in the way. Spencer was worse than conservative, especially about his wife's property. But given the chance, Ema was sure she could persuade him.

Once the baby was born she planned to be as active as possible in the new partnership. The fact was, she was still a salaried employee and that was not her goal in life. Besides, society parties, once her cherished idea of glamorous high-life, had begun to seem trivial; the making of money would never be that.

Furthermore it was apparent to her that she had nothing to do with the important part of the *Star*—there was more to a newspaper than the women's page, after all! Harding made policy and what he said had meaning; he could influence public opinion. By comparison, who would care in a hundred years whether Muffy Pedersen wore taffeta or velvet for her debut? Trivial. She had thought several times lately of hiring someone to do the society column while she wrote about issues of real importance to women—or of leaving the paper altogether to devote herself entirely to business.

Still, she would not abandon her position at the *Star* even when the business took hold; it was hers, she had built it, and she relished the influence it gave her, no matter how limited its scope. Besides, she needed the *Star* to keep busy. She needed as many ways as she could find to hide all the secrets within her.

She met the Atwoods the next day as soon as school was out. The buildings were badly in need of outside repairs and the interior was shabbier than she remembered.

Spencer was interested, despite his caution. "I gather it's an advisory service you want to run, not a catering establishment, but you plan to ask only a small advance deposit from the clients. We in turn will have to give deposits to all the suppliers and pay them in full, probably before the clients pay us the balance."

"That's right," Ema said. "The rich pay only for services duly received, and they take a long time doing it. That's why we need so much bridging capital. It'll cost something to rent offices and furnish them and hire staff, but the bulk of our cash will be tied up between the time we pay the suppliers and the time the customers pay us."

Spencer looked worried. "That's a major drawback in this kind of business," he said. "The people you want to work for are extravagant. Suppose we have to order five hundred favors from Tiffany for a ball?"

"Oh, Spencer, don't be such a goose," Ema said. "The more extravagant they are, the more we'll make on our cut when we're paid."

"*If* we're paid."

Ema was impatient. "Of course they'll pay us—eventually. Why wouldn't they? They'll want to use us again." She stopped talking for a moment, and when she resumed she spoke calmly. "I would never involve you two in anything really risky, you know that. I have money beside what I plan to invest with you, enough to fill any gaps—but there won't be any gaps once we start rolling. We won't be able to keep up with ourselves. Aside from all that"—she looked from Kate to Spencer—"the Treadwell Academy is no longer viable. You have to do something soon. There'll be prep schools for the boys, all kinds of things. Here's a way for you to get them. And I need you, there's no one else I can trust."

The Atwoods looked at each other, then smiled. "All right, Emanuelle," Spencer said. "We've got a partnership."

"Wonderful!" Ema hugged each of them. "I'll tell my lawyer to do the contracts with you, Spencer. It'll save us time."

"What will we call it?"

"RSVP—for *répondez s'il vous plaît*. You like it?"

"It's perfect," Kate said. "I can't wait to close this place down. I'll need some business clothes too." Her eyes sparkled. "Let's have a glass of wine."


Spencer turned to his wife as soon as Emanuelle had gone. He had caught the enthusiasm Ema always generated. "I've figured out a way for us to raise the money," he said. "We can sell two of these brownstones and rent an apartment while we renovate the other two for us to live in. I know we can realize enough on the sale to pay for the construction and our half of the partnership too."

"Wonderful, darling," Kate said, settling close to him on the worn, comfortable couch of their sitting room. "Trust you to find the best way!" She turned to smile at him, then her expression changed and she asked, "What is it, Spence?"

"Are you absolutely sure you want to do this? Ema is very persuasive." He shrugged. "A lot more than I am."

Kate took his hand. "That isn't so. I want to do this because it's a good idea and we needed one badly. I know you agree, so why worry?"

Spencer nodded, only half satisfied. "I just want to be sure you're doing it as much for yourself as for Ema."

"I'm doing it for *us*, Spence, for you and me and the children." Kate was very emphatic; it was a new side to her character that had been growing since her marriage. "It's true," she conceded with a little nod of her head, "that I worry about Ema. She races so fast."

"Ema's running after something she'll never have—and I think she knows it. So does Harding. It's a damned shame, too, they're meant for each other."

Kate took his face in her hands. "You're a very perceptive man, Spencer Atwood. Why did it take you so long to know I was in love with you?"

He kissed her. "I knew. I just didn't dare to believe it."

She moved closer to him. "But you believe it now," she said softly.

"Yes, even if I'll never understand what a woman like you sees in a dusty old bookkeeper."

"A woman like me? Oh, my darling," she whispered passionately. "You're the reason why I'm a woman like me."


Ema went home, her head buzzing with ideas for launching and running RSVP, but she made herself wait to tell Harding the news until they were alone in her study that night, having coffee and cordials.

"I know it's what you've always wanted," he said, hiding his resentment that she still did. "But why now, when you ought to be taking it a little easier?"

"Harding, I'm as healthy as a horse; I always have been."

"But why the secrecy about your market investments?" His voice betrayed him now.

"Superstition, I suppose," Ema said, aware of the discord between them but trying to make light of it. "You know us French peasants." Then her high spirits took over, and her face was unguarded and jubilant. "I'll make a fortune, Harding, I'm sure of it!"

He nodded. Casting a shadow on her pleasure made him a dog in the manger. "Ema, you'll succeed at whatever you do, but I'd like to help you."

"No, this has to be mine," she protested. She looked at him anxiously and hurried on. "I'm going to call it RSVP. Do you like that?"

He nodded, silent again, sipping his brandy.

"What's wrong, Harding?"

"It occurred to me that I've never given you anything you really want."

"Yes, you have, you do all the time!"

"I don't mean furs and jewelry, I mean something lasting that really matters to you." He leaned back in his chair. "I want to slay the dragon and protect the castle for the woman I love. Most men do."

She put down her glass. "You helped me get away from Tillie in the first place, Harding. You gave me the *Star*. I could never have done it without you."

He shook his head. "Oh, yes, Ema, you'd have done it, you didn't need me. I don't think you ever have."

"I don't understand you!" She was confused and vaguely alarmed. "You've always said you wanted me to fly alone."

"Not alone," he said, still disconsolate. "With your own wings."

The room was very quiet; she felt threatened by a nameless danger. Suddenly she knew what to say to him and she went to sit on the arm of his chair. "There *is* something I want very much, Harding."

He looked up at her.

"A castle," she said, smiling. "I want a house on the Hudson."

"You? Leave the city?"

"We could keep this apartment, couldn't we, for entertaining and nights in town—and buy land not too far away. Oh, Harding, I want a real house with a driveway and a green lawn and a carved oak door—and a rose garden—and elm trees! I want this baby to grow up in a house like that."

He took her gently on his lap, his hand on her swollen belly. "I think you really do want it," he said.

"Will you do it, Harding?"

He kissed her hand and his dark eyes shone again. "If you'll promise to slow down until the baby's born." When she agreed, he smiled. "Don't you know I'd have done it long before this if you'd told me you wanted it."

She had always wanted it, her shining palace, even before she knew it existed in the Kentish countryside of England, but now she had to have it.

She leaned back against him. "I *do* need you." She took his hand and held it fiercely, protectively, against her face. "I do, I do. Not for the house, not for that. I want you to be happy, Harding." It was an ardent plea.

"My darling, I am. There's only one thing that would make me happier."

"What is it?"

"For you to trust me, Ema, and not keep secrets from me."

She nodded, not looking at him, keeping tight hold of his hand.

# 47

FEBRUARY 1927

Harding waited in Ema's hospital room, trying to read the proofs of Sunday's editorial page, but it was impossible to concentrate.

The doctor had assured him it would be an uncomplicated delivery, but Harding was worried about Ema's mood. During the last three months of her pregnancy she had been frantically busy, refusing to acknowledge her condition until he made a point of it, and he was sure she was preoccupied by something she still did not choose to tell him.

"Pregnant women often turn inward," Kate had told him, soothing and imprecise. "She'll be her old self when the baby's born, wait and see."

He had not been comforted. And he was impelled to seek the key to Emanuelle, no matter how many times he reminded himself that he had accepted the limitations she had placed on their relationship from the start.

"We're so much alike," he had told Kate pleadingly. "We're both stubborn, determined to get what we want, always wanting more. I understand her! Why must she keep part of herself closed to me?"

Kate went to him impulsively and put her arms around him. "She's had to close a lot of doors in her life, Harding. Be patient, in time she'll open them all." She looked up at him. "She does love you, more than she knows."

He had nodded, wanting to believe it, grateful to her for saying it. He kissed her cheek. "You're a lovely woman, Kate. I never had a friendship with a woman before; it's a rare and wonderful thing."

Kate's parting words that day had given him pause. "Until the baby's born, though, it might be better to leave her to herself."

Not easy for a man in love, Harding reflected. And Emanuelle *did* love him, he was sure of that, despite her independent nature. She was more herself with him than with anyone else; that was the important thing.

From their first night together she had begun to let her hair down when they were alone. He knew that however sophisticated and proper she appeared in public, lest the slum child emerge to humiliate her, she preferred having a beer with the people from the *Star* to making bright conversation with the social élite. She enjoyed a hearty laugh at an off-color story, and sometimes told one herself. She had a wonderful laugh, deep and rich, like her body when they made love, like her mind and her heart, deep and rich. She was a complicated woman, but that was what attracted him to her. He was never bored with Emanuelle, but there were moments when she eluded him and he could not bear that.

He walked to the window and looked out over the city. He knew Emanuelle would not have married him so soon except for the baby, but he was convinced she had begun to accept her condition, even to be glad of it. Yet she had changed again after the imagined glimpse of her dead husband and it hurt him to acknowledge that the man still had a far greater hold on her than did Harding or the child now being born.

He wondered if things might have been better had they not been counseled to avoid sex in the last months of her pregnancy. He wanted her, but it was not only desire that impelled him; he needed to know she wanted him. He wanted his to be the face she saw when they were not together, but his instinct told him it was not.

Harding was convinced that sex revealed more about a woman than anything else. In bed he could tell whether a woman was selfish or generous, suspicious or trusting, calculating or honest. No matter what had happened to Ema before he knew her, she withheld nothing there.

But would she now? Or would the shadow of that old love come between them physically, as it had in other ways? Once he had been fool enough to think it was better than a living rival, but now he knew it wasn't. He did not know how to fight a ghost.

The door behind him opened and he turned from the window. "You have a daughter, Mr. Ellis," the nurse said, smiling benevolently. "A beautiful little girl. Six pounds, four ounces."

"My wife?"

"Fine, but sleeping now. You can see your daughter, though, she's in the nursery."

Full of gratitude and wonder and that insidious cheat, hope, he followed the nurse down the corridor to see his baby.


Emanuelle woke a few hours later to a desolating sense of déjà vu. Then her eyes flew open and with relief she saw the flower-filled hospital room and through the window the towers of New York. What a different experience from that long travail at Silvermoor! But the cry she heard through the whiff of anesthetic they gave her at the last had been the cry of her unknown son.

She dozed again until the baby was brought to her and put into her arms. She felt the warmth of the little body, looked down curiously at the tiny face, and was totally unprepared for her reaction to the sight of her daughter. She had expected the natural protectiveness of her maternity, but not this overwhelming love, unlike any she had ever felt before. This beautiful little creature, miraculously, belonged to her completely, the only person in the world who did or ever had. She was Ema's to care for and love and protect. She pressed her lips to the baby's head. "My darling," she whispered, "my beautiful little girl, you'll never be sorry you're mine."

She looked up from her blissful contemplation only when Harding came in. "How are you, darling?" he asked, bending to kiss her.

"Harding, will you do something for me?" She had already turned back to her baby.

"Yes, Ema, anything." He sat down near the bed and folded back the pink blanket to look at his daughter. "What is it?" he asked her, love for them both in his voice, in his eyes.

"I want you to settle a million dollars on her as soon as you can."

She did not look up to see his face, nor did she notice how hollow his voice sounded when he answered. "I've already arranged a much larger settlement than that, Emanuelle. You and I are joint trustees. All my lawyer needed was the baby's name."

"Dana Katharine Beranger Ellis, as we planned," Emanuelle said, smiling up at him now. Harding's mother had been a Katharine too. "And thank you for the settlement, Harding, I'm grateful."

"Grateful?" He was incredulous. "For God's sake, Ema, she's my daughter too."

"Yes, of course she is, that was stupid of me. Oh, look at her, Harding, just look at her." She took his hand for a moment and then was once more absorbed in her child. "I never dreamed she'd be so beautiful, did you?"

His hurt and his anger faded, watching her, and he reminded himself that inside Emanuelle Beranger Ellis there still lived a little girl who would naturally think first of protecting her infant from the kind of poverty she herself could not forget. That was why she had seemed mercenary in their first moment together as parents. She adored the child she had been so reluctant to have, and that in itself was a blessing.

Love me, he pleaded silently, love me the way you loved him.

*　*　*

Emanuelle had already engaged a nurse, but she decided not long after she came home from the hospital that they must have an English nanny.

Harding had no objection to a nanny. "Not on principle," he said, "although the English are inclined to be rather cold, in my opinion."

Ema waved away his concern. "We'll insist on a warm nanny, then. But really, Harding, they're the best, and I want only the best for Dana."

Dana was two months old when Nanny Mills was hired, and Emanuelle went back to work a month later. She was touched by the deluge of mail that welcomed her return and the many gifts of booties and bonnets and rattles that readers of her "Star Gazer" column had sent. The gifts from people like Tillie Blessing were far more elaborate but not nearly so touching.

"I never expected them to take such a personal interest," she told Harding as she dressed for a dinner party after her first day back.

"It's because you give them what they really want," Harding said. "Not only embroidered sheets and scented soaps and how many maids it takes to dust the chandeliers, but a different way of looking at life."

He was already dressed in the white tie and tails that always made him uncomfortable, no matter how well he looked in them, and he sat in an armchair in their bedroom while Ema finished her makeup. She wore a black chiffon dress of Georgette, a square slip of a dress at the top, a short swirl of layered pleats and handkerchief points below. The mirror reflected the bronze highlights of her smooth, cropped hair and the emerald and diamond necklace, bracelet, and earrings on her dressing table, Harding's gift to her when Dana was born. She was beautiful and vibrantly healthy. She had gone for a last checkup that morning and Harding had called her doctor afterward to see how she was. Fully recovered, the doctor had said, adding that she could resume a completely normal married life. The euphemism for sex had made Harding chuckle at first; then it had made him think.

"Well, those are the things I always wanted to know," Ema said, smoothing eye shadow onto her lids.

"Precisely. You have the common touch."

"I don't think that's funny." Ema glanced at him in the mirror, her tone as cool as the emeralds.

"Oh, come off it, darling, you know I meant it as a compliment. People have always said the same of me."

"I'm sure the ones who said it were all richer than you," she said, turning to check the narrow straps of her dress in the mirror. Her breasts and her silken legs were in profile to him. Desire engulfed him.

"I'm richer than they are, now," he said.

She smiled then, an apologetic little smile. "All right, I'm sorry, I was being stuffy." She picked up her lipstick.

"Don't put that on yet," he said, making himself sit quietly in the chair. "I'm going to take you to bed and make love to you, very slowly." He waited for her reaction.

Her smile changed to one of seductive complicity. She put the lipstick down and stood up, pushing the straps of her dress from her shoulders. "We may miss the governor's gala."

He went to her and undid the dress, putting his lips to the tips of her naked breasts. She sighed at his touch and leaned back, letting the dress slip to her feet. She undid the waistbands of her slip and panties and stood naked except for her gartered stockings.

"Damn the governor, it's been a long time," he said, holding her. His hand slid gently down her back, stroked her hips, and moved forward.

"Oh, yes," she said, "too long."

She loved him; tonight he was sure of it. Emanuelle could never take a man with such delight or so enjoy his taking her unless she loved him. It was in the way her body moved, the sound of pleasure in her voice. Her eagerness banished his sense of loss. He almost told her so, but it seemed wiser not to speak about that curious and painful interval when she had been so far away from him.

# 48

In the rare moments when Emanuelle was alone—it was incredible, but she was almost never alone these days—she took down the framed souvenirs of Montmartre that no one else had ever seen and looked at that other country, that other life.

Julian had been living safely in the province of her past, in the letters he had written to her, but now he was alive, part of her future, possibly a threat to Dana unless she was very careful. Harding was neither a fool nor a saint. He would never tolerate a liaison, emotional or sexual, with another man.

I should never have married him, she told herself. But it was for Dana she had married him! Harding and Dana were irreplaceable—but so was Julian. She loved them differently, but she loved them all. She had no clear idea yet of how and when she and Julian would meet again, nor even where, but she knew they would.

She had the London *Times* delivered to her office every day, and when Dana was three months old she read, with no visible reaction, the announcement of the birth "on 29th May 1927, at Stridings, Kent, to Major Julian Andrew Saxon, VC, DSO, and Davina Fitzross Saxon, a second child, their first daughter, Juliana Carole."

Not even Kate was aware that Ema planned to see Julian again, even though the two women worked so closely together. Emanuelle was adept at guarding secrets, at partitioning her life.

With her usual dispatch Emanuelle had found offices for RSVP just before Dana was born. Kate and Spencer had ordered the furniture, with a few suggestions from Ema, while she was recuperating, and they were ready to open for business soon after she returned to the *Star*.

"I don't know how you do it all," Spencer had said when the four of them celebrated the inauguration of RSVP.

"I don't do it all," Ema said. "The secret of success is to delegate responsibility."

"And to get us clients," Spencer said. Boxes of announcements just
delivered from the printer were stacked on the floor in a corner, and there
was a huge bouquet of red roses from Harding in a vase on the window-
sill.

"Spencer, will you stop worrying, for God's sake? As soon as those are
mailed we'll have more clients than we can handle."

Tillie Blessing was at breakfast when she received the announcement.
"Clever," she said to Thomas. "Very *art moderne,* very Emanuelle."

The announcement had *RSVP* splashed in angular lipstick-red script
across a shiny black ground. Inside there was an invitation to New York
hostesses to bring their party problems to RSVP, a unique and exclusive
party service. Emanuelle's name was prominent on the convenient little
business card enclosed.

Tillie passed the announcement to her husband. "Those bitches were
always trying to hire Emanuelle away from me—and now they'll have her,
even at the shocking price she'll charge."

"Well, I'm sure she's worth whatever she charges for her services,"
Thomas said with a wink, returning the card.

Tillie's hackles rose, and she thought briefly about starting some scandalous rumors about her former secretary to make Emanuelle's husband
more watchful, but she was sure Emanuelle was faithful to Harding Ellis.
She had always been distant with men, except for Rupert McAllister, and
she had hoped to marry him, foolish girl. Her husband was an attractive
man no matter what his origins; one way or another Emanuelle had managed to have all the trappings of status she craved—money, an entree into
society, an influential husband. Oh, she's very clever, Tillie thought.

"But if I looked like her," Matilda said to herself when her husband had
finished breakfast and left for his office, "would I have been faithful to
Thomas?" Tillie decided to keep a closer eye on Emanuelle. Heaven knew
what she did on her trips to Paris! There might be something interesting
to put a large dent in that halo. Who was she, after all, but a little upstart?
It was Tillie who had discovered her and taken her in, like a viper, to her
bosom.

"I taught that little bitch everything she knows," Matilda muttered,
"and I'll never forgive her for leaving me. Nobody leaves me."

Emanuelle kept busy. RSVP's success was immediate. Spencer hired
three secretaries in addition to their receptionist when winter bookings

poured in with requests that certain musicians and chefs be reserved in advance, that Kate or Ema call at the Pace-Abercrombie mansion or the Titus Stanhopes' town house to discuss menus, decors, and favors. RSVP was in demand and Spencer's profit forecast for the coming year kept growing.

"Provided, of course, that they all pay us," Spencer always reminded the two women.

"They wouldn't dare not to; I'd print it in the *Star,*" Ema said, heady with success.

She enjoyed being a rich man's wife, but piling up her own fortune was a delicious, almost sensual experience. She was making money on the market, too; it seemed she could not lose on anything she touched. Even Harding's investments became more speculative throughout the winter of '27; it was hard to resist a quick and easy profit, and the house was bound to cost a huge sum.

Whenever she and Harding had a free day together they looked for land on the Hudson, and in November they found exactly what they wanted, a site overlooking the river but high enough to be dry.

"I can see the house and the garden already," Ema said.

"And I can see the pool and the tennis courts."

"And trees, Harding," Emanuelle said, spreading her arms, "dozens and dozens of trees."

"As many as will fit, darling."

He bought the land outright as a Christmas gift to Emanuelle. Now his money had a purpose beyond the satisfaction he always took in acquiring it. His chief pleasure was in the string of newspapers and magazines he owned, but he had expanded his interests to include the developing air transport industry. He was heavily invested in the market, too, that leaping, soaring bull market that was the wonder of the economic world, keeping America booming while Europe was in a slump.

Emanuelle, armed with clippings of English country houses and her own sharp memories of Stridings, began to interview architects.

Except when she was alone, she thrived on her busy life. She was even glad when Tillie Blessing swept into the *Star* just before the new year, swathed in leopard and obviously bursting with momentous news.

"I'm going to give a June gala in Venice," Matilda said.

"Taking a page from Cole Porter's book?"

"No, his party last summer was all jazz. This will be a costume ball, absolutely authentic, in one of those sagging pink palazzos on the Grand Canal." She perched on Emanuelle's desk and smiled her flame-red smile.

"And you'll let me come if I give you a full-page spread in the *Star,*" Ema said. She tilted her chair back and put her hands behind her head.

"Two pages," Tillie bargained.

Emanuelle thought for a moment, gazing calmly at the ceiling. "I'll give you two pages if you can hook the Prince of Wales for your ball. He's the big catch these days."

"Brilliant!" Tillie said. Her eyes blazed with green fire, anticipating the certain envy of her friends. "Thomas will arrange it—he knows everyone."

"You'll have to invite some English nobs to accompany him," Ema suggested, lighting a cigarette.

"And who better than the queen of the columns knows which English nobs to invite?"

"Who, indeed?" Ema returned with a cool little smile.

# 49

"I'll make the changes," the architect said, beginning to roll up the elevations they had just approved. "Your wife has very definite ideas about how she wants the house to look; it simplifies my job enormously."

Kate glanced at Harding, standing with his daughter in his arms.

"She has definite ideas about everything." Harding was smiling at Emanuelle, glad of her impassioned interest in their new home. "And I like her taste." He went to see the man out, carrying Dana with him.

"More coffee?" Ema asked. Spencer accepted, Kate refused. It was Sunday afternoon and the Atwoods had come to lunch to celebrate Dana's first birthday. Kate's two husky sons could be heard playing upstairs in the nursery when Harding came back with his daughter.

Dana was Emanuelle in miniature. Her hair was darker, almost as dark as Harding's, but she had Ema's mouth and her gray eyes. She was a dainty little thing, always dressed exquisitely in handmade smocked dresses and coats and bonnets from Paris and handmade soft kid shoes from Florence.

Emanuelle approved every detail of Dana's routine, but Nanny Mills had complete charge of her most of the time. And a good thing, too, Kate thought, Ema wants so much for her, she might expect too much.

"I forgot to ask him when it would be finished," Ema said, taking Dana.

Spencer laughed. "Give the poor man time, Ema! He has to draw up plans, order materials, hire contractors."

"He won't break ground until late summer," Harding said, "and winter will slow him down. I don't think it'll be finished until the autumn of 'twenty-nine—but he'll do a good job. It's worth the wait." He had signed the contract with the architect and paid him a large deposit. Looking at his wife and child, he felt it was the best investment he had ever made.

Harding wanted a home that was solid and substantial. He dreamed every now and then of more children to fill it, at least one of them a son, but he said nothing of that to Emanuelle. It was much too soon and there was time; she was only twenty-eight.

Nanny Mills came to take Dana upstairs, and Emanuelle lit a cigarette. "I've thought of a way to triple our profits," she said to Kate and Spencer.

"I thought this was a birthday party," Spencer protested, but he smiled. Ema was always full of ideas and he had to admit most of them were sound—daring, but sound.

"I think we should buy our own catering facilities," she said. "I've been looking into the catering business and it comes down to this. Potatoes cost forty-three cents a bushel and we're paying many times that for the article we deliver to our clients. That's too much, even though we charge them more and collect a commission from the caterer on that price."

"The preparation costs something," Kate said, "and the delivery. It's a fair markup, more or less."

"Of course. But why not pay the markup to a company that belongs to us?"

There was a reflective silence for a moment. Harding nodded approvingly, but he never interfered in RSVP's business unless he was asked.

"I think you've hit on something," Spencer said. "Although I thought RSVP was supposed to be an advisory service."

"At the start, yes. But no one gets ahead by staying in the same place."

"I'll bet you have a kitchen picked out already."

Emanuelle nodded happily. She had been waiting for the right moment to broach the subject, and after they had talked it over, Spencer and Kate agreed to look at the place she had found.


"What a lovely day it's been," she said to Harding that night. He didn't even ask whether she was talking about Dana's birthday or the expansion of her business; he knew she meant both and that she was expanding for Dana's sake as much as her own. She wanted to do as much for their daughter as he did, and he was convinced that if she went on at this rate, she certainly would.

But it made him feel extraneous, excluded from the center of her life. It was not her success he begrudged but the fact that it made her need him less. There were moments when he hoped RSVP would fail. He berated himself for it, but there were moments.


RSVP had no trouble financing the purchase of a block square two-story establishment on the upper west side, equipped to prepare ten-course dinners for five hundred people. RSVP also financed a fleet of specially equipped trucks to deliver the food. Emanuelle had a lot more in mind, but she had learned to proceed cautiously with the Atwoods.

She was cautious with Matilda Blessing, too, not turning a hair when acceptances to the invitations began arriving.

"I've hooked the big fish!" Tillie said triumphantly on the telephone. "HRH graciously accepts. Do I get my two pages?"

"Of course, that was the deal." The acceptance from the Saxons was far more important to Emanuelle; for all she cared, Tillie could have had eight pages.

"What are you wearing?" Matilda demanded.

"Sorry, that's a secret. And I'm late for my fitting as it is." She hung up and called Kate. "Can you meet me at the dressmaker?" she asked. "I want to be sure I made the right choice."

When she came out of the dressing room and climbed on the fitting platform, Kate nodded, her eyes round.

"I know the other women will all wear hoops and powdered wigs and patches," Ema said. "I want to be different."

She was dressed as a page, with her own Eton-cropped hair untouched. The costume was black velvet ruffed in pleated silver tissue, its full sleeves slashed with silver lamé. The fitted doublet was so luxuriously embroidered with crystal beading that shafts of light radiated when she turned for Kate under the lights. The short, puffed pants were cuffed at the thigh over long black hose. She wore black silk shoes, high-heeled and silver-buckled, and a tilted black velvet pouf of a hat with a small brim and a silver plume.

"Ema, that's the most provocative thing I ever saw," Kate said.

"That's what I thought. But it's not—well, *vulgaire*, is it?"

"No, darling, not a bit. Harding will love it. Has he seen it?"

"It's a surprise. He'll see it at the ball."


But when she sailed for Europe in June Harding wasn't with her. He had gone to California two days before she left, on business that would not wait.

"It's an airplane factory," he told her excitedly while he gathered some papers. "I can buy it for a song if I get out there before anyone else."

"Then you must go. But what do you want with an airplane factory?"

Harding closed his briefcase. "It's the future, Ema. Someday you won't sail to Europe, you'll fly there."

"Not I," Ema said. "I'm still not sure what keeps them up."

He came to kiss her. "Will you mind going to the Blessing ball alone?"

"Of course not. I'll be with Ken and the rest of my staff."

On the ship, while the distance widened between what she had and what she had been waiting for, she did not congratulate providence for letting her come to this fateful meeting alone, any more than she questioned the not-very-social Saxons' acceptance of the invitation. Harding would not be in Venice, that was all. She would have seen Julian in any case.

The forces that shape destiny were better left unquestioned. She had merely given fate a push by putting Julian on the guest list.

She disembarked at Genoa and arrived in Venice two days before the ball.

# 50

There were few places that lived up to Ema's expectations as Venice did. It was a city that suited her mood, dreamy and unreal, and as she wandered the narrow streets or floated along the canals in a gondola, the magic grew, reflected in the water. Sun and cloud, dipping, darting birds, church bells baritone and treble—all were echoed in that soft lapping water, and it mattered little whether the city had enchanted Ema or a meeting so long desired had put a spell upon the city. Coming here she had passed from one room of her life to another.

The city had calmed her by the time she dressed for the ball. She went out to the balcony. She was in Venice at the Gritti; Julian was in Venice at the Danieli. From their separate balconies both of them could see the Campanile of San Giorgio Maggiori on its private island in the lagoon, shimmering in the June sunlight.

"Are you ready, Mrs. Ellis?" Kenneth Conan's voice accompanied his rap on her door promptly at nine o'clock. She wanted to be at the palace about an hour before the bulk of the crowd arrived.

"I'm coming, Ken," she called back. He always addressed her as Mrs. Ellis, but this time it seemed more than a sweet attempt to camouflage his love for her, it seemed a reminder that she was Harding's wife. She shook her head; she needed no reminder. What she was doing did not involve Harding. She put on a black cape that covered her to the floor, took up a black mask from the dressing table, and went to join Conan.

"I like that hat, but you're still keeping your costume a secret," he said, looking young and austere in a monk's cassock.

"You'll see it as soon as we get there," Ema said. "Are you sure you took enough film over this afternoon?" They took the lift to the lobby, and the steward helped them into a gondola at the landing. "To the Rezzonico Palace," Ema said, grateful for the gloom as the graceful craft glided away from the Riva degli Schiavoni and turned into the Grand Canal. Ema leaned back against the velvet cushions, her heart pounding under the gorgeous costume. The eerie calm of the past few days had deserted her. She felt as if she were suspended between the darks of sky and water, breathless, wondering where he would be when she saw him, what he would say when she let him see her.

"Emanuelle," Kenneth said. In this fairy-tale city it seemed natural that he should call her by her name. "Are you happy?"

Impulsively she touched his hand. "Kenny, dear, why do you ask me that tonight?"

"I don't know. I always wonder if you are."

"Oh, yes," Ema said softly, "happier than I've been in a long time."

"I'm glad," he said, gazing down at the water. "I want you to be happy. I love you, you know."

"Yes, I know. I wish you didn't."

He shrugged. "Everybody's somebody's fool."

"You're not a fool. Love is not a matter of choice."

He made no answer and the single oar lapped on until the gondolier brought them to a stop. *"Ca' Rezzonico, Signori,"* he said. A tall black man, dressed in the splendid livery of a seventeenth-century royal footman, helped her onto the landing. Kenneth paid the boatman and followed her up a torchlit street to a palace that had been begun in 1660.

"Mrs. Blessing said it would be authentic," Kenneth said, holding her arm, "and it is. It's all torchlight inside, too, and purposely dark in the corners for the usual hanky-panky at these things, so watch your step. The only concession to the twentieth century is modern plumbing in the rest rooms."

More footmen waited to take their wraps at the entrance to the palace. Kenneth shook his head; the cassock was all he wore. His eyes were on Ema as she unfastened her cloak. In the dancing light of the torches her doublet glittered and her legs gleamed through the sheer silk hose. For a moment Kenneth could only look at her. Then he said, "You're beautiful, Ema."

She nodded her thanks, too nervous to speak. She put on her mask, replaced her hat, and went into the palace to find out what the rest of her life would be like.


An hour later a throng of gorgeously arrayed people made a hum in the lofty rooms of the palace and were spilling over onto its terraces. Only minuets and chaconnes had tinkled delicately on the balmy night air at first. Long before the royal party arrived the main hall was a revolving wheel of dancers.

Emanuelle gave last-minute instructions to her staff and spoke briefly to Tillie Blessing, magnificent in a red satin farthingale and a Renaissance headdress.

"You sparkle like Van Cleef's window," Tillie said with some venom. "I should have known you wouldn't wear a dress—take care no one bites you on the thigh. I just hope your people know what they're doing as well as you do."

"Don't worry about it," Ema told her, retreating as soon as she could to a shadowed recess from which she could watch unseen the main entrance to the palace.

She saw him come in shortly after ten o'clock and stop to greet Matilda Blessing. No costume could disguise his physique, or that walk, with the barely perceptible limp from Passchendaele. He was dressed as a cavalier in a garnet velvet frock coat and breeches, with a frothy lace jabot and cuffs. He carried a plumed hat under his arm—he had never liked wearing a hat. He was masked but she would have known his face among a million faces.

She made herself stand quietly for a while, just looking at him. He was infinitely more to her than a memory of love. Her life would have shriveled into bitterness without him.

When he started across the room she looked at the Marie Antoinette in blue satin and lace walking at his side, and her face changed. Davina was regal, splendid; the role of a queen became her. With the curled and powdered wig she wore a smile for the room at large, but whenever her husband spoke, she turned her dazzling face up to him and gave him her devoted attention.

Ema tried to stop the trembling of her body, breathing deeply before she stepped out of the recess and followed them into the next room, but Davina stayed at his side and Ema waited in the shadows for nearly an hour before the opportunity finally came to talk to him alone. The music was louder and the party noises deafening when at last a small Mephistopheles led Davina out to waltz.

Julian walked to one of the buffet tables and asked for a brandy. By the time she reached the other end of the long table he had taken a cigarette out of a gold case. Her breath caught in her throat at the sight of those hands, and then she looked more closely at his face, so well beloved, so long remembered.

He was not as painfully thin as he had been in New York, but there were deep lines at the corners of his mouth, the lines of a person accustomed to pain. There were wide streaks of white in his dark hair, and the somber look of those first days in Paris was upon him.

She still could not speak. In all the months since that fateful glimpse of him, her thoughts had brought her only to this moment, not beyond it.

Her love for him had never faltered; her other loves had to exist beside it, life lines that never touched. But what did he feel for her after all these years? He must be happy with his wife and children now. The very sight of Emalie Bequier might embarrass him; he might regret every moment that had passed between them, every word and sigh and touch of love.

She stood there hesitating amid staccato bursts of high-pitched laughter and a constant crescendo of music, and then he took the glass from the waiter and raised his head and saw her.

His face paled. His eyes behind the mask closed for a second, opened again, and widened in amazement. He put his glass down on the table and moved toward her.

"Ema? Emalie? Is it really you?" He pulled off the mask and a light suffused his face. "My God, how I've longed for this!"

She could only nod.

"Take off your mask, Ema, I want to see your lovely face again."

They stood then, gazing at each other as their separate memories mingled, until he moistened his lips and spoke again. "I tried to find you, but old Vaillant didn't know anything about you. Where did you go?"

"New York," Ema said, careless of anything but that he *had* tried to find her. They moved apart when a troupe of hilarious maskers blundered between them, and when they came together again she felt his touch on her arm through the velvet and the sparkling embroidery.

"We must be alone somewhere, Ema; there is so much to say. Can you meet me tomorrow? At noon?"

She gave him the address of a café and he nodded, understanding that no one they knew would go near that quarter of Venice.

The waltz reached its whirling climax, but he was reluctant to leave her side. He stood looking at her in that way that made her feel he had invented love. "Say my name again," he said, "the way you used to." He watched her lips move as she said it, and there were tears in his eyes when he replaced his mask and turned back to the dancers.

She watched him, dizzy from that brief exchange of words. She was shaking from the control it took not to put her arms around him no matter who might see them. But not here, not now. Tomorrow.

Her mind, unbidden, raced ahead. And what then, what would happen after tomorrow? But for this man, she would never have loved anyone and no one would have loved her, but now someone else did, a man and a child, and what of them?

She shook her head. She had only one life, and half of it belonged to Julian. She could not live without her second half again.

She skirted the dancers and went up a short flight of stairs to a raised gallery, where Kenneth was hard at work with two of the girls.

"I'm leaving, Ken," she told him. "I've got a terrible headache. No, thanks, I'll be fine, the landing's just down the path. Sheila, even if they're drunk as lords, get the names right!"

Near the dance floor Julian watched her while he made polite conversation with his hostess. "Who is the page in the suit of lights up there?" he asked Matilda Blessing.

"But you must know Emanuelle Beranger," Tillie said, appraising him more carefully. He was a very handsome man, but withdrawn, like all the English. "She's the society editor of the *Star-Tribune*—the queen of the columns, I call her."

He smiled, hiding his surprise at the name, as Emanuelle went down the stairs and made for the door. "I'm afraid I don't have time to read the American press as thoroughly as I should," he said.

"You must ask your wife, she'll probably know."

"Know what?" Davina was returned to him by Mephistopheles.

"About Emanuelle Beranger, the columnist."

Davina's masked eyes were turned briefly on her husband. "I've heard of her. Is she here?"

"Busy working." Tillie studied the pair, then added with a sly little smile, "Your husband was just asking who she was. She helped to organize this ball, you know, did the guest list and such; she used to work for me."

"Fascinating," Davina said. "Darling, I'd like some champagne."

"Of course," Tillie said, her black eyes shining. She watched the couple move off. Beautiful people, she said to herself, but cold, cold as ice. Then she sailed off into the thick of her stupendously successful party.

# 51

In the clear light of day they sat at a small table on the café terrace like two well-mannered children, separated by nine years and divergent lives.

"I thought you were dead," Ema said, her hands clasped tightly on the table. "For years I thought you were dead. Tell me what happened."

He told her in the same way he had always talked about the war, haunted by its horrors. "My country is proud of me," he said when the story was finished. "I was awarded the Victoria Cross for killing those men." He took two cigarettes from the gold case she had seen the night before and offered her one, lighting them both. He sat looking at her, and his expression changed to the one she remembered best.

"I love you, Emalie," he said, his voice low but fervent. "That will never change. Other things have changed, though, for both of us. I have two children now, but it's my son I adore." He inhaled deeply, looking at the sky. His hands were still beautiful, like his face.

"I didn't know he existed for a long time after they brought me home," Julian went on. "When I wasn't raving with fever I was thinking about finding you as soon as I could."

The shouts of the boatmen came to them on the warm breeze, and an occasional voice was lifted in a song of love. It was always love, she thought, the whole world is besotted with it; but the sun on her arm did not warm her.

"You see, my darling, all my sermons about honor and duty didn't matter a damn when I went home on that last leave, no matter how noble I thought I was to keep my marriage alive. I even made love to Davina that night. It was what she expected—nor could I refuse if we were to go on together." He flushed and stopped speaking for a moment. "Fool that I am, I only made things worse. I knew that night we couldn't go on together. I told her so, that she must divorce me after the war because I was going back to you."

Holy Mother, if I had stayed in Paris! If I had kept my son! The magnitude of what she had thrown away appalled her.

"I would have written to you," he was saying, "I would have come to Paris to tell you, but I was ordered directly up the line," he was saying, "and then I didn't wake up until April, in Munich, and my father came to identify me."

April? She had been only in her seventh month in April of 1919!

And Sir James had not come to Silvermoor Cottage to see her that month. Her head ached violently as the pieces fell into place, one by one. She crossed her arms, hugging herself as she had in the taxi that day with Davina. What a colossal trick the Saxons had played upon her and Julian! Despite their breeding, they were no better than she was, no, not as good. Her agreement with them was based on the assumption of Julian's death; that had been implicit! But they were determined to hold on to him whether or not he wanted to stay—and they had used her son to do it. She almost told him everything then, but shock and an old habit of caution kept her quiet.

"What a terrible punishment it is to be cherished by people you plan to betray!" Julian shook his head. "When I began to mend I told myself I wasn't hypocrite enough to keep up a marriage for appearance' sake. After all that had happened, I couldn't care a damn about appearances anymore." He shrugged.

Silence fell between them again while he lit fresh cigarettes. "Before I could tell them that, they brought me Drew. He was thirteen months old." He sighed. "I was astonished that I had a son, a dark-eyed little boy who looked at me in that trusting way only babies have. He still does. He used to play near my bed, very quietly most of the time, as if he knew I needed quiet. It helped just to look at him." He took her hand, holding it tightly. "To me he was all of them come back, William and Tony and all the German boys I'd killed. And because I'd lost you, Ema, in a way he was you too. You'd like him; he's a wonderful little boy." Julian almost smiled. "I had to stay with him. Even now I can't resent him for coming between us, I love him too much. I could never leave him with his mother."

She felt a different kind of anger. "Why not? Is she unkind to him?"

He hesitated. "It's just that he's always been more mine than hers, as our daughter is more hers than mine."

As clearly as if he had said the words, he was pleading with her to understand what he himself could not comprehend: Davina's dislike for her son. But you must know why, Ema shouted silently, you must feel it in the marrow of your bones!

"I tried to find you once in Paris," he said, "but Henri Vaillant told me you'd just vanished and I left it at that. I had nothing to offer you but a secret meeting now and then, in some place where no one would know us—like this." He looked around the little café. "The kind of affair other people have. It was never good enough for you."

She did not speak for some time. She wondered if he had a picture of her son, but she could not bear to look at Drew, not now. She could hardly bear the weight of all she had lost for the want of just a little more courage when it mattered most. She knew it was fatal for her to look back in judgment, but the knowledge gave her no comfort.

As never before, she wanted her son. Until Dana was born she had not realized how possessive she was of what was hers; no one had ever belonged to her before. She did not ask now if love were at the heart of it. She simply wanted her son because he was hers, but she knew she could never have him, any more than she could have his father.

"I have a daughter," she said, suddenly needing Dana very much.

She could tell that her child came between them in a way his did not. "I assumed you were married," he said, "because of the name."

"Beranger is the name I took when I went to America." Tears filled her eyes. "I still use it professionally. My daughter's name is Dana. My husband is Harding Ellis."

"What sort of man is he, Emalie?"

"Don't," she pleaded. "I haven't asked you about Davina."

"She hasn't changed, but she's never reproached me. I admire her for that." He waited. "Tell me about your husband, please, Ema."

"He has nothing to do with you, with us."

Her marriage was not the question now. She ached to tell him the truth about his sainted father and his noble, forbearing wife, but the moment was gone when he would have renounced his heritage to live with her. He wanted his birthright for his son and heir, the future baronet. The only feeling Ema's son had ever evoked in her was pain; it would not help to add Julian's to it. It would avail her nothing, nothing, nothing.

What was revenge compared to the contempt he would feel if he knew she had sold his son for a thousand pounds?

"People were saying last night how successful Emanuelle Beranger is," Julian said. "Emanuelle is very beautiful, but I can still see Emalie in her eyes. I remember that first morning in Neuilly, when you told me all the things you wanted. I wanted to give them to you. I hope you have them now." His hand touched her cheek. "Don't cry, my darling. I can't bear to see you cry."

"But I'm a great success," Ema said, "why would I cry?" She took a handkerchief from her handbag, cursing the tears that would not stop. She left the table and walked across the café's little terrace to look down at the canal. He came to stand behind her, and she leaned against him. His arms enfolded her and she felt again the joy it was to be held by him.

She would not give him up, ever. She had been used more cruelly by his father and his wife than she had supposed, and she would even that score, but until she did they could no longer hold Julian hostage to their rotten little schemes. She would protect him—and Harding and Dana too—but she would never give him up.

It was an enormous compromise, but her whole life had been a compromise with necessity. She knew how to hide the wrath that flourished inside her like a poisonous plant, but this man she would not punish with it, this man she could only love. Of all of them he had had the courage to tell his truth. He must not be tormented by hers.

"Must I lose you again, Emalie?"

"No, my love," she whispered, "never. I'll be with you whenever I can, but there are other people involved now; there are rules to keep, no matter how many we break."

"We both know that, Ema."

"I'll be in Paris for the collections this winter."

"That's months away!"

She nodded and turned to look at him. She touched his face and stroked his hair.

"All right," he said with the sweet smile she remembered. "I'll meet you in Le Havre. We can drive down together if you come a few days earlier."

They spoke as quietly as if they were arranging a business meeting. They parted in the same way, a brief embrace all they dared allow themselves, but in the gondola that took her back to her hotel she could feel the sun on her skin again and, when she let it in, warm anticipation sat side by side with her cold anger.

# 52

Emanuelle packed when she got back to the Gritti and left for Paris that evening. "All of you have a night on the town," she told Kenneth while her bags were being put on a gondola. "The *Star*'s treat."

He frowned. "Why can't you wait and go with us in the morning?"

"I don't need a chaperon, Kenneth," she said frostily, and then felt that the time for explanations had begun. "My oldest friend lives in Paris, I want a long gossip with her. I'll meet you at the boat train day after tomorrow."

She needed that solitary night to put herself together, to see ahead. Desperation had made her blunder tragically in the past. What she did now would be with calm deliberation, no matter how long it took. She even welcomed the absolute secrecy to which she and Julian were committed.

With Julian, she could never openly be either the woman she had made of herself or the girl she had been. The former was too well-known and lived another life; the latter was locked away forever. With Julian she would be not only the other woman but another woman entirely.

In Paris, after a near sleepless night, she told Danielle nothing about what had happened in Venice. In fact she was confronted with a new worry as soon as she saw the unmistakable signs of poverty—Danielle's frayed cuffs, her worn shoes, and mended gloves. She knew the reason for it five minutes after they were in the taxi: Danielle could not afford to replace her outdated equipment, and the ambitious young women who could afford tuition were going elsewhere to train for office jobs.

"*Mon Dieu, c'est ridicule!*" Ema finally resorted to anger to make Danielle accept the money she offered her. "You gave me your money and your heart and your shoulder to lean on—and plenty of advice I never asked for, in the bargain! All I offer you is a loan so you can keep up with the times, and you shall take it, *un point c'est tout.* I'll make the transfer as soon as I get home."

"I've never taken a sou from anyone in my life," Danielle said dolefully, accepting what she could not refuse. "Not even from my husband, that *minable*—I earned every penny he left me."

"I'm not your husband." Ema put her arm around her melancholy companion. "Dani, I wish you'd come to America, just for a while! There's no slump there, believe me. You'd get rich overnight playing the market."

"*La bourse?* Emalie, you mustn't gamble on the stock market!"

"I don't gamble! I invest."

"I thought you were happy with your own business." Danielle accepted a gold-tipped cigarette and a light. "It's still the best insurance for a woman."

"Of course I am, but a little flutter now and then never hurt anyone." It would be tactless to tell Danielle about RSVP's expansion. It would take every penny she could make on the market. They had just bought and remodeled two more catering kitchens and hired the best French chefs to run them. Spencer was negotiating right now to buy more delivery trucks, a separate factory making fine chocolates and confectionery, and a wholesale floral distributorship. RSVP never turned down a contract, and their cash reserves ebbed and flowed with the seasons, high in spring, sinking from summer onward, when they needed tremendous amounts of cash.

"Where shall we go?" Danielle asked. "After Thiboux, of course."

"To a bistro on the Left Bank for lunch—I'm dying for real French food. What passes for it in America is beyond belief. Then we might go to the museum, the way we used to."

Danielle shook her head. "To visit your statue again? Ah, well, we French are merely romantic, but I gather people still believe in love in America. It's clear from your letters you love your husband."

"He's a wonderful man," Emanuelle agreed. The way she said it made Danielle look at her sharply.

"But you still haven't forgotten your English milord."

"How could I? A love doesn't leave you just because it's gone, Danielle."

"Does your husband know you don't love him?"

"That isn't true!" Ema said, flushing. "I'm devoted to him. I'd never do anything to hurt him."

"*Calme-toi, ma chère.*" Danielle shrugged. "I suppose it's possible to be faithful to a man with your body and betray him in your heart—or even the other way round."

They said nothing more until the taxi stopped at Thiboux, and when they came out they went to the Luxembourg Gardens to watch the children roll hoops and sail toy boats on the fountain pond. They had tea in the gardens, enjoying the early summer day, and stopped at the school on the way home. It looked as frayed as its owner.

"Fresh paint and new equipment will change everything," Ema said. "You're still the best teacher in Paris. I'm living proof." She stood looking at the place where Emalie Anne Bequier had counted out her registration fee in sous.

"It's true; you could stay at the Ritz instead of on my couch," Danielle said.

"I like your couch," Ema told her, and they went home.

The next morning she dropped Danielle off on her way to the boat train, relieved to see that the worry lines in that long face had faded.

"Here," Danielle said, giving Ema a package before she got out of the cab. "This is a dolly for my little namesake."

Ema kissed her. "You'll see her soon, I promise. *Au revoir,* my darling Dani."

The parting saddened her, but she felt better when she saw Kenny and the others waiting for her on the platform. As soon as she boarded the ship it seemed she was leaving one life for another as she had done so often, as she would do again. The sadness lifted.

When the *Ile de France* docked in New York she was out on the deck, eagerly scanning the crowd until she found Harding on the pier with Dana in his arms. "There they are, there they are," she shouted to Kenneth. It was good to see them there. She waved wildly.

# 53

Davina selected a half-dozen art and fashion magazines before she climbed into the railway carriage at Dover. Julian, already seated, helped her in and returned to his window seat opposite. As always, they had booked the whole compartment; his valet and her maid traveled in second class.

They had not gone abroad very much; the trip to America for the branch bank had been their first venture out of England apart from a few days here and there in Paris, Deauville, and Monte Carlo. The week in Venice had started as a welcome diversion for Davina, but she wondered what would happen now. He would certainly travel a lot more, but he would go without her, to meet that woman.

She looked at him, apparently absorbed in the English newspapers he had bought at the station. He had always been handsome, but there was something about him now that mesmerized everyone, men as well as women. No matter what nonsense he talked in his pacifist causes, people were swept away by his passionate sincerity. He devoted far too much passion, Davina thought, to disabled veterans and the League of Nations. It was all very dreary to her, but ordinarily he would have been eager to return to his work; it was what mattered most to him after his children. His son, to be precise.

Now, she was sure, he did not even see what he was pretending to read. He was still in Venice with Emanuelle—or did he call her Emalie? Davina did not know where they had made love, only that they had. What else would he have been doing for three hours yesterday, hours she had not even mentioned.

"It was a lovely ball, darling, don't you think?"

He looked at her, his dark eyes distant. "What? Oh, yes, spectacular, even for the Americans."

"What a hag that Blessing woman is. I thought she'd never leave you alone. But I mustn't take any notice; all women make fools of themselves over you."

He said nothing, returning to his paper.

His father must do something about this, Davina thought. If Sir James could make him stand for a seat in the Commons, he would have to stay in England.

His infatuation with that woman was intolerable, but Davina knew it must be borne in silence; she had learned that long ago when he came home on leave. She held two trumps she hadn't had then: Drew, for obviously Emanuelle had been too clever to tell Julian the truth about his bastard son; and her own daughter, Juliana. It was time for Julian to give her another child. Her knees parted slightly in anticipation of sex. There had been none since the night before the costume ball.

She looked at his hands, wondering how he would touch her now. He would never leave her or his children, she knew that; at least she would never be a laughingstock. But he might not sleep with her at all, and that would be almost as unbearable as public humiliation. Then she decided that he would not desert her bed; his conscience would not permit it.

For a moment she almost choked on the very honor that bound him to her when what she wanted was for him to love her as gluttonously as she did him.

He felt her watching him and looked up. His eyes were still remote, but after a moment he smiled and she felt as if he had stabbed her with that smile, so courteous, so kind, so absolutely devoid of passion.

He must sleep with her! Her lust for him was so enormous that it had always been hard for her to control herself until his natural appetite made him turn to her in bed. Then she could abandon her wifely-motherly pose for the erotic skills that made him avid for her, made him remember her, by God!, remember who she was! But would he even turn to her now that he had found the woman he'd been dreaming of for all these years?

Her eyes lingered on the hollows of his face, the outline of his mouth, the sweep from his shoulders to his hips to the span of his thighs. She was swollen with desire, determined to conceive again as soon as she could, to prove to him that he belonged to her and always would.

Julian was staring blindly at his paper, but her desire for him was so perverse he could feel it encompassing him, try as he would to ignore it. She slept by his side, it was her rightful place; he knew he would soon sink between those breasts, tantalized by the scent of her, be tangled in those arms and legs, plunge again into that frenzied body—and long all the more for Emalie.

How was it that two passionate women could be so different? Ema had enfolded him; Davina devoured him. Emalie was ardent and Davina voracious. Sometimes, no matter how hotly he coursed after the scent his wife laid down for him, he felt he would drown in her, be swallowed up by her in her savage need to possess him utterly. He was a phallic ritual to Davina; Emalie made him feel like a man in love with a woman.

"I can't wait to see the baby," Davina said, "can you?"

"And Drew," Julian said. He did not think she really loved either child.

"Of course, darling. Juliana's my precious little girl, but Drew's at an interesting age now; he notices everything."

He wondered suddenly if she knew he had gone to meet a woman in Venice, although she could not know which one; he had never told her Emalie's name. He looked at her, but her face was as open and sunny as it had been when she was a little girl. He turned to the countryside outside the window, seeking escape in his own thoughts.

Davina took out her needlework, glad that the rocking train masked the trembling of her hands while he took her in her mind. Her breath quickened, her body felt the kiss of her silken underwear as if it were his mouth. She crossed her legs tightly to enclose him and moved with the same rhythmic rock the train made rushing over the tracks.

After a while she relaxed and began to rip out the botched stitches she had just placed in her needlework. She was calm now. After all, what she had of him—his name, his body, his children, his guilt—was more than any other woman would ever have. Emanuelle Beranger had a husband and a career that kept her in New York—and a child, too, but not the one she wanted.

The train glided on toward London, and Davina contemplated her flashing needle and smiled.

# 54

"I could come with you," Harding said a few months later, on their way to the theater.

She kept her face calm and her voice even. "To Paris for the collections?"

"No, just on the crossing if you can go a week later on the *Dresden*. I want to have a look at Germany." He sighed. "Conditions are going from bad to worse there. It doesn't seem to matter how much money pours into that country from American investors looking for bargains. It's like our south after the Civil War. The economy's so inflated, everything is cheap to anyone with hard currency—plant, equipment, labor."

"Are you going to invest?"

"Maybe. Mainly I'm going to report."

"I never cared much for Germans," Emanuelle said. "They were threatening Paris when I was only fourteen. There was never any love lost between them and us."

"My love," Harding said, "you're a Yankee now—except for your elegance and what you would call your *je ne sais quoi*."

"Do you really think so?"

"No doubt about it. You're energetic, decisive, and you take risks. That's typically American."

She appreciated the compliment, but in certain ways she would have preferred to be typically English. She wanted an English education for Dana and, of course, English furniture for the house. She planned to order it in London. "If I go to England to buy furniture, will you come with me?" she asked as the Rolls came to a stop in front of the theater.

"If I can. Otherwise I'll leave the furniture to your impeccable taste." The chauffeur opened the door and Harding got out of the car. "Except for my study. I have plans for my study." He took her arm and they went into the theater, but her mind was not on the play, it was on two lines that had to be kept parallel and were in danger of crossing. It was on a meeting in France only three weeks away.

She did not sail on the *Dresden;* her schedule did not permit it, although she would not have gone with Harding in any case. She needed time and distance to separate her from her husband, even temporarily. It was the only way to still an inner voice she could not identify. It was not a sense of sin, for Ema no longer believed in sin. She believed in survival.

Julian came aboard the liner at Le Havre to find her, and she ran down the long corridor outside her stateroom to meet him. He held her, kissing her eyes, her cheeks, her mouth, as if he could not believe she was really there. They went ashore together, happier than they had ever been before. Whatever stood between them now, death did not.

"I always loved the way you drive," she said in the Hispano-Suiza he had brought across from England with him.

"Do you drive?"

"Oh, yes, when I have the time."

"Tell me about your life. I want to hear all about this famous Emanuelle Beranger I've just met."

In a way, as she told him some of what had happened in America, she, too, felt that they had just met. She was very different from the girl he had known, and she wondered if he was aware of that.

Then, and she did not know what word or look released it, desire engulfed her, like a flash flood.

He felt it too. They had stopped talking before they reached Rouen; they were both silent when the door of the hotel room closed behind them. Then they were in each other's arms.

They heard the church bells of Rouen toll the quarter hour and then the half before sound no longer intruded in this mingling of flesh and fantasy and remembrance.

Her hands caressed the latticework of scars on his back. "*Grand Dieu,* what they've done to you," she whispered as much about his father and his wife as the German shells. "But I kept you safe, do you remember, and I always will."

She touched her mouth to the marks on his body as if she could heal them and banish his pain. She kissed the livid scars of his belly and the velvet flesh of his groin. It was an acknowledgment of manhood and the man himself, of his strength and his vulnerability and that essence of him that was the other half of her.

"I love you," she said.

He drew her up along the length of his body and reclaimed her once again and, with her, the joy of his youth.

They did not mention Harding during this first meeting. They had only three days together and she wanted those hours for themselves alone, without intrusion by her husband, his wife, her daughter, his son. She had given Danielle a later arrival date, adding that she would stay at the Meurice because it was more convenient to the collections. It would be wiser not to spend too much time with Danielle, even after Julian left for England; her old friend was far too perceptive.

"Damn the collections," Ema whispered to Julian when they woke in Paris on their last morning. "I won't go."

"You must go, Emalie," he answered, kissing her, "you'll regret it if you don't."

"No!" She had said it passionately, ablaze with her love for him. "I'll never regret a single second I spend with you." She wanted to fill her eyes with the sight of him and her arms with the feel of him.

He was leaving at noon and she missed Balenciaga entirely that morning and was very late to Chanel. Up to now she had prided herself on never resorting to official handouts for fashion reportage, but he was more important than looking at clothes for a lot of bored, idle women.

She dined only once with Danielle, who was too busy discussing repayment of her loan to notice Emanuelle's new serenity. Perhaps it wasn't visible, even to Danielle, that warmth within her where once there had been a loneliness that neither husband nor child had eased. She did not go home by way of London; she put off buying furniture and went directly to New York, in haste to resume her life there and restore the balance.

When she saw Julian again the following February he was a Member of Parliament. "My father finally persuaded me to stand for a by-election," he said, "and perhaps he's right. Perhaps people will listen if I speak from the House of Commons. Except for the Colonel Blimps who have always lived only for the next war, people want to forget it and what it did to England. I can't let that happen. I won't let them sweep that cataclysm under the rug. That makes it too easy for them to start another one."

"It's the same in America, Julian. People say that what goes on in Europe doesn't concern them."

"But it *does* concern them," Julian insisted. "So many thousands of them died on the Western Front. They'd be involved in another war, like it or not. Wars make money, even for wealthy countries like America. They appear to solve the problems of unemployment in poorer ones. What does your husband think about it?" Julian asked it as a matter of course, and she made herself answer in the same way.

"He doesn't want America involved in any more wars, but he says peace in Europe won't last if people are starving. He's gone to Germany again because the situation there is even worse than in France and England. And he's curious about a feud between two newspapermen vying to be the official party organ for the National Socialists."

"Yes, Gregor Strasser and Joseph Goebbels. I've heard about them."

"He met Goebbels on his last trip—a sinister man, he thought, not a journalist in the true sense of the word. Harding thinks it's damned peculiar to have party-owned newspapers in a republic. You can't have a democracy without a free press. Suppose the National Socialists took office in Germany—who would print the opposition's arguments?"

"I agree with you and Harding." On Julian's lips her husband's name sounded strange to Ema. One was born at Stridings and the other in a Chicago slum. It had never occurred to her before that the two men would think alike.

"And you, Ema?" Julian asked. "Tell me more about RSVP."

At first she had regretted having told him about her catering service—she knew what the English aristocracy thought of people who were "in trade"—but she was constantly glad she had. He always listened attentively to her ideas for expansion, he always applauded her triumphs. He was the only person who had absolutely no reservations about her ambition or her success.

She had been back in New York for a month when the *Times* of London announced the birth of Julian's second daughter, Alexandra Margaret. She felt betrayed, then worried because Julian hadn't told her—and then she realized that he could not have told her any more than she could tell him about her sexual relations with Harding.

A strange feeling seized her when she read the announcement, even in the elegant warmth of her own library. It was not jealousy but something far more complicated. Even with Dana safe beside her, she felt the new baby was in some way a message from Davina, possibly a threat. She had never felt that about Juliana—or Drew. Emanuelle had yet to see a picture of Drew; she could not bear to be shown Drew's likeness and to utter banalities about her own child while Julian looked on.

"*Que fais-tu, ma petite chérie?*" She put her arm around Dana, who was busy with a pencil and pad. She usually spoke French to Dana, who answered in either language.

"*Les notes,*" Dana said.

"Why do you make notes?"

"To be like you, Maman."

Emanuelle bent to kiss her child. "You want to be like me? My darling baby, that's the loveliest thing I ever heard." She lifted Dana onto her lap. "But you'll never have to work, not a day in your life."

She would see to that! Dana would be so armored by money that nothing and no one would ever hurt her, but Emanuelle, not Harding, had to provide the lion's share of it. Emanuelle's determination sprang from corners within herself she could not examine. She was well on her way to accomplishing it; the next step would be to persuade Kate and Spencer to open RSVP branches in Palm Beach and Boston.

Comforted by the prospect, she put away the paper and with it her apprehensions about Davina Saxon's baby.

# 55

"Do something," Davina hissed.

"There's nothing to be done," Sir James protested. "Be reasonable, Davina, I can't forbid Julian to see her."

For all her venom and his alarm they were speaking very softly. They were in Davina's bedroom. He stood near the tiny Alexandra's lace-draped bassinet.

"Then—forbid—*her*!" Davina bit the words off one by one. "It's bad enough that they meet in Paris, but now she's here in London!"

Sir James shook his head. "She hasn't seen him or called him; she seems to be buying furniture. And she's booked to sail on the *Carinthia* in two days."

Davina shredded the handkerchief in her hands. "She comes closer each time, like a creeping fungus. Damn it," she whispered explosively, "why must I go on having these wretched girls?"

He looked at her, uncomprehending.

"I'm going to have a son, d'you hear?" she said vehemently. "I'll keep at it until I do, and then I'll make short work of that rotten little bastard you and Julian are so mad about."

"Davina, for the love of heaven!"

She looked at him, her blue eyes blazing. "Only the eldest *legitimate* son can inherit the title, that's the law."

He left the bassinet and approached the bed. "What do you mean?"

"If you're too dim to understand, just wait until I have a son." She watched his face darken. "Ah, the penny finally drops."

"If you challenge Drew's legitimacy, we'll all be ruined—and you'll lose Julian!"

Her face twisted. "I'll lose him anyway unless you keep that woman away from him. You have ways. Use them!"

Sir James glanced at the door. "Keep your voice down, Davina. Very well, I'll go up to London and try to see her tomorrow." He stood looking down at her, his expression impenetrable.

She smiled slyly. "You'll like that, you always fancied her. You used to come back from Glengowrie looking like a cat without a canary. It's a pity you didn't marry her yourself before we found Julian."

Without a word he left the room as the infant began to cry.

"Nurse!" he heard Davina call. "Get her out of here, I can't stand that bloody wailing!" and he was grateful Julian didn't know what an insufferable bitch she was.

"No, I will not stop seeing him," Emanuelle said.

"You may destroy him." He stood in the salon of her suite at the Ritz, a tall, spare, distinguished gentleman, as handsome as a knight, caught in a web of his own making.

"Not I! He's alive again, even you must see that. You destroyed him by tying him to a woman he doesn't love. You could have stopped it, there was time."

"There was no time! Everyone had been told she was expecting a baby."

"She could have lost the baby. But you wouldn't let him make his own choice. You preferred to lie to him, to protect him from a creature like me."

He was amazed by the change in her, even though he had followed her career in America. She had the sleek elegance of a wealthy woman of fashion, in black silk and emeralds, but now she had authority, too, not the harsh belligerence he had seen before. There was nothing left, either, of that young girl asleep in the garden, so vulnerable, so gloriously helpless. She was a fully achieved woman now; no wonder Julian was alive again.

"What do you hope to gain by it?" he persisted.

"Nothing, in the sense you mean. What I wanted was for Drew and he has it."

Sir James shook his silver head. "Maybe not. Davina talks of persisting until she has a son."

For a moment she frowned, puzzling over that. Then she understood what he meant and her brief, derisive "Ha!" brought back for an instant the girl who had walked into his office ten years ago. "Even so, she'll never tell Julian because she's afraid to."

"And you?"

"I won't tell him because I love him."

He could not deny it. It was in her face, along with her terrible loss and her courage. Her spirit had captivated him from the start, as much as her shining sensuality. Character like hers was hard to credit in a woman.

"I must trust you for that," he said.

"I trusted you once; you have the better deal by far." She lit a cigarette. "Is that all?" she asked through the smoke.

He nodded. "I want to tell you that I also have had bitter moments. It wasn't easy, seeing him like that, an empty shell. I love him too. But there was nothing else to be done."

"Tell me about my son," she said. She drew on her cigarette and listened to him intently.

"He's a fine boy, the best in the world, very quick and bright. But that's not it; he lights up everything around him, as his father did before him." He hesitated. "I see you in him sometimes. I wonder Julian doesn't."

"Do you have a picture of him?"

He reached into his breast pocket and handed her a photograph of a nine-year-old with eyes she would have recognized anywhere and a brilliant smile. He wore a round Eton collar and a blazer, short pants, and knee socks—I would have dressed him in long trousers by now, she thought. It was a posed picture, but the charming essence of the child was irrepressible. She could not tell what quality predominated—intelligence or that hint of wistful sadness that gave his father's face its magic. "He's just like Julian," she whispered.

"We must see to it that he keeps what he has."

Her gray eyes examined him at length. "You're merciless," she said finally. "What do you want of me now?"

"Ah, so much, so much," he said obliquely, certain she knew what he meant. "But I ask only that you be even more discreet—Paris is full of the English, and Julian is well known—and that you stay out of England. She was . . . frantic when she heard you were here."

"Yes, all right, but from now on don't tell her everything your spies tell you! It's Julian she wants; if she has him, she'll be quiet, whether or not she has a son." She handed him the picture.

"Keep it, I brought it for you. But no picture can really do the boy justice."

She heard true feeling for his grandson in his voice and understood why Julian loved this stubborn, imperious man. "How could you let him live with her?" she asked.

"One does what one has to do." He took up his hat and his gloves. "I wish you understood that, just a little." He was not imperious now. "Good-bye, Mrs. Ellis."

He left her alone with her wrath and her pity and the picture of her beautiful, lost boy.

*　*　*

On a Sunday in the autumn of 1929, Emanuelle and Harding drove up to see the house, taking Kate and Spencer with them in the Rolls while Nanny Mills and the children followed in the Packard. The house was finished but still empty, waiting for the antique furniture Ema had bought in England to be repaired and shipped when it was ready. She was reluctant to order anything else in the meantime, and English craftsmen were slow about their matchless work.

The house stood atop a wooded bluff, fairly level for several acres before it sloped down to the river. The lawns had been turfed in the spring and the garden was still in flower as the cars rolled up the elm-lined gravel walk and stopped in front of the carved oak door.

Liberated, the children ran about noisily, playing tag under the trees, while Harding and Spencer went in to look at the house again and Kate and Ema walked past the gardens and greenhouses toward the river.

"It's one of the most beautiful houses I've ever seen," Kate said, her eyes glowing happily behind her glasses. "Have you decided what to call it yet?"

"Silvermoor."

Kate stopped. "Oh, Ema, why keep a painful memory alive?"

"It isn't only painful. I felt safe at Silvermoor for the first time in my life."

Katharine took her hand. "You're safe now, darling."

"Yes, I am—and Dana will have everything I didn't have. A home like this, a governess, the best schools. Maybe she'll even marry a title."

Kate shook her head. "You mustn't force Dana to live your life, Emanuelle, it isn't fair!"

"Force her?" Ema objected almost angrily. "I'll never force my child to do anything she doesn't want to do. I want her to have choices. I had none." She turned to Kate. "Neither had you, Kate. You were raised to be a spinster schoolteacher!"

"I know," Kate said. "And I would have been, except for you. I promise I won't scold you, but talk to me, Ema, let me help. I know something's wrong; you run as if the Furies were after you."

"I do talk to you," Emanuelle said.

"Not about Julian. You've been seeing him in Paris, haven't you?" Kate persisted.

"Yes."

"You can't go on with it."

"I can't go on without it—and you said you wouldn't scold."

"But where will it end, Ema?"

"I don't care, I don't care, it's something I *must* have." She turned away from Kate, looking down toward the river. "It's not some rotten little affair, you know that."

"Harding will think it's a rotten little affair."

"He won't know! I swear it, Kate, he'll never know."

"Don't you love Harding, Ema?"

"Yes, yes, I love him, but it's not the same." Ema shook her head. "I can't explain it." She turned back to Kate, and her face, shaded by the brim of her white straw summer hat, was drawn. "It isn't fair to involve you in it, to make you keep my secrets and tell lies for me. It's better for you to stay out of it."

"All right, I will." Kate put her hand on Ema's arm. "Unless you need me."

But Kate knew she would share Emanuelle's risks as she had shared her rewards. At least she wouldn't have to worry until Emanuelle went to Paris again.

That worry was completely overshadowed by a monumental crash on Wall Street at the end of October. The bulk of the Atwoods' money was either invested in RSVP or had been spent on the renovation of their house. But Emanuelle had gambled every extra penny she owned on the stock market and she watched helplessly as it disappeared, apparently forever, just when RSVP needed it most.

# 56

"It's bad, Kate," Spencer said. He closed his ledger and let his head drop to his hands, rubbing his eyes. "We've used up all our available cash and we're still in debt. Some of our clients simply can't pay outstanding bills from as far back as last summer and there's precious little new business coming in now. We have a big payroll to meet and we owe people like Cartier and the musicians, not to mention the notes due the banks." He looked at his wife, sitting next to him behind the desk. "I blame myself for letting this happen to you, especially now that you're pregnant."

Kate shook her head briskly. "No, Spencer, I won't listen to that kind of thing. We're not the only ones this happened to and it isn't your fault the stock market crumbled. We've just had bad luck, that's all—except for the new baby."

Spencer almost smiled. He took her hand and kissed it. "Nothing seems to frighten you anymore."

"Not as long as I have you." It was true. Sometimes she looked for plain, fearful Kate, as if she lurked in the mirror or just out of sight in a corner of a room like a plaintive ghost. But that woman had vanished over the years of her marriage to this quiet, unassuming man who loved her. She stroked his thinning hair, and it was some moments before he spoke again.

"I don't think Ema knows how bad it is."

"Then she must be told."

"Told what?" Ema, her steps muffled by the thick carpeting, came into the office. "If it's more bad news, please say it quickly."

With a last look at Kate, Spencer described their predicament again. "And if we can't pay them soon," he finished, "we'll have to declare bankruptcy."

"Not bankruptcy!" Ema knew that the stigma attached to bankrupts would ruin them all. And there was more at stake than RSVP; there was her own reputation as Dana's mother. She walked to the window and pushed aside the curtain.

It was only a little past four in the afternoon, but it was already dark outside. "I hate March," Emanuelle said angrily. "All we need is a high wind and a driving rain to complete the picture." But the night was crisp and clear.

"If we don't declare bankruptcy," Spencer went on, "our creditors can put liens on our property."

"What property?" Ema turned and looked around the office. "Do you mean furniture—or my paintings and jewelry?"

He shook his head. "They couldn't touch your paintings and jewelry— they're in the apartment and the lease is in Harding's name. But they could take everything else that secures RSVP, probably your land at Silvermoor and certainly our house and any money we have."

"Never!" Emanuelle got to her feet. "I won't let that happen, or bankruptcy either. My God, Spencer, you two are in this mess because of me!"

"It was a wonderful idea," Kate said, "and we all made money. Our timing was bad, that's all."

Ema went around the desk. She put an arm around Kate and extended a hand to Spencer. "You're a good man, Spencer Atwood, one of the few. And it's still a great idea. I'll get the money somehow."

"From Harding?"

Ema didn't answer. "Let's go home; we can't do anything more to-night. How are you feeling, Kate?"

"This pregnancy isn't as easy as the first two. You'd think I'd have the hang of it by now." Kate smiled ruefully.

"Just don't worry too much," Ema said. "I'll think of something. Don't ask me what. I just will."

She decided to walk home; she thought best either sitting in a hot bath or walking along Park Avenue. The avenue looked just the same, as if the bottom had fallen out of some other nation's economy. But there were some desperate people still hanging on behind those patrician façades, hoping for a miracle; others had already moved to humbler addresses. And there had been a few suicides by men whose fortunes had vanished, men whose positions she had always considered impregnable. She could understand their fear; poverty terrified her too.

She must do something until the rich began spending and RSVP began earning again. She couldn't watch everything she had accomplished for Dana vanish like ashes on the wind because she had been overly greedy to make a lot of money quickly. Nor could she see harm come to Kate and Spencer, their two boys, and the baby on the way. She tried to concentrate on her immediate problem—cash to pay the creditors and the bank and money to keep RSVP from declaring bankruptcy.

She would never part with her land. She could sell her paintings and her jewelry, but that took time and heaven knew what they were actually worth right now. "You can own the Taj Mahal," Harding had said a few days ago, "and if a dime is the highest price anyone can afford to pay for it, a dime is what it's worth."

She had her hefty collection of gold napoleons—in the wall safe, no longer in the mattress—and the securities Harding had given her, but they would all have to be starving in the streets before she would sell those, and they were a long way from that, *Dieu merci,* thanks to Harding.

She did not want to ask Harding for the money; Harding had lost a great deal on the market himself. He expected no miraculous turnaround on the market and predicted the slump would run a long course, a year, possibly two. Businesses were failing in ever greater numbers already, and as a result advertising revenues on all of his publications were falling sharply and so was circulation. Soon he would need most of his own capital just to keep the *Star* staffed and running.

"I don't want to fire anyone if I can help it," he had told her just this morning on his way to a budget meeting at the *Star,* with a more worried frown than usual. Of all the things he owned, he loved his newspapers best and the *Star* most of all; he would never jeopardize the *Star* for RSVP—not even for her. She was not blind to his mixed feelings about her success; she had simply chosen to ignore them up to now.

It was infuriating! When it was operating, RSVP pumped money, but like any pump, it had to be primed. Until the still-rich began spending again, Ema's business couldn't function and pay its debts. But there must be money available somewhere! She thought fleetingly of Sir James and his bank, but that was a last resort. It was risky; Julian might find out about it. Nor could she ask Julian. Money had never been a part of their relationship.

"I'll just get a personal loan from my own bank!" she said half-aloud as she walked on. Borrowing had always been anathema to her, but she moved among the very rich and it was time she accepted that borrowing was the way they did business. She had a sound reputation and bright business potential to offer as collateral, even if RSVP's other assets were mortgaged to the hilt.

A loan would pay off the bank notes and the salaries for a few months; they had to keep their highly skilled chefs and florists for the time when people started booking parties again. The drivers and lesser personnel would have to be fired.

A loan would protect Kate and Spencer and avoid the stigma of bank-

ruptcy for all of them. And from now on RSVP would demand in advance
at least fifty percent of the projected expenses for a party. Ema had her
solution.

When she reached home she found a message from Harding that his
budget meeting would keep him late at the *Star*. Worried, she had supper
in the nursery with Dana and Nanny Mills. She read Dana a fairy tale
before she kissed her good night, then took a long, hot bath and got into
bed, idly turning the pages of a magazine until Harding came in at eleven,
looking even more weary than usual. She ran a tub for him and sat with
him while he soaked, waiting to hear the results of his budget meeting.

"So we're going to have to trim your staff," he finished, "and probably
suspend your trips to Paris too. I'm sorry."

"I understand," she said, hiding her alarm. Was Harding in deeper
trouble than she had thought? "I expected the staff cuts. As long as I have
Kenny and Sheila I can manage. There won't be many big parties to cover
until the summer, and who wore what to where isn't the kind of thing
most women want to read right now."

"Will they want to read anything at a time like this?" He said it in passing, thinking of other things.

She massaged his shoulder muscles while she considered it. "I think
so. If I were a woman whose husband was out of a job or afraid of being
so, I wouldn't give a damn about world news or some rich girl's debut. I'd
want to know how other women were coping, what kinds of shortcuts
they had found to feed and clothe their families, you know, inexpensive
recipes, how to make clothes over, things like that. I'd want to know
where I could get help if I needed it—and most important of all how not to
have more babies."

He craned his neck to look at her, his interest piqued. "Except for birth
control—that's too controversial—you're right. Why don't you have a
crack at it?"

She looked at him in surprise. "You mean do an article?"

"Not one, a series. Why not make it a woman's page in the real sense of
the word? Women are in trouble and the *Star* can help."

"Yes, it can." She was proud of that. "Of course I'll do it!"

Her momentary elation faded as she got back into bed and lay there
worrying until he got in beside her. "Harding, how bad is it? Please tell
me."

He turned out the light and put an arm around her before he answered.
"I'm not ruined, you mustn't think that. Almost everything I invested in
Wall Street is gone until the market recovers—and that may take a long
time. The rest of my holdings didn't vanish in a puff of smoke when the
market crashed. They're still out there, but the cash is tied up in factories

that will close down and mortgages that will default, even banks that are failing already. It would be pointless to sell now, even if I could find a buyer."

"You'd be selling the Taj Mahal for a dime."

"Yes." He laughed briefly, without humor. "But it will take every available dollar I have to hold out. I should be back in the black a lot faster than the rest of the country, from the look of things, but I can't hang on unless I cut spending for a while."

"And Silvermoor?" The beautiful house, only partially furnished, was sad and untenanted, like a jilted bride.

He sighed. "I'd rather wait. Anyway, I feel more on top of things here in the city."

She agreed—and waited, but he didn't mention RSVP; either he could do nothing about it or he didn't want to. She did not want to know which it was; either way it created a breach between them. But she had finally built something for herself and she would keep it, no matter how. "I'm glad I know how to cut corners," she said finally.

He turned to her. "I knew you'd understand, Ema. You're wonderful, you know."

But she did not want him to make love to her and he sensed it. They said good night with her worries still unspoken between them. She knew she was no safer than she had ever been. Even married to a man like Harding she was not safe.

# 57

She was in her bank manager's office by noon the next day and learned to her astonishment that she would need better collateral than her name to get a personal loan.

"The business assets, as you know, are all mortgaged," the manager said. "We can't extend any more credit on them."

"Are you saying your bank might repossess our property if we default on the payments?"

His eyes shifted, confirming her fears. "Now, now, we're talking about a personal loan, Mrs. Ellis." She was about to offer her jewelry as collateral, when he added, "And of course you can't obtain a loan without your husband's countersignature, no matter what collateral you offer."

"That's ridiculous," she protested. "I made that business; my husband had nothing to do with it."

"I'm sorry, Mrs. Ellis, that's the law," the bank manager said gloomily.

"Then the law ought to be changed," she said imperiously as she left. She headed automatically for the *Star,* but on an impulse went to a quiet speakeasy and had a brandy, thinking furiously while her temper cooled.

After a while she nodded, with a grimace of distaste. She finished the brandy, made a telephone call, and then took a taxi to Thomas Blessing's office on Wall Street. She went not only because of her clear responsibility for Kate and Spencer, but because she had secret obligations, too, that were not so easy to identify. They had always cost her dearly.

"So you see," she told Thomas Blessing across his desk a half hour later, "we need a loan only to tide us over until people start living again. Life goes on, Thomas; girls have to make their debuts and get married. There will always be charity balls and funerals." She smiled at him, aware that she smiled in a very particular way and that he responded to it on cue. "We want to be ready when it all begins again, so I came to a friendly banker who wouldn't tell me a lot of nonsense about needing Harding to co-sign."

Thomas Blessing's attention shifted. "Won't he? Is Harding in trouble?"

"No, of course not, he doesn't even know about my little setback. Anyway, RSVP is mine and I want to keep it that way."

"You always were a feisty little lady!" He offered her a cigarette and came around the desk to light it for her. He sat on a corner of the desk and looked down at her with what he fancied was a persuasive smile. "I'll approve your loan, Emanuelle. I'll even lend you the money interest free. After all, we're old friends, aren't we?"

She smiled again. It was about to be made, the offer she had steeled herself for.

"But first spend a weekend with me."

She raised her brows. "You're not serious, Thomas."

"But I am. I've always admired you, you know that. I'm a happily married man, but I like an occasional fling."

"Occasional? You're the worst womanizer in New York, everyone knows that." She said it languidly, to mask her disgust.

He was pleased. "One has one's little accomplishments. But you're not just a passing fancy, Emanuelle, I've been waiting for you a long time. You won't be disappointed, I assure you. I know how to make a woman happy." His eyes traveled expectantly up and down her body.

She smoked in silence, balancing the trouble she was in against what it would cost to let Thomas Blessing get her out of it. The man standing over her was not a monster, even if he was a fool, yet she shrank from accepting the proposition she had risked by coming here. *Idiote*, she called herself, *crétine*. What had such niceties to do with the despoiled Emalie Anne Bequier? Still she hesitated, and she wondered why.

It had nothing to do with virtue; hers had been destroyed long since. It was not a moral issue, either; she did not believe in morality. Maybe it was honor, not Julian's code, but her own. She had done many things inconsistent with Julian's concept of honor, yet she had sacrificed much to protect other people from the consequences of what she did. Still her mind cast about frantically for another way.

She thought of Sir James again and decided she would rather swallow her pride and go to bed with him than with Thomas Blessing. She could trust Sir James to keep a secret, but Blessing was a small man who would relish telling Harding, sooner or later, that he'd been to bed with her. He wouldn't care if Tillie knew it, either.

Tillie! The thought of Tillie brought a sudden smile to Ema's face, and she relaxed in the chair for a moment, her eyes closed. Then, with a flourish, she crushed out her cigarette and gathered her handbag and gloves.

"Well, what do you say?" Blessing asked as she headed for the door.

"I say thanks, Thomas, but no thanks."

"Isn't that why you came to me?" He looked comically confused.

"*Mais non*. I came for a loan," she assured him, laughing, "for money, not for your little pink *zizi* on a plate."

She took a taxi back to the *Star*, striding past the half-deserted desks of a gloomy City Room with a smile that cheered people up a little.

"Hello, Kenny," she called to him, "any coffee left?"

"Good morning, Mrs. Ellis, I'm just making some fresh."

"I have a call to make, then I want to see you and Sheila about changes for the page."

She rang the Blessing mansion and finally got Matilda on the telephone. "I have to talk to you this afternoon. It's important and it won't wait."

"I'm in the middle of being waxed," Tillie complained. "What's it about?"

"Something you won't be able to resist. Can you be here by two?"

Grumbling, Tillie agreed. When she arrived, her reaction to Emanuelle's financial difficulties was predictable. "I'm grief-stricken, of course," she said with a smile, "but I warned you not to get in over your head. Why tell me about it?"

"So you can provide the money I need to tide me over. In return I'll make you a silent partner. It's a booming business in a temporary slump— a really sound investment."

"Don't be ridiculous. Why on earth should I invest in your miserable business?"

"So I won't have to ask Thomas."

The two women took each other's measure in silence.

"I don't think I should ask him," Ema said ingenuously, "although I'm sure he'd make me an offer."

"No," said Tillie faintly. "I don't think you should ask him, either." She recovered almost immediately, taking her checkbook out of her bag. "How much?"

"Two hundred thousand for ten percent of my half."

"I'll give you fifty now, the rest in a week," Tillie said, writing.

"I'll have the papers drawn up."

"Clever," Matilda said. "You were always very clever. Take care you don't outsmart yourself someday." She put the check on Emanuelle's desk and left the office.

# BOOK III

The last temptation is the greatest treason:
To do the right deed for the wrong reason.

—T. S. ELIOT

# 58

Emanuelle hurried down the wide central staircase of Silvermoor, carrying her briefcase, handbag, and gloves. It was just before eight o'clock and the car was waiting in the drive already, but she stopped briefly on the landing. The two-story entrance hall was bathed in cool light, but the hand-rubbed woods of the furniture and paneling made the hall warm and welcoming.

It was full of the treasures Emanuelle had so lovingly chosen, first in London, then through dealers in New York. There was a large French tapestry behind each of the Sheraton sideboards, and, on the sideboards, Sheffield silver bowls of fresh flowers from the Silvermoor greenhouses. An imposing grandfather clock towered in one corner, and a graceful nude clung modestly to her wisp of marble drapery in the other.

Replete with the satisfaction that every corner of Silvermoor brought her, Emanuelle fluffed the organdy jabot of her white blouse, settled the jacket of her hand-tailored gray broadcloth suit, and turned at the bottom of the stairs to go to the breakfast room. Harding and Dana looked up as she came in and the two Great Danes, Castor and Pollux, rumbled a greeting.

"I know I'm late," she said, kissing Dana's glossy dark hair, "but all I want is coffee." She poured a cup and sat down before she realized how quiet the other two were. She looked inquiringly over the rim of her cup.

Harding was lighting his pipe. "We were talking about school," he said. "Dana thinks you want her to go to England next year."

Emanuelle glanced from her daughter's troubled face to Harding's. "Only if she wants to."

"She doesn't," Harding said. "And I certainly don't want her to."

Flushing slightly—Dana's education was her most treasured project—

Emanuelle shrugged. "It was only a thought," she said. "And this is no time to discuss it, we're late." She finished her coffee and rose from the table. "Ready, Harding?" She stopped again at Dana's chair, meeting the child's enormous gray eyes. With a pang of remorse she saw how troubled they were. She touched Dana's cheek. "Don't worry about school, *chérie*. It was only a suggestion."

A smile of worshipful relief lit Dana's face. "Really, Maman? You're not disappointed?" She stood. She was only ten, and the awkwardness of adolescence was not yet upon her. She put her arms around her mother's waist.

"*Mais non, ma chérie*, I could never be disappointed in you. What will you do today?"

"Go to Caro's—we're working on our albums. May I sleep over?"

"Yes, if Miss Prescott is willing to take you." Emanuelle approved of little Carolyn George, farmed out every recess to her grandparents' house on the Hudson by her globetrotting socialite parents. "But change before you go, darling; that dress is wilted." With another kiss Ema smiled and left the room, hearing the two enormous dogs scramble up to follow. The butler put her Russian broadtail coat around her shoulders and handed Harding his Chesterfield. Husband and wife went out to the Silver Ghost waiting in the driveway.

"Go on, you two," Harding said to the dogs, "go back inside to Dana." He waited until the chauffeur had closed the door. "You're angry," he said immediately in the stillness of the car's plush interior. "Well, so am I."

"I don't see why," Emanuelle said.

"This compulsion to send Dana off to private school in England is ridiculous, and you know I'm against it."

"She'd be safer in England, for one thing," Ema said. It was not only the Lindbergh kidnapping; the *Star* had reported over two thousand abductions for ransom in the two years before that poor baby was murdered.

"Nonsense, Miss Prescott is as much a guardian as a governess. We have an alarm system and three Dobermans on the grounds as well as Castor and Pollux in the house." Harding shook his head. "I don't think that's any reason at all."

"But her future *is*, Harding. She has to go to prep school eventually, and there's no better education than an English one."

"Horsefeathers! We have some fine prep schools right here. Anyway, she's American. She ought to be educated in her own country."

"I didn't think you were so insular," Emanuelle said frigidly. She had always felt smothered when he tried to impose his will on her. Furthermore Harding was shortsighted; girls formed the right connections at school, and after school came marriage.

"It isn't insular to want my little girl here, not thousands of miles away." He said it so fiercely that Emanuelle abandoned the fight temporarily.

"If you feel that strongly, we'll drop it. It was just an idea."

"Maybe," he said, mollified, "but Dana thinks your ideas are Holy Writ. By the way, what kind of album is she working on with the little George girl?"

Ema smiled. "Movie stars. They cut their favorites out of screen magazines and collect them in scrapbooks. They use a nauseating paste made of flour and water."

Harding raised his eyebrows. "Some of those actresses are too raunchy to have little girls mooning over them."

"The little girls don't know that—to them they're heroines, all pure as the driven snow."

They settled back, both of them relieved that the argument was over, although Ema knew it had only been postponed until Dana was ready for prep school. She was reluctant herself to be parted from Dana now, but she had her heart set on Rodean, a prestigious school where Dana would meet not only the daughters of the English peerage but of European nobility—or what was left of it—and begin to move in the right circles. Ema wanted her to be presented at the Court of St. James's, in a white gown with a train and the requisite three-feathered headdress on her shining hair.

She glanced at Harding. He looked much younger in profile, not so absolutely dominant as when he faced her and his dark eyes blazed. They rarely argued over anything except his attempt to exert his authority, and she was uncomfortable when they did; it felt as if he had withdrawn his total approval of her. But if the price of approval was subservience, the price was too high. She remembered all too well what it was like to surrender her will. It had made her suspicious of marriage in the first place.

She respected Harding and was proud to be his wife, but the RSVP argument still rankled although a year had gone by. It had been the fault of Tillie Blessing's big mouth wagging over cocktails that night, announcing that she was still Emanuelle's business partner.

*     *     *

"Until tomorrow, anyway, and I'm not at all sure I like selling Ema back my share," Tillie babbled with a knowing glance at her husband. "RSVP's positively rolling in money now."

"What in hell is she talking about?" Harding demanded of Ema.

"Later," Ema said, "I'll tell you later."

"No, damn it, you'll tell me now!"

But just then dinner was announced and the two couples joined the guests moving into the dining room. Harding was obviously furious throughout the evening and had barely waited until they were homeward bound to demand an explanation.

"It was the Crash," Ema said. "Too many people couldn't pay us and RSVP was on the verge of bankruptcy. I had to have money and I got it from her."

"Why not from *me*?" He waited a few seconds, but she did not reply. "Emanuelle, I have the right to know. Why not from me?"

She turned her head quickly, regarding him with well-ripened rancor. "Because *you* didn't even ask me if I was in trouble, Harding! All you talked about after the Crash was *your* predicament. You weren't in the least concerned about RSVP; it could have gone under for all you cared!"

He shook his head vigorously, denying it to himself as well as to her. "That isn't fair, Ema. Why should I begrudge your success? I just had too many things to juggle at the time."

"All right, then! So I solved my problems without adding to yours! What on earth is wrong with that?"

"Nothing, to hear you tell it. But there ought to be complete confidence between us. You're always doing things I know nothing about."

She said nothing.

He shook his head again, impatient at her silence. He had told himself again and again that their marriage was based on a bargain, that she had only promised him what she had to give him, not what he had to have. But as time went on, that bromide wasn't strong enough for the pain.

It made him do things he didn't like—about Dana, sometimes at the *Star*. It made him jealous and he hated that. It wasn't physical jealousy, thank God, that would be the ultimate betrayal. There was no other man in Ema's life, except in her memories. But that was what he could not bear! He could live with her, share her bed, reach her physically, but her memories were her own; he could not enter there. And her other secrecies were a constant reminder of that.

"I'll pay Tillie off today," he had said at length.

"No, Harding, I'll pay her off myself."

"For God's sake, Ema, why refuse now what I should have offered then?"

"But there's no need, I have more than enough money!"

"And RSVP is *yours*," he said hotly, "that's the real reason, isn't it? What did you think I was going to do, demand a share the way she did?"

"Oh, stop it, Harding, just stop it!"

*    *    *

The argument had eventually worn itself out, but it was the first of many confrontations like this morning's. She knew he resented her independence no matter how he denied it.

But I'm not sorry I married him, she thought, glancing at him again, and I hope he's happy. She knew he would have liked more children, but he never said so and she pretended not to know it. By now she felt it was really too late; she was thirty-six.

Sometimes she was afraid of her good fortune in such troubled times; it had often amused the gods to give her what she wanted only to wrench it away from her again.

Harding's cash position had improved after two nervous years, largely because of his holdings in the flourishing radio industry which made consistently huge profits in the depths of the Depression. The American public, needing surcease from the country's malaise—poverty was a shameful thing, it meant a man was shiftless—had turned to soap operas and comedy shows, accepting in exchange the miraculous claims on behalf of soaps, dentifrices, and nostrums for everything from indigestion to sore feet. The advertisers paid well for radio time.

Harding had been right about the aircraft industry too; its civil possibilities were mushrooming. Celebrities like movie stars and the Prince of Wales flew on short trips everywhere, and transatlantic service was just around the corner. The rich had their lavish private railway carriages and yachts; they would soon want luxuriously appointed private aircraft. The military's interest was less public, and Harding was watching German aircraft development with some alarm at its technological progress.

They had finished Silvermoor and moved into it two years ago. Nanny Mills had been replaced by an English governess, Miss Prescott, who stayed on even after Dana started day school in Manhattan. The governess was a special comfort when they were away, Harding in California and Canada, Emanuelle in Paris and, as often as she could manage it, in Germany with Julian. They were far less likely to run into people they knew there than in Paris.

Ema opened her briefcase and resumed counting her blessings. True to form, the rich had resumed their social activities, although they were more discreet about them with long lines of starving men waiting at soup kitchens all over the city.

RSVP now owned catering facilities and wholesale florists in New York, Boston, and Palm Beach and had recently opened a small French coffee shop in Manhattan as an experiment. The Café Vendôme had been so successful that they were moving to larger quarters on Madison Avenue and adding a retail counter for the sale of Vendôme pastries and chocolates. Cautious from her brush with ruin, Emanuelle still planned to es-

tablish a Vendôme chain outside New York as soon as possible. It was a
sure thing.

"Circulation is up again," Harding said, tapping the page in front of him.
He turned his head to look at her. "You still get more mail than anyone at
the *Star*."

"More than Edison Carter?" She laughed.

"By ten percent this week."

"Just wait. If the king decides to marry Mrs. Simpson, Edison will have
star billing."

Harding went back to his figures and Emanuelle smiled with satisfaction. In the spring of 1933, when she had started writing about women's
special problems during the Depression, she had hired Edison Carter to
help with the society column. He was a bitingly clever man, Social Register, who had lost everything in the Crash and now had to work for his
caviar. She had given him a by-line a year later, alternating his society
column with hers.

"Everyone knows which columns are yours," she had told him. "And if
they don't, it's high time they did. You've earned it."

"Darling," Edison crowed, kissing her in the antiseptic manner of
homosexuals touching women. "I always knew you were true blue, no
matter what stories that Blessing bitch told when you left her."

"Tillie? What did she say?"

"She denied your ducal ancestry." Edison had paused a moment, but
Emanuelle remained noncommittal about the story, as she had always
been. "She said you were a bastard, if you please, trying to worm your
way into society on your back."

Emanuelle laughed. "Dear Tillie. But that was years ago!"

"She still doesn't like you, Emanuelle. I'd be wary of her if I were you.
Her grudges hold up better than her face. A propos, I'm off to the dog
show. You ought to enter those Baskerville hounds of yours; they'd win
by intimidation."

Now Emanuelle took a folder from her briefcase with notes for a new
series of columns. She had written about everything from household
budgeting to food—"Don't throw wilted lettuce away, braise it with a little
bacon"—and fashion on a shoestring—"Turn the collars of your big girls'
dresses and cut them down for the little ones." She had done a long series
of interviews with working women, bluntly listing the discrimination,
sexual and economic, they faced. She had reported interviews with soci-
ologists about coping with domestic depression in a time of crisis; men
without work made their women's lives doubly difficult.

Emanuelle stirred uneasily. Now she wanted to write about something
that would almost certainly stir up a hornet's nest, no matter what hap-

pened to Edward VIII and Wallis Simpson. She wondered how Harding would react to a detailed report of the methods of birth control.

Birth control still embarrassed some people as much as it angered others, who considered it immoral, Catholic or not, but Ema thought it was a far better option than abortion. She still shivered at the memory of that kitchen table. But she had no precedents. She would have to rely on her own intuition about how much her readers would accept.

One thing was certain—she would not consult Harding before the first column appeared. He would certainly try to stop her as he had this morning about Dana, since he was just as proprietary about the *Star*. But this was her column about her own sex and she refused to be censored by anyone. The opening article was ready; with any luck he would be away when it was published.

"Ema?" She realized he had said her name more than once. "Are you all right?"

"Yes, of course, why?"

"You looked so—I don't know, fierce." He took her hand.

She shook her head. "I was just thinking."

"What about?"

"My new series."

"It must be something controversial to make you look like that. Tell me about it?"

"No, it's too soon, it hasn't set yet." She smiled and he went back to his work as the car reached Manhattan and headed for the *Star*. She closed her eyes briefly, thinking of Julian, not as her lover but as her escape.

The ugly facts of her life never surfaced when she was with him. They talked about real things—like the rash of dictatorships spreading around the world and the precarious situation in Spain—but with Julian she lived in a world apart. She basked in his presence, as if privilege canceled out the dark underside of human nature.

She knew firsthand that it did not, but Julian himself had no darkness in him. When they were together they acknowledged reality, but because they met so seldom they did not have to live in it.

"We're here," Harding said. "I wonder what you think about when you're miles away like that."

"New ways to make money."

"Are you going on or coming in?"

"Going on. I want to talk to Kate and Spencer."

"How many tigers do you have to take by the tail?"

"As many as there are," she answered enigmatically.

"Will you ever trust me enough to tell me?"

"Trust you? I'm married to you!"

He shook his head and got out of the car. She watched him go into the building, then signaled the chauffeur to drive on. She was eager to see Spencer's figures on Vendôme's proposed retail expansion.

# 59

"Good for you!" Kate said, putting down the *Star* with the page folded to Emanuelle's most recent column. "That description of an abortion was terrifying! And obviously based on fact."

Kate stopped talking and glanced at Harding, who had just come off the tennis court at Silvermoor with Spencer.

"Harding wasn't very pleased at first," Spencer said, and Kate winced.

"Want some lemonade?" Ema asked the two men.

"It's no secret I thought she'd gone too far when I saw the first column," Harding said crisply, accepting a glass. "I just wish she'd let me see the piece before it ran."

"Why should she? You'd only have stopped her." Spencer said it good-naturedly. Kate and Ema avoided each other's eyes.

"I'm the publisher of the *Star*. What Ema does with RSVP is her business. Anything printed in the *Star* is mine."

There was an uncomfortable silence among the four friends. Kate had long been aware of the strain between Harding and Ema, of the almost daily disagreements over one thing or another. She knew they had argued about the column hotly in private, Harding standing on his authority, Ema insisting she had taken on the column to handle as she saw fit.

"I would certainly have toned things down a little," Harding said stubbornly into the silence.

"But reaction to Ema's plain speaking has been mostly favorable, hasn't it?" Spencer said, trying to make amends.

"Public reaction is beside the point!" Harding said, exasperated. Then, with an effort, he calmed himself. "What's your next project after this series?" he asked Ema.

Ema hesitated for a split-second before she relented. "You'll approve of this one," she said. "The boom we had in the 'twenties makes our Crash more dramatic, but France, for example, has been in trouble since the war ended. There are whole communities in England existing on the dole. I'd like to do a series on how European women have been coping with hard times."

Kate looked at Emanuelle again. Didn't she know it would be risky for her to see Julian more often than she already did?

"I think it's a damned good idea," Harding said. "America's inclined to forget there are people on the other side of the ocean in as much trouble as we are."

"Where will you go first?" Spencer asked.

"France, of course. Danielle will have plenty of material for me on the secretarial job situation—and I'll deal with fashion, too, but only as an industry that employs women. If women want fashion, they can read *Vogue*; the glossy magazines are monopolizing it anyway. Then I'll go on to Belgium and Holland. I don't particularly want to do Germany, but it's always a possibility."

"Why not start in England?" Harding suggested. There was a silence and Kate sprang up to empty the ashtrays. "I'm going there myself," Harding went on when Ema made no reply. "I want to meet with some of the British press, particularly Lord Broadhurst. He shares some of my concerns."

"The Fascists," Kate said, glad to change the subject.

"Yes—and the pacifists."

Emanuelle thought of what Julian had told her of his heated discussions with Broadhurst, who was determined to have a hero in his corner—just as determined as Julian was not to be there. "You're not suggesting a similarity between pacifists and Fascists, surely!" she demanded.

"No, of course not. It's just that militant pacifists, however sincerely motivated, make things easier for militant Fascists. We can't deny that belligerence is on the rise worldwide—Italy in Ethiopia, Germany in the Rhineland—and that little toad Goebbels has started a suspicious campaign against the Czechs." He sighed. "We might have to protect ourselves against the spread of dictatorship someday and we can't hope to do that with our inadequate army and outdated weapons."

"Harding, you can't mean war!" Kate said, her astonishment outstripping her alarm over Ema's project.

"No, I'm talking about defense."

"Oh, Harding, please!" Ema objected heatedly. "You can't pretend that munitions are manufactured for tea parties! They're made for killing. If we make them, we'll use them—and nobody wants another war."

It had become a private argument again. Harding did not reply and the Atwoods sat in embarrassed silence.

"I'm sorry," Ema said, thinking that she must control herself. "I got carried away."

"I didn't know you were such an ardent pacifist," Spencer said.

"I was in Paris for four years of war and the trenches were never far away. Once you've heard those guns and seen what they can do to a man, you're bound to be angry at even the mention of another war."

Nervously she lit a cigarette, ignoring the one smoldering in the ashtray. Her face was bleak and in Harding's eyes she was a frightened young girl in Paris; she was a war widow, mourning a slain soldier she could not forget.

Harding took her hand, ending the argument. "Now, how about starting your series in England? You've been there only once—amazing for such an Anglophile. Kate, did she tell you she wanted to send Dana to school in England next year?"

"All right," Ema agreed quickly, avoiding Kate's eyes. "I'll start in England. When do you plan to go?"

"In about a month. How long will you have to stay?"

"Hard to tell," Emanuelle said, intent on the smoke from her cigarette. "A few weeks, I'd say, maybe a little more. And I'll come back to see Dana before I go on to France—unless," she said suddenly, "you'll bring Dana over for the summer as soon as school's out. I could rent a villa for us on the Riviera."

"Very glamorous," Spencer said.

Ema smiled, the tension completely dissipated. "You two must come as well, with the three boys. And Danielle in August! It would be a wonderful summer. Harding?"

"Sounds good. I couldn't stay the whole summer, but I could manage a few weeks here and there. How about it, Spencer?"

They made excited plans until the two men went back to the court for another game. Kate pretended to watch the ball. "Ema, you're playing with fire," she said sharply.

Emanuelle shook her head. "The articles are bona fide, Kate."

"But you're not supposed to go to England at all!"

"I've had enough of being told what I can do! Those two will just have to accept that I'm going to travel where I like. After all this time they must know I'm not going to change anything." Ema leaned back in her chair and closed her eyes. "Drew is almost seventeen," she said after a moment.

"You won't try to see him!"

Ema shook her head.

"But you'll see Julian, won't you?"

"Yes, whenever I can. He's not free to come and go as he chooses, either."

"I hope you know what you're doing," Kate said, shaking her head, but Ema did not answer and avoided the subject in the weeks that followed. She was busy locating sites for Confiseries Vendôme and setting up interviews with the help of newswomen in London and Paris.

She sailed with Harding on the new, opulent *Queen Mary* in June.

"It's going to be a treat, having you to myself for almost a week," Harding said after dinner on their first night at sea. They had come back to their suite to get coats for a turn on deck.

"I love ships," Emanuelle said. "You can be anyone you want to be on a ship."

He put her pale gray broadtail coat around her and held her for a moment. "Who do you want to be, Ema?"

"What a question! Myself, of course."

"I sometimes wonder. There's so much you keep hidden from me."

She stepped away from him and tied a chiffon scarf around her head. "Harding, please let's not argue about that anymore. I'll never run a column again without giving you advance notice, if that's what you want."

"I mean what goes on here." His hand touched her forehead, then her breast. "And here. You've never forgotten him, have you? It's why you're reluctant to go to England."

Her voice was even as she answered him. "I told you, long ago, he'll always be a part of me." She turned to him. "But Harding, he has nothing to do with us, I promise you that." She kissed him softly, but she was troubled. In all these years this was the first time she had crossed the Atlantic with Harding. There would not be enough time or distance between her present and her past, Emanuelle and Emalie, the dreamer and the dream.

He was comforted by her assurance, and they went up on deck to watch the moon-silvered wake from the stern for a while, saying little, both exalted and diminished by the dark vastness of water and sky. She knew he would make love to her that night, and he did, with that passion to possess that was so much more than physical, as if he could reach what he wanted of her by way of her body, as if he could come closer to it the more intense her pleasure in him was.

He was an irresistible lover. They were in a state of heightened sexuality throughout the trip, making love when they napped in the afternoon and again every night. The excitement hovered just below the surface when they were with people; they even welcomed companionate meals and games of bridge and shuffleboard, relishing the erotic feast they would consume when they were alone.

The fever had run its course when they checked into the Connaught in London. They were a husband and wife again, loving, physically attracted to each other, but not, under ordinary circumstances, ravenous for sexual consummation several times a day.

"I'll ask Broadhurst if he can do anything to help you," Harding said, brushing his dark hair for his first appointment.

"I'd rather deal with women columnists for the most part," Ema said. "They're feminists and you'll find Broadhurst isn't."

"It's up to you, but you know he's asked us for dinner tonight. I'll be back in time to dress."

He went off and she waited a few minutes before she called Sir James, saying she was a client referred by the Paris office.

"It's Emanuelle Beranger," she said briefly when he came on the line.

"Yes?" he said, alert and cautious.

"I'm here in London, with my husband. There was no safe way to give you advance notice."

"I understand. Will you be here long?"

"Several weeks, but not too long in London. I'm on assignment. It might be reported in the press."

"Yes, I quite see." A pause. "Can we meet?"

It was what she wanted. "I'm free right now," she said. "After that I'm busy every day."

He gave her the name of a discreet hotel well off the beaten track. "In an hour?"

She agreed and broke the connection. She took off the dark wool jersey dress she had chosen to see her through the day and put on a navy blue Chanel suit, lined in pale yellow and bound in blue and yellow braid. She added some heavy gold chains and bracelets, taking confidence from their weight. A navy felt hat, tilted well forward like a military pillbox, completed the ensemble. Her hair was arranged in the style English fashion reporters called "ready for the bath." The king's favorite, Mrs. Wallis Simpson, had made it fashionable to smooth hair close to the head and roll it up at the ends. Ema checked her makeup, picked up a cape, and left the hotel.

# 60

At first sight he did not appear to have changed, but when he stood to greet her in the private parlor he had reserved for their meeting she saw that age had finally come upon him. He was handsome still, a tall, straight figure in his elegant clothes, but there was a translucence to his skin and a hesitation in his movements that had not been there at their last encounter, or when he had bent to kiss her with repressed desire in Glengowrie seventeen years ago.

"Mrs. Ellis," he said, taking the gloved hand she offered him. "You never change except to grow more beautiful." He handed her into one of the wing chairs. "I've ordered tea."

"I would really prefer coffee," she said.

"Of course." He went to the door for a moment and gave the order. "I seem to remember your drinking tea at Silvermoor Cottage," he said, coming back.

"Only under protest." She took off her gloves and looked up at him. "Have you told her I'm here?"

"Not yet. I will tonight." A waitress in a starched white cap and apron came in with a tray. When they were alone again, he said, "She will accept it, since your husband is with you."

"Tell me about Drew," Ema said, careless of whether Davina accepted it or not. She poured tea for him, remembering how petrified she had been of being asked to do so at Stridings.

"Better and better. He'll be at Oxford soon, but he is abroad at the moment." He seemed anxious.

"You needn't worry, I won't try to see him," she said curtly. She drank some of the weak coffee. "My husband is meeting with Lord Broadhurst today. It seems they take the same dim view of many things, including the pacifist movement."

"I see," he said. "Will your husband want to meet Broadhurst's friend, Julian Saxon, one of England's leading pacifists?"

"He might. I don't want him to. Is there any way to prevent it?"

He shrugged. "I shall try. It must happen eventually, in any case. Julian is planning to take his crusade abroad, to your country."

She took a deep breath.

"All of us throw pebbles in the pond every day we live," Sir James said. "The ripples expand. The misfortune is that they sometimes touch—you and Davina, perhaps Julian and your husband."

"You're so quick to condemn adultery, aren't you?" she said in a furious rush. "Mine, at any rate. Yet you accept Julian's because men are expected to do that sort of thing."

"On the contrary, I deplore it equally. But you're an unusual woman, Emalie. Over the years I have come to admire you and to understand you better than I did when first we met."

Gratitude overcame her at that, as if he had opened a door in the high wall between her world and Julian's. She understood him too. He did what he had to do, but at least she knew where he stood. He could be trusted to be faithful to his own concept of honor, no matter what it cost. For him it was *noblesse oblige;* but admire her or not, he would never see it was the same for her. All at once she despised both his admiration and her gratitude.

"You'd still ruin me," she said coldly, "to protect your own."

He nodded.

"But they're mine too!" she pleaded, needing the very approbation she despised. Why else had she called him but to let him see how prosperous she had become, how worthy of his respect? "Why can't you see that? Why can't you trust me to protect Julian and Drew?"

"Because of Davina and my three granddaughters."

"Davina!" The three syllables were heavy with scorn. "I pity those little girls."

"Nevertheless I made her a party to the whole affair—and, consequently, her children with her."

"She was a willing accomplice; she'd have done anything to hold on to Julian, surely you know that!" Her vehemence embarrassed her and she got hold of herself. "Why did you want to see me?" She was crisp now, businesslike.

"Just to—see you again. I'm getting on, one wants to see the people one thinks about constantly."

She flushed, amazed by even this subtle avowal of affection—no, it was more than that!—from such a man as this, furious because she knew it had started at Silvermoor Cottage as a purely carnal impulse he could not deny. She was not to be mollified so cheaply, and with deep satisfaction she degraded his love to the level of commerce, where he had put hers.

"I almost came to you for money, once," she said.

He blanched, but answered nonetheless. "I would have given it to you. I would have given you anything."

"Except what was mine, Julian and my son." Suddenly her barrier of pride was shattered again. "How could you ruin our lives the way you did?" she demanded, her gray eyes dark with disdain. "A man like you? You threw me away after I had served my purpose, that was to be expected. But you condemned *him* to a marriage he had already renounced. You used his love for you to manipulate him, not for his sake or Drew's, but for yours, *your* heritage, *your* title. His beliefs embarrass you; you'd prefer that he keep them to himself. But he won't. He has more courage and more principle than you and Broadhurst put together."

She took a deep breath, and when she resumed it was with baleful calm. "I despise you for what you've done. Your 'admiration' for me," she said with a contemptuous movement of her shoulders, "can't change that."

He made no reply, and she went quickly through the door, closing it behind her. Outside she walked for several blocks, utterly shaken by the conflict of emotion she felt, this Emalie desperate for his unqualified approval—for everyone's, the world's—and unable to accept what was offered in its place. She might never see him again and she was as anguished by the loss as she had been by her mother's passing. Each had known an aspect of Emalie Bequier that no one else, not even Julian, would ever see: the victim and the desperate winner.

Leave me alone, she told Emalie Bequier, hating herself for clinging so perversely to the very identity she had been fleeing all her life.

Still shaking, she came to a little square and sat on a bench to smoke a cigarette and recapture the disciplined restraint that was second nature to her. *Second* nature, she thought, there's the rub. But she was afraid of her real nature; it was too rebellious for the world she wanted to live in.

She knew Sir James would try to keep Julian and Harding apart, as she would. Her motives were different from his, considerations not of property but of the flesh, hers and that of the two men in her life . . . but it was dangerous to think of that.

At length she made herself hail a cab for Fleet Street. She had an appointment with Mary Alice Chandler, society columnist for the *Daily Gazette*, whom she'd first met in Paris several years before and rather liked. Her hands were still trembling when she was shown into Mary Alice's office.

"Well, you're looking a bit frazzled," Mary Alice said, "stunning, but decidedly off color. That's Chanel, of course," she said, nodding at Emanuelle's suit and cape.

Emanuelle nodded and accepted a cigarette. "London doesn't agree with me," she said.

"Maybe it was the crossing. I always sicken when I have nothing to do." Mary Alice was a dark-haired, sharp-featured woman whose upper-class accent was too perfect to be anything but acquired by hard work, as her position had been. "I have plenty of interviews set up for you, most with working-class women, a few with nobs."

"No nobs," Emanuelle said, visualizing Davina. There had been enough of Davina to last her a lifetime, Davina and her wretched brood of daughters. There were three of them already; after Ema's visit there would probably be a fourth.

"Why not interview a few aristos fallen on hard times? They're feeling the pinch too."

"Recently pinched women don't interest me; I want the ones who've been black and blue all their lives. They know how to fight, how to survive." She looked steadily at Mary Alice.

"Right," Mary Alice said after a moment. "Can you meet me here at nine tomorrow morning? It's on the way."

Ema nodded. They discussed the next day's schedule, then Mary Alice accompanied her through the clattering main room of the *Gazette* and pressed the button for the lift. "All newspapers look and smell alike," Emanuelle said.

"Wonderful, isn't it?"

"Yes. Oh, I almost forgot—anything special I should know about Lord Broadhurst? He's asked us to dinner tonight."

"Hide-bound traditionalist," Mary Alice said. "He's violently anti-German, and was, even pre-Hitler. Hates Bolshies like the plague. Can't stand Mrs. Simpson, either, thinks the king ought to be locked up in Fort Belvedere until they can ship the bloody woman back to you lot."

"The British press still doesn't mention the relationship?"

Mary Alice shook her head. "All reference to her—as the king's mistress, that is—is excised from the foreign press as well, before distribution to our news agents."

"That could never happen in America," Ema said.

"You don't have a monarchy in America. Our royals mean a lot to us; we don't like the king consorting with a gay divorcee."

"What about marrying one?"

"Never. Fancy a queen of England who's been to bed with two other blokes and they still alive to tell about it!"

"Ha!" Ema laughed. "I thought the flap was about status and pedigree, but it's really about who had prior access to Wallis's private parts."

Mary Alice laughed. "You might say that—but I advise against it."

"You're probably right." She got into the lift and held the door open. "I won't, but when you think about it, everything *is* about sex, one way or another. Back to Broadhurst, what does he think of women in general?"

"That they have their place," Mary Alice said. "Pedestal, ballroom, bed, nursery."

"Oh, God," Ema said, thinking that any impression she made on Broadhurst might get back to Julian.

She said it again, to Harding, while she dressed for dinner in a gray chiffon, draped à la grecque by Madame Grès. She had had enough of English aristocrats and their code today.

Yet she was agreeably surprised by Broadhurst. He was some fifteen years Sir James's junior, a vigorous, attractive, forceful man with a somewhat eccentric bent. He came from a wealthy county family, had become a Member of Parliament while he was accumulating his newspapers, and was created a peer by Lloyd George for his ardent support of the ultimately disastrous Great War. Broadhurst had a rakish charm of which he was certainly aware; his blue eyes were intense, his skin had a healthy pink glow.

"I admire your husband enormously," Lord Broadhurst said to Emanuelle after dinner in the lofty drawing room of his London mansion.

"So do I," Ema returned. "He's an honest man." She looked across the room to where Harding stood in conversation with a ferret-faced man who owned a string of newspapers almost as big as Broadhurst's.

"He'd have to be, to be married to you. Those columns you've been writing have made quite an impression here." He smiled at her warmly. "You are a very outspoken woman."

"You disapprove?"

He laughed. "I'm in no position to disapprove. My business, like yours, is to turn the public in what I think is the right direction. How I do that is irrelevant."

"Your influence is far more political than mine."

"Yours could be," he said, serious now. "Women have the vote. If they can all be persuaded to use it, they'll be a potent force in politics."

Emanuelle nodded, liking him for that. "I suppose I've been moving in that direction," she said. "Trying to change certain laws, I mean."

"Ah, but politics, real politics, deal with larger issues. International issues. These are parlous times, people's passions are aroused and an aroused populace can be easily led."

Lady Broadhurst, dressed in beaded pink and looking like a Gainsborough, joined them, and the conversation became general. "As if," Emanuelle said to Harding back in their room at the Connaught, "she were too delicate to hear about passions. These pale English beauties! I wonder how they reproduce. With runners, do you think, like strawberries?"

"Come off it, Ema, Broadhurst's a good man."

"He's a crafty son of a bitch."

"What's wrong with that?"

"Nothing, as long as he doesn't try to influence me."

"Or me," Harding said. "He's far too clever to try."

"*Mon oeil*! I'm too clever to let him," Ema said. She prepared for bed, relieved that her period had arrived. Both her children had been conceived during such ardent, repeated sex as there had been aboard the *Queen Mary*.

Both her children. She wondered if Julian knew she was in London and when they would meet, but that was a disquieting prospect somehow.

She worked steadily through the next few days, going from one interview to another, until a week had passed with no word from Julian, and Harding was ready to return home.

"Public opinion about Germany is as varied here as at home," he told her as he packed. "I wonder what will happen, though, if there's civil war in Spain. When a republic is threatened, free people are bound to react."

"No one cared when the Weimar Republic got hitlerized," Ema said. "Britain is dead set against war. Aside from that, the English are imperialists, don't forget. They want freedom for themselves, but the wogs of the world are meant to do as they're told. You and I, Harding, qualify as white wogs. Anyway, the British hate communism more than they hate fascism."

"The Spanish Republic may be red, but it isn't Bolshevik. That's a distinction most people forget to make." He snapped his valise shut and smiled. "I intend to remind them. Any idea how long you'll have to stay in England?"

"Three weeks at most. I'm going to Manchester and Birmingham, then to Edinburgh. That was Lord Broadhurst's suggestion. After that I'm off to Paris."

"You'll be easier there," he said.

"Do I seem uneasy here?"

"Yes, you do, damned if I know why." He put on his coat and came to kiss her. He took her hands and pulled her up, putting his arms around her. "I'll miss you," he said, "come home soon."

"I will. Kiss my baby for me."

He stopped in the corridor when he had closed the door behind him. Miss her? That didn't begin to describe it. He always hated leaving her, but it was worse when he did not leave her safe at home. He shook his head. As if home made any difference. Ema was the same no matter where she was—evanescent, the core of her always somewhere just beyond his reach.

Ema left London the same day, glad to escape from the city. She was depressed by the provincial drabness of Manchester and Birmingham and worked steadily, finishing her interviews in a week. Edinburgh was a welcome change and she felt her spirits rise as soon as she arrived. She had been there only once before, to buy summer clothes for her voyage to New York in 1919.

I was better at mental discipline then than I am now, she thought en route to her hotel. She could not help confronting the reason why she and Julian had not even spoken to each other in London: Harding was the reason. Harding had to be protected. He was not practiced in deception.

But it isn't like that, she reminded herself. She and Julian did not meet for the thrill of deception, but simply to be together for a little while, to have privately what Sir James and Davina had made it impossible for them ever to have openly.

She took a long bath when she got to her hotel, made a few telephone calls, and was looking through her notes when the telephone rang.

"Darling?"

"Julian! Where are you?"

"In London. But I can be there tomorrow, even if it's only for a day."

"Oh, darling, yes, please come." She hesitated. "How long have you known I was in England?"

"Since you arrived. Broadhurst raved about an extraordinary newspaperwoman from New York with brains as well as beauty. I knew it was you before he mentioned your name. I heard about your projected series of interviews. You're wonderful, Ema, you get better and better at everything you do!"

She wished she could have seen his face when he said that. "How did you find me here?"

"Broadhurst again, when I returned from Paris—I had some urgent business at the bank for Father." He sounded hurried. "I have to run, darling, I'll see you tomorrow."

Anticipation made her wakeful throughout the night, and she rose early and tried to work on her notes while she waited for him. Those waiting hours were always the same, like a familiar perfume or a magic elixir that made her heart sing and her body crave to see him again, to feel his arms around her. She was still in her negligee when he arrived; she always wanted him to make love to her the moment he touched her; it was only then that she could be completely herself.

She lay looking at him afterward. The taut, strained look had faded, like the scars on his body. He was still very slender, but he had filled out of late. His face and arms had a touch of sun—from working in the garden, he said—and except for the widening streaks of gray in his hair, he looked very like he had on the day he walked into the bank in Paris.

"Do I?" he said, smiling down at her when she told him so. "So do you. I was such a bleak character until I met you." He kissed her. "My darling heart, you gave me the only real springtime there was. You still do."

She drew him down to her, missing him already. "Come to France, Julian, I'll be on the Riviera looking for a summer villa. It's still off-season. We could have a few days together."

He shook his head. "Too risky, Ema. You must be careful."

She guessed that Broadhurst must have told him about Harding, a man Julian already knew by reputation, but she did not say so. The two men must not meet. "Germany, then?"

"Yes, Germany, for as long as we can. I can count the days we've spent together. Not nearly enough, but for me there's a lifetime in every one. I love you, Emalie, I love you. All ways," and his arms went around her, "and always."

When he left they had arranged to meet in Munich and drive to a town too far off the beaten track for any of the sophisticated travelers who might recognize them. The prospect made their parting a little easier, and Emanuelle rushed through her interviews in Edinburgh and left for Paris two days ahead of schedule, as if traveling toward their meeting would make it come faster.

# 61

The flagstone terrace of the villa on St.-Jean-Cap-Ferrat overlooked the Mediterranean, and it was there that Ema ordered a special farewell dinner served at summer's end. Kate and Spencer and their three sons—Skip, Emmett, and Paul—were there, along with Emanuelle, Harding, Dana, and Danielle.

The summer of 1936 was the best Ema could remember, with all the people she loved most—save one, for she had not seen Julian again since June—together in the unspoiled beauty of the French Riviera. Yet she was eager to get back to New York. She had been busy writing her articles on the women of England, Scotland, France, and Belgium, and filing regular society columns on Riviera high life, as well; but she missed the hubbub of New York. There was too much time for memory and introspection here in the pervasive quiet of sea and sky—and the outbreak of civil war in Spain made her uneasy: Spain shared a border with France.

"I wanted to go to Spain," she said when the children had gone to bed and they were having a nightcap in the lounge, "but of course that's impossible now."

"I still can't figure out which side is which," Kate complained.

"Neither, it appears, can they," Danielle said. With her usual industry she had mastered English in order to make her secretarial school more competitive.

"Ask Harding," Ema said. "He has it all straight."

Harding collected his thoughts for a moment. "The situation, vastly simplified, is this. The monarchy—one of the most oppressive in Europe—fell in 'thirty-one and Spain became a republic. The Republican government is a mixed bag—leftists, Socialists, Communists—the vast majority of them idealists trying to make a democracy out of a seventeenth-century feudal kingdom."

"Some of those idealists are anarchists!" Kate said.

Harding shook his head. "The anarchists are against *all* organized government, including the Republic; they'd bring it down if they could. Unfortunately the government itself hasn't yet agreed on the best way to achieve land and labor reform in Spain, although they've made a start."

"They need time!" Spencer said. "You don't make a democracy overnight."

Harding agreed. "And despite its troubles, the Republican government was reelected again this year. That was when the old establishment rose in an attempt to reinstate the monarchy, and a civil war started. On one side are the Loyalists, that is, loyal to the Republic. On the other side are the monarchists, the church, and most of the army; they say they're fighting to preserve the Spanish nation—some call themselves Nationalists."

"And General Franco?"

"He led the military rebellion. And I think he'll let the Falange—the Spanish Fascist party—join him, along with anyone else who'll help reinstate the old regime. F for Falange, F for Fascists, F for Franco." Harding went to the bar for another brandy. "I'm opposed to fascism."

"Even though the Spanish government is Communist?" Spencer asked him.

Harding nodded. "Even though. Because this is a uniquely Spanish struggle, not part of the Russian revolution. A Spanish Communist isn't a Russian Communist. Or a Stalinist. People sense that. It's why the Loyalists have found such strong support in America, regardless of the Neutrality Act. People know the Loyalists need help, that they have nothing to fight with but spirit."

He glanced at Emanuelle. "Still, I want to know what the Soviets would demand in return for aid to the Loyalists before I commit the *Star* either way." He sat down beside Ema again. "So I've arranged to go to Spain."

"No!" she said, putting down her drink. "It's too dangerous. Harding."

He took her hand. "Ema, I won't go where there's any danger. I'll be able to see what the political picture is *before* the real fighting starts."

Ema bit her lower lip nervously. "Then I'll stay on here until you come back. Dana can go home with Kate and Spencer. Miss Prescott's going to meet us at the ship, anyway."

"Dana won't want to leave without you!" Kate said. "Anyway, you can't sit alone in this villa and wait."

"Darling . . ." Harding began.

"I'll go to Paris with Danielle," Ema said stiffly. "I'm used to Paris, especially when there's a war on."

"Ema, it happened a long time ago," Danielle said in French. "*Calme-toi.*"

Ema looked at her and nodded after a moment. She turned to Harding.

"I'm sorry, I don't know why I'm carrying on like this. Go, if you must, but for God's sake be careful."

When he left she was only half convinced that there was no danger, particularly for journalists, since both sides wanted favorable publicity and foreign support.

"Your Harding is an admirable man," Danielle said, boarding the train for Paris that afternoon.

Ema nodded. "And like most men he dashes off to the first war that's going."

"It's the nature of the beast. Mankind is combative."

"Not *all* men. Not women. I haven't gone off to war, have I?"

"*Ma chère*, you must tend to your private war with yourself."

"Danielle, please, none of those cryptic observations just as you're leaving. We'll argue about it next time I'm in Paris."

Ema waved until the train was out of sight, glad that Danielle knew nothing about Julian or his resurrection, or about Drew. She went back to the villa to direct the packing, and two days later she drove to Genoa with Dana and the Atwoods to board an Italian liner for New York. It was an uneventful crossing, in that end-of-holiday atmosphere of summer regret and winter anticipation, but she was anxious about Harding.

They were often separated by business obligations, but this time it was different. He was in a country at war; he was in danger. She had not been anxious in quite this way for a long time—and never about Harding. Again she felt that confusing sense of déjà vu.

# 62

"I miss Daddy," Dana said disconsolately one night soon after school had started.

"So do I, darling."

"What are Fascists, anyway?"

"Briefly, people who don't want other people to think for themselves." Ema looked at her daughter, wondering why she asked.

Dana's lowering expression was comical, she looked so much like Harding. "No wonder Daddy's against them, then, they must be worse than the reds."

"Where did you hear all that?"

"At dancing school. Claire Blessing said the *Star* ought to be called the Red Star and Daddy is a Communist, just like the president. I thought Communists were bad."

"*C'est ridicule!*" Ema was annoyed. "Those big girls never even bother to say hello to you little ones, much less talk politics to you! Your father's not a Communist! He's as American as the Blessings. He'll explain it all when he comes home and you tell Claire Blessing I said so."

"But when is Daddy coming?" Dana sighed. "I don't like school very much this term."

"I'm sure you'd be happier in England." When Dana made no reply Ema went on. "Cheer up, darling, we'll spend the weekend in the city. We'll have tea at the Plaza and see some new movies."

"And go to the Metropolitan? I want to see the Egyptians again."

Emanuelle hugged her. "Of course, we'll go anywhere you like."

Dana didn't have as many school friends as Ema had hoped, but that was because she was intelligent enough to be selective. Ema was glad of the time they spent together. In a few years—come hell, high water, or Harding—Dana would be in England.

She called Tillie Blessing the next day. "Your daughter's bothering mine," Ema said, repeating what Dana had told her. "And Claire can have heard it only at your hearthside."

"Nonsense," Tillie said too smoothly. "Everybody's keen on politics these days. Claire could have picked it up anywhere."

"Then kindly tell her where to put it, at least where Dana's concerned— or I might print some Blessing items I've picked up."

"Now, now," said Tillie, backing down. "I'll talk to her. There's no need for you to behave like Lady Macbeth; it's not your style."

"When it comes to Dana, Tillie, you ain't seen nothin' yet," Ema said, and hung up. "Nasty old bitch!" Ema muttered. "I despise her as much as she despises me."

When Harding did come back from Spain a few weeks later, he was committed to the Loyalist cause. "Although I saw some things I didn't like," he told Emanuelle. "I don't think there's a church in Spain that hasn't been vandalized."

"That's because the church was as oppressive as the monarchy in Spain. It always has been, even before the Inquisition."

Harding shook his head gloomily. "There have been random executions on both sides already. But no matter how people try to disguise it, this isn't a religious fight."

"The press calls it a revolution," Ema said. "Is it?"

"All the factions want far-reaching reforms, even the Spanish Fascists. But the government and the Communists insist the revolution must wait until the war is won; and the Anarchists and Socialists insist that the only way to win the war is to extend the revolution. It's a civil war within a civil war."

"Is it true that women have been given the kind of freedom unimaginable in Spain before?"

Harding nodded. "Abortion on demand, prostitution abolished, women replacing men as workers, deputies, soldiers." He raised an eyebrow. "The anarchists disapprove of marriage, but the mothers of Spain are appalled by free love."

"I can sympathize with the mothers of Spain," Ema said. "What happened?"

"They invented something they call revolutionary weddings." He shook his head. "But what's happening in Spain can't be compared to the Russian revolution. In the first place, the Republic was legally elected— twice. And this is a purely Spanish battle between a Republican government and a disgruntled pack of would-be dictators. Anyone who values democracy will support the Loyalists."

"You'd better explain all of it to Dana. The Blessing girl at dancing school said you were a Communist and the paper ought to be called the Red Star. Tillie put her up to it."

"I'll talk to Dana," he said. "She'll be hearing a lot more along the same lines, I'm afraid. The *Star* will openly advocate sending the Loyalists everything they need."

"You mean arms too?" Emanuelle asked. "Wouldn't that violate the Neutrality Act?"

"It's an untenable law. How can anyone be neutral on a shrinking planet? And I *do* mean everything—food, medical supplies, arms, even men. They're volunteering already."

"You're not!"

"No, my darling. I'm no warrior."

"Aren't you, Harding, when you advocate war?"

He looked at her, perplexed. "Ema, that's not true. I don't advocate war, I deplore it. But this fight will be waged no matter what I do, and now that the die is cast I'm bound to support those I believe to be right. Wouldn't you?"

She agreed with him, but Julian would have no part in it now, except to stop it in any way he could.

Emanuelle felt, uneasily, that she stood somewhere between the two men on the issue. And it made her face up to what she had never admitted before, that she stood between the two of them literally, touched by both, when up to now she had kept them rigidly apart.

She had to take a public stand on the issue, though, or forfeit her right to call herself a columnist. A few days later she handed Harding a column on women and war that reflected her confusion.

> Men are warlike by nature because they are so far removed from the life force once their part in it is over. They even transmit life in a moment of violent thrust. For them war is an outlet for the energy that women expend in bearing and raising children.
>
> And yet in all but mindless brawn women are much the stronger sex. They suffer more pain and discomfort than men in the ordinary course of their lives, but they manage to live in a hostile world without killing each other off at regular intervals. Women have never organized mass slaughters.
>
> The rare man who is a pacifist deserves respect. There is great moral courage in a man's refusal to glorify war, no matter what the provocation.
>
> But sometimes it seems that there is no other solution. Franco's attempt to overthrow the elected government of Spain *is* a gross provocation. The women of America, as the women of France, sup-

ported revolution in the name of freedom not so very
long ago. It is time for us to do so again.

We can help by raising money to send food, clothing, and medical supplies to the Loyalists, who are
fighting for a form of government that, like ours, respects the free expression of opposing points of view.

"Is this what you really think of men?" Harding asked, coming into her
office at the *Star* with the typed pages in his hand. "It seems a brutal
assessment."

Her father blundered once more into Ema's thoughts, and she avoided
Harding's eyes. She pulled on her gloves and concentrated on working
the soft leather well down on each finger. "It's not only what I think; it's
how they are."

"All men?"

"I think so," she said. "They just try to dominate in different ways."

"I never knew you felt that way," he said. His voice carried resentment
at being grouped with other men in Ema's eyes.

"It's an article," she replied with a shrug. "One has to overstate the case
for dramatic effect."

"You never do, that's what gives such impact to everything you write."
She made no reply, and he shook his head slightly and looked at the typed
pages again. "I can't tell from this whether you're supporting the Spanish Loyalists or world pacifism."

"It's an honest confusion. I think most people will find it hard to choose
in this one. No sane person wants war—or fascism." She was putting on
her coat. "I must go, Harding, I have an appointment at RSVP."

He turned the pages. "Well, we'll run it and your readers can take it in
whichever way suits them—but I'm killing that stuff about 'a moment of
violent thrust.' This is about politics, not sex."

Ema stopped on her way out the door and whirled around to face him.
"That's what *you* think!" she said angrily. "This is *my* column. It's meant
to say what *I* think. And *I* think that one way or another, everything's
about the war between the sexes."

"So Dr. Freud insists. But the public isn't ready to have the life force
thrust upon the women's page."

"The public be damned," Ema said heatedly. "And you, too, if you
touch my copy."

He ignored the last, trying to veer away from a serious argument.
"Who said that, about the public?"

"William H. Vanderbilt and I. He's dead and I'm late." She stalked out
of the office.

Harding watched her go, as angry as she was. She had always objected to his changing a single word she wrote, but never so vehemently as this. He looked at the article in his hand for a long moment, then took a blue pencil from his vest pocket and struck out the offending line.

"Damn it," he said softly, "at least I still run the *Star!*"


Even without the line the column produced bags of mail, far more than Emanuelle's articles supporting birth control a year ago. Angry men wrote about bloodthirsty females in history: Medea, Messalina, Isabella and her Inquisition, Bloody Mary. Some women protested that Ema's ideas were blasphemous, quoting Ephesians 5:24. Others, more practical, argued that women owed obedience to men in return for men's support and protection. But the majority of women sided with her.

"We can keep this going for weeks," Harding said. "We'll print all points of view."

"Except mine," Ema told him.

"Ema! It was a question of policy!"

"No, it was a question of power."

"I'd like to know why we argue all the time."

"You're in a better position to change that than I am."

The argument was swept off the women's page, at least, early in December, when Edward VIII of England abdicated to marry an American divorcee. The country was once more awash in a tidal wave of romance.

"He can't reign without the help and support of the woman he loves! It's absurd!" Edison Carter said in Ema's office at the *Star*. "Everyone wants to see this abdication as a glorious sacrifice."

"How do you see it?" Ema asked him.

"As a clever way for the Brits to get rid of a Nazi sympathizer."

"Edison, for God's sake! You have no foundation for that."

The dapper society reporter snorted. "He's said often enough in private that he admires Hitler."

"He never said it as a matter of policy, so keep it out of your column," Ema warned. "Harding would be first on line to sue you."

"Never fear, Ema darling, I'm not about to kill the golden goose who lays so well, although what la Simpson has that charms him so, I'll never know. She's a frightful creature, cold as a witch's tit. She'll lead him a merry dance because he didn't make her queen of England, wait and see." He put on his bowler hat.

"Damn it, Edison, you're unfair! How do you know what really made her what she is? How can anyone know that about another person?"

"Ah, well, my business is gossip, not psychoanalysis. *Au revoir*, my pretty, I'm off to El Morocco to gather new scandals. Keep on defending the fair sex; someone has to when a woman just cost a king his throne!"

Ema watched him parade across the City Room, then went back to work. She was as busy as ever, but she was anxious, too, and unsettled. She felt she had suddenly lost control of her life, that some nameless force she could not identify threatened, like a whirlwind, to destroy everything she treasured.

# 63

"My God!" Julian exclaimed. "It's either ancient Rome or a Wagnerian opera!"

He put a protective arm around Emanuelle as a hush fell over the crowd in the stadium, and in the distance, through the quaint medieval streets of Nuremberg, came the crack of jackboots against the cobblestones. The rumbling tattoo of drums echoed their rhythm and carried it to the stadium crowd, waiting breathlessly. Then a blare of martial music heralded the entrance of the storm troopers, and a roar rose from the crowd. By torchlight the men goose-stepped into the stadium, carrying bloodred banners with hooked crosses at their centers and beaked bronze eagles atop their staffs. Scores of the same floodlit banners glowed imperiously from niches in the colonnade of the vast arena. One hundred thousand Germans welcomed them in a frenzy of adoration while overhead searchlights stabbed the night sky to a height of twenty thousand feet. It was the last, climactic night of the Nazi party rally.

The seats from which Ema and Julian watched had been reserved for them by Major Siegfried Brand, Ema's official escort to the rally she had come to report. She would see, he had promised, proof of the German devotion to its führer. She would take back to her country the glorious message of the new Germany, strong, proud, and with faith in the future. His attitude to Julian, who had arrived that afternoon, was the same; he called him Major Saxon.

Ema was chilled to find herself hypnotized by the drums and the trumpets and the delirium of the spectators, their faces alight with a near-religious ecstasy.

"It's madness," Ema whispered to Julian when an expectant hush had settled over the throng.

"A contagious madness," Julian added grimly.

A mighty ovation greeted Adolf Hitler as he came to the rostrum. Above him soared a burnished metal eagle sixty feet high, wings outstretched, a drawn sword clutched in its talons. It lent ferocity and stature to the man below as he began to speak. He used his voice with the force of an evil baton, electrifying the air, rousing and controlling the crowd so that, on cue, it bellowed with a single voice or was instantly stilled.

Major Brand's face, as he shouted "Sieg, Heil!" was a mirror-image of every other face, ablaze with the sensuous ecstasy of utter surrender.

The torches, the banners, the ranks of warriors—for these were more than soldiers—were pagan. The Germans were transported, but to Ema it was fearsome and Julian, too, was troubled; she could see it in his face. She had been bombed and threatened by Germans, and Julian had fought them face-to-face, but neither had seen anything to equal these mass responses, this tribal bloodlust tied to death and sacrifice by the black wreaths and the death-head insignia on Major Brand's cap. He was a member of the SS, Hitler's elite guard, which also ran the state police.

It was very late by the time the major drove Ema and Julian to where her car was parked on the outskirts of Nuremberg, repeating as he left that he would be at Ema's disposal if she decided to visit Berlin.

They drove toward the quiet of Ema's inn near Munich, reflecting on what they had seen.

"All Hitler's talk is of peace," Emanuelle said, "but what he does points to war. How do you stop a man like that?"

"He's a bully," Julian said. "If we stand firm, he'll back down without a fight."

Ema shivered, still oppressed by the spectacle. "I'm sorry we went."

"I'm not," Julian said. "It's the kind of thing I want to know and talk about at home. A threat of war exists—but war has always existed. We have to find ways to avoid it, ways that will have an effect on people like these."

"Julian, do you know what I think? I think we've waited too long for this time together to share any more of it with the Nazis."

"Then we'll make our own pact," Julian said, putting his arm around her. "We won't mention Hitler again while we're here."

But the turmoil in Europe filtered into every conversation they had. Harding was in Spain again. As he had predicted, Franco had accepted the support of the Fascists—the Spanish Falange, the Germans, and the Italians—and the civil war had clearly become a testing ground for the awesome Nazi arsenal of guns and planes.

And Drew, although still at Oxford, had started flying lessons right after German planes demolished the civilian Basque town called

Guernica five months ago. "I like flying," Drew had said, but Julian was convinced that outrage, not pleasure, motivated his son. "I made him promise not to run off to Spain to join the Loyalists, at least not before I get back."

The very houses and fences they passed sprouted Nazi flags like poisonous mushrooms, intruding on the peace of the countryside. It seemed to Ema that love was the only escape.

"Long live love and lovers," she said as they lay together the next morning, drowsy and content.

"Amen to that—even the Duke and Duchess of Windsor."

"Yes, poor things. How the British establishment hates her! Is she so terrible?"

"Have you never met her?"

"No, but I'd like to, so I can judge for myself. Do you know how many American women dream of marrying into the English nobility—and even they never aspire to a king! But Edison's doing the society column almost exclusively now; I cover the political stories."

"The Windsors will be here next month, on a tour of Germany. I may be here too. If you can come, you'll meet them."

Ema looked at him in surprise. "Why on earth would they tour Germany, after the rumors about the duke's admiration for Hitler?" She shook her head. "And is it wise for you to be seen with a suspected Nazi sympathizer, Julian?"

"I think his admiration is more for what Hitler's accomplished. Germany is in far better shape than we are since the Nazis—"

"No," she said, rolling over to lie on top of him. "No Nazis. I don't want to talk about them, about anyone but us." She kissed him to push away the strangers who had invaded their bed. She moved against him, letting him feel the heat and warmth of her, then she took him into her, rising and sinking on him in a frantic need to escape, so eager for climax that it eluded her, and he stopped the movement of her hips, withdrew, and turned her onto her back.

"Emalie, what is it?"

"I'm afraid, Julian."

"What of, darling?" He gentled her, kissing her hair, her eyes, her cheeks.

"That something will separate us and take even the little we have away from us."

"No," he said, cradling her against him. "We gave up a lifetime for moments like this. Nothing will take them away."

She could believe that when he held her, when he touched her. There was bliss in his touch, and she lay back and let desire mount at its own

pace until she felt that moment of breathless quiet near the crest of fulfillment, that pause before the final surge when all but joy was left behind.
*"J'ai le coeur joie,"* she whispered, clinging to him.

But the next day a telegram from England shattered her fragile happiness. Julian's youngest daughter was very ill, and Davina called him
home.

"How did she know you were here?" Emanuelle asked.

"I have to leave an address these days," Julian said, "with Father fading
so fast. I'm sorry, darling, but I must go to Jenny, you understand."

Of course she understood—far better than he. She was certain he
would find his youngest daughter completely recovered by the time he
reached Stridings. This was just Davina's way of demonstrating her
power to take him away from Ema whenever she chose.

They parted at the station in Munich, Julian for England and Ema to
drive their hired car to Berlin. She had decided to see Major Brand about a
project she had in mind, but she went as much to fill in the time before
Harding was due to arrive in London the next day. She would meet him
there and they would sail home together.

She did not enjoy the drive to Berlin. Depression over Julian's departure overwhelmed her. It was nothing new; she had always known there
was no hope for them beyond the little they had, but she had known it
with her mind and had been able to reason it into a corner. Now she knew
it with her heart and soul and they were not amenable to reason. Julian
still owned those, but he inhabited them too rarely. She felt more desolate
than she had in a long time.

In Berlin she turned in the car and spent an afternoon with Major Brand
in his black beflagged Daimler, touring the Third Reich's new buildings
and monuments and statues. She felt threatened by their colossal size.

"I'd like to come back with my photographer," she said when they went
back to Brand's office in the imposing building occupied by the Ministry
of Propaganda on the Wilhelm Platz. "I have an idea for a series of articles."

"Ah, but we have excellent photographers of our own, Miss Beranger.
There is no need to bring yours." The inference was clearly that it would
not be permitted. His manner was indulgent; obviously he did not take
women seriously as journalists. He looked far more forbidding seated
behind his desk than he had seemed throughout the rally; there was
none of that wild elation in his face. He was very blond, sternly handsome, and immaculate to the point of sterility. He had a thin face, with
prominent cheekbones and a wide mouth that turned down at the
corners.

"What subject did you have in mind?" he inquired, his pale blue eyes
examining her. She had the feeling that the question was suggestive.

"Women in the new Germany. I'd like to interview them, all ages, all walks of life."

She saw she had aroused his interest now. "An excellent idea! I am sure something can be arranged—if you can give me a little time?"

"I wouldn't be free to come until after the new year, sometime in the spring."

"Excellent, excellent. I shall make the arrangements and advise you in New York." He took some information from her and, after another pause during which his blue eyes resumed a speculative warmth, he asked her to dine with him.

"Thank you, but I'm leaving tonight for London."

"A pity," Major Brand announced. "Still, we shall see each other when you return."

She nodded deferentially. If it would get her in to do these articles, she wasn't above extending a vague promise of unspecified favors. She had done it before and never delivered.

He rose and came around to her chair. His white teeth showed in a vulpine smile, and he raised her hand to his lips. She felt the same kind of horrified fascination as she had at the rally. There was the same ruthlessness about him.

She forgot about the major as soon as she boarded the train. She and Julian would have traveled back separately, in any case, but the lonely journey seemed a fitting punctuation to their ruined holiday. It was an effort to shift her mood in the taxi to the Connaught.

"Harding?" she called when she was shown into their suite. Her voice sounded strange, even to her.

"In the bath," he called back. "It'll take at least three more baths in Rinso to get me clean."

She walked to the bathroom door and put her head in. He waved a soapy sponge at her. "Hello, darling! How was life among the Nazis?" He thought she looked strained.

"Disturbing. How was life among the Loyalists?"

"The same." He took a nail brush from the rack and scrubbed his hands. Something was wrong, but it would do more harm than good to ask what it was. She would tell only if it was something she chose to tell; that was what had always plagued him. "I'll be glad to get home," he said.

"Yes," Ema agreed, the knot in her throat beginning to dissolve. "So will I." She managed a smile.

"We've been invited to Lord Broadhurst's tonight," Harding said. "All right?"

"Fine. Keep scrubbing, I'm going to call Dana."

"Do, she's waiting."

"You called her?"

"The minute I got in."

"You're a good man, Harding Ellis," she said, meaning it, and it was hard to keep her voice steady. "You deserve to have everything you want."

"I have everything I want," Harding said, espousing the falsehood again.

And I, Emanuelle thought, going to the telephone, have all I'm ever going to get.

# 64

"Hitler raves on about the glorious place of women in the Third Reich," Emanuelle said later that night to the little circle gathered around Lord Broadhurst. "I want to see just how much glory there is in Germany. From what I hear, motherhood is all they're selling now."

Across the magnificent drawing room she saw her reflection in a towering mirror framed in carved and gilded wood. She was glad she had chosen black velvet and pearls; it was dramatically different from the other women's pastel silks.

Englishwomen have class, she thought, but most of them look like doilies.

"But will they let you in?" Broadhurst asked.

"Oh, yes, they love publicity. Dr. Goebbels spends about fifty million dollars a year on propaganda outside Germany. There are over three hundred German-language newspapers published abroad and he has financial holdings in as many foreign papers, if not more."

"I think it's a brilliant idea," Harding said. "As long as they don't suspect what my wife is really after."

Emanuelle smiled. "They think the sight of a baby addles a woman's wits."

"But it will take a lot of advance preparation," Broadhurst added. "And they won't let you wander round Germany without a nanny from the Ministry of Propaganda."

"There's plenty of time to prepare," Ema said. "I don't fancy tramping around Germany in the dead of winter. My nanny is a Major Siegfried Brand." Ema wrinkled her nose in distaste. "A pure Aryan type, of course, devoted to *Volk* and Wagner and *Deutschland über Alles*. I keep expecting him to wear a horned helmet and carry a spear."

Broadhurst had turned to include more guests in the circle. "Ah," he said to Harding, "here's someone you wanted to meet. Julian Saxon, Harding Ellis."

As if from a great distance, Ema watched while two hands she knew so intimately reached out and clasped. She looked at Julian's seal ring and the onyx with a diamond center she had given Harding, at two starched white cuffs and their gold cuff links, at the black broadcloth of two dinner jackets. She forced herself to raise her eyes and nod politely when Julian was introduced to her and again when Davina, her gilt blondness made more stunning by scarlet silk, said, "Charmed," in a cool murmur.

Why had Sir James permitted this? Ema wondered angrily. And then she realized that he was no longer omnipotent, that he could no longer protect her.

"I've heard a lot about you, Mr. Saxon," Harding said. "I admire your courage."

Davina's eyes met Ema's briefly, then turned back to the two men. She's enjoying this, Ema thought, wanting to run; but she stood without moving, clutching her glass as if it might contain a magic potion to make her invisible.

"Even though you disagree with my views," Julian said amicably, his dark eyes intent upon Harding.

"Of course," Harding said. "One thing has nothing to do with the other."

"I'm glad of that." Julian smiled. "His Lordship sometimes despairs of me."

"Not of you, Julian," Broadhurst countered, lofty and avuncular. "Rather of England's ability to defend herself if she should do as you propose and fail to rearm." Broadhurst looked around the circle. "Do you know that our war ministry's budget includes fodder for horses in the event of war? Horses! After what Mr. Ellis has seen in Spain, I don't think we can count on mounted cavalry to defend ourselves."

"Will the Loyalists lose, Mr. Ellis?" Julian addressed Harding as if the two men were alone in the room.

"I'm afraid so," Harding said. "American law forbids arms sales to warring nations—our ships are even prohibited from transporting them for third parties. And Russian matériel can't match what the Germans have developed."

Julian shook his head. "It will be a catastrophe if the Spanish Republic falls."

"Precisely!" Broadhurst said. "And we must avoid the same catastrophe here."

"We're not threatened by civil war, Milord," Julian said. "In any case, I can't support rearmament; it's always a prelude to war." His eyes went back to Harding again.

"Darling," Davina said, "not here."

Julian acquiesced gracefully. "My wife is right, the place is ill-chosen. My apologies." He bowed, a bow Emanuelle had first seen long ago, under the lamplight in the Place Vendôme. The muscles of her neck felt tight, as if she had not moved since then.

"Another time?" Harding said. "I'd like to continue this discussion."

"With pleasure," Julian returned, and the women's eyes met again.

"It's madly exciting," Davina said to Emanuelle with another charming smile, "to be a hero's wife."

Bitch, Ema thought, you know he hates that kind of thing.

As if he had heard her, Julian's manner changed. "I make no claim to heroism, as my wife knows very well. I don't trust heroics and I have no faith in gallantry."

"Sorry, darling," Davina said with the kind of smile a woman gives a talented but overly modest child of whom she is very proud.

She glitters with pride of possession, Ema thought, as if he were her rubies.

"You mustn't sell gallantry short," Harding said. "It comes out of what's best in a man. It's what brought us out of the caves."

"Here, here," Broadhurst rumbled enthusiastically. "Your Victoria Cross was gallantly won, Julian."

"Do you think it sane to send anyone to war for a piece of beribboned bronze?" Again Julian spoke directly to Harding.

"No," Harding said, "only in defense of a good cause."

"And who is to judge which cause is good?"

Dinner was announced and the little group separated with obvious relief and moved toward the dining room with the twenty other guests.

Ema, going in on Broadhurst's arm, wondered if she would get through the rest of the evening. She was seated at Broadhurst's right, directly across from Julian. At the other end of the long, richly decorated table, Harding and Davina faced each other.

It was an enormous effort for Ema to make conversation, but fortunately Broadhurst talked most of the time, asking Julian all about the spectacle at Nuremberg. She watched Julian's lips move without hearing what he said. She had never done this simple thing with him before; she had never sat across a dinner table from him with people they both knew, and it shook her, like a nightmare within a dream.

"How did you find Germany, Mrs. Ellis?" Broadhurst said, turning to her.

"Berlin is spectacular—the new buildings and the statues are all of colossal size. They're meant to be intimidating, and they are." She was relieved that the conversation then switched to art. Her head throbbed violently, but she turned politely to speak to the man on her right, as dinner party etiquette required. At the other end of the table Davina seemed to be amusing Harding and Lady Broadhurst, but her blue eyes turned often toward Ema and Julian.

Naturally, Emanuelle thought, a real lady can rise to any occasion. She felt gauche and awkward again, as if she had accomplished nothing, as helpless as she had been at fourteen. It was hard for her to breathe, to get air down to the bottom of her lungs.

The meal went on interminably, course after course, hors d'oeuvres, soup, fish, roast lamb, chocolate mousse, and cheeses. She barely touched any of it. Another age passed while the men retired for brandy and cigars and Ema, consigned to the drawing room with the other women for coffee, avoided Davina. The separation of the sexes after dinner made her even more furious tonight. It wasn't to spare the women cigar smoke, it was to spare their smaller brains the effort of serious conversation—and Julian and Harding were certainly talking to each other.

They were still deep in conversation when the men came in from the library, but Ema reminded Harding that they were sailing the next day and so she escaped at last. She leaned back in the limousine and closed her eyes.

"I like Saxon," Harding said. "There's something very fine about him, quite aside from his spectacular face."

"Yes," Ema said, "I agree."

"He has integrity, no matter how unrealistic his ideas are. He's the kind of man I once imagined leading the Charge of the Light Brigade."

"And dying," Ema said. "They all died."

"I know, that's the other side of it. Still, I hope he'll come to America."

She opened her eyes and turned to him in surprise. "Is he planning to?"

"I suggested it. He's been approached already and he's considering it. We've got a lot of people at home screaming for disarmament, neutrality, isolation—but no one to argue the pacifist position as honestly as he does."

"But you don't agree with him!" Emanuelle said, mystified. "Why would you want such a formidable opponent?"

"Because I prefer peace to war—if it's possible. He thinks it is. Maybe he has some ideas we haven't thought of." Harding smiled. "Anyway, the only worthy opponent is a formidable one."

The limousine stopped at the Connaught and they went upstairs. "I'd like a brandy," Ema said. "I have a terrible headache. I think I've caught a cold."

"You've been looking flushed and uncomfortable all evening."

"Really? I didn't think it showed."

"Not to anyone else, but I can always tell when you're not feeling up to snuff. Get into bed with the brandy and I'll get a hot water bottle and some tea from the maid."

Presently he got into bed beside her and put an arm around her.

"Harding, I really feel rotten."

"I'm not going to ravish you, Ema, I just want to feel you close to me again, it's been two weeks." He took her hand. "You *are* sick; your head's hot and your hands are cold as ice. I hope you'll be well enough to sail tomorrow."

"Nothing will keep me from boarding that ship!" After a moment she added, "What did you think of his wife?"

"Beautiful, of course, but brittle."

"What do you think she's like in bed?" It was a question she often asked about the women they met together.

"Carnivorous. A man would have to check when it was over to be sure he still had his balls."

"But exciting?"

"If you like making love to a cobra." He kissed her cheek. "I prefer lush, warm velvet, like you. Now go to sleep before I do ravish you."

She lay awake for a long time. The evening had been a wrenching experience. It was devastating to see the only two men she had ever cared for take each other's measure and find it good. In another kind of society it could have made her proud and happy, but people would make a nasty scandal of it and that would be unbearable, for her and for Harding. The rigid walls she had so carefully constructed had been breached and she felt threatened. She wanted to run for home as quickly as she could.

She slept badly and woke with a sore throat and a heavy chest cold, but she flatly refused to postpone their sailing. She spent the entire crossing in bed and Harding, working on a series of editorials for the *Star,* slept in the living room of their suite until, at last, they were home and life took on a semblance of normalcy.


"Oh, my God," Kate said when Ema told her about the encounter at Broadhurst's.

"I'm sorry, Kate, but I had to warn you. Harding's bound to mention him. He liked Julian very much."

"What are you going to do now?"

"Nothing. What can I do?"

"I mean if Julian comes here?"

"Fall in with whatever Harding arranges."

"I hope he doesn't come," Kate said. "He must have known how upset you were."

Ema thought not. Once Julian had agreed to deception, the precise extent of it was irrelevant to him. It was an honest approach and a rational one: infidelity was infidelity, whether or not he and Harding knew each other. Secret lovers must always surrender some rights, among them jealousy and exclusive possession.

But three months later the news that Julian was on his way unnerved her. It was not guilt she felt, but the same foreboding that something outside themselves would tear them irrevocably apart.

I won't let that happen! she told herself angrily. They've taken enough from us already!

Her foreboding did not lighten when, in March, Germany invaded Austria, and Harding, waiting until they were alone in their bedroom at Silvermoor, told Ema he wanted to borrow Ken Conan.

"Of course. What day do you need him?"

"I need him a few weeks." He went to undress and came back from his dressing room with his briefcase. "I want to take Ken to Europe with me—Austria first, then Spain."

She had watched him sort papers from his briefcase like this many times before, but this time it disturbed her. "Harding, what good will that do?"

"I want to see what's going on for myself." He tapped a thick file. "I have some investments in Germany and I want to liquidate them if Hitler's appetite for expansion still hasn't been satisfied."

"The Germans won't let you bring your own photographer," she said irrelevantly. "I already asked."

"We'll still try—and the Spanish will. Ken wants to do it in the worst way."

She looked at him mutely, really frightened.

"Ema, there are horrible things going on all over Europe and every attempt to call attention to them is glossed over by a policy of total appeasement. People ought to know the facts, pleasant or not, before they make up their minds."

"And of course you're the only one who can tell them." She stopped arguing and shook her head. Nothing she said would stop him. "What about Julian Saxon?"

"I wired him that I won't be here when he arrives, but he wired back that he can't postpone. His lecture tour's already booked." He shrugged, going back to his papers. "The Anschluss with Austria weakens his position a lot. Well, I'll be sorry to miss him, but if he needs any help, you'll be here."

She sat on the edge of the bed, her hands clasped. "Be careful, Harding, please, please be careful."

He looked at her and put the files down. "Don't look so desolate, darling," he said, coming to kneel in front of her.

She cradled his head against her breasts. "I can't help being frightened. Something might happen to you."

"Nothing will," he said, "I'm too mean, only the good die young." He kissed her, first comforting, then ardent.

"Ema?" He seemed uncertain.

"Don't say anything, just hold me."

He opened her satin peignoir and pressed her gently down on the bed, still kneeling beside it. He rose to let his lips travel up the length of her body and down again to linger persistently between her thighs until he felt her trembling response. "I'll never let you go, Ema," he said when she lay still again, his cheek pillowed on her belly, his arms stretched wide to cover her. "You're mine, you know."

"Yes, Harding, I know I am." Still tingling with pleasure, she held out her arms to him, her eyes closed.

He moved and lay beside her on the bed, holding her against him while he opened her thighs again. When at last he went into her, was clasped by her, felt another rolling shudder start deep inside her, she heard what he was saying without heeding it.

He made love to her in that seeking way he sometimes did, as if Ema were more vulnerable in love, as if the phallus could plumb depths that always eluded him. Then he was silent, moving with her until climax overwhelmed them and they slept.


After he had sailed the next day, she went to her office at the *Star* and tried to work, but she was thinking that in the very act of having her he had said, "I want you, Ema," as if he had yet to take her. She gave him all she had to give him, but he wanted more. She was still thinking about it, feeling torn apart, when the telephone rang.

"I never see you since you went all political," Tillie Blessing said.

"It's nice to be missed."

"You'll never guess what I heard from the pacifist contingent," Tillie went on, "you know, the ladies who want to ban toy soldiers and Decoration Day."

"Come on, Tillie, you're dying to tell me."

"Remember that perfectly gorgeous Englishman you invited to my ball in Venice?"

"I invited a lot of gorgeous Englishmen, as I recall."

"Not like this one—Julian Saxon, the one with the bitchy blond wife."

"What did his wife ever do to you?"

"Nothing in particular, but as you have cause to know, I can tell a bitch when I see one."

"Well, it takes one to know one," Ema said. "Anyway, what about the Saxons?"

"He's coming to do some lectures." Tillie paused for effect and was disappointed. "Or did you know that already?"

"We met the Saxons in London. Harding told me he might come."

"Did he? Well, never mind that. I want Saxon to be guest of honor at a peace party."

"Then ask them. The ice is broken, the Saxons have already been your guests."

"She isn't coming. In a delicate condition, I understand. I can just imagine them together, like the gods on Olympus. Fascinating, isn't it?"

"Mesmerizing."

"Will you cover the party for the *Star*? I won't have that nasty little pansy Edison in my house!"

"Have I ever refused you anything?" Emanuelle said. "I'll be there, just let me know the date. Now I have a call waiting. Good-bye, Tillie."

She put down the receiver and sat looking out of her office window. Leave us alone, she said to something far more threatening than Tillie Blessing, damn it, why can't you leave us alone.

# 65

Julian stood at the lectern waiting for the applause to die away. Even at nine in the morning the enormous concert hall had filled with women who rarely rang for their breakfast trays before ten.

To them he's Sir Lancelot and King Arthur, Emanuelle thought, and they're not even in love with him.

He was, of course, an extraordinarily handsome man, but it was more than that. He was an irresistible combination of the good, the true, and the beautiful, even though most people preferred to admire such a man from a comfortable distance. Suddenly Ema grasped that living with a man like Julian was in itself a punishment for Davina and Sir James: Julian trusted them completely and his trust was a constant rebuke for what they had done.

I am of baser metal, Ema thought, but Julian doesn't know that. He would never forgive *me*, either.

Julian had no idea what she was really like, where she came from, who she was. He would never understand what had made her surrender Drew for Drew's sake and—she made herself admit it—her own. Julian would not be proud of some of the things she had done since—still contemplated doing—in order to be worthy of him and her son. She would never be their equal. But Dana could be, Dana could surpass Drew.

Tillie Blessing, sitting in the first row next to Ema, whispered, "Thomas in his prime was like that."

As well compare Galahad to Torquemada, Ema thought.

Finally the applause died away and Julian began to speak, and now it was his integrity that held people. It had ruined both their lives and others besides. Except for it, he would never have said good-bye to Emalie in Paris in the first place. What made him human and vulnerable was his love for her, his one infringement of the rules. He had to struggle between duty and desire like everyone else; he had to lose too.

"I believe there is a political solution," he was saying, and that intimate quality of his voice was more seductive than any booming oratory. "And we must find it.

"Once it begins, war has nothing to do with bugles and banners and parades, nor even with principles. War has to do with death, only death. It is brutal beyond belief, beyond anything you can imagine. It makes one despair for our species that it has such madness in it. War is not an acceptable way for men to die."

His voice dropped even lower, into memory. "You can smell a battlefield long before you see it because of what has happened there. The second time we fought in Flanders—and the third and the fourth—the shell bursts threw up bodies of men fallen in battle the time before, beckoning with rotting fingers for the living to join the dead." A faint shudder seized him before he went on, his hands holding tight to the lectern. "A generation of young men perished that way—French, British, German. And for what? I shall tell you.

"We couldn't find clean ground to bury our dead. For fifty yards around our trenches the earth was alive with maggots feasting on the old dead. It was the maggots, not the British or the Germans, who owned that pitiful few yards of ruined earth, taken and lost and retaken at the price of so much precious young life. When they hold parades and make speeches, think of that."

He leaned forward and Ema thought of William Poyndexter's golden head beneath the muddy water and Tony Holland with a neat bullet hole in his brain.

"I speak for them," Julian said. "There is talk of rearmament again in England and even here. You are told it is for security, for peace, but a nation rearms only to make war and I for one will not stand by and let war come again. Will you?"

He stepped back and for a few seconds there was absolute silence before applause rocked the huge hall again.

"I never expected anything like that," Tillie said, uncharacteristically subdued. "He didn't spare us the ghoulish details, did he?"

Ema shook her head as she got up to go. "I have to rush, I have an appointment. I'll see you at your party tomorrow night. Will Thomas be there?"

"Yes." Tillie's black eyes glittered suspiciously. "Why?"

"Tom's a munitions manufacturer—Saxon can't be one of his favorite people."

Tillie made a face. "Don't be dreary, Emanuelle, it's a party, not a board meeting. Pacifism's in fashion right now and Saxon's very decorative—and quite harmless. Everyone wanted him and I got him!" Tillie pulled on her gloves. "The British ambassador is coming, so try to be on time."

Emanuelle made certain to leave the hall alone. She walked a block, turned the corner, and got into a waiting taxicab. She and Julian would be able to talk more freely there than in the Ellis's chauffeured Rolls. "We'll have to wait a little longer," she said to the driver.

"It's your money, lady."

Ema nodded. It certainly was. Her salary as an editor and columnist was generous but negligible by comparison with RSVP profits. It had become a very big business in a party-oriented society. Thank heaven for debutantes, Ema thought. They were the new American celebrities, as slavishly worshipped and copied as Hollywood stars, and grist for two of Ema's mills, the women's page and RSVP.

Times had changed. Very few girls were quietly presented to their parents' friends at home, with a glass of champagne and a string quartet. The public was avid for glamour girls like Brenda Frazier and Esme O'Brien and Cobina Wright. The press and the slick magazines, always happy to give the public what it wanted, followed the young women on their rounds of Café Society's favorite haunts—the Stork Club, the Empire Room, El Morocco, the Persian Room, El Rio, the Cotton Club. *Life* magazine featured current debs on its cover and next year's crop in photo essays.

The *Star*'s society page covered lavish charity balls and cotillions, as well as private debutante teas and dinner parties and sumptuous debuts, many of them arranged by RSVP. The Depression might have put an end to the era of flaming youth and jazz, but in their place—even though the economic slump dragged on—were swing and garishly painted jalopies piloted by hepcats and, above all, glamour.

After the debuts came the engagement parties, bridal showers, and weddings, followed by baby showers and christenings and birthday parties, large and lavish affairs that used RSVP's services.

"We're sensational," Ema had told Kate and Spencer when they moved to larger offices on Fifth Avenue.

"And how," Spencer agreed. "We billed a quarter-million in flowers alone last year in New York. Add the Boston and Palm Beach figures to that."

"And look how much more we did in food! I always knew there was a fortune in food." Ema had nodded approvingly over the RSVP books. "We're getting very, very rich, aren't we?"

But Kate had been more interested in talking about Ema's trip to Germany. "Europe's like a tinder box; I'm afraid it'll blow up and there you'll be, trapped in the middle of another war. Everyone is sure one's coming."

Julian won't believe that, Ema thought now, watching for him to round the corner. Julian had met Hitler several times and he was convinced the German leader could be stopped short of war. He was in favor of Prime Minister Chamberlain's appeasement policy—to which Harding, now on his way back from Europe with Ken, was totally opposed. The *Star*, following Harding's instructions, would run Julian's arguments and Harding's rebuttal side by side on the front page tomorrow.

She had read Harding's article. It praised Julian as a man he personally admired, "but whose very integrity can turn our honest desire for peace into the illness called appeasement. It is an illness that may leave England too debilitated to defend herself from what is coming. And after England, America."

The two men would surely meet again before Julian finished his lecture tour and sailed for England, and the prospect was not a pleasant one for Ema. A different light—Harding's—had been turned on her relationship with Julian. She was uneasy with him, as she never was in Europe.

It was because of Harding. Harding might understand what she had done all those years ago, but not what she had been doing since. She could not bear the idea of his discovering it; she could see the look in his eyes, and the prospect made her shiver. This new relationship between the two men was intolerable. And it made discovery a dangerous possibility. Still she shrank from the obvious solution. How could she give him up? She must see Julian alone once more, in Germany, before she decided anything.

She shook her head in dismay and confusion. Julian mustn't see her in this state. From her briefcase she took the German grammar she had been studying and stared at it blindly.

She knew a little German already from her mother's stories of Alsace. She remembered Sylvie speaking it from time to time, a sound that was harsh, unforgiving, like Sylvie herself.

She was unable to concentrate. She put the grammar away and in another few minutes she saw Julian rounding the corner, his velvet-collared overcoat thrown across his shoulders. He wore a soft black Borsalino hat and carried the silver-topped cane his father had given him. When Sir James is gone, Ema thought as she waved from the taxi window, there will be no one to keep Davina in check. She'll have him all to herself.

"All right, cabbie," she said as Julian got in. "And close the partition, please."

The driver grunted and slid the glass shut and they were alone together, on the way to Silvermoor.

"It was very good, Julian."

He shook his head. "I hate dredging all that up, but I can only fight horror with horror."

"Then we won't talk about it. Tell me about the children."

He sighed heavily. "Drew's having a hard time steering a course between what I believe and that old devil glory. He's furious about what's happening in Spain—how else could he feel?—and he thinks a European war is inevitable and we ought to prepare for it. My son admires me, I know that, but he thinks I'm tilting at windmills. The little girls know nothing about politics, of course, but now and then they eye me with more suspicion than hero-worship, the way Davina does." He closed his eyes wearily.

"Julian, don't talk anymore, just have a rest until we get home." It was good to have the care of him, even in so small a way as this. He leaned back and Ema looked for a few seconds at the face she loved so well before she turned away, wondering what would happen to him and Drew if war should come.

# 66

She touched his arm when the taxi turned into the drive forty minutes later. "Silvermoor," she said.

He straightened, waiting for the house to come into view. He turned to her in surprise. "Ema, it's like Stridings!"

"Yes, I had it copied from pictures. It was a dream I had, to live in a house like yours."

"It was a dream I had too." He said it as if he had just realized it would never come true. "And that must be Dana, between those two enormous dogs."

It was lovely to watch him with her child. No wonder Drew adored him; all children responded to real kindness.

Dana stayed on after lunch, asking questions.

"Aren't you a lord?"

"No, baronets aren't peers, so they don't sit in the House of Lords, even though they have hereditary titles. I'm just called Mister—or sometimes Major—but my father is called Sir, and so shall I be after him and my son after me."

"Where do your daughters go to school?"

"Juliana will start at Rodean next term. Alexandra is still at boarding school, but Jenny's too young to go; she has a governess."

"Maman wants me to go to Rodean," Dana said, her interest piqued, "but Daddy doesn't."

Julian glanced at Ema.

"He'll agree when you're the right age," Ema said.

"Is school in England very strict?" Dana persisted.

"Yes, and it's meant to be," Julian said. "Privilege implies discipline and responsibility, that's what *noblesse oblige* really means."

It was what the best of the British aristocracy had always tried to teach its children, and Emanuelle was more determined than ever that Dana must have an English education to prepare her for marriage to a titled Englishman.

"I'm glad I'm not *noblesse,*" Dana said. "I'd rather live at home and go to day school."

Miss Prescott came into the room. "Caro is here, Dana."

"*Je puis la présenter, Maman?* I want her to meet Major Saxon."

Ema nodded and Dana ran into the hall, coming back with Carolyn George in tow. The two were the same age and the same height, but Carolyn, with her pale brown hair and hazel eyes, was a shy contrast to Dana's strong personality, so like Harding's. The girls stayed for a few moments asking questions about England, then made their curtsies and were shepherded out by the governess.

"Would you like to see the grounds?" Ema asked when the silence in the room seemed strained.

They went out, past the gardens and greenhouses to Ema's favorite view of the river.

"It's a beautiful house, Ema, a perfect setting for you and your exquisite daughter. You must have been just like Dana at her age." He touched her hair for the first time. "Except for this. At the front I used to think about the sunlight on your hair."

Ema, as conscious of that touch as if it had been on her naked body, did not want to think of what she had been like at Dana's age. But it was not Dana who troubled her, it was Harding's meeting with Julian in London and the memory of those two clasped hands.

It's what I've always been afraid of, she thought, something as simple as that.

"Julian," she began, and hesitated, hardly knowing what she wanted to say.

"I wish you weren't married to him," Julian said, taking her hands in his. "Or anyone else. But he's a good man and I admire him."

"He thinks the same of you."

"I'm aware of that irony." The bitter irony of mutual admiration between Ema's husband and her lover was in his face.

They looked at each other. "I wish you'd never met him," Ema said suddenly, despairingly.

"Ema, so do I. The idea of you with him is unbearably real now, but it changes nothing else. Knowing him makes it harder for me to betray him, but that's for me to deal with. Has anything changed for you?"

She shook her head hopelessly. "I never thought of it as betrayal before. I don't know," she said, "I just don't know."

His hands gripped hers. "Ema, I can't give you up, you're the only thing that makes that other charade bearable. You're not just my love, Ema, you're the only real love of my life."

"I never wanted anything to change," she whispered. "I just wanted things to stay the same."

"Darling, they will. I'll come to Germany when you're there; we'll both see things differently."

"Yes," she said, wanting desperately to believe they would.

They stood in each other's arms for a moment and she thought that life would hold no real joy without him. Then they walked back to the house and she ordered the car to drive him back to the city.

"He's very nice," Dana said as the two girls came running to see him off.

"He's wonderful," Carolyn sighed. "Is he really a hero?"

"Yes," Ema said, looking down at two expectant faces, Carolyn's ready to believe, Dana's questioning, "he really is."

She went into the house and the two friends set off to finish their game on the other side of the garden.

"I'm going to marry a hero," Caro said.

"If you can find one. A hero has to be perfect and my father says nobody's perfect—but I know he thinks Mother is."

"So do I! She's not only kind and beautiful, she's clever too."

"Yes, but it takes all of her time," Dana said.


Emanuelle saw Julian briefly at Tillie's party, but not again until he returned from his lecture tour one month later, when she and Harding had dinner with him on the night he sailed. She sat between the two men, uncomfortable and silent.

"You've gathered enormous support," Harding told him, "but some of your sponsors only pretend to be pacifists. They're either Fascists or they're heavily invested in Germany, as I was, and they don't want anyone interfering with Hitler's good works against bolshevism. The Fascists are betting Hitler will destroy the Soviet Union for them. Your name is being linked with Nazi supporters and in this world guilt is very often decided by association."

"I can't help that," Julian replied. "My convictions are my own, no matter who my hangers-on may be."

"Julian, I don't want a war, but it depends, unfortunately, on a man who obviously does."

"Not with Britain. Hitler considers us his natural allies, however grotesque that may be, and besides, we have nothing he needs except in the far reaches of the Empire. He wants the coal and oil fields of Europe, he wants the mineral deposits and the Skoda munitions works in Czechoslovakia."

"Are we supposed to give him everything he wants so he can make war on Russia for us?"

"We're agreed that a lot of people would like him to do just that," Julian said. "*Communist* is a word that drives reasonable men berserk. They talk about the 'red menace,' conveniently forgetting that it was Allied troops, including Americans, who invaded Russian soil and occupied Murmansk after the revolution. Is it any wonder the Soviets are as suspicious of us as we are of them? And is suspicion worth a war? Suppose we had a mutual assistance pact with Russia, as we do with France? Hitler would never start a two-front war."

Harding shook his head. "No one in the West would have made a pact with the Soviets even before Stalin and his bloody purges, much less now."

Julian predicted that they would, and Emanuelle, watching, thought they were as totally different as two men could be. Harding's dynamism was bright as a new penny; Julian's charisma lay in his polish and in a strength one sensed rather than saw. Harding was an American success story and very proud of his country's new power; Julian represented centuries of tradition and the habit of dominion over an immense empire.

After dinner they drove him to the pier and watched him board the ship. "He's like Don Quixote," Harding said, echoing what Julian had said about himself, "tilting at windmills, but he's fine, very fine. I would like to have been his friend."

"Why can't you be?" Ema said, startled.

"He's to the manner born—I'm not." He helped her into the car.

It was what she thought, but she didn't like the way it sounded. "You don't have to be!" she protested. "Anyway, he's not a snob, and even if he were, this is not Europe!"

"My lady wife," he said, taking her hand, "the truth is that you *are* a snob, however much you resent the class system when it shuts its doors to us! Still, there are things. Take Lord Broadhurst, for example. I've known him for several years and he still calls me Mr. Ellis, not even Ellis. That's to remind me we can be colleagues but never friends."

"And Julian Saxon? Does he remind you?"

"No, he doesn't have to, there's just something about him. Now, tell me," he said, uncomfortable with the subject, "how is the German tour working out?"

She described the itinerary, but she was wondering how it would be when she and Julian met again in Germany. Too many things were pressing in on her, and she could not overcome the dread, remembered from so long ago, that each time she saw Julian might well be the last.

# 67

"The Führer believes in the family," Frau Gruner said in heavily accented English, "but marriage is not a young girl's primary goal in the new Germany; motherhood is. Our girls aspire to motherhood above all, they are exalted only by it." Her fervor sat ill upon her broad, scrubbed face. "It is a woman's destiny."

"Destiny aside," Emanuelle said dryly, taking notes, "I see your birth rate has increased dramatically since 1933."

Frau Gruner nodded proudly, as if she had done it all herself. "You must remember that after the war there were three million more women than men in Germany, two million of them of marriageable age. Most were denied the bliss of motherhood and our Fatherland its harvest of children, but that will never happen again"—and her blue eyes rose to heaven—"thanks to the wisdom of our Führer."

Even after two weeks in Germany it still surprised Ema to hear Adolf Hitler invoked as the deity. The frenzied worship of that pale, unprepossessing man still seemed faintly comical to her, but she remembered Nuremberg and realized that his power over his people was potentially more dangerous than the military presence she saw everywhere. He was every German's heroic father. His asceticism, even his vegetarianism, made him noble and virtuous to them. It was something Ema could understand very well. How many real fathers were like that?

The stories she wired to the *Star*, however, remained glorified travelogues for the moment. She had been told she was free to file what she liked, but she knew discretion was definitely the better part of valor in Germany, where Dr. Goebbels, the gnomish Minister of Propaganda, reigned supreme over all channels of information. Foreign journalists had been evicted before for embellishing the official press releases.

But her official trip would be over today, and Julian would meet her in Regensberg tomorrow, a meeting she longed for differently from any in the past. Make it all right, she pleaded with the doubt inside her the moment she awoke, make it all right again.

The black car bearing Frau Gruner had come early that morning to collect Ema at the Hotel Continental in Munich. It was now approaching a *Lebensborn,* or fount of life, a maternity home, and Emanuelle was eager to see it. The *Lebensborn* program had been inaugurated by Reichsführer-SS Himmler; it was mainly for girls pregnant by Hitler's elite guard. The SS—Major Siegfried Brand was one—were the Nazi chosen, perfect "Aryan" specimens according to the physical standards Himmler had created. The girls selected to mate with them were members of the *Bund deutscher Mädchen,* the post-puberty level of the girls' youth movement, and pure "Aryan" too.

To Ema it sounded either like a mass fertility cult, with all the hysterical sexuality of pagan ritual—how cleverly the Nazis used ritual!—or as mechanical as stallions covering mares. She hoped to determine which by talking to the girls.

"Why the high wall?" she asked as the car turned off the road into a leafy park. The wall was obviously new.

Frau Gruner confided earnestly. "You are a writer on women's issues, Miss Beranger, you know how people fear new ideas. We don't want our mothers harassed by outdated notions of morality. In the new Germany the only morality is the state."

They entered the large handsome stone house, a former spa requisitioned by Himmler, and Ema was given a tour of the premises. The bedrooms were large and luxuriously furnished. In the sun-drenched nursery the bassinets were beruffled in pink or blue sprigged cotton.

"Charming," Ema said, privately shocked by the extreme youth of the girls she saw strolling on the grounds or sitting in groups on the wide veranda. Most of them were under sixteen and in a late stage of pregnancy.

She was annoyed to discover that she would not be permitted to question the girls at length, even through Frau Gruner, but she gathered that most of the girls had met their men at party rallies like the one she had attended with Julian last year.

"What happens to them after their babies are born?" she asked Frau Gruner as they went to inspect the delivery rooms.

"The state takes care of them, of course," Frau Gruner said, again with Rhinemaiden fervor. "We honor them as the cradle of the race. We expect them to conceive often, by the same man, should they marry, or by others. As Reichsführer Himmler has said, the unmarried mother, during and after her pregnancy, is not a married or an unmarried woman, but a *Mother*. She is officially addressed as Frau, not Fraulein." She smiled conspiratorially. "As you probably know, our German feminists have been demanding that for a long time. The Führer is a feminist at heart."

Frau Gruner pushed open the door of a well-equipped delivery room. A large photograph of Adolf Hitler loomed on the wall, his fierce gaze riveted on the table where a woman in labor would lie, her legs strapped into stirrups for the delivery. "What a place for a picture!" Ema said.

"We do not believe in anesthetics. Women in travail call upon the Führer to give them strength."

"Frau Gruner," Ema said impatiently, "have you ever had a child?"

"Four," the woman replied, inflating her ample chest.

"Then you must know that's utter rubbish! Pain is pain, no matter what's hanging on the wall!"

"Not in here. Shall we proceed?"

A Valkyrie, Ema thought, but Germans were all a little insane. She followed Frau Gruner into the spacious dining room for a robust lunch of sausage and potato salad. Then they were driven away to visit a *Jungmaedel* group, the junior division for girls ten to fourteen, healthy children dressed in navy blue skirts and white middy blouses with blue ties. She was not allowed to question them, either, but she knew enough German to understand what they were reciting in the classrooms like a catechism; it was the Nazi party line.

She was grateful when the long day ended and she escaped all that stultifying chauvinism for the more rational atmosphere of her hotel room. She took a hot bath, ordered a dry martini sent up, and made notes of the day's impressions for the columns she wanted to do.

She understood the appeal of the German credo. There came the man, penis in hand, to say, "Woman, lie down and be fertilized. In exchange you shall be honored, cherished, and secure." It was a tempting offer; what woman did not yearn to be worshipped just for what she was?

Yet such adoration was on too primitive a level to satisfy a woman who knew she was more than a womb.

"In America," Ema began to write for a future column, "even adoration on a sexual level is more difficult to come by; it has to be earned. A woman's face and body must conform to the fashion"—she thought of Kate—"and she must be—or look—young, eternally, exhaustingly, sometimes grotesquely young." That was Tillie.

Ema picked up one of the propaganda primers and checked on a passage before she resumed writing.

"Dr. Goebbels, the German Minister of Propaganda, says a woman's task is to be beautiful and bear children, to preen her feathers in order to attract a mate. Elsa Maxwell, international columnist and social arbiter, says women should be beautiful, exquisitely dressed, and not too smart. Emily Post warned debutantes not to outthink or outplay a man or they would be out looking for another one. Maternity might not be the sole object of the American exercise, as it is of the German one, but in both societies seduction is."

Emanuelle nodded with satisfaction. That would stir things up!

For a moment she reflected that everything between the sexes *was* about sex, the luring and the yielding. Then she reminded herself it was certainly not all she felt for Julian or for Harding. If she never slept with either man again, she would still love both of them.

There was a knock on her door and she went to answer it. It was a page with a telegram from Julian. Sir James was dying and Julian had canceled his trip to Germany. "I'll ring you as soon as I can," the message ended.

She went back to her chair, disconsolate. This meeting was a crucial one, and its cancellation a part of the new pattern that was pulling them apart; family considerations were coming between them more and more often. And she couldn't be with him when he needed comfort!

"*Sainte Vierge*," Ema muttered to herself, "I'd see more of him as his friend than as his mistress."

She made herself think of Sir James, but it was with a tangle of emotions. She was filled with remorse over their last meeting, remorse that she had not—but no, she *could not* have accepted what he offered her at such cost to himself. But he was a man of many facets; acknowledging one would not have meant she condoned all that he had done. How much would a little kindness to an old man have cost her?

Even if he had deprived her of her son, he was still the kind of father she would have wanted, capable of anything to protect his child. She had both despised and respected him, and so she had punished him for not admitting that he had been wrong, that she *would* have been worthy of his son and his grandson.

Ema wondered if Drew knew his "mother" hated the sight of him. She was certain, from things both Julian and Sir James had said, that he sensed it.

Sometimes days went by when she didn't think of Davina, who had to steal what she could not keep. Maybe vengeance fades, like beauty, Ema thought. Maybe love is the other side of vengeance. But not a love like hers and Julian's. It would never fade, no matter what happened.

Suddenly she ached to see her son. It was a yearning that did not often overwhelm her, but tonight it was especially painful. She wanted to comfort him, too, Andrew James Julian Saxon, the future baronet. And Julian would soon be Sir Julian—with Lady Davina at his side.

* * *

Sir James could hear their voices clearly and turned back once again from the benediction of final sleep, of surcease for his overburdened heart.

"Julian," Davina was saying, "come and rest for a while."

"No, I'll stay with him." Julian's tone was terse, less controlled than it usually was when he spoke to his wife. My dear son, Sir James thought, I wish I could have made your life happier.

"What for?" Davina persisted.

"Good Lord, Mother!" That was Drew, constantly dismayed by her, by her covert resentment of his very existence. "Grandfather might speak to us again."

"Don't be ridiculous, Drew, he's almost gone."

"That's enough, Davina!" Julian's whisper was angry now. "He might hear you! Leave if you want to."

"No, darling, I'll stay with you."

Sir James listened to the silence in the room, the same barbed silence that always reigned when Davina was with Julian and Drew, clutching one, despising the other, and he longed again to put down the intolerable burden he had carried so long.

But he must save Drew. Heaven knew to what lengths Davina might go once Sir James was not there to protect him. Her bitterness, insidious as a low-grade fever, had already made Drew tentative, wary, even self-centered in his need to defend himself.

Was there no comfort Sir James could give his grandson? Julian had Emalie, but Drew had no such sweet easement.

He took a ragged breath and felt a hand grasp his. Was it Julian's or Drew's? He formed a name with his lips.

"Yes, Father, what is it?"

"Drew," Sir James said.

"Yes, Father, I'm listening."

"Tell Drew . . ." The father's strength failed him again.

"Julian!" It was Davina's voice, urgent now. "He's dying! Get the doctor!"

Sir James sensed a quick movement at the bedside and felt another hand stroke his brow. "It's Drew, Grandfather. Just rest for a while."

I had to take you from her, Drew, Sir James wanted to say, but he made no sound. Forgive me, my dearest boy, there was no other way, but Drew . . .

He felt a prick in his arm and flinched away from the hypodermic needle, but the medicine eased the pain and gave him strength to speak,

"Your mother loves you very much," he said to the sobbing boy just before he died.

"Father," Julian murmured, leaning over the bed again. He held the frail hand for an instant to his cheek. "My beloved father." He released the hand and touched Sir James's face gently, then he put an arm around his weeping son. "Did he say anything, Drew?"

"Yes, darling," Davina answered him tenderly. "Something about your mother, about Margaret."


Ema, alone with her thoughts, was lighting another cigarette when the telephone rang. It was Major Brand, inviting her to dinner. She had not seen him since her arrival in Berlin, three weeks ago, and she hesitated only for a moment. Julian's wire had depressed her, and Brand was a way to get through the evening. She would try to make him tell her more about the all-night induction vigils for the new SS members—positively medieval, she thought with a little shiver—and about the blood oaths and the secret tattoos.

She got up and began to dress.

# 68

She put on a high-necked white crepe gown with a pleated drape from left shoulder to right hip, and added simple gold jewelry. Her hair was rolled high at the forehead and worn in a shoulder-length pageboy behind.

"Ravishing," Major Brand said when she met him in the lobby. With a sharp click of his heels he bent to kiss her hand, then appropriated the coat she carried and held it for her to put on. "I've reserved at one of my favorite restaurants. The food is excellent and you will find the atmosphere"—he paused and smiled briefly—"romantic."

She was led out of the lobby and put into the Daimler—there was no other way to describe his manner of command. It was a very short drive to the restaurant, and beyond asking if her tour had been successful, he said little until they were seated at a candlelit table.

"Do you like it?" he asked.

"Very much, especially the Gypsy violins," Emanuelle said, wondering what this man really thought of the Aryan myth. "I thought Gypsies were persona non grata in the Third Reich."

He smiled his humorless smile. "The music may be Bohemian, but the musicians, I assure you, are pure German. Shall I order for you?" He did so without waiting for a reply, choosing pâté, trout, asparagus, and squab dressed with rice, with the appropriate wines. "The wines," he said, "are French, of course. I could offer a Parisian no less."

"How did you know I was French? I pride myself on having no accent left."

He offered her a gold-tipped cigarette and lit it. "I know everything about you," he said, suggestively it seemed to her. "We investigate our foreign guests very carefully, journalists in particular." He drew deeply on his cigarette. "I was especially interested in you."

Ema raised an eyebrow, refusing to ask why, but she was surprised by what he said next.

"Here was a woman, well known and highly regarded in her field, married to an American millionaire, with only one child and a thriving business of her own. All that is unusual in a woman, especially one as seductive as you are. Why do you work? Furthermore, your husband must want more children, a son at least. I wondered if he was too insistent about it, if that was why you came so often to Germany alone—until I discovered it was to meet a lover." He raised his wineglass. "But I commend your choice. Major Saxon is not unknown to us, he sympathizes with our cause."

"No, Major Brand, his only cause is peace," she said angrily, "and what you said about me is equally offensive." She felt violated by his gross exposé of her life, yet she hesitated to get up and leave the restaurant. He was too unpredictable and, she was certain, capable of violent behavior.

"Then I apologize, it was not my intention," he said, his pale blue eyes expressionless as they studied her. "I was merely stating the obvious. Ah, the pâté. I hope it is up to standard."

The conversation was impersonal for the rest of the meal, but his scrutiny of her was not. She felt threatened; she was in a country dominated by men and particularly by SS officers like Brand who answered only to Hitler. He was very handsome, a perfect Aryan specimen, she thought, and there was something about him that was as mesmerizing as that madness at Nuremberg.

It was power, she realized suddenly, grasping the answer to his perverse fascination for her. She would not be the only woman to confuse power with sexuality, whether the symbol of power was brawn or money or a uniform.

He was the kind to demand what he wanted and he did, in the Daimler. But first he took her hand and removed her white kid glove, rolling it down her forearm slowly, then urging it expertly from her fingertips with his. He opened her hand and kissed her palm with warm, insistent lips. She felt the tip of his tongue lick her flesh, and she shuddered faintly.

His blue eyes pinioned her. "You will sleep with me." It was a statement, not a request.

"No," she said.

"Why not? You desire me." His eyes once again examined her body and her mouth.

She withdrew her hand as the car stopped in front of the Hotel Continental.

"You're mistaken, Major," she said, the flat tone of her voice puncturing the bubble of eroticism he had created. "Aside from everything else, I could never desire a man who wears a death-head insignia."

"It is a mark of honor."

"Not to me. It says things about you I don't like." She replaced her glove deliberately.

His tall body unfolded out of the car and he reached down to draw her out after him, briefly holding her against him. He accompanied her into the lobby and for a moment she was afraid he would come upstairs with her, but with another click of his heels he bowed over her hand at the elevator.

"*Auf Wiedersehen,*" he said. "I have been called back to Berlin. I trust the rest of your stay will not be lonely, even though Major Saxon cannot join you." He left her and she went up to her room and turned the key in the lock.

The invitation to sex from an SS officer had unnerved her completely. Brand was like this country, mad and loveless. There were violent passions here, certainly, but there was no tenderness in Germany. It was all lust and death, blood banners and black wreaths and men who pledged themselves to die for another man.

Brand had assumed that because she was unfaithful to her husband with one man she would be with any other man who wanted her, that she made no distinction in her choice of sexual partners. It was a mean assumption, but then, it was a mean world.

He had demeaned her in a way that all the years of meeting Julian in secret had never done. She felt incomplete, without total validity in either Julian's life or her own. You can fill a novel or a movie with stolen moments, she thought, but not a life. Some women knew better than to try.

"But not the romantics among us," she said bitterly, removing her jewelry at the dressing table. She loved Julian too honestly to let a Nazi major sully it. What did it matter how it looked through Brand's eyes?

Or Harding's? Ah, that mattered. She had never come to terms with that.

She had just stepped out of her gown when the telephone rang. "Harding? Oh, Harding, I was never so glad to hear anyone in my life."

"Ema, what's wrong?"

"Nothing, I'm just tired. It's been a rough trip."

"Come on, Em, tell me what happened?"

"My German nanny, Major Brand, invited me to bed. Actually it was more like an order."

"The rotten bastard! But I've seen you crush would-be Casanovas as if they were gnats."

"It's different with SS officers, let me tell you. They expect a woman to keep her legs open and her mouth shut. This one thinks he's God's gift."

"It's time you got out of there."

"I finished sooner than expected. I'll leave tomorrow and have some time with Danielle. I'm glad you called, Harding."

"So am I. Good night, my love, get some sleep and hurry home."

She left for Paris in the morning and met Danielle at Maxim's for dinner. "How are your winter enrollments?" she asked when they had given each other that loving scrutiny they always exchanged when they met.

Danielle, who had repaid the last of Ema's loan months ago, nodded contentedly. She was completely gray now, but otherwise unchanged. "I've hired two more assistants. And you?"

Ema told her about the sensational articles she would publish about Germany—and about Major Brand. "He's like the whole damned country, off center."

"On the contrary, for a man he was right on target. He wanted to play with your toys, so he naturally assumed you wanted to play with his."

Ema laughed. "The gospel of sex, according to Sainte Danielle. But some men are exceptions to that rule, thank heaven." She studied the menu. "I think I'll have crêpes for dessert. I can't get real crêpes Suzettes in New York, not even in a so-called French restaurant."

"Open one of your own," Danielle suggested.

Ema worked on her notes during the crossing aboard the *Normandie*, but Julian preoccupied her. She had always felt threatened by her past; now it was the future that appalled her, because there was pain in it no matter what she did.

# 69

From the back seat of the Rolls Emanuelle and Harding could see the crowd in front of the *Star* and they smiled at each other. Ema's long, thoughtful series of articles about German women, published weekly, had created a satisfying furor. The publication in America of Hitler's *Mein Kampf* in English underlined everything Ema wrote and kept public interest high.

"Listen to this!" Ema exclaimed to Harding when she read the book. "'The German girl is a State subject, she becomes a State citizen only when she marries.' That's enough for four columns."

Pacifists called what Ema wrote deliberately provocative, a sensational attempt to turn the American public against Germany—"Although," Harding said, "fascism and communism are the issues that concern Americans, not the Nazis as such."

"Then let's make it the Nazis," Ema said. "It's time someone did."

Anti-Fascist and Jewish groups called the articles the best inside look yet at Nazi totalitarianism, because they brought political theory down to a personal issue everyone could understand.

Those who believed a woman's place was in the home said Emanuelle was a woman in pants, like those other insults to their sex, Marlene Dietrich and Katharine Hepburn. They accused her of using the material as an excuse to champion the most radical feminist ideas.

The feminists supported her, as usual, hailing her scathing comparisons on the way both societies treated women.

This morning the various groups were carrying signs in front of the *Star*.

"You're quite a woman," Harding said when they had pushed their way through the crowd and were inside the building, "but I worry about

Dana. You know how cruel other children can be when one of them is in the spotlight."

Why must he always weaken a compliment like that? Dana was coming home from Foxcroft the next day for summer vacation. Ema had enrolled her for the second semester there as soon as she had returned from Germany after another heated argument with Harding.

"She's made of sterner stuff than that," Ema assured him now.

"Yes, but she's only eleven. It's hard when people picket your mother, and your father is called before the House Committee on Un-American Activities."

"And defends himself brilliantly, don't forget that. Are you going to stop printing what you believe, Harding?"

He shook his head.

"Neither am I. Dana's not like most children her age," Emanuelle said with satisfaction. "She's different, I've always said so."

"I wonder if she thinks she's so different."

They separated to go to their offices, anger just below the surface again.

As always when she was troubled, it helped Ema to be very busy. Little things kept adding to the confusion she felt, like the condolence note sent to Sir Julian Saxon, Bart., from Mr. and Mrs. Harding Ellis when they learned of his father's death.

It placed Harding, all unknowing, in an ignominious position; yet she was the cause, she had no right to resent him for that. He had not come between her and Julian by design. But sometimes she felt crushed by the weight of the loyalty she owed him and had not rendered up.

And there were special reasons for resentment. Drew was going to inherit his father's title, but Dana could surpass him by making the right marriage, if only Harding didn't stand in the way. "And I'll see that she does," Ema said, "no matter what it costs and no matter how much Harding objects."

She turned to the list of appointments her secretary had typed out and put on her desk. The morning was fairly free, and she would use some of the time to write an article comparing the diminishing number of women in the American job market with the same phenomenon in Germany since 1933. In both countries the jobs were reserved mainly for men, no matter what the women's needs or qualifications, and women who did find jobs were paid abysmally low salaries by comparison.

The afternoon schedule looked good. She had a lunch appointment with the Atwoods in the RSVP conference room—lunch to be catered by their own kitchens, of course; and another with the French chef at La Caille after his luncheon rush was over. For months Ema had been pondering Danielle's suggestion about opening a restaurant, and if both meetings turned out as she hoped, she intended to do just that. She was rich enough already to insure Dana's future—with her money, not Harding's—but when it came to money, more was always better.

She lit a cigarette and made herself work steadily until she stopped to answer the buzzer on her desk. "There's a man from the German embassy to see you," her secretary said. "Mr. Gerhardt Rausch."

That was unexpected. "Send him in, please."

He was a pleasant-looking man, quite nondescript except for his Hitler mustache. Thank God they're not all like Major Brand, Ema thought.

"Please sit down, Mr. Rausch. What can I do for you?"

He wet his lips. "Dr. Goebbels is concerned about the articles you are publishing in the *Star*."

She bristled. "Dr. Goebbels is not Minister of Propaganda in America! He doesn't edit every word that's published *here*."

Mr. Rausch looked pained. "You misunderstand. He feels you were misinformed when you were in our country. You make it seem that we coerce our children into . . . intimate relations."

"The German American Bund made the same objection, but I still think you do. There are many ways to coerce young girls into sex, some of them apparently benign."

"The woman who escorted you in Bavaria . . ." He consulted his notes. "Frau Gruner."

"Ah, yes. Apparently she was not cooperative."

My God, Ema thought, what'll they do to the Valkyrie? "But she was very cooperative, I assure you."

Mr. Rausch coughed. "I gather you were not allowed to speak to the young ladies."

"I'm sure that directive came from Dr. Goebbels."

"Perhaps. In that case he regrets it and invites you to return to question the girls freely."

"That's kind of him, but I really haven't the time."

He was surprisingly persistent. "Perhaps not during the summer, but in the autumn?"

Ema considered. Personal interviews with *Lebensborn* mothers and the *Jungmaedel* children would be quite a coup—and she could meet Julian in Berlin! Things might be as they were before if she could be alone with him. She would call him and arrange it.

She nodded. "All right, but I'll have to see how it fits into my schedule before I set a date. Please thank Dr. Goebbels for the invitation—and tell Frau Gruner I look forward to seeing her again." Maybe that would help. The woman was a fool, but she had only been following orders. The Nazis liked finding scapegoats for their own mistakes, and Ema despised them for that.

She knew Harding would object, but she would have to cross that bridge when she came to it. She was going to Germany, and that was that.

"Not again!" Kate protested when they were eating poached salmon and cucumber salad at RSVP. "Far be it from me to say I told you so, but I told you so. They almost had a war last month over Czechoslovakia."

"Yes, my darling Kate, but almost doesn't count. Hitler did back down. Now Dr. Goebbels has offered me a closer look at his baby factory and I can't resist it. His nose will still be out of joint once I get back here and print those interviews, but I'm not going to tell *him* that."

Spencer shook his head. "Don't underestimate the Germans, Ema. They aren't playing games."

"I know that, my friend, and I appreciate your worrying about me, but you needn't. I know what I'm up against."

Kate and Spencer looked at each other unhappily, but dropped the subject. Once Ema made up her mind . . .

When the coffee cups had been cleared away, Ema opened her briefcase. "I came to ask your opinion about something important. I'm not suggesting that you two put money into this; I really want to do it on my own."

"Do what, for heaven's sake?"

"Open a restaurant, the most lavish, expensive, *authentic* French restaurant in New York—not another American effort that's neither one kind of cuisine nor the other. It was Danielle's idea and I think it's a good one."

The Atwoods studied each other, and after a moment Spencer nodded his approval. "A luxury restaurant is a money-maker provided it's well run. Will you run it yourself?"

"No, I don't know anything about running a restaurant. And I don't want anyone to know I own it—although I intend to patronize it so often myself that Café Society will follow me there in droves."

"But they'd come in droves if they knew it was yours."

Ema shook her head. "I know, but I have my reasons. RSVP has cachet because no one connects it with those unglamorous kitchens we own, but a restaurant is something else. I don't want the smell of onions in my clothes—or Dana's."

"Who'll front for you?"

"Monsieur Étienne, the chef at La Caille. He's the best French chef in New York and a born snob; he hates working for anyone else. I think he'll jump at the chance of a quarter share in his own restaurant. Do you two have any idea what the profit is in haute cuisine and wine? Caviar's one dollar and fifty cents at the Russian Tea Room, and let me tell you that's one hell of a profit."

She handed Spencer the papers she had taken from her briefcase. "Here are a few good locations that never made it back after the Crash—

and what it will cost to redecorate in high style. I'll leave the figures with you. Look them over and tell me how long you think it'll take to crack that nut. I'd like you to handle the administration, Spencer, and watch the books. Like a hawk. I wouldn't trust a French chef as far as I could throw him." She headed for the door. "I have to run. Dana's room still needs some finishing touches."

"Will she ever stop?" Spencer said to his wife when Ema had gone.

"No," Kate replied. "She can't."

"Why the hell not?"

"Whatever's chasing her might catch her."

"And what would that be?"

Kate shook her head. "I've never been sure, Spence." But she wouldn't have told him even if she had been.

# 70

"Oh, Mother!" Dana said the next day. "It's beautiful."

"I'm glad you like it, darling." Ema watched with Harding while Dana inspected her room. The canopied bed had been replaced by a four-poster with a cream velvet spread and bolster. The lacquered white furniture and pink glazed-chintz chairs were gone, and delicately carved oak pieces—a desk, two chests, a wardrobe—stood in their place on a soft, pale green carpet. There were two down-cushioned easy chairs in the bay window, upholstered in the same green and cream cut velvet as the window seat.

"I'd like to stay home and live in it," said Dana. She didn't look at her parents, and Ema said, avoiding Harding's eyes, "Come see your summer clothes." She opened a large closet, hung with the silk, linen, batiste, and organdy dresses Ema had ordered from Thiboux with Danielle's help. There were hats on the shelves above and a selection of handmade T-strap shoes and sandals on the shoe racks.

"Fashion is not my forte," Harding said. "I'll leave you to it." He headed for the corridor.

"Nice," Dana said, ruffling through the things, "but I'll need some overalls, too, and some hiking boots for Maine."

"To poke around in moldy old caves? I was hoping you'd outgrown that."

Dana flung herself into one of the velvet chairs, still wearing her school skirt and blazer, bobby socks and saddle shoes. She sprawled there, awkward and ill at ease. Her features had lost the sweet blur of childhood, although her body had not; her face was her mother's, with the same changeable gray eyes and wide-bowed mouth and the same coloring except for Harding's dark, almost black hair. Her quick temper was Harding's, too, and sometimes her expression when she took a stand. Right now, though, she was unsure.

"Is anything wrong, darling?" Ema asked, aware of the unaccustomed tension between them.

"Yes," Dana said softly. "I hate boarding school. I want to live at home and go to day school again."

"Darling, we've been through this a hundred times. You can't get the best education or meet the right people in a day school."

"Oh, Mother, I don't care about the right people," Dana said.

"You will when you're a little older, take my word for it."

Dana stared past the embroidered Swiss muslin curtains of the bay window. "Sometimes I think you just don't want me around anymore!"

Dismayed, Ema resisted the impulse to give in. "Dana, you know that isn't true! Are you going to hurt me, just to have your own way?"

Dana, in a lightning change of mood, shot out of the chair to hug her mother. "I'm sorry, Maman, I didn't mean it." She hesitated, then looked up at Ema, her gray eyes watchful. "But will you at least think about it? I hate it there."

Emanuelle smoothed Dana's rumpled hair and kissed her cheek. "I think I know why. Your father was right, the girls *are* bothering you about us, aren't they?"

Dana nodded. "But it isn't only that. I just want to be at home with you and Daddy," she said.

"That's nonsense, Dana. Daddy and I are away half the time. What did the girls say?"

"Oh, Mother," Dana sighed, "I don't remember all of it, but I shut them up. I told them *their* mothers can't change anything but their hairstyles, but you're different, you try to help women."

They walked to the door, arms around each other. "You're different, too, darling," Ema said.

"But I'm not, not the way you mean." Dana said it with heat, not envy.

"But you are! Even to a passion for archaeology at your age! *Mon Dieu*, do you want to be like everyone else?"

Dana broke away and ran to the top of the broad staircase. "There's different, and different," she called back as she descended. "I'm going out for a run with Castor and Pollux."

"Then please be back in time to dress for dinner," Ema called after her. There was no reply, but Dana came down to dinner bathed and dressed in the white ruffled organdy dress with a wide blue satin sash that Ema had put out on her bed. She wore white knee socks and hand-turned Mary Janes. A blue satin band held her shining shoulder-length hair in check.

"You look beautiful," her father said.

"I hate these clothes. I'd rather be wearing my uniform."

"I still think you look beautiful," Harding said, and Dana smiled at him, tranquillity apparently restored.

* * *

On a warm night in August after Dana had gone to bed, Ema came into the library and sank into a chair. "I never dreamed *Oh, Mother* could be said so many ways," she said to Harding.

"She's at a difficult age," Harding agreed.

"And how! Hiking boots, caves, and arrowheads! She slumps in a chair like a bag of cornmeal—after all those dancing and deportment lessons."

"Ema, she's not happy at boarding school. If she doesn't want to stay there, why insist, just to produce a social butterfly."

"I don't want her to be a social butterfly! I want her to be—a real lady. She'll get used to boarding school—and if she were at school in England, she wouldn't have to defend our politics. She could just be a little girl getting on with her education!"

"No, Ema, Foxcroft is far enough! I don't like her being involved in our battles, either, but the situation in Europe's too volatile right now."

"Nonsense, Chamberlain will do anything to avoid war." She was determined to go to Germany at the end of September and, deciding she could no longer put it off, she told Harding about her projected trip.

"You can't go, not after what you've printed about them, let alone what happened when you were there last time!"

Ema shrugged that aside. "They've invited me back to set the record straight—not that it'll help them—and nothing happened, not really. It's a chance in a million to get inside Germany while there's a crisis on, and just imagine how sensational those interviews will be!"

"That's beside the point. I don't want you to go, Emanuelle."

"The interviews are very much the point! I didn't want you to go to Spain last year, either, to get a story, but you did, and that was a shooting war. Hitler's only prolonging his tantrum over Czechoslovakia. You're afraid I'll be the most important columnist on your paper, that's all." She felt her anger swelling like a wave, carrying her too far.

"Are you saying I want to stand in the way of your career?"

"I think you do, especially when I have a chance at something really big!"

"For example?"

She lit a cigarette, on the brink of recalling RSVP, of bringing up all the times he had killed an idea for an article or censored what she wrote; but that had all been said already. "For example now. I want to finish what I started, just as you'll want to be in Spain if the Loyalists surrender. I must decide those things for myself, just as you do. Harding, please let's not argue. It's a month off and I'll be perfectly safe."

"Even from Major Brand?"

"Darling, how sweet," Ema said, seizing the opportunity. She went to sit on the arm of his chair. "You're jealous, that's what this is all about."

"Don't flirt with me, Ema, I'm serious."

"No, you're jealous. I think it's lovely." She slid from the chair to his lap and kissed him. She knew she was using her body to solve a problem that was not sexual, but men did that all the time.

He put his arms around her. "Have I any reason to be?"

"I'm *your* wife, *n'est-ce pas*? And a damned good one, if you ask me."

"The best," Harding said. "That's why I don't want you taking risks."


It was not the end of the running argument, but it was the last time they made love before she left. Harding persisted in sharing a bed with her no matter how violently they clashed after that temporary truce. She made it clear, in the subtle ways a woman has, that she did not want sex; she even hoped he would move to a separate bedroom. But although he did not attempt to make love to her, he slept resolutely at her side when he was at home.

The worst argument came just before Ema sailed for Europe, when Harding insisted he now had legitimate reasons to worry. The German clamor to annex Czechoslovakia had grown very loud. When France mobilized, the peace of Europe seemed to hang in the balance.

"The British are issuing gas masks and ration cards and digging trenches," Harding insisted. "Their fleet's in the North Sea, ready to blockade Germany! You can't sail off into a war, for God's sake. I won't let you."

"Sweet Jesus, when will you stop telling me what I can and cannot do? There isn't going to *be* a war because no one's ready to fight one, you said so yourself! And if there is, I'll come back."

"You might be interned for the duration; how would you like that?"

"If you really want to know, I'd like it better than living with you for a jailor!"


They were barely speaking to each other on the day Ema sailed. "I hate this," she told him, "but I refuse to be bridled, like a brood mare."

"I'm not trying to bridle you, Ema. Damn it, you don't know what love is if you don't understand the difference!"

"Love is a very good excuse for a man to tell his wife what to do, but I know more about love than you do, Harding! Love has open hands, for one thing, love knows how to let go. You've always wanted your own way, with me and with Dana, but you can't have it, Harding, you just can't."

A few times she thought he suspected that another reason fueled her defiance, but it was her own guilt—something she had never felt before—endowing him with a clairvoyance he could not possibly possess. And by now she had to go, she had to get away from him for a while to decide how she would live the rest of her life. All her other doubts aside, Julian was the one link she had left to her son. Still, the way she and Harding parted made the crossing utterly wretched for her.

# 71

SEPTEMBER 1938

By the time Ema's ship docked in Bremerhaven, the British Prime Minister was in Munich making a third attempt to pacify Hitler. Those who were fed to the teeth with appeasement grumbled when the Munich Pact was signed, but they were in the minority. Those who knew Britain was not prepared for war quietly began to make ready, even as Chamberlain returned to his reprieved people with the promise of "peace in our time."

Ema, absorbed in her own turmoil during the entire crossing, went directly to the hotel to meet Julian. Her face showed the strain of many days of introspection and her growing anxiety about Harding.

"You don't have to say it," Julian said as soon as they were alone. "It's in your eyes. You want to end this—us."

She shook her head. "I wish I *did* want that! It would make things so much easier. But I've had some time to think and I know I can't—I can't go on living with Harding and deceiving him, not anymore. And I don't want to leave him." She sat down, wearied by her confusion. "Everything's changed since you met each other, I can't keep the two of you separate anymore. I don't understand why that should be, but it is, it just is, and it's a heartbreak, no matter what I do about it."

"Hush, darling, don't cry." He knelt by her chair. "I can't bear to see you like this."

She smoothed his hair; the shape of his head was familiar after years of intimacy. "Julian, how can I let you go? You're half of my life. I love you, you give me joy, you always have, but this is too much for me too. I never thought anything could come between us. I never felt I was betraying him, but I do now and it's—unbearable. I don't even think guilt describes what I feel."

"You've never seen us through his eyes before."

Or Dana's, she thought, flinching.

She looked up as if he had given her the last piece of a puzzle. "Yes, that's it, only through my eyes, no one else's—and now I hurt for him. We're so far apart now, all we do is argue, but I'm arguing because of *this*, you and me, more than other things. He doesn't know it and that's not fair; that *is* betrayal. Lately I've wanted to tell him. It's the kind of thing he'd understand in the abstract, but not about me, Julian. He'd be furious and humiliated. He trusts me; that's the worst of it."

"No, the worst of it is that he loves you, Emalie, I'd be a fool not to see that. And you love him."

"It was never like us, Julian, but yes, I do. It's—I never realized before this how important my life with him is to me, I wouldn't know how to get on without him. Yet we were hardly speaking to each other when I left." She touched his face, traced the line of his mouth. "And then I see you and nothing else matters."

He took her hands in his and got to his feet. "Emalie, you need time alone, away from him and Dana and from me, too, before you make a final decision. I'm going back to London, there's a train in two hours."

She stood protestingly and put her arms around him. "Oh, Julian, no," she said. "Is this the way we say good-bye?"

"It's beyond me to say good-bye to you a second time. But we can't go on like this—you can't." He took her face in his hands. "Ema, I've hurt you too much already, I won't do it again."

"I don't understand what you're saying."

"Only that I'll abide by any decision you make, but *you* must make it, fairly, while you're away from both of us." He kissed her mouth tenderly and she clung to him. "If I stayed, I would persuade you, darling, every way I know how." Deliberately he put her from him and she watched him while, as if in slow motion, he took his coat and picked up his packed valise. Don't go, she pleaded, but she did it silently.

"I'll go down with you," she said, and followed him out of the door. Even a few more minutes with him was better than nothing. The lavish elevator rose in its glassed-in cage, doors crashed open and shut. Arm in arm they sank to the street level—and at the street level came face to face with Thomas Blessing.

"Ema!" Blessing said, a broad grin on his large handsome face. Then he noticed her arm in Julian's and his expression changed to lewd appraisal. "I don't have to ask what *you're* doing here." He chuckled at both of them. "It's Sir Julian Saxon, isn't it, the English pacifist; I'll bet you're pleased with yesterday's work at Munich."

The men shook hands. "Very," Julian said.

"I've just arrived," Ema explained, knowing she should not. "And Sir Julian's just leaving."

"Good-bye, Ema," Julian said politely. "I must go or I'll miss my train. Have a good trip." With a barely courteous nod to Blessing he left, striding through the lobby to the hotel's entrance and out into the street without looking back.

She wanted to run after him, but she got back into the elevator with Thomas. She chatted overbrightly with him and refused a dinner invitation, which obviously included the night.

"Why not, Emanuelle? It's obvious we both do as we please on our travels." He raised an eyebrow. "Harding will never know about it from me."

"Know what? That you've been here making deals with the Nazis?"

"No, that you've been making love with that lucky bastard who just left."

"Thomas, you have a feverish imagination, you really have, and I'm busy tonight." She left him, feigning reluctance that she could not dine with him, and went quickly to the window of her room, as if she might still see Julian in the drive below, wondering how she could have let him go.

She loved him with the same essential innocence that had characterized their feeling for each other from the start, but as if with another self. And she could not explain that to anyone.

Dana would never believe her either. Children have such clearcut ideas about loyalty, and Dana, already embarrassed by her parents' sexual relationship—the double bed, the closed bedroom door—would defend Harding with all the fierce devotion of an adolescent girl, taking the side of her father against the woman who shared a part of his life no daughter could.

And he deserved devotion! With a little sob Emanuelle wished she could talk to him. He was the one person capable of giving her sound advice on the only problem she could not put to him.

A decision was beyond her. She knew it from the moment Julian was gone. She was unable to take a step in either direction, to hack away either half of herself. She knew that for once she would do nothing, nerve-racking as inaction was to her; she would let one day become another day, one year another year, until the time for making this choice had passed or life had decided it for her, just how she could not imagine.

She kept to her room for the next two days, avoiding Thomas Blessing, trying to think, but it was not in Ema's nature to roost long upon a problem she could not solve. She left Berlin on the third morning after her arrival for her tour of the *Lebensborn* homes in the south.

What she heard from the girls confirmed her suspicions: they met their babies' fathers only once or twice before they entered into a "biological marriage." The men were officially called "conception assistants," not lovers.

The government organized many occasions for the purpose; the most popular were the spring festivals and the party rallies in September, but the *Lebensborn* homes had become glorified brothels for the SS.

Not your typical high school proms, Ema thought. She envisioned bunting and banners in the social hall: "Class of 1938. Meet, Mate, Propagate."

She was spared the company of either Major Brand or Frau Gruner; evidently they had both had enough of her. The much younger woman assigned to escort Emanuelle this time said very little, although her contempt for Ema's decadent French blood was apparent from time to time.

She planned to print most of her conversations with the girls *verbatim:* the Nazis would be hoist with their own petard when she did. These girls made her grateful that Dana was safe, that she had a mind of her own no matter how difficult she was getting to be.

"We will go now to talk to the mothers in the garden," her guide directed on Ema's last day, at a *Lebensborn* home in Baden, and Ema followed her. It was a beautiful October day, awash with sparkling clean air and sun and something—the rustle of fallen leaves, the crisp scent of autumn, a play of light through the trees—reminded her of a park in Paris when she was very young. She felt another pang for her youth, gone like that of the adolescent mothers before her in the garden, tending their newborns like dolls.

One of them was singing, but it was not the girl's voice Emalie Anne heard crooning a German lullaby, it was Sylvie's, out of that long ago when there had been some kind of tenderness and trust between Emalie and her mother, some kind of love, before it was ravaged away on a rainy afternoon in the Rue Momette. She yearned for that first lost love as much as she yearned for Julian, and sudden tears filled her eyes.

She didn't give a damn what Hitler did with German youth. Why should she? She had lost her own girlhood to rape and her youth to war and an impossible love she could not surrender and must not keep.

"*Ach, so,*" her escort said. "Even you see how it is beautiful to be *Kindersegen,* blessed with children."

"Yes," Ema said, wanting her son, grateful she would soon be with Dana. They were too much for her, her loves and her irretrievable losses. They buzzed around her divided heart like bees, stinging. She was wounded and she wanted to go home and rest from all of it. She left Germany with relief.

Harding was waiting at the pier when she reached New York and she
eyed him anxiously in the moment before he held out his arms to her. "I
put a notice in the *Star,*" he said. "'Harding come home, all is forgiven.
Signed Ema.' Say it's over, Ema, whatever it was."

She put her arms around him gratefully, aware that she must negotiate
a new relationship with him and not let him know she was doing it. "Yes,
of course it is—at least until the next time."

"There won't be one, this time was enough. How did it go, any trouble?" They walked to the customs shed on the pier.

"No, the Germans are still a lot more interested in Dr. Goebbels's
shiner than the Munich Pact."

Harding laughed. "Who hit him?"

"Well, he has dozens of mistresses—amazing, isn't it, for such a little
worm—and last spring one of their husbands socked him in the eye. The
Germans are still laughing about it."

"Good for the husband! But did you get what you went for?"

"Oh, yes. The Nazis give themselves away, just being what they are. I
have a great series of articles."

"How about dinner at the Stork Club to celebrate?" He was too festive
and she realized that he was uneasy about the moment of sexual reconciliation and wanted to put it off.

"No newspapermen, no politicians? Just the two of us?"

"Just the two of us, the way it used to be before you were rich and
famous—if you can remember what that was like."

She remembered what it was like. There were things about it she could
never forget.


It was a comfort to lie in his arms again. He was as tentative as she was,
then as gently loving. Their bodies were well attuned, they satisfied each
other, but she wondered if they had seen the last of real passion together.

# 72

"I'm beginning to like flying," Ema said, getting into her berth aboard Pan American's *Yankee Clipper* to Southampton, "even if I still don't understand what keeps these damned things up." They had surged into the air from Port Washington early, spent the morning reading and waiting for the last sitting in the plane's dining room to have a champagne lunch. They had played bridge in the lounge, and by now it seemed a good idea to sleep through part of the trip.

The compartments were designed to seat ten people on short hops and sleep six on overnight trips, but Harding had booked a private cabin suite for the twenty-four-hour flight.

"I always knew you'd love it," Harding said, pulling down the little shades before he got into his own berth.

She had been nervous on her first transatlantic flight aboard the *China Clipper* with a press party, but not for very long. The enormous craft, with two decks, a bar, and a galley, apart from its passenger compartments, felt perfectly solid.

Harding's long-term bet on the future of aviation was paying off. Apart from the plants he owned in California for the manufacture of smaller craft, he had been foresighted enough to buy patents on steering and wheel-assembly mechanisms for the huge passenger planes that were coming into their own. And he was buying land for the long-runway airports of the future, for planes that would not have to be built, as the Clippers were, to take off and land on water.

She stretched out gratefully, one ear still attentive to the sound of the motors that somehow kept the forty-two-ton airboat aloft. She knew she would wake at each of the three stops in New Brunswick, Newfoundland, and Ireland before they reached Southampton, but she wanted the time to think as well as to rest.

Almost a year had passed since Berlin, and there had been no telephone calls, no cables. She was deliberately trying to make a future without Julian, and the resolution had changed her life with Harding, almost as if he sensed it. There was a great void within her, but the burden of conscience that had afflicted her since the two men met in London was gone. These days they rarely argued; they hardly disagreed except about Dana.

Much as Emanuelle still wanted to send her to school in England, the consensus was that Europe was headed for war. Ema would not put Dana in harm's way until the issue was resolved. The wrangle about boarding school had continued until Dana's friend, Carolyn George, entered Foxcroft, too, and Dana was at last content to stay there, "even though," Harding said at the time, "I still don't understand why you want her so far away."

"It isn't what *I* want, Harding," Ema insisted. "I'm thinking of Dana's future." In a way, though, Ema was protecting herself too. Someday Dana would leave her—sooner or later everyone did. It was wiser to put a distance between them, to practice for a parting that was bound to come.

Dana was spending August in Maine with Carolyn and her grandmother, "and *she* doesn't care if we wear overalls to dinner," Dana had announced with satisfaction while Caro blushed to the roots of her pale brown hair.

Ema smoothed the sheets and turned her thoughts to business. Monsieur Étienne had accepted her very liberal offer and the Louis XV decor was almost complete. Her restaurant, Danielle's, was scheduled to open in October, just as the winter season in New York got under way in earnest. She had left the work in the Atwoods' hands until she got back in September for the opening.

The color scheme was cream and ivory "because," Ema said, "we don't want anything to clash with the women's clothes." In addition to etched mirrors, a Lalique fountain, and Baccarat crystal, the restaurant boasted the most modern kitchen in New York.

"But I shall have no interference in my kitchen," Monsieur Étienne had reminded her again only last week, waving his doughy little hands. His eyes were always bright under his pillowy lids and tufted reddish brows. *"Vous êtes toujours d'accord, Madame?"*

"Yes, yes, I still agree. For my part, I shall have no interference in the restaurant's administration."

*"Mais non,* the preparation of exquisite food is an art. I leave the ledgers to you."

"Just get the best prices you can for whatever you buy, Monsieur Étienne. You may be an *artiste culinaire,* but I'm a businesswoman and I intend to make money on this venture." She was certain she would, and Harding agreed with her once his initial surprise had passed that she was the secret owner of the new restaurant.

"I sometimes wonder what else you haven't told me," he added, but the change in her—and he couldn't really put his finger on what it was—had made him soften the remark with a smile, and there had been no further argument between them.

A few months ago he had declared that Ema needed a holiday. "We both do. We've been working too hard and we've never really seen the British Isles. I know you don't like London, but we'll stay only a few nights before we start touring the provinces."

She had agreed to the trip, although she suggested France as a better alternative.

"The French think all Americans are barbarians," Harding said.

"So do the English."

"Yes, but they have the good manners to hide it."

"Perfidious Albion," she said, agreeing.

"There's something to be said for perfidy; it spares a lot of feelings."

There was no longer reason to flinch inwardly when he said such things, and that in itself was a relief. She would not call Julian while she was in England, but Harding probably would—irony upon irony!—because he wanted to know what position Julian would take in the event of war.

"It's a damn shame he has to choose at all," Harding had said only last night in bed, "but if England goes to war, what else can he do but join forces with Broadhurst and the others?"

"Maybe," was Ema's noncommittal reply. She had been glad of the dark.

"He'll have to. The English want peace, they'll have to be jolted into belligerence. Saxon is one of their war heroes and the Establishment is bound to put pressure on him to reverse himself."

Ema turned now in her berth to look at Harding in the dim light of the compartment. He had the happy facility of falling asleep as soon as he closed his eyes. He was forty-five, but aside from the first traces of gray in his dark hair he looked it only when he was tired. His high energy kept him youthful. Her energy had diminished considerably.

"Although," Kate had said, sympathetic as always, "your lassitude would be wild activity in any other woman."

"I don't seem to have any joie de vivre."

"Maybe," Kate suggested, "you're still looking for it in the wrong place. At least you're peaceful."

"Peace is for cows," had been Ema's tart rejoinder.

\*        \*        \*

After the second series of articles on Germany she had turned her attention to RSVP, the restaurant, and society, writing only occasional political commentary for the women's page, and that puzzled Harding. So did their lovemaking; it was steady but uncharacteristically serene—or did that happen to all couples after years of marriage? he wondered. He told himself it was enough, that he did not miss the lusty eroticism that once left them both shining inside and out—but it puzzled him.

He was grateful that their period of confrontation was over. He still believed his major rival for the sole possession of her was Ema's long-beloved ghost. Too proud to be jealous of a phantom, he preferred to see Ema's fidelity to her lost love as a touchingly tender streak in her otherwise guarded personality. He convinced himself that the threat of another war had dredged up memories that explained the subtle change in her.

He was not an analytical man, but he felt she was asking him wordlessly for something he could not identify. It was too nebulous a feeling to discuss with her, but it was there between them.

On Ema's side, she had willingly dispensed with ecstasy; all it had ever brought her was heartache. She wanted Harding to fill the corner of her life she had once kept only for Julian. She was glad of the restored comradeship between them, but it was not all she needed, and she tossed in her berth, apprehensive about the future, his and hers and the world's, while the Clipper roared on.

Since the fall of the Spanish Republic in the spring, Americans were disillusioned with noble causes. They had put war at the bottom of their priority list; neutrality and isolationism were the watchwords. People were visiting "The World of Tomorrow" at the World's Fair and avidly reading all about the upcoming crop of debutantes for 1939–40. It was of importance to very few that Hitler had broken his word about Czechoslovakia and shifted his greedy eyes to Danzig and the Polish Corridor; or that Britain, France, and Russia *had* agreed on mutual assistance should any of the three be attacked, precisely as Julian had predicted. Americans saw Hitler screaming like a madman in the newsreels and didn't much like him, but he was Europe's problem, not theirs.

He was Ema's problem, though. What would happen to Julian and Drew if England went to war? The question never ceased to torment her.

She did not agree with Harding that Julian would reverse himself about war. He would find some way to help his country if war came, but he would never yield to any demands except those he made upon himself.

Damn Broadhurst and the others, Ema thought, punching her pillow, Julian's worth all of them put together. She knew he would resist coercion, as she did, fiercely and often unwisely, rather than act against her will.

She fell into a restless sleep.

# 73

They stayed longest in Devon, in a great Victorian pile of a hotel in Sidmouth. Ema loved the narrow leaf-shaded country lanes meandering through the high lush pastures on either side. She was up early to walk in the soft wet mist of morning, enjoyed the gentle light that lingered so late in the evening. She liked the courteous people and the games of cricket on the green and the tender concern of the hotel staff for the splinted pigeon, surrounded by its family, that was recuperating on their balcony and must not be moved.

"In France they'd have eaten him," she told Harding one morning as they drove toward Torquay. "The English love animals and the animals respond. English cows are better-natured than French cows."

"What would a Parisian know about cows?"

"I spent a few days in the country once."

"Where? Doing what?"

She turned toward the window. "Just looking, like this. Do you have the camera? Dana wants pictures of Kent's Cavern."

"Right here," he said, reaching down to pat it. "I have a whole roll of Stonehenge and another of Tintagel. I never thought my baby would grow up to be an archaeologist."

"Dana's not going to be an archaeologist!" Ema said. "It's no career for a young woman."

"I wouldn't make any bets."

They had left Devon and were driving back to London when they heard the news of the German-Soviet nonaggression pact. It was universally seen as a sure prelude to war, and in London the Tate Gallery began to move its treasures to safety. In Canterbury the cathedral's irreplaceable stained-glass windows were removed, crated, and placed in subterranean vaults. This war, they already knew, was not going to be fought in trenches on a well-demarcated field of battle. Airplanes would bring it wherever there was shipping or strategic industry.

"It's hard to believe," Ema said. "Hitler's such a rabid anticommunist. What'll he tell his people now?"

"Anything—and they'll believe him," Harding said. "He can't have Stalin at his back, can he, if he plans to attack Poland. I'm afraid Julian pinned too many hopes on the Allies' mutual assistance agreement with the Soviets."

"Talk about perfidious Albion, Stalin takes the cake!"

"He's expecting the whole world to attack him eventually and he bought time to prepare. I hope England can do as much."

They found a kind of desperate gaiety in London as people tried to believe war would be averted. "We might as well join the party," Harding said. "I think Beatrice Lillie's at the Café de Paris."

In the lavish nightclub, gorgeously dressed Londoners danced to "Deep Purple"—and why not, they told each other. Hitler's poised armies had not moved on Danzig after all. Maybe he could be propitiated again. Surely the Poles could be "persuaded" to give him Danzig as the Czechs had surrendered the Sudetenland. Anything was better than war. "Why Die for Danzig?" demanded a headline in the French paper *L'Oeuvre*. What was the free port, anyway, but an artificial creation of the Versailles Treaty?

Harding called Lord Broadhurst the next day and his expression was glum when he put down the telephone. "He says Hitler's delay is only temporary and may God help England, she's not prepared to fight yet. The French have the best army in Europe but no heart to use it. Would you mind if I stayed on another week?"

"I'll stay with you. If England declares war, she'll need her women again and that's right up my street." She would be near Julian and Drew, too, but that was small comfort when she couldn't see them. She must find a discreet way to learn what was happening to them.

On September first, a hot, humid morning, Ema called Mary Alice Chandler at the *Gazette* and invited her to lunch.

"Lunch?" Mary Alice shouted. "I haven't got time to go to the loo! Haven't you turned on the wireless? Hitler's attacked Poland and we've told him to get out or else! I'm on my way to Charing Cross Station, they've started evacuating the children. If you want a story, that's where you'll find it."

Ema saw story enough in the streets of London. There were banks of sandbags everywhere and the streetlights were shrouded in black shades. The trees and curbs had been ringed with white paint to guide motorists

and pedestrians through the blacked-out nights ahead and Ema saw a
policeman wearing a steel helmet instead of the familiar domed hat of the
London bobby.

There was organized confusion at the station, and Ema reflected that
even English children knew how to queue up politely, something the
French and Americans had never learned. There were long lines of
youngsters boarding trains for the country, each clutching a valise and a
gas mask, with their names and addresses tagged around their necks.
The little ones wailed for their mothers, and the mothers smiled and
waved reassuringly until the trains pulled out and they could collapse in
tears themselves.

Ema found Mary Alice and watched the heartbreaking scene with her.
"Damn the Germans! I wish I could do something besides file a story,"
Ema said.

"If you stay on, there'll be plenty to do, never fear."

"I know," Ema said. "I've been through a war before."

Mary Alice looked skeptical. "Not like this one. I hear the Germans
aren't sparing civilians in Poland. Now we know what *Blitzkreig* means, it
means women and children first." She turned back to Ema briefly.
"Where are you staying? I'll try to ring you when I can."

"At the Connaught. Please try."

Mary Alice nodded and plunged into the crowd and Ema left the station. She walked ten blocks before she found a taxi to take her to the *Star*'s
office in Fleet Street. Until last year it had been a small headquarters for
the *Star*'s overseas reporters. Now its foreign correspondents occupied an
entire floor.

Harding was there, bending anxiously over the teletype, and she joined
him. "What about France?" she asked, peering at the clattering machine.

"Nothing yet, she doesn't want to fight."

"Who does, with all those dead? My poor Danielle, what'll happen to
her?"

He put an arm around her. "It's incredible that it's started again only
twenty years later." He shook his head. "Armored columns against Polish
cavalry—it'll be a slaughter."

"What will you do, Harding?"

He looked at her. "I was thinking of staying on to do a series of broadcasts from London. Britain needs aid, and where's it going to come from if
not America?"

"Broadcasts?" She nodded emphatically. "Yes, you'd be good at that.
What line will you take?"

"Just describe things as I see them. If the reports from Poland are anything to go by, that should be enough." He turned to her. "I think you'd
better go home."

"Soon," she said, temporizing. "Let's see how things go."

There was no call from Mary Alice until two days later. It was early, but Harding had gone to Fleet Street already and Ema was poring over the Sunday papers. The sultry weather of the past two days had broken after some ferocious thunderclaps the night before, and it was a lovely sunny morning.

"The news is grim," Mary Alice said. "If Hitler doesn't start withdrawing from Poland by eleven this morning, we'll declare war. The Commons was in an uproar last night; they smelled a second Munich and they weren't having any."

Ema looked at her watch. It was ten o'clock. "What are the chances he'll pull out?"

"Nil—and that leaves us up the bloody creek with no weapons and the pacifists to thank for it."

"Mary Alice, you're not going to print that!"

"No, of course I'm not. We need every scrap of morale we can muster, pull together, don't let down the side, all of that." Mary Alice sighed. "People are so admirable in wartime, it makes you wonder. Switch on the wireless at eleven. I'll call you tomorrow. Tonight I'm going to get drunk."

Chamberlain, crooning dolefully in his nasal voice, declared war at 11:15, as the church bells rang out all over England for morning services. Half an hour later the air raid sirens wailed, but that was a false alarm and people who had rushed to the inadequate shelters came shamefacedly out of them.


And, incredibly, life resumed. Almost overnight women appeared in the uniforms of army and navy auxiliary forces or to fill jobs as army and ambulance drivers and clerks. They replaced the nation's men as Ema had seen them do in France, but this time everyone carried a gas mask in a case that often housed compacts, lipstick, and ration tickets as well.

In America—thank God for America, Ema thought—Eleanor Holm was the top attraction at the World's Fair, the wasp-waist corset had arrived from France and been picketed by women who objected to more girdling than a two-way-stretch provided, and Congress refused to amend the Neutrality Act to permit the sale of planes to belligerents, including England and France.

"Are they blind?" Harding demanded. "This is America's first line of defense. If Europe falls, Hitler will polish off the Soviets and then come after us."

"He would never dare!" Ema said. Then she thought of the madness at Nuremberg, the drums and the banners and the crowd's voracious roar, and she knew that Harding was right.

# 74

Emanuelle met her son two weeks after the Second World War began. She did not see him at first. She saw Julian and Davina over the maître d's shoulder as he showed them to a table in the Ritz bar. The Saxons did not look up, and she would have walked on, but Harding stopped.

"Saxon!" he said. "I'm glad to see you, I've been hoping to speak to you. But it's Sir Julian now—and Lady Davina. We met at Lord Broadhurst's."

"I remember, Mr. Ellis," Davina said. She smiled brightly at Emanuelle. "Good evening, Miss Beranger. I'd like you to meet my son."

Her eyes met Julian's briefly and closed for an instant before she looked at her son. He was wearing the uniform of the Royal Air Force, it was the first thing she noticed. He looked very much like Julian, but he was taller and broader and his features were not so finely drawn.

He shook hands with Harding and smiled politely at Emanuelle, with a nod of his handsome head. It was a brilliant smile, with the brio of youth in it. "I've heard so much about you both," he said to Harding and Ema.

What had he heard, what had Julian told him? And Davina, for God's sake?

"Flattering, I hope," she said dryly, but she was glad that her deep wine jersey dress, its shirred softness stitched flat at the midriff, was elegant and understated, even severe.

"Of course," he returned with a real smile this time, and she thought unexpectedly, he is as irresistible to women as Julian, but in a different way. It was not the kind of appraisal she had anticipated making about her son. But then, she had never dreamed she would meet him except on some carefully designed stage set of her mind. She held her myriad feelings at arm's length, like a loaded gun.

"Won't you join us?" Julian asked as if none of it had ever happened—

Paris, Neuilly, Venice—as if she had not let him leave her in Berlin without the courage to tell him that it was for the last time. Maybe he doesn't know it yet! she thought with a start. But when she looked at him again she saw that he did know and was as desolate as she, as bleak as he had been that first time in Venice, before their being together had given him something more than honor.

"We'd like that," Harding said, "if we're not intruding."

"Not at all," Drew assured them. "You can help me celebrate. Please, sit down." He gave Ema his chair and snapped his fingers with easy authority, signaling the waiter to bring two more.

"Celebrate?" Harding asked, smiling at the young man's high spirits.

"Father's not opposing my leaving Oxford to join the R.A.F. I knew he wouldn't once we were really up against it."

"Did you? How very clever of you." Davina let Julian light her cigarette. Her enameled nails glowed crimson in the light; they matched the clear red of her dress, the most dramatic choice for a blonde who can wear it, Ema thought, and Davina still could. "I'd have sworn he wouldn't let you go to war even if hell froze over. At least he won't go himself." There was affection when she spoke of Julian; her disdain was for Drew.

Julian said nothing and Drew's exuberance vanished. He sat down between Ema and Davina. "He can still serve without having to fire a gun, Mother." It shocked Ema to hear him call Davina "Mother," but more shocking still was the look Davina flashed him, imperious and patronizing. Apparently he was accustomed to it. He lit a cigarette for himself. His hands were like Julian's.

"I'm sorry you might have to make the choice," Harding said to Julian. "It was a case of too little, too late. If the Allies had started mending their Soviet fences back when you suggested it, there might not have been a war."

"It's not much of a war," Davina said. "The French are sitting on their Maginot Line, the theaters have reopened here, and those blasted sirens have stopped going off every time a bird flies over. Even my gallant son"—and she put a hand on his sleeve—"has to restrain his impatience for action."

Drew colored, but he made no attempt to argue the point, and Ema wondered what he would have been like had she had the raising of him. He would have been less tentative, certainly. Dana—and for the first time she thought of Dana as his half-sister—was only twelve, but she spoke her mind more freely than he seemed to.

Drew left Harding and his father to their conversation and turned back to Ema. "I've read most of your articles on Germany, Miss Beranger. I thought they were smashing."

"Sensational," Davina said ambiguously.

Ema ignored her. "Thank you, but who showed them to you?"

"Fenella Bayliss—a friend of mine." Drew looked at his watch. "She ought to be here any time now, she'll be glad to meet you."

He asked some questions about the articles and Ema thought, not without pride, He's very bright and he has more English charm than ought to be allowed. But she didn't think Drew would ever suffer a conflict between love and duty. He had learned to deal with difficult situations by withdrawing from them.

If he were hurt, I couldn't bear it, she thought. Her eyes were on the wings of his well-tailored uniform, but she saw the scars that covered Julian's body. She thought, Most mothers knew a child's body minutely in its infancy, but I've never even touched him, not even on the day he was born.

She had to touch him. She asked him for a cigarette and when he lit it for her, her hand cupped his for a protective instant and all she had felt for him, collected and hidden away for twenty years, surged inside her with a force that startled her.

He was hers, her flesh and blood, and the same feeling that had overwhelmed her when she first looked at Dana engulfed her now.

She felt Davina watching her, and returned the look with eyes the color of slate. It was Davina who looked away first. Mercifully Drew saw Fenella Bayliss and left the table to bring her back.

She was one of those clear-skinned, fair-haired English girls who are not beautiful from across a room but seem so almost immediately after you meet them. Drew introduced her proudly and his eyes rested tenderly on her. Her lips were pink and perfect, like the hint of cleavage showing above the line of her rose velvet dress.

They're in love, Ema thought with a pang while she answered Fenella's eager questions, and they're much too young for love and war.

The Saxons departed soon after for a private dinner party and Ema sighed inwardly and picked up the martini that was not cold or dry enough.

"A strange man," Harding said.

"Who?"

"Julian. He lives under a cloud."

"Why wouldn't he, with a war on and his son in the R.A.F.?" She knew what it had cost Julian to let Drew go before he had to.

"That isn't what I mean." Harding searched for the right words. "I've met men like him before. It's as if something bars their way to happiness and they've never known it fully, even for a moment, and never will." He took her hand. "When I first met you, I thought you were like that."

She made herself smile. "Well, you soon found differently."

"I'd like to think so." He paused, looking at her. She knew that look. Tell me, it said, I don't care what it is, I want to know.

I can't tell you, don't ask me! she told him mutely. "I must say, you're being very fanciful tonight, Harding—but I'm starving. Can we go on to dinner?"

In the next few days she felt on edge, but she kept very busy, filing stories almost daily on preparations for a war that didn't seem to be starting. A state of war had been declared, but no great battle had been joined, and there was the curious feeling that if everyone carried on as usual, it might just go away. But by the end of the week she decided to fly home, fleeing what she could not face. Danielle's was due to open; it would make a good pretext if she needed one.

She had managed to get through to Danielle in Paris when Harding returned to their hotel suite. He seemed very preoccupied as she pleaded in vain for Danielle to leave everything and come to America.

"I've been through one war," Danielle said, "and I'll get through this one—if it ever starts."

"What's wrong?" Ema asked as soon as she gave up and put down the telephone.

"I just heard a very troubling story about Julian Saxon," Harding said. "He wants to go back on active service—intelligence or an equivalent, he was too badly wounded last time for a field commission—but they might not accept him. He was in Germany in thirty-seven with the Windsors and several times before and since. Some people are threatening to say he's pro-Nazi, that he advised Hitler on the negotiations for the Munich Pact." He went to get himself a Scotch while Ema listened, riveted. "They're calling the Pact a devilish instrument, designed to lull Britain into a false sense of security while Hitler brought his war machine to maximum strength. They're linking the pacifists to it and Julian's one of the best known in England."

"Who are 'they'?" Ema demanded.

"Some anti-Establishment people. They'll do anything to attack the government, even at a time like this."

"But why, for God's sake?"

"So they can bring it down and take over themselves—otherwise the Conservatives will be in for the duration. Britain isn't ready for war, she needs all her spirit, all of her famous bulldog tenacity to hang on. A scandal about a German sympathizer in the officer reserve corps is the last thing the government needs."

"But it isn't true!" Ema said, aghast. "You know it isn't true."

He sat down and took off his shoes. "Of course it isn't. I think Julian's a fine man, you know that. But unless this is quashed, he might not be permitted to go back on active service. He might even be arrested or interned for the duration. He would certainly be pilloried from one end of the country to the other if the rumor even got out."

"That would kill him," Emanuelle said desperately.

Harding looked up at the sound of her voice. He nodded agreement but his eyes questioned her.

"I can't stand vicious slander," she said by way of answer. "I've had it thrown my way."

"No more can I," he said, hanging his jacket and trousers on the mahogany valet. "But if I know the British Establishment, they won't let it get that far. I need a hot bath." He went into the bathroom.

Emanuelle shivered as she sat down to apply her makeup. Julian had been with her on most of his trips to Germany, but he would say nothing about their meetings. Nor could she. Yet how could she let his whole life be put in question and his honor with it just when she—the reason for his dilemma—had abandoned him.

Damn his honor; it had brought them nothing but grief! Yet it was one reason she loved him. The two of them would not have been caught in this web were it not for his principles, but he had never compromised them, except for her, and certainly not in the monstrous ways she had. His principles were what he was, and what he was had always been between them, almost as much as what she was.

She went to the bathroom door. "Harding? Is there anything you can do to help him?"

"I'm damn well going to find out," he said. "I forgot to tell you the good news. It looks like the broadcast idea is arousing some interest." He turned to look at her, his hair and ears snowy with lather. "I'll know in a few days."

Despite her anxiety she was glad for him. "The CBS broadcasts have been good, but yours will be better."

He splashed water over his head. "Have you thought about going home?"

"Constantly. I'll decide in a day or so."

She went back to the dressing table and looked at herself. There were shadows under her eyes and she was shaking inside, but her hands were still and her mind made up. She could not leave London until Julian's fate was decided; she owed him that much. If she had not arranged that meeting in Venice, his reputation would not be threatened now.

It was a few days later that Harding answered a telephone call while they were at breakfast in their suite.

"Broadhurst," he said when the call was completed. "He says Churchill wants to see me at the Admiralty tomorrow. He's all for the broadcasts, even wants to ask their majesties to come on with me."

"That's wonderful, Harding!"

"I'm convinced he'll be the next prime minister," Harding said. "And I hope the broadcasts will help him get American aid for Britain, short of war." He looked up from the toast he was buttering. "Broadhurst also asked me to meet him this morning at the *Star*, along with a general and an MP—and Julian."

"Julian?"

"They want to hear his side of things, and my office is less likely to attract the British press than any of theirs. I know for a fact that he gave no quarter to the Nazis in America and Broadhurst thinks that will help his case." He bit into his toast.

"They don't want to hear his side of it," Emanuelle said. "They want him to hop on their bandwagon."

He nodded. "That's part of it. But he's not helping. I've met Julian several times this week, and he won't say anything beyond what he's told Broadhurst, that he was there as an observer, or on holiday."

"Maybe there's nothing more to tell," Ema said, getting up from the table, her napkin clutched in her hand.

"We believe him, but we're his friends."

"So were they," she said. "They once polished his Victoria Cross as if it were the rood to get the veterans' vote. Now they want to use him for something else." She turned away and a familiar anger smothered her. Sir James had used Julian—and Ema—and Drew, whose eyes glowed with absolute faith in his father. "I have to get dressed, Harding, I have an appointment."

He came around the table to kiss her. "You're worried, I know, you like him as much as I do. Call me at noon, I'll tell you what happened."

She nodded and went into the bedroom, shrugging off her robe. She closed the bathroom door and let the water run hard into the sink. "*Assez!*" she said. "Enough—haven't they done enough to you?" But whether she meant Julian or Drew or Harding or even herself she did not know.

# 75

Ema's taxi struggled through the crowds that thronged the newspaper district, waiting for news of the war that, having been declared a month ago, still hadn't started. One of America's foremost isolationists, Senator William Borah, had already dubbed it the phony war; some British wags called it the bore war.

She got out of the cab and quickly climbed the two flights of stairs to Harding's private office, past the familiar clatter. She crossed the second floor as if she were enclosed in a bubble of calm. She could see shadows moving through the clouded glass panels of Harding's office before she opened the door to confront her husband, her lover, and her son. They stood politely, along with a silver-haired brigadier general, Lord Broadhurst, and a third man who must be the MP Harding had mentioned.

Harding made the necessary introductions before he asked, "Ema, what are you doing here?"

"I came to help if I can," she said, avoiding the warning in Julian's eyes. "No one in America questions Sir Julian's loyalty. I'm surprised anyone would in England."

There was an embarrassed silence while she took a chair in a way that left no room for anyone else to question her presence at this meeting. The men sat too. She looked at Drew. He was obviously anxious, but he gave her a look of admiration that flooded her with pride. Then they all turned to the brigadier, who was talking in a tone both stern and apologetic. He was obviously an army man to his marrow, sworn to defend his officers, and a staunch admirer of gallant men like Major Saxon. He was clearly ill at ease while he put his questions, addressing Julian as Major and insisting that there was no need for Julian to defend his loyalty to him, personally.

"But it's these rumors that the army must consider," the brigadier said, glancing at Harding and Emanuelle. "You can't deny that you've been in Germany very often in the past several years."

"No, and I don't deny that I met Hitler several times and was photographed with him, and in particular with the Windsors when they were there. I knew His Royal Highness before the abdication; it was natural that I be invited to a reception for him."

"He seemed kindly disposed to Hitler when he was king," the MP remarked coldly. He smoothed his thin black mustache fastidiously.

"I will not presume," Julian said, "to speak for His Royal Highness; as for myself, I was there for personal reasons—primarily," he added quickly, "to get some idea of what Hitler might have been planning."

"How did you go about that—by personal meetings with the Reichschancellor?" pursued the MP caustically.

Julian bristled. "Not beyond a few casual encounters, no. I used my own observations, which I reported to the responsible persons in the government whenever I thought they deserved attention."

Emanuelle glanced at Drew again. He was watching his father loyally, but with a pleading look in his eyes. Darling, Ema said silently to Julian, you'll have to do better than that, you'll have to prove it.

"Can you deny," Broadhurst continued in a far less hostile manner than the MP's, "that you were in Germany when the Munich Pact was signed?"

"I was there," Julian said, "but not in Munich. I swear on my honor that by then I had not seen Hitler alone for many months, nor ever mentioned anything I knew of Britain's defense plans. The implication that I advised Hitler on how best to hoodwink Britain until he was better equipped to conquer us is absolutely untrue, and I repudiate it."

"But you approved of the Pact?" the MP said softly.

"Yes. It kept us out of war." Julian looked around the circle of men. "I am not the only one who abominates war."

"Then why do you want to go back on active service after years of denouncing it?" Broadhurst asked.

Julian paled. "What do you want me to say to that, Milord?"

"That your country is in danger," said Broadhurst, "and you are willing to help her in any way you can."

Julian nodded slowly, his expression that of a man who has accepted the lengths to which Broadhurst would go. He was ready to force Julian to champion this war, not as something inevitable, but as something glorious. But all he said was, "My request to return to active service should be proof enough of that."

"Not quite," the MP said sharply. "In almost any other circumstance your word would suffice, but this is war, by God. The country's in an uproar, there are people base enough to make political capital out of a former hero, a holder of the Victoria Cross, the highest honor this country can bestow—and, heaven help us, people frightened enough to listen to them! They're going to ask why you were in Germany so often—and curiosity or tourism just won't answer in a case like this."

"It's all I can say," Julian replied, his face still pale.

"Which implies that there is something you can't say," Broadhurst observed. A silence fell until Broadhurst spoke again.

"It just won't do, Julian," he said, echoing the MP. "I regret it, but if push comes to shove with these people, how can I champion you for a position of trust?" He glanced at the brigadier, who mournfully agreed with him.

"I don't think that's all of it, Milord," Julian said angrily. "You've always wanted me to glorify war, and this is a convenient way to force me to do it. Britain has to defend herself at all costs, but that is not a reason to rejoice."

"We must do more than defend ourselves, Julian," Broadhurst said. "We must win, by whatever means we can." He gestured toward the windows. "You know as well as I do what the mood of the country is about the war—apathetic, unwilling. Britain needs her heroes. If they are not with us, they'll be assumed to be against us."

"That's blackmail," Julian said furiously, "and you know it."

Broadhurst crossed his arms. "I said by whatever means we can, Julian. I for one will stop at nothing."

He had finally said it, Ema realized. Julian would have to recant publicly everything he believed in or he would be thrown to the mob, dishonored as only a fallen hero can be dishonored, and most cruelly of all, in the eyes of his son, the one person he had left to love. It was not enough that Julian was willing to join the war, he must exalt it, too, against his will. It was always the same, power prevailed, whether it was the kind of power in this room or brute force.

Damn them, Ema thought, damn them all to hell. She got out of her chair.

"No, Emalie," Julian said, "no, you mustn't." The others watched as she went to stand behind Harding, her hands resting on the back of his chair so that she could not see his face nor he hers.

"Julian was almost always with me when he was in Germany," Emanuelle said. "When the Pact was signed we were in Berlin, not Munich."

The men's eyes narrowed to examine more intimately the elegant woman who had just declared—hadn't she?—that she was Sir Julian Saxon's mistress. But Harding had only to look at Julian to know it was true, and his hands came up to cover his face.

The brigadier cleared his throat, but Emanuelle continued. Her meetings with Sir Julian on that occasion and many others before it were entirely personal and very private. They had nothing to do with politics, quite the contrary. Her voice was even, her gaze direct, but she spoke as if she weren't really there with them. She knew Drew was looking from her to his father in utter amazement, but she avoided everyone's eyes. When she had finished, there was another silence.

"Am I to understand," the brigadier said, trying to state the case delicately, "that you and Major Saxon met frequently in Germany for—for romantic assignations?"

"Yes," Emanuelle replied, "we have been lovers for many years."

Harding took a short, sharp breath. The other men looked at each other, embarrassed but intrigued that this supposedly virtuous matron had been intimate with a man they knew, not once, but repeatedly, over a long period of time. They turned back to her, visualizing her now in the wanton, unwifely abandon of their fantasies.

There was nothing more to say. Harding's shock was proof enough that he hadn't conspired with his wife to help a mutual friend.

"I hope this will remain confidential," Julian said to the others.

The men flushed, and the brigadier assured him that it would, Julian had his word as an officer and a gentleman. He would also make an announcement to the press that Major Saxon was now on active service and his duties highly classified. That would stop the rumors meant to embarrass the government. "Lord Broadhurst will see to the rest?" the brigadier finished, and the press lord nodded.

"It will be reported in the American press as well," Broadhurst said. "When an ardent pacifist like Julian joins the battle, we want people to know it. I'm sorry, Julian, but we need you. Convictions be damned. A hero doesn't belong to himself, he belongs to his country, to use as she sees fit."

There was silence again, thick and breathless, until Harding raised his head, and he and Julian looked at each other for a long, agonized moment. Julian was the first to look away. He left with Drew.

"Harding," Ema began, still clinging to the back of his chair.

He shook his head. "Not now. Later. Tonight. Just leave me alone."

She followed Julian and Drew and they went quickly down the stairs and out to the street without speaking. She turned her smoke-gray eyes on each of them before she got into a cab. Father and son watched her go.

"I never thought you were interested in other women, Father." A change had come into Drew's voice, even into his posture as he stood next to his father. Their relationship had altered, as if, because the father had yielded to unsanctified desire, he was no longer his son's idol, but rather his equal in transgression.

Julian shook his head. "Only in *that* woman. I can't explain it to you,

Drew, but she isn't someone who just happened to take my fancy. I met her in Paris during the war. I have loved her for a long, long time—as long and as much as I've loved you—but it was entirely apart from you and your mother. Your mother never knew we'd met again—and if you don't tell her, she never will. Can you trust me enough to spare her?"

"Of course, Father, I'm not a sneak and it's your affair"—Drew colored at the word—"not mine, but I still can't quite grasp it. You're the most honorable man I ever knew."

"But still a man," Julian said, "not a hero, not some kind of god, just a man."

Drew nodded, but it was hard to think of his father in those terms. "You'll be on active service soon, then," he said.

"Yes, there must be some way for me to help." They looked at each other guardedly again.

"Well, I must be getting back to the base," Drew said uncomfortably, flagging a cab. For the first time in his life he did not embrace his father when they parted, that brief placing of hands on shoulders that was acceptable between men; he just shook Julian's hand and climbed into the cab and Julian realized, with a dull pain that would always be with him now, that Drew was glad to leave him.

He went to a call box to ring Ema, but she had not yet returned to her hotel. He almost went back to the *Star* to confront Harding, but he couldn't risk making matters worse just to ease his own conscience. He knew he must not try to call Emalie again, either. She had made her choice and he had no right to interfere unless she asked him to. He only hoped her marriage could bear the strain that had just been placed upon it.

He set off for the house in Regent's Park, walking like a man with an intolerable burden.

# 76

"Since the war!" Harding said, and the sound of his voice was worse than the sight of his face would have been. They sat in the dark living room of the suite, the windows open to let the crisp air in.

She had been waiting all day for him to come back and ask the questions he had a right to ask, but he had poured himself a brandy without a word. He had turned out the lights, pulled back the blackout curtains, and opened the windows before he spoke, and it was impossible to know which feeling, contempt or anger, humiliation or astonishment, dominated him most. All of them colored his voice while they talked, while the tip of his cigarette moved in the dark and she told him all she could bring herself to tell him. But it was not enough, even as what Julian said had not been enough.

"Yes, I was seventeen when I met him."

"My God, Ema, you could have told me the truth before you married me, you owed me that much. I thought you'd been widowed in the war."

"Harding, I thought he was dead! I didn't know he was alive until a few months before Dana was born."

"When you saw him at the opera! Why didn't you tell me then?"

"We were married, with a child on the way. He had two. I hoped I'd never have to tell you."

"Of course not! It was easier to go on with your filthy affair."

"It was never that. You know him! He was more to me than an affair."

"He was all that I wanted to be and wasn't, is that it?" It was unbearably painful to hear him. "Oh, Ema, that wasn't fair, that wasn't like you, to pretend you loved me."

"But I did, I do, I love you very much."

"Jesus," he exploded, "be honest, at least. A woman can't love one man and sleep with another."

"She can love them both, for different reasons! And because she met each one at a different time of her life. And it's been over since you met each other."

"I see. That was too much, even for you."

She wanted to put her arms around him, to take away the scalding bitterness. "I had to choose and I chose you. I won't see him again."

"Damn it, do you really think that wipes the slate clean after years of lies? You never loved me the way you loved that damn fool hero of yours! And you still love him, after all these years. But why?—never mind all his endearing young charms—why? We have a child together, we have—we had a marriage. What the hell did he ever do but seduce you when you were hardly more than a girl?"

The familiar smothering sensation seized her and she made her way to the open window before she answered him. "I wanted him to seduce me, not for sex, but because he could get me out of the . . . the place I lived in." She leaned against the drawn blackout curtain, holding on to its inky new stiffness. "I never thought I could love him—or anyone else after that place."

Harding said nothing for what seemed a long time, and when he did speak, his voice made her shiver. "The bastard! And I admired him! I couldn't stand what they were trying to do to him, I tried to help. And he let me too! How noble of him, after making love to my wife behind my back! Did he have you in our bed at Silvermoor too?"

"Harding, no! Please don't. He was ready to be ruined today rather than compromise you."

"But you made a different choice, didn't you?"

There was nothing she could say; she knew it seemed she had deliberately chosen to humiliate him, but the impulse that had driven her to speak was far more complicated, too complicated to explain to this scornful, angry man. She could never stand by and watch anyone be ruined, particularly not Julian and the son whose love was all he had left.

She heard Harding coming toward her and she turned to him, hoping still, but he only pulled the blackout curtains closed. Then he put on the lights and went into the bedroom without looking at her. She followed him. He was packing a small case with overnight things.

"Don't go now, Harding, we have to talk about this."

"There's nothing more to say. I'll send for the rest of my things as soon as I decide what to do."

She watched him pack, remembering how many times she had watched him before and how different this time was.

"When will you leave for home?" he asked her when he had snapped the case shut.

"I'll stay on in London for a while, you might—need me."

He shook his head in bitter contempt. "Don't pretend you're staying for me," he said. "Not after what you did today."

"But they would have destroyed him!"

"Emanuelle, did you stop for a single second to think what this would do to me?" He jammed his hands into his pockets. "I made a pact with the devil when I married you. I said that whatever you could give me would be enough. I was wrong. It was a bad bargain." He turned away from her. "Except when we made love. I thought I had all of you then. It was all I was sure of, and today you took that away from me too." His hands came up to smooth his hair in a nervous gesture. "That was the ultimate betrayal, Ema. Our bargain is concluded."

He left her standing where she was, stunned because, no, she hadn't thought of him, or of herself, or of anyone but Julian today. She had chosen Julian's honor over Harding's pride.

But Julian was her youth, her *bohème*, her shining palace! With him she had touched what she dreamed of. He was hers to protect even if he could never be hers to acknowledge.

But that was no excuse to offer Harding, only an explanation that would never be enough. For her and Harding there were two truths, hers and his, and they were incompatible because hers was incomplete.

She almost went out, just to walk, but walking in a blackout was a slow, stumbling process, not the headlong flight she wanted. She undressed automatically and got into the double bed, lying rigid on her side of it until dawn broke before she fell asleep, knowing she owed Harding the truth about herself and about Drew, no matter how difficult it would be—if only he could forget his pride long enough to let her tell him.

She woke at noon to the sound of his key in the door.

"Harding?" she called, steeling herself for what she had to say.

He said brusquely that he had come only for the rest of his things. He obviously had not slept and he looked every bit his age.

"Harding, wait," she pleaded. "There's so much more I have to tell you." She shivered thinking of it, her son, her father.

His face was closed. "I have no time," he said. "I'm attached to British Army Intelligence now, I did it this morning. I saw something of German tactics in Spain; they think I might be useful to them." He went into the bathroom to see if he had left any toilet articles, talking as he did so. "I'll be billeted somewhere outside of London, I don't know where and I couldn't tell you if I did." He came back into the bedroom, avoiding her eyes.

"What about the broadcasts?"

"I don't know; maybe, whenever I'm in England." Finally he made himself look at her. "This war will get a lot worse before it's over. You should go home, for Dana's sake, at least. Or doesn't she matter as much to you as he does?"

"Stop it, Harding. I told you already that it's over."

"Do you expect me to believe you?"

"Yes, because it's the truth! Try to understand. I fell in love with him long before I ever met you and I was honest about that from the beginning."

"Honest? Oh, yes, enough to try aborting my child without telling me why. You didn't want her and you didn't want me."

"That's enough," she said in a strangled kind of scream, as furious now as he was. "I didn't want to get married then, that's true, and I thought I didn't want her until she was born, but all that changed and you know it. I don't deserve this from you."

"Don't you? I think you do, after years of adultery."

She shook her head violently. "I know that's how you see it, but any time I spent with him had nothing to do with you and me." Her voice dropped. How could he believe it—but she said it anyway. "I was loyal to you in my own way."

"In your fashion, Cynara!" He was shouting at her now. "But that isn't good enough, Ema, it's not what the contract called for. You were my wife, but you loved another man, you sneaked off to meet him, you made a fool of me and my feeling for you." He took the valise roughly off the bed and started for the door, then he stopped without turning.

"What was that name he called you yesterday?"

She was not surprised that he remembered it, he had a journalist's talent for detail. "Emalie."

"Why did he call you that?"

"It was my name," she whispered, "before I came to America to start a new life."

"Jesus!" he said, shaking his head. "I don't know much about you, do I, except that you're capable of anything!" His voice broke. "It's been hard enough to deal with your separate life, but a separate *secret* life! That's too much, even for me. How could I have been fool enough to love you?" He walked out, slamming the door behind him, and she stood near the bed, thinking that she could never tell him now, not in the face of all that rage between them.

She had been alone many times, in many places, but none that felt as empty as this hotel suite. Anxiety engulfed her as the hours passed.

She thought of Drew's look of admiration when she first appeared at the office yesterday to help defend his father. What joy that look had given her! But then had come the pain, after her admission that she was Julian's mistress. She shook her head, wishing the memory away.

She moved restlessly around the suite, thinking of her child—but which child, the one safe at school in America? Or the one here who was in mortal danger? It was an agonizing dilemma. She knew she could not save Drew by staying here, but now that she had seen him, touched him, how could she leave him if there was any chance of seeing him again before it was too late and he was gone forever?

It was mid-afternoon when she made the decision to stay on for a while to sort herself out—without Julian or Harding, even without Dana. She went to bathe and dress, then ordered coffee. She knew she had lost the habit of living without a man, but there were worse things, she thought for the first time in many years. She had never stood morally naked before her own son, the child she had never owned and never would, or her husband—both of whom judged her harshly.

Only Julian judged no one but himself, and that was what made him so rare.

She told Mary Alice over dinner that Harding had joined British Army Intelligence and she was going to stay on. "But it's dreary in a hotel. I'm going to look for my own place."

"There's a kind of bed-sitter going in my flat if you want it. Roland—that's my next husband—used it for a study, but he's gone off to the wars so you can have it—unless you're too delicate for the sounds of passion you'll hear when he comes back on leave." She smiled and her sharp face softened. "At least he left me for another war, not another woman. I prefer the war, let me tell you. I'm not used to living alone."

"Neither am I," Ema said. "I'd like to come."

She packed that night and waited until it was late afternoon on the East Coast before she called Dana.

"Daddy's going to help out here, darling, and while you're at school I'd like to stay on too."

"Is there really going to be a war, Mother? People say it might never start."

"Maybe not, but they have to be prepared and I can help with that. But it's up to you, Dana. I won't stay if you don't want me to."

There was a pause. "Stay," her daughter said. Then her voice dropped to an almost accusatory whisper. "Mother, when am I going to get my period?"

Ema almost laughed. "Next Friday at two P.M. Dana, stop worrying about it, it'll arrive when your body's ready for it."

"And breasts?" Dana implored.

"Those too. Why?"

"Caro's started, and a few other girls. Maybe something's wrong with me."

"I didn't start until I was thirteen, and there's not a single thing wrong with you, not in any way. You're the best daughter any woman ever had."

"Maman? Are you crying?"

"A little. If I miss you too much, I'll have to come home, but thanks for letting me stay a while."

"It's all right," Dana said, noble and doubtful at once. "Kiss Daddy for me."

"I will, darling, I will. He may not be able to call or write for a while, but you mustn't worry. Good-bye, Dana."


Dana ran back to the room she shared with Carolyn George and flung herself into a chair, breathing rapidly. Caro watched her for a moment, then put down her book.

"Your mother?" Caro asked.

Dana nodded, close to tears as she repeated most of the conversation to Caro. "So she's off on one of her crazy crusades again," Dana finished.

"Be fair, Dana," Caro said. "It isn't crazy to help England at a time like this."

Dana kept her eyes on the wall, but her hands closed into fists. It was always that way; everything her mother did seemed wonderful to everyone else. She *was* wonderful, that was the trouble. There was no hope in the world that she, Dana, could ever match Ema, could ever be what Ema wanted her to be. Sometimes it seemed to Dana that she was walking down a narrow, endless corridor with the walls pressing in on her and no possible escape except a turn she did not want to take.

On the table beside her chair Ema and Harding smiled from a picture taken at Silvermoor last summer. They stood near the sea of full-blown roses in the garden, with their arms encircling each other, Harding in slightly rumpled tennis clothes, Ema in pristine white linen and turquoise jewelry, cool, confident, and perfect, the most overwhelming woman Dana had ever known.

Oh, Daddy, Dana pleaded silently, I can't be like her. I don't *want* to be like her.

Caro waited until Dana's hands relaxed and the red blotches on her forehead began to fade. "I know you're proud of her when you're not angry," she said.

"Yes, all right, I'm proud of her!" Dana answered. "But she's always away somewhere, doing things that get talked about, so everyone will say 'Isn't Miss Beranger wonderful, isn't Miss Beranger marvelous.' She's

never been just Mrs. Harding Ellis, just my mother." Dana sighed, de-
jected now. "And you know what she has planned for me."

"You're supposed to be a brainy glamour girl and marry a prince." Caro
nodded. "You could do that without half trying, even though you hate the
idea." She went to put an arm around her friend. "Never mind, Dana,
you won't be getting married for a long, long time."

Dana finally smiled, a tight little smile with no joy in it. "You bet I
won't, and never to anyone Mother chooses!"


Ema, preoccupied by her own misery, moved to Mary Alice's flat in
Portman Square the next morning, leaving the address and telephone
number at the Connaught.

"I have to do more than write about British women at war," she told
Mary Alice while she unpacked in the handsome, book-lined little study
that was to be hers. The studio bed was covered with summer clothes and
cocktail dresses; she would have to buy a few practical winter things before the shortages got serious and there was nothing left to buy. "I'll go
round the bend if I don't do something to help."

"What can you do beside look stunning and fight for women's rights?"

Emanuelle thought a minute. "I know about food. I can order it for ten
people or a thousand and tell people how to make it go a long way. I know
how to distribute it too."

"Good," Mary Alice said. "I'll fix up for you to see the Food Ministry,
I'm sure they can use you. Now I'll make us a nice cup of tea, it'll be ready
by the time you've settled in."

Ema nodded, thinking as she finished unpacking that she had been
trying to get away from food since the Rue Momette, but she had gone
from Tillie's dinner parties to RSVP to Confiseries Vendôme to Danielle's.
Next week her sumptuous restaurant would open without her.

# 77

By the spring of 1940 Ema felt utterly twinned. She had lived in two worlds, with a man and his child in each, and all of them were out of touch and out of sight now. She telephoned Dana at school several times each week, using a priority phone at the *Star* and trying not to hear the resentment in her daughter's voice. And she spoke to Kate every day. The restaurant's success was reassuring, but Kate was clearly anxious for Ema to come home.

"This fake war can't go on forever, Ema."

"I can't leave England, Kate, not now."

The world itself seemed to be split into two different planets. Hitler was called tyrant, liar, and murderer on both sides of the Atlantic, but in America antiwar letters still flooded Congress and "Keep Us Out—Stay Neutral" tags sprouted on license plates like weeds.

"Are they blind?" Mary Alice demanded after reading a stack of American papers.

"They just don't want to be involved," Ema said. "You can't blame them for that."

"I won't have to," Mary Alice fumed. "You wait and see; they'll blame themselves when they get caught with their knickers down."

Even in London, hovering on the brink of disaster, there was Hungarian music at Claridge's and superb Italian food at Quaglino's. There were tulips and blue hyacinths in Hyde Park and azaleas in the hotel window boxes, like any other April.

And then in May Hitler put an end to the phony war by invading Norway, Denmark, Belgium, Holland, Luxembourg, and France. The war moved closer, complicating the dilemma Ema had to resolve of whether to stay or go.

By the end of May all but France had been gobbled up by the Nazis, and the British Expeditionary Force was stranded on the beach at Dunkirk.

From across the Atlantic Americans saw the lightning metamorphosis of the map of Europe. The isolationist tide slowly began to turn and the newspapers reflected it.

"But this time they aren't buying any hogwash about making the world safe for democracy," Mary Alice said. "This time to hell with the world, it's their own necks they have to save. The penny has finally dropped."

Ema was not so sanguine about American aid. She thought of Spain, closed to foreigners now under a regime more repressive than the monarchy had been. The short-lived republic was a monument to the world's indifference. "You can't trust what the East Coast papers and magazines say, Mary Alice. There's still a whole country beyond New York, more interested in *Gangbusters* and *Kitty Foyle* than in Hitler."

"All the same, Roosevelt got his appropriation to build fifty thousand planes."

"That's to defend us, not you."

"Wait and see. They'd far rather we did the fighting—and when the Germans invade, we'll have nothing to fight with but brooms and pike-staffs unless we get help." Mary Alice looked at Ema speculatively. "Your husband's in aircraft, isn't he? He'll help you put an air force together—and they'll call him a war profiteer for his pains."

"People aren't that stupid!"

"People judge things by how they look, my poor innocent! Remember what they tried to do to your friend Saxon?" Ema looked at her warily and Mary Alice nodded. "Rumors like that have a way of getting out, but no one printed them, not even the gutter press. I hold no brief for the pacifists; they're partly responsible for our pikestaff defense, but I know Saxon was never a Nazi sympathizer any more than your husband's a war profiteer."

Emanuelle had not seen Harding since the day he left her at the Connaught. He had called her once to discuss what they would tell Dana—not the truth, at the moment. The conversation had left her feeling chilly and barren, like London after dark, when wardens patrolled the streets for stray beams of light and people dimmed their flashlights with tissue paper to find their way, fearing the moonlight that had once delighted them. In the daytime the city went about its business, past windows taped against flying glass, along streets almost devoid of children.

Ema's recurrent nightmare started then. Night after night she wandered through darkened, empty streets calling, Where are the children, where are my children? only to come upon Dana as she was now and Drew as the nine-year-old boy in the picture Sir James had given her. In the dream her children clutched each other's hands and called to her across a sea of dead bodies Ema could not bring herself to cross.

She felt she had to stay on, although Dana's school was ready to break for the summer.

"You can go to camp with Caro this summer," Emanuelle said on the telephone, trying to sound calm and persuasive. It was a fashionable camp, more like a country club.

"I don't want to go to camp!" There was a pause, then Dana continued. "If you and Daddy aren't coming home, I want to go to Colorado on a dig."

"Alone?" Ema frowned. It was not the sort of summer she would have chosen for Dana.

"Oh, Mother, of course not. With a junior group from the University of Colorado. Skip Atwood wants to come too."

"If your Aunt Kate lets him go, so can you."

"But you promised you'd come home if I asked you to." Dana, having won her point, was close to tears. "I don't like being all alone."

"Darling, there are French refugees pouring into London every day. I can really help as an interpreter while you're away for the summer."

"Oh, Maman, will France surrender?" Dana said, shocked out of her own concerns. "Where's Tante Danielle?"

"Still in Paris."

"Make her come away, Maman, and as soon as she does, bring her home with you."

But Ema could not get through to Danielle. Paris was in chaos as the government fled. The impenetrable Ardennes Forest had been penetrated in the first days of the attack, and the Germans had gone around the indestructible pillboxes of the Maginot Line. What remained of the British Expeditionary Force was being evacuated from the beaches at Dunkirk in a national cross-Channel effort that was called a miracle. Along with the navy destroyers and minesweepers had gone an armada of private pleasure craft, fishing boats, anything that could float, to take over 300,000 British and French troops off the beach.

"We're good at miracles," Mary Alice said.

"I remember another miracle," Ema replied. "The miracle of the Marne. But they had to do another miracle four years later."

"Chin up, Ema, France will hold out; Winston's been over again to buck them up."

In addition to her work at the Food Ministry, Ema filed a regular column about the working women of London, some of whom had sent their children away to safety; it was the first time most of them had ventured outside their homes and they were amazed by their own efficiency.

They were fully prepared to fire rifles when the Germans invaded—if there were any rifles to fire. Most of the British Expeditionary Force's equipment had been left behind on Dunkirk beach.

Ema was at the Ministry when the incredible news came that France had capitulated. People gathered in anxious little groups. "It can't be true!" one of the men said fearfully. "Jerry will be across the Channel before we know it!" He answered the jangling phone morosely. "For you, Ema," he said, handing her the receiver.

It was Julian, and the sound of his voice was a comfort. "I had to call you, darling, as soon as I heard the news."

"I'm glad you did." There were tears in her eyes. "I hate to think of Nazis in our city."

"Are you all right, Emalie?" He asked it tenderly, and she knew he was not referring to the war.

"It's so good to hear your voice."

"Have dinner with me?"

"Not yet, Julian, not for a while."

"All right, darling, I won't press you." In the background someone called him. "I must go, Ema. I'll ring as soon as I can. I love you. Take care of yourself."

They spoke to each other often after that. It even made the coming invasion seem less frightening to her. Julian's headquarters was charged with home defense, and he was often away—in Scotland or on the southeast coast, Ema presumed—where everyone knew the first German attacks would come. He had turned the Regent's Park house over to the Royal Air Force for use as an officers' club and had rented a small flat in Mount Street.

"Drew needs a place for his romances," he told her in one of their long nocturnal telephone conversations.

"What about Fenella?"

"That's serious; a gentleman mustn't . . ." A pause. "I wasn't much of a gentleman, was I?"

"I wasn't much of a lady."

"Yes, you were, Emalie, and you are."

She was sure Drew did not share his opinion.

Davina was at Stridings with the girls most of the time—it was safer—but Julian never pressed Ema to meet him at the flat. He knew she would not.

She felt foolish, sometimes, for keeping her promise to Harding. She did it as an almost religious act of contrition rather than from any moral principle. A *Götterdammerung* was no time for morality. Yet this seemed a time for keeping promises as if, in return, fate would deal more gently with the ones she loved.

Harding did a broadcast almost every week. It was a relief to know when he was in England, away from the fighting, but it was hard to hear him speaking to her as impersonally as he did to thousands of other people. It was eerie altogether to communicate only across wires and air waves with the two men she cared for.

Except for what Julian told her, she had no communication with Drew at all, and it was Drew she was waiting for, however impossible it was for her to see him now. She had fantasies of changing that appraising look he had given her at the *Star*. And she worried about him, with good reason. Royal Air Force fighter planes were the only barrier between the German bombers and their targets: the docks, factories, and, in particular, the airfields of England from which the R.A.F. pilots scrambled to intercept.

She was alone in the apartment late one night when Harding called her. "I'm going home for a while," he said. "There are things that need doing." She knew he must mean gearing all of his aircraft factories on the West Coast to war production. "Then I'll be somewhere else, on assignment. What about you?"

"I'll go home soon. The Free French need me for a while longer."

He considered that before he went on. "Then what shall I tell Dana?"

She sat up, her anger flaring. "Nothing about us, Harding!" They would tell Dana together, or not at all.

"No, no, this is no time to think about—our personal differences." He had almost said *divorce* and the unspoken word hung between them. "I mean about your staying on."

"Dana knows I'll be here for the summer. I told her she could go to Colorado with some archaeology group. Skip Atwood's going too. I hope that was all right?" It was a ridiculous conversation to be having with him, so cold, so remote. She would have preferred it if they shouted at each other.

"Fine." He paused. "Ema, it might get very bad. Before the Germans invade, they'll try to bomb Britain into submission, or starve her. You ought to get out while you can." He sounded almost like the old Harding again and her anger faded.

She sat holding the telephone. You always like to tell me what to do, she pleaded silently with him. Tell me to come with you now, please, please, tell me.

"Ema? Are you alone?" His voice changed and she knew what he was thinking.

"Mary Alice is still out, so I'm alone. I'm always alone, Harding, I told you I would be."

"It's none of my business, I shouldn't have asked."

She sighed. "I'll be back before Dana comes home from Colorado, tell her that, will you?"

"Yes, I'll tell her. Good-bye, Ema, be careful." It was the sort of thing everyone said these days; she found no hope in it.

She hung up and looked for a cigarette, but the packet in her bag was empty and the only tobacconist within walking distance was closed by now. She went back to her chair and sat down, trying to make some sense of what she hoped to accomplish by staying on, by keeping Julian at a distance.

# 78

The summer of 1940 was apocalyptic, and Ema waited with the rest of England for the sounding of the church bells that would signal invasion. The weather was fair and warm, but a gray fog was welcome whenever it hung protectively over the southeast, where so many of the battered airfields lay.

"You act," Mary Alice said one evening when Ema came in feeling especially glum over the casualty reports, "as if you had a lover in the R.A.F. Don't look at me like that, for heaven's sake, you wouldn't be the only woman to go off the straight and narrow during a war. Life is short and love is warming."

Ema shook her head with a thin smile. She had a son she hardly knew and no lover at all. It was the war that had made her a middle-aged ingenue, when both she and Julian needed all the comfort they could get. "I apologize for my bad temper lately."

"Never mind, everyone's on edge waiting for the Hun. Take a pew and put your feet up." Mary Alice was wearing her favorite tatty bathrobe. Her black hair was rolled in rag curlers that wagged comically when she moved. She had a teapot in her hand. "Want some?"

"No, thanks." Ema stepped out of her shoes and took out a cigarette before she dropped her handbag. "Only the mad English drink hot tea in weather like this." The telephone rang. "I'll get it," she said. "Once I sit down I won't be able to stand up."

"Ema?" It was Julian.

"Hello," she said, careful not to say his name. "How are you?"

"Ema, it's Drew."

"What? Tell me what?" she demanded. Mary Alice came to stand by Ema's side.

"He went down in the Channel today. Broadhurst just called to tell me. I haven't—I haven't told anyone else."

"My God, oh, my God. Where are you?"

"At the flat, but I'm going out there to wait"—she thought he meant the airfield at Hendon—"as soon as I can organize a car."

"I'll get one. I'll be there in half an hour, wait for me." She put down the phone and went quickly into her bedroom.

Mary Alice followed her. "What happened, Ema? Who was that?"

"A friend—his son went down in the Channel." She struggled into the uniform she used for the motor pool. "He needs a car; we're going out to the field to wait for news."

"Hold on, where will you get the car?"

"From the motor pool." Ema put on her shoes and her cap and picked up her bag and her gas mask.

"They won't give you a car just because you ask for one!"

"I don't intend to ask." Ema was already halfway down the stairs. How long can a man live, she thought desperately, in the English Channel?


She and Julian reached Bentley Priory, on the outskirts of London, before the late August light faded. Lord Broadhurst had used his influence and obtained permission for Julian to wait for news at R.A.F. Fighter Command Headquarters.

"Broadhurst said Drew was reported definitely clear of the aircraft," Julian said on the drive. "And his parachute opened. Our boats just haven't picked him up yet."

"They will," Ema said, but her heart sank. She knew from whispers at the *Star* that R.A.F. losses in this kind of situation were far too frequent. There were no spare English aircraft for use as spotter planes, and too many pilots who managed to get out of their planes either drowned in the cold, rough waters of the Channel or were fished out by German patrol boats and carted away to prison camp.

"Thank God you're with me," Julian said, and then they sat in silence until the sentry waved them into the drive of the eighteenth-century mansion.

They were admitted by a young lieutenant and escorted to a small room that had once been a back parlor. Now it was furnished with desks, chairs, and an array of telephones. Julian went out with the lieutenant, and Ema dropped into one of the chairs and put her head down on her crossed arms. Through the open windows came the sounds of the country at twilight.

She looked up when Julian came back, but he was shaking his head. "No news yet. All the reports won't be in until after the light fails."

"But he's been out there for hours!" she gasped.

Julian stood near the desk opposite and looked at her the way he had at

Cesar's the night he said good-bye. His hair was all silver now, like his father's.

"Ema," he said, "there would have been more planes to search for him, except for me. I didn't want them to build planes."

She shook her head. "No, Julian, you weren't powerful enough to stop them by yourself. If Drew is—lost—you'll have to bear it without the luxury of guilt." He could not know it was what she had tried to do, and that it had become impossible. Maybe it had always been impossible.

Julian's eyes closed for a moment and then he nodded. "You're a strong woman, Emalie." He held out his hand and she got up and went to him. She had not felt his arms around her for a long time. Her fingers touched his face and the smooth, close-cropped hair at the back of his head. She wondered why she had denied him love after loving him so long. What good was physical celibacy when she still belonged to him the way she always had?

They walked to the open window. It was almost dark and their hopes faded with the light. They stood together, looking out at the lawn and watching the green trees grow black and blend into the night.

At last there was a knock on the door. "I'm sorry, Major," the lieutenant said, "all the regular boats have reported in and they haven't got him." He paused. "But you mustn't give up hope. He might still be picked up by a fisherman—or by the Germans. They're eager to keep our lads out of the sky." He tried, but there was no conviction in his voice.

"What's the longest a man has survived in the Channel?" Julian asked.

"Twenty hours, as far as we know, sir. Some might have been out there longer that we—that we didn't get to."

Ema felt Julian's body shudder. "Thank you, Lieutenant," he said. "Is it all right for us to stay here?"

"Stay as long as you like, sir. Just call if you need anything. I'm very sorry, Major."

Ema didn't hear the door close. She wept silently at first, leaning against Julian, and then she cried as she had not let herself cry in a long time.

"Emalie." He held her close. "I'm glad you're the one who helped me keep watch for my son."

She was certain Drew was dead, or worse, dying out there, alone in that cold black water. She took Julian's face in her hands and looked up at him, blinded by love so long denied. She put her cheek next to his, tasting his tears, and said it softly, quickly. "My son, Julian, he's my son too. Ours. I gave him up before he was born, but he's still mine."

He stepped back to look at her, confusion mixing with his terrible grief. "*Your* son, Ema? Drew? I don't understand what you mean."

She brought two chairs to the window and placed them side by side. "Come and sit here with me, Julian, and I'll tell you."

Her voice was as hushed as the dark room while she told him about Sir James and Davina and Silvermoor Cottage in Glengowrie. It was the revelation she had always dreaded making to him, and so had never risked.

"I should have known it," he said at length, staring out at the invisible trees that rustled in quiet lamentation. "I should have known why I loved him so much, why Davina didn't. My poor darling, I should have understood that look on your beautiful face whenever I talked about him." He fell silent again, but he turned toward her in the dark when next he spoke. "Why didn't you tell me in Venice when you realized what they had done to us, Davina and my father?"

"Because of my daughter—and our son. Would you have told Drew he was a bastard whose mother had abandoned him? That his grandfather was a party to it? And you could never have left him with Davina! She hates him, she always has."

"I don't know what I would have done," he said with anguish, the shock of discovery past, the scope of what she had told him fully realized. "But think what our lives have been because you didn't tell me! Davina and I—you and Harding. That was a decision for both of us to make. You should have given me the chance."

"Should I?" She had never spoken to him in anger before. "When it would have changed nothing? How can you know what I should have done? I should never have given him up in the first place, that's all I know, but I had to, he had a right to everything, he still has a right, illegitimate or not! He's your son!"

He reached for her hand. "I didn't mean to blame you for it, Ema. You and he are the only two people in the world I really love."

Her voice dropped. "Yes, I know, I know." She leaned against him. "I saw him only twice, Julian. I want you to tell me all about him."

It took them through the night, the recital of a boy's life that eased his anguish as much as hers. It was not told in sequence—Drew was twelve, or two, or seventeen. He was by turns angelic, rebellious, amusing, impossible, but always irresistible.

Davina was part of the story, fully comprehended now by the man she had manipulated, but never to be understood by the boy she had doubly cheated, first of his mother's love, then of her own. Julian's daughters were part of it, Juliana, Alexandra, and Jennifer. They adored Drew. And Sir James was in it, too, as incredible as his actions were to Julian.

Tea was brought them at midnight and again at four. A false dawn grayed the sky, then it lightened enough for them to see each other, both of them beyond tears for this day at least.

"We must get back to London," Julian said. "I want to tell the girls about Drew. And Davina has to know too."

Ema nodded and gathered her things, her emotions as worn as her clothes. The HQ had been stirring for a while, with the morning sounds of people in the corridors, but they were both startled when the door burst open.

"He was found, Major!" the lieutenant shouted. "Last night, by some dotty old fisherman who wasn't on the telephone and didn't hike to the post office till this morning. Your son has three cracked ribs and he was frozen blue, but he'll be right as rain in a month or so." The lieutenant approached, his hand outstretched. "I'm very happy for you, sir, for all of us." He nodded at Ema, not certain who she was, and left them alone again, still separated by life and joined by Drew, their arms around each other.

"What now, Ema?"

"I don't know. He's alive, that's enough for the moment."

They left Bentley Priory and drove slowly back to London in the early light, too tired to talk. When she stopped the car at his headquarters he turned to her.

"I always wondered why you wasted your life on me, Ema, why you didn't live happily with Harding. He loves you—and he's right for you."

"He isn't you," she said quietly. "He's an extraordinary man, but he'll never be you."

"Emalie," he said after a moment, "I have to leave London for a few days, but when I come back I must see you. There is still a great deal for us to talk about."

"Yes, Julian."

He touched her cheek and got out of the car. "I love you very much," he said. "More than I ever did."

She drove off, thinking about what he had said. He thought Harding was right for her because they were both self-made, cut from the same cloth. She was someone else now, but Julian would not have wanted Emalie Anne Bequier to raise his only son. And Emanuelle Beranger was not the kind of woman Drew would want to acknowledge as his mother.

"Andrew James," she said softly. "Welcome back. What a pity we can never really know each other."

She returned the car to the motor pool and stopped at the *Star* office to see when she could get on a flight to New York. Even though there was a waiting list, she would still be there when Dana came home in ten days.

But that night bombs fell on Greater London for the first time, and the code word Cromwell, signaling "imminent invasion," went out across the country. Diplomatic priorities on flights to New York tripled, and Emanuelle was shunted to the bottom of the waiting list.

There was no invasion. The bombs had probably been a mistake, the people who knew concluded, dropped in the dark by a German pilot bound for home who preferred not to land with bombs aboard. But Britain was outraged and her morale needed bolstering. There were four retaliatory raids on Berlin and then, after Julian returned to London, the terror bombing of London began in earnest.

# 79

---

"Marry you?" Emanuelle said softly. His body was silhouetted against the fading light of the living room window, but his face was in shadow. He was still the same man she had seen from her desk at Saxon, Vaillant, where her dream of marrying him began.

"Yes, Ema. Drew is a man—war has a way of making men out of boys. And the girls are at school." He walked back and forth, a slender figure against the light, and her mind darted away from decision, around the living room of the Mount Street flat. It was decorated in pale blue, like the small drawing room at Stridings. It made her uncomfortable; it was Davina's, but it was the only place they could talk undisturbed. Even the Germans respected their privacy, there had been no sirens yet today.

"We should have married long ago," Julian was saying, "and we would have, except for Father and Davina and my own incredible stupidity."

"Julian, you're forgetting Dana."

"No, darling, I'm not." He stopped pacing and faced her. "I know what she means to you. But you say there's very little hope for you and Harding; will he give you custody if he divorces you?"

"Not the way he feels about me now," she said. And certainly not if she married Julian. Her marriage to Harding seemed irreparable, but both her children would be alienated if she married Julian.

Yet it was what she had always wanted.

He had kissed her when she arrived, but since then he had not even touched her hand. This decision was too important to be based on that fatal attraction between them. She loved him in more ways than she could ever say, but she had always expressed part of what she felt without words, by making love to him. She had not done that for two long years. They were gone forever, those precious moments of her life, and her pitiful attempt at honor had changed nothing. She still loved him.

"You're saying this because of the war," she said, still unbelieving.

"No, Ema. Because we love each other and because of our son."

They had already agreed to keep that secret. A war was not the time to tell Andrew James Julian Saxon, once future baronet, that he had no right to the title. Drew's sense of himself would be turned upside down when he needed a cool head. Maybe the time to tell him would never come.

She thought of Drew's appraising expression that day at the *Star,* of Dana's certain bewilderment and inevitable anger. "Julian, it's too late for us."

"No, Ema, it isn't. We'll have to wait for our children to accept us and that will be hard, but one day they will, when they're older and wiser. Marry me, darling. Be my wife for the years we have left."

Her hands moved nervously; her eyes pleaded with him. "I love you, you know that, but I can't answer you until I've seen Dana and spoken to Harding. Wait until I've done that, please, Julian."

"Oh, Ema," he said, shaking his head. "Would I hurt you more than I already have? Of course I'll wait."

He held out his arms and she went to him. Together they had always recaptured their past—but how much of the past can anyone recapture, Ema thought. How much of what they were feeling now was only a longing to bring back youth and love and memories so gilded by time that they could never be relived except in a passion of the body. Harding had said cynically that she loved this man for all his endearing young charms. Yes, of course she did, but her soul was as much enchanted by him as her hands, her mouth, her body, pressed close to his, wanting him.

"I've missed you so, Ema."

"Yes, but not here, Julian, not in Davina's flat."

"No, not here. Somewhere else. We'll have world enough and time now."

"What about Davina?"

"I won't live with her, whatever you decide. I'll tell her so as soon as I can get another few hours' leave and go to Stridings."

"You need more leave than they give you, you look so tired. Sleep now, I have to go on duty anyway. I'll come back for you tonight." She looked at him and saw her reflection in his eyes. "Have you any idea how much I love you?"

"Oh, yes," he said, "but it still amazes me."

She left him lying on the couch. At Hyde Park Corner she boarded a tram going in the direction of St. George's Hospital and stared out of the window. She had learned to live with the burnt-out shells of buildings and the mounds of rubble elsewhere, but the West End was still intact. The three hundred bombers in the first raid on London were only a promise of what the Germans had sent since. Ema had resigned her position at the Food Ministry the day she made arrangements for her now-deferred flight to New York, but since the bombing began she had been driving an ambulance.

The air alert wailed a few minutes after night fell and the tram jolted to an abrupt halt. Ema scrambled out with the other passengers and ran for a shelter just yards away. She found a space to sit down on the floor, glad of her ambulance driver's coverall. She waited to see how close the bombs would come. They were falling closer to her today than ever before. Each time the earth shook, little puffs of dust drifted into the shelter. She lit a cigarette and covered her ears, trying not to scream every time a bomb exploded.

What am I doing here? she thought, trembling, I want to see Dana again! But how could she explain divorce and remarriage and separation to a young girl? How could she beg Harding for permission to see her own child, the one being in the world who had ever belonged to her.

The explosions were moving away, like a thunderstorm, but she put her head on her knees and covered it protectively with her arms. She thought of Julian, standing in front of the window. He was still the most beautiful man she had ever seen, and he understood her instinctively, but he didn't really know her.

She felt unreal with him because of all he didn't know about her, the side that was ineradicably the Rue Momette, the side Harding had always accepted, even cheered. Julian had never lived with her drive that knew no limits, her ambition that had no bounds; he knew nothing of what she had done to pile up mountains of money, first for herself and then for Dana. Money had never been something he had to fight for the way she and Harding did.

Julian had never heard the pungent language she used with Harding, he did not suspect her toughness, what she would do to get a story, how she would fight to have it printed exactly as she wrote it—even the way she had scared money out of poor old Tillie Blessing. Harding would have laughed at that if he'd ever let her tell him about it.

Most of all, Julian didn't know what she came from and the street rules she lived by—no honor, no traditions, no principles for her, except those she made for herself. Julian had been her guiding principle; she had lost Drew's respect for his sake, and she had lost Harding, but she could not sacrifice Dana, too, no matter how much she loved him. That was what she would have to tell him tonight.

Her body flinched away from the prospect, as it had from the bombs. To be Julian's wife! Lady Emalie of Stridings! That would have been well worth perpetuating the role she had always played with everyone—not even Harding knew how it began and why she had played it. But it was not worth Dana.

She would tell him tonight, and she would stay with him. Once more the world was crashing down around them, and once more they could give each other shelter.

The all-clear sounded and she went out into the street, dumbstruck at the sight of flames only a few blocks away. Her uniform got her a ride to the hospital in another ambulance.

"Glad to see you're in one piece," the dispatcher told her. "They've been all over the place this time, the House of Lords, the Abbey, the West End."

"I know, I've just come from there."

"Jerry is democratic, he showers his love all over town, never mind if it's nobs or slobs. You're for Piccadilly."

Ema just drove when she was on duty, trying not to see what the rescue teams pulled from the ruins, not to hear the sounds of pain from the back of the ambulance. It was very late when she had finished her shift and she tried to ring Julian, but the telephone lines were down again. She was lucky enough to find a taxi and gave Julian's address.

"You've not had an easy time of it today," the cabbie said, noticing her uniform.

"No. It was bad today." She sat rigidly in the back of the taxi, willing him to go faster through the blackout, but their pace was agonizingly slow and he had to stop two blocks away because of the safety barriers that had been flung up all along the street. She paid him off and walked as quickly as she could toward Julian's building, in dread of what she saw.

There was a heap of rubble where several blocks of flats had been. Only one section of Julian's building still stood, a line of bathrooms with tubs teetering crazily on the edges of shattered flooring.

She could not even hope. The bombs had hit not twenty minutes after she left him to sleep; those must have been the first explosions she felt in the shelter. Julian never went to air raid shelters; he said they reminded him of the trenches on the Western Front, close-packed and dark. He said, "If they didn't kill me out there, they won't kill me in London."

She stood there, shivering in the light of dying fires, while the rescue crew went on excavating Julian's tomb, and knew she had had her share of miracles. There would be no resurrection this time.

Someone said, "Not yet, Milady," and she gasped at the sound of a title she had been offered today. Davina stood about five yards away, dressed for the country in a tweed skirt and cashmere sweater with a single strand of pearls and the ubiquitous English cardigan over her shoulders. Her gaze traveled away from the wreckage and met Ema's. Davina moved a little closer and her blue eyes glittered in the firelight. "You met him here, didn't you?" Davina asked.

"Yes," Emanuelle said.

"If he'd been at his headquarters, he'd still be alive. Now I've lost him, because of you."

"You lost him long ago," Emanuelle told her.

"I was his wife, damn you, his *wife*! He was supposed to love *me*!"

"You're a fool, Davina, if you think he ever loved by contract."

"He loved me when we were children and when he married me—and he would have gone on except for you. Why couldn't you leave him alone?"

"Why couldn't you—you knew he didn't want you. You used my son to keep him."

"What was I supposed to do?" Davina said. "Let him go? Let everyone know he'd stooped as low as a creature like you?"

"If you cared about him, yes, you'd have let him go. But you never cared about anything except yourself and your right to a man who couldn't love you, no matter what you did to make him." Emanuelle stopped, her anger overcome by something worse. "Go to the devil, Davina. I won't stand here"—she pointed to the mound of debris—"and argue with you."

Davina's eyes narrowed. "What did you talk about with him?"

"About Drew, about our getting married."

"Then I'm glad he was killed. It's a pity you didn't die with him."

Emanuelle shivered again and turned away from Julian's malignant wife, toward his funeral pyre.

"What about Drew?" Davina said. "Have you told him? Will you?"

Emanuelle shook her head. But tomorrow loomed. She would look into the maw of morning and know that Drew was out there where death waited for him as it had for Julian, cheated for so many years but not to be denied. And she would know nothing about him; there would be no one to tell her.

"Milady!" One of the rescue crew approached. "We've got him out. He's dead." The man paused. "Milady, there's no need for you to identify him, he had his military ID."

"No, I want to see him, just once more." With a last venomous look at Emanuelle, Davina moved away.

Emanuelle stood alone and saw Julian young again, the way he had been in Paris. He was all she had to remember of beauty in her youth, a time so terrible, so tender, and so brief. Now he was gone forever, and she could not bring him back except in those magic moments when what has been still is.

I love you, Julian, she told him, you made the world shine for me and I will love you as long as I live.

She found her way past the wreckage and walked away into the darkened street.

# 80

She stayed at Silvermoor for three months. For the first month she saw no one, not even Dana, who had a dozen excuses for not leaving school. When Ema could think, she realized that it was Dana's way of punishing her for her long absence.

"You can't blame her," Harding said on the telephone on his first day back in London. After his quick trip to America he had been away on an intelligence mission for many weeks—she guessed it was either to North Africa or Burma—and apparently had not heard about Julian yet. She could not bring herself to tell him. He would find out soon enough.

"I don't blame her," she said, sorry she had confided in him. She was cool and distant now, taking her cue from him, although it was not how she had planned to be.

"I'm having Ken come over to work with me," Harding said after a moment.

"All right," she said.

"He's been begging to come, Ema, I'm not doing it to spite you!"

"It's all right, Harding."

He paused again. "I have a favor to ask of you. Will you run the *Star* for me while I'm away?"

She was truly surprised. "But what about Hennessy and the others?"

"I'd feel better if it were you."

The colossal irony of it seemed to escape him—that he would trust her as his managing editor but not as his wife! But she had been too weary of confrontation to comment and from then on she was too busy to dwell on it.

Managing the *Star* was a demanding job. She had Harding's staff—only a few had been young enough for the draft—but her job was to keep circulation up and policy as Harding wanted it. The male staff at the *Star* resented taking orders from a woman, but that was to be expected and Ema ignored it.

Things brightened when Dana came home for Christmas. She was overcome with remorse for her stubborn absence when she saw how thin Ema was.

"But I'm fine, darling, I just lost some weight and haven't had time to gain it back. And you're all grown up. I'm so sorry I missed that."

"So am I, but you're home now and you're going to stay!" Dana had Ema's gray eyes, but she had inherited from Harding a boundless energy and a determination to have her own way. She was mature beyond her thirteen years. The things that made young girls squeal were not of primary interest to her. She agreed with Ema that they should close Silvermoor, and after the Christmas holiday they moved permanently to New York until Harding came home.

"I still don't know why he wants to be there instead of home with us," Dana grumbled, regarding her mother with suspicion as she left for the spring term at school.

"England's in danger, he wants to help." But it sounded hollow, even to her.

By the following Christmas America, too, was in danger, far more than she realized even after Pearl Harbor was attacked and the Pacific overrun the way Europe had been. It was doubtful that most Americans knew how close they came to losing the war in those precarious months after Pearl Harbor; anger buoyed them up. RSVP began flourishing wildly. As soon as they recovered from the shock, people celebrated at the drop of a hat.

"It's all a divine bacchanal," Matilda Blessing told her at a war bonds gala. "People are humping like goats. I know you appreciate that part of it."

"Oh, shut up, Tillie. I've lost my patience for your nasty innuendos."

"My, but you're a bundle of nerves. Running the *Star* hasn't done you any good at all! I only meant you'd have plenty of scandal for your society column." Tillie's black eyes, opened wide by too many face lifts, observed Ema knowingly. "It must be bad in London."

"It's unbelievable. I don't know how they live through it."

"Some don't." Tillie arched her plucked brows with difficulty. "I heard your dashing baronet was killed."

"He wasn't my baronet," Ema managed to say. It was true; Julian had never been hers.

"Really? Thomas saw you with him in Berlin."

"Thomas saw me with a lot of people in a lot of places. Now, tell me, who is that tarty-looking woman talking to your husband?"

The scandals of Café Society were more trivial to Ema now than ever, but they were safe and uninvolving. The night life kept her out of the apartment until she was ready to drop into bed. She did volunteer work at the air base and the Stage Door Canteen, promoted scrap drives and bond drives and the American Women's Voluntary Service. Most days she relaxed during the cocktail hour at Danielle's where people who had any items of interest could find her.

Monsieur Étienne, in despair at the shortage of luxury food and French wine, had expanded the restaurant's chic little cocktail lounge. Hard liquor was guaranteed to blunt his clients' palates. Ema added a pianist.

"To play Debussy, *bien sûr*," Monsieur Étienne had agreed, pursing his lips.

"To play love songs," was Ema's response. "There's a war on. War is love, didn't you know?"

"Madame, you have become a cynic."

"Monsieur, I always was."

Was she? Was she any of the things she—or anyone else—believed her to be? Dana, a young woman who still preferred dungarees to Hattie Carnegie gowns, had another opinion of her. "You care about the wrong things, Mother," Dana objected frequently. "I don't think you even know what my philosophy is."

"Mine is to see that you have everything you want."

"You don't really *know* what I want."

"Tell me, then."

But Dana, in dramatic resignation, always said it was pointless, Ema would never understand.

Life, in Ema's view, left a woman little time for philosophy. She still wanted Dana to have everything Drew had, everything Davina's girls had. More. And marriage was still the way for her to get it. Dana didn't agree, but then, Dana made it a point to disagree with almost everything Ema said. At times Dana seemed to blame her for Harding's absence, almost as if she knew her parents were estranged. And as soon as an end to the war was in sight, she began waiting for Harding's return as uneasily as Ema did.

Ema would, of course, step down when he came back, but she had her own little empire to run. For other women it was different, and her column scorned the subtle propaganda that began well before the war in Europe ended.

> The future is clear: after doing a man's job all through the war, Rosie the Riveter will be sent back to the delivery room, whether she likes it or not.
> Why should woman's sole task be to replace lives lost in a war created, declared, and glorified by men?

But no one cared about women's rights at the moment; the Allies were winning the war, the lucky ones would soon be coming home, sex and motherhood were in the air. Any other role for women was not acknowledged, much less championed. With so few men to go around, women couldn't risk being labeled unfeminine.

The war affected Dana's college plans too. She wanted to go to Northwestern, but coed colleges were reserving space for veterans applying under the G.I. Bill. By the time the Americans entered Paris in August 1944, Dana was packing for her first semester at Smith.

The newsreels of the liberation of Paris made Dana reach for Ema's hand in a gesture that was becoming rare these days.

"I'm happy for you, Maman," Dana whispered. "And Tante Danielle."

Dana had left for Northampton when Harding sent back the news that Danielle had died several months before of pneumonia complicated by lack of medicine, adequate heat, and decent food.

"I can't bear it," Ema told Kate, crying over Danielle's likeness in the black enamel locket. "Why didn't she come here? I'd have done anything for her."

"She knew that, darling."

"It frightens me, Kate, who am I going to lose next?"

But Kate could offer no assurance; the odds in Europe were not in favor of survival.

Emanuelle hovered constantly over the incoming press bulletins when Harding went north to cover the Ardennes offensive in December and then east with Patton's Third Army. He and Ken Conan reached the concentration camp at Buchenwald in April 1945.

"My God," Ema said aloud when the first lines of Harding's story began to appear.

"What is it, Mrs. Ellis, are you all right?"

All she could do was point to the teletype. A small group of people gathered near it and from the press room others, sensing something out of the ordinary, crowded around the machine.

Harding's descriptions of Buchenwald, written in the simple language of a man shocked beyond the power to express shock, made a silence in the room that spread throughout the building as copies of the story were distributed. What frightened Ema most was that Harding sounded totally devoid of hope.

> If ever a man looked into the face of evil, I did here today. They were men who did this, husbands and fathers like me, not fiends. I must now believe, with Immanuel Kant, that out of the crooked stuff of which man is made no good can ultimately come.

This war exposed a bestiality that we, in our fatuous
ignorance, thought civilization had gentled out of us.
It took the Nazis to make evil manifest on such a scale,
but it is still there in men, in all men, no matter how
we turn away in denial.

"We can't run this on page one!" Derek Hennessy said when Ema
sent down the makeup for the next day's edition. "Particularly not with
Conan's pictures; the whole thing's horrible."

"He didn't write it to be buried, Mr. Hennessy, and I certainly won't let
it be."

A few weeks later, while the West was still reeling from the nature and
extent of Germany's crime, the war in Europe ended.

And Drew—Sir Andrew Saxon now—survived. It was hard for Ema to
believe her son was twenty-six years old, that he had the title she had
coveted for him, that she must celebrate all that secretly, except for Kate.

His picture appeared on the cover of *Life*: THE FLYING BARONET, the cap-
tion said. He still looked amazingly like Julian, but the face was more
rugged, the handsomeness more picaresque than perfect. The story carried photos of Drew's illustrious father and grandfather and Lady Davina
at Stridings, of his sisters and his fiancée, Fenella Bayliss. *Life* applauded
his decision to go straight into the family bank without finishing at Oxford. "The Wing Commander has made history; there is no need for him
to study it." That issue of the magazine had been placed with Ema's hidden cache of treasures. She wondered if she would ever be able to display
them openly, the silhouettes from Montmartre and Julian's letters and all
the clippings about the Saxons and Stridings, still wrapped in linen on a
closet shelf.

And now Harding was coming home. She guessed from his letters that
he was greatly changed, and worried about what the change implied for
the two of them.

# 81

"If waiting time counts for getting into heaven," Emanuelle said, "women have nothing to worry about." She prowled around the library on Park Avenue, taking books off the shelves and putting them back unopened, glancing repeatedly at her watch. Finally she went back to the desk and took a cigarette from the gold-tooled leather box.

"Most of our lives we wait for lovers and husbands and babies," she said, lighting the cigarette and exhaling smoke. "We wait for wars to start and telegrams to come. We've just waited years for a war to end." She raised her hands in frustrated disgust. "Men make all the trouble and we just sit and wait."

"You never just sit," Kate said. "And if you smoke any more, you'll be too hoarse to speak to Harding when he gets here."

"What can I say to him, Kate? What happens to us next is up to him."

"Why should it be?" Kate demanded. "I'll never forgive him for being so cold to you the only time he called you from England."

Emanuelle looked lovingly at her friend. "Ever my loyal Kate. But he didn't know about Julian—and he did ask me to run the *Star*."

"Because he knew he could trust you! He'll take it away from you as soon as he comes home—and censor half of what you write." Kate settled her glasses on her nose, her round face earnest and sober. "Ema, I was always afraid your love for Julian would destroy you, and in my opinion there's not much to be said for adultery, not even in circumstances like yours. But Harding's pride in your success was always half-reluctant, even before he knew about Julian. He resented your independence; it meant you didn't belong to him completely."

"Maybe if I had given him more, he'd have demanded less."

Kate shook her head. "If! If is a crooked word. You'd have to live a second life parallel to this one to know what if. In this life, submission was never in your nature."

Emanuelle looked at her watch again. "We'll soon find out. He'll be here in an hour."

Kate rose to go. She was even rounder than she had been the day Ema met her. Her hair was feathered and streaked with gray, but her face, at fifty-five, was virtually unlined.

"You're a beautiful woman, Kate," Ema said, embracing her.

Kate blushed and put on her coat. "I'm beginning to believe that."

"Well, you are. Spencer always knew it and the boys too."

"Well, they would, they're mine."

The two women walked down the stairs of the duplex toward the door of the apartment. "I'm yours too," Ema said. "I'd never have made it this far through life without you."

"Call me tomorrow," Kate said, waiting for the elevator. "I want to know how things went." The elevator door opened. "Go and sit in a hot bath; that always makes you feel better."

But Emanuelle had already had two hot baths. She went back to the library, fixed herself a stiff drink, and made herself sit down, smoothing the overskirt of her black silk crepe lounging pajamas. She sat there smoking and sipping brandy, too apprehensive to think coherently, until the doorbell rang again.

She shot to her feet. She had given the staff the day off and she ran to the door to let Harding in. She had expected it to be a difficult moment, but the sight of him, so gray and thin, made her forget that. She put her arms around him and held him as she would have held Dana, taking as much comfort from his nearness as she tried to give.

"Oh, Harding," was all she could say, "oh, Harding." She could feel his body trembling, like hers.

Oh, my God, he thought. He had hoped for only one thing, blessed indifference. He did not know yet what he felt, but it was not that.

"How are you, Ema, are you all right?"

"Yes, I'm all right now," Ema said. "Come and sit down. Are you hungry, or would you like a drink?" She went with him into the library.

"A drink first." He stopped on the threshold and looked around the room before he walked into it. "I always imagined you and Dana here, somehow, never at Silvermoor."

He was happier here, she thought; Silvermoor is English, like Julian.

He eased himself down into his chair, trying it on like a favorite jacket, and she brought him a brandy. "You're so thin," she said. She wanted to touch his cheek, but did not dare. His skin was still tanned, but the lines that fanned out around his eyes were deep and white.

"So are you, but beautiful as ever." His voice was hoarse. He sipped the brandy and she sat down in the chair facing his. He glanced toward the door. "Where's Dana?"

"She'll be down from school tomorrow, I wanted to have this evening alone with you."

"Yes, so did I. How is she?"

"Brilliant. Lovely. Serious. She never swooned over Sinatra or anyone else; she doesn't do the silly things most young girls do. She has plenty of boyfriends, but she prefers to be with Skip Atwood, rummaging in ruins. Poor Skip is in love with her. She's missed you very much."

He nodded and sat for a while in silence, looking at nothing. The clock struck seven and he started, then looked at her. "My nerves," he explained. "But I'm much better than I was." His eyes did not leave her face.

"Mother of God," she whispered, destroyed by the look of him and by all that had happened to bring them to this meeting.

"You've done a wonderful job on the *Star*," he said, looking directly at her for the first time. The *Star* was safe terrain.

"It was always your favorite dream," she said. "I couldn't let anything happen to it."

He did not reply immediately and she realized she had blundered into the heart of the matter. He shook his head. "You were my dream, Ema." He had to stop before he could bring himself to say it. "The way Julian was yours."

The tension mounted but at least she could answer him honestly now. "I never gave him anything that was yours, only what was already his long before I met you. Whatever was left in me to give to anyone you had, you still do, you always will. There can never be anyone else for me but you." She shook her head. "But what difference does it make, when you can barely look at me?"

"Oh, can't I?" His despair was more rending than his anger had been. "Do you think I thought of much else for the past five years except the sight of you?"

"Or I of anything but you, us, this moment?" she demanded with soft vehemence, suffocated by all she could not say. "But I gave him up for you. Maybe you'll believe that now that he's dead."

"Christ, Ema," he said explosively. "Why didn't you tell me he was dead when I called you from England?"

She was startled. "How could I? You were so . . ."

"This *is* why you came back, isn't it, because he was dead?"

"No, Harding! No! I knew I was coming back during an air raid, right after Julian asked me to marry him." She sighed in hopeless desperation. "Would it have made any difference if I'd told you that too?"

He looked down at the brandy in his glass. "Maybe not," he said after a moment, "maybe it took death to do that, all those other deaths as well as his. I admired the man, you know, he was one of the best."

"Oh, Harding, don't." She felt her face crumple and tears well up that she had vowed she would not shed.

Harding shook his head fiercely, determined to say it all. "When I first heard about him I was glad. I thought, now it'll be my face Ema remembers in the winter of her life. I'm not very proud of that, but it's the truth, God help me." He put the glass down and leaned back in the chair, covering his face with his hands. "A long time later, when I could think about him without seeing him with you, this came to my mind: 'When he shall die, take him and cut him out in little stars, and he will make the face of heaven so fine, that all the world will be in love with night.'"

"But you said that in a broadcast last year!"

He nodded, in control of himself once more. "I said it for him. By then I could say it and mean it." He looked at her again. "I've had a lot of time in the last five years to think about you and him, you and me. I wasn't blameless, there were—a lot of things. I *was* jealous of your success, I thought it would take you away from me." He shook his head. "How could I lose what I never had? I think you'll always be in love with night, Ema, you'll always be in thrall to some darkness I don't understand. But whatever you and he did, it was for love, not for blood and power. There isn't much love in the world."

"I could have told you that," she cried, "I should have told you—everything." If he asked her at this moment, she would.

"It doesn't matter now," he said. He pushed himself out of the chair and walked to her. "Don't cry, Ema, or I will, too, and I haven't any tears left. I want us to let all of that rest and go on together if we can."

"Yes, oh, yes. It's what I want too."

"It won't be the same, I know that, but there's Dana. And I—I couldn't care for anyone else either. We can make a go of it if we try."

He held out his hands and she took them and got out of the chair. After a moment's hesitation she put her arms around him and they held each other like long-lost friends. His body felt unfamiliar to her, strangely fragile, and his trembling had not stopped. She touched her lips to his cheeks, to his eyes, to his hands, wanting to show him how dear he was to her, unable to say it.

He was right, it would never be the same, and she would always mourn that old sharing between them that had transcended all their grievances.

They walked out of the room together. They could give each other only what was left in them to give, but she loved him with all of her sadder, wiser heart, with everything she had.

But sometimes there has to be more than love, she thought, sometimes love is not enough.

# BOOK IV

If you bring forth what is within you, what you
bring forth will save you. If you do not bring
forth what is within you, what you do not
bring forth will destroy you.

THE GNOSTIC GOSPELS

# 82

Dana came down the wide, curved staircase of Lord Broadhurst's mansion in Stanhope Gate, enjoying the feel of her satin taffeta gown. Her mother had chosen it. The gown was deep ruby, strapless, and fitted to the waist; then it billowed out over wide petticoats to her ankles. For dinner she wore a matching jacket, a dramatic pouffed sacque with a high, standaway collar.

Dana's near-black hair was cut in a gamine bob, like Zizi Jeanmaire's, and she wore the diamond-set rubies her parents had given her when she sailed off to do post-graduate work in archaeology at Cambridge. Oh, yes, she was at school in England. Mother always got her way in the end, even though it was Dana's choice to earn her master's degree at Cambridge.

This was her second and final year, and living abroad had given her a better sense of herself. She no longer resented anything merely because her mother approved of it. Dana had her own flat at Cambridge, comfortable but not half as luxurious as home. "Tacky English," Ema had announced approvingly when she saw it, "the upper-class kind." Dana enjoyed feeling imperial when she stayed with the Broadhursts, as her mother preferred her to do whenever she came up to London because she would meet the "right people" here.

Ema had always been concerned about things that never worried Dana overmuch: clothes in the latest style, friends from the Social Register— "but *we're* not in the Social Register," Dana had protested—and above all dating only eligible men.

"What *do* you think about—besides ruins?" Emanuelle had asked just before Dana sailed away to England for this final year at Cambridge.

"What the ruins tell me: how ancient civilizations lived, the gods they worshipped, their customs and beliefs."

"And what will you do with all that knowledge?"

"Get accepted to go on a dig in Israel, if I'm lucky—and I'm sorry if that shocks you."

She isn't sorry at all, Ema thought, but she smiled. "I'm unshockable by this time! When the other girls were ga-ga about Dior's New Look, you were rhapsodizing about the Dead Sea scrolls. Israel's very far away, though."

"Does that bother you, Mother?" Dana was ashamed of herself but she hoped it did, the way her mother's decision to stay in England when the war began had bothered Dana and still did. They had always been engaged in a private little war of their own, but it had become far more apparent since then.

"Yes, but I'm proud of you; you're the new woman I'm always writing about. I just wonder if marriageable men frequent tombs these days."

"I don't want to get married yet."

"You're on the brink of twenty-four, isn't it about time?"

"There speaks the ardent feminist! Mother, you're a fraud. I'm not getting married until I meet someone I love as much as I do Skip but in a different way."

She still wished she could love Skip in that way, but it wasn't possible. They had almost made love one summer in a cool, dark cave in Maine that had always been their special hiding place, but she had burst into tears when she felt the tip of his penis trying to slide into her, and Skip had stopped because he was that kind of boy.

"Now you'll hate me," she had sobbed, curled in a ball and too embarrassed to pull on her panties and jeans.

"No, Dana," Skip said. "I love you, I've always loved you. That will never change." She knew his thin, freckled face was peering at her anxiously in the gloom of the cave and she felt a surge of remorse. He resembled his father, but he had Kate's warm brown eyes. "I shouldn't have let things go so far." He turned away considerately and they both put their clothes back on.

"It's not your fault!" Dana told him, overcome again by his willingness to take the blame for any mischief the two of them had got into since childhood. "That was a terrible thing to do to a friend."

"It's more than friendship. I'm going to marry you," Skip had told her on the way back to the rambling house her father had bought for summer holidays in the Maine woods.

She had thought about it for over a year, knowing it was not the kind of marriage her mother had planned for her. That was probably why, for a while, Dana wanted it. But Skip deserved better of her than that, and she had told him, before she sailed for England, that much as she loved him, it wasn't in that way.

It was the hardest thing she had ever had to do, and the look on his dear face still haunted her. Lately she had begun to think how superior he was to the men she'd met. Her virginity was getting to be a burden, too, but there was no one Dana wanted in that way.

She took a last look at herself in the hall mirror and went toward the buzz of voices in the drawing room. It was a discreet buzz, not like the roar of an American party. Dana liked English manners and English breeding, but it was unsettling to be constantly in the company of people who were far too well bred to say what they really thought. Sometimes she was blisteringly frank, just to stir things up. It had earned her a reputation as an "original," something between an eccentric and an intellectual, not as peculiar as the first and far more amusing than the second. It tickled Dana to know that. She walked into the drawing room.

"Ah, here you are," Lord Broadhurst said from his chair. He sat most of the time to spare his knees, but otherwise age had been kind to him and his color was as healthy as the first time she had met him. He was still a power to be reckoned with. "My dear, come and meet our guests."

She moved around the small circle of people, directed by Broadhurst's lordly hand. There were three press barons and their wives whom she had already met with her parents. The young people included an American attaché's daughter and her cousin, both members of the Princess Margaret set; two eligible marquesses in their twenties, one pale, one ruddy; and finally a handsome dark-haired man who was slightly older and whose expression sharpened when he heard her name, as hers did when Broadhurst introduced him.

"Last but not least, this is Sir Andrew Saxon."

Never least, she thought, never. She extended her hand and, as soon as general conversation began among the others, she said, "I met your father once."

"I met your mother—and your father too."

"Really? When?"

"During the war, in your father's office in Fleet Street. And you?"

"Your father was in America lecturing. He came out to Silvermoor for lunch."

"Silvermoor?"

"Home. On the Hudson." Dana took a glass of sherry from the tray the footman offered her. Sir Andrew replaced his empty glass, took another whisky, and added water from the crystal pitcher on the tray and some ice; she noticed that because the British liked everything to be tepid or bland, the way they were. He wasn't in the least bland, though. She watched him while he fixed the drink; he looked a lot like his father. She and Carolyn George—Caro was married and having babies in Chicago— still remembered Sir Julian as a picturebook prince, startlingly handsome and heroic, almost unreal. His son was handsome, but very real, more Lochinvar than Galahad. He was taller than his father had been.

"What shall I call you?" Dana asked when he turned back to her.

He smiled; for the first time she knew what other girls meant by a devastating smile. "I don't answer to Sir Andrew, " he said. "Most people call me Drew. What are you doing in England?"

"Getting a master's degree in archaeology at Cambridge."

He did not make a flippant comment, as most other men did when they heard that. "I knew a chap during the war who wanted to study archaeology. He was shot down over Burma a few months before the war ended."

"You were in the R.A.F.! I remember a *Life* magazine article about you. What did they call you—The Flying Baronet." She raised her glass to him in a quiet little toast. He acknowledged it. "What do you do now?"

"I'm a banker. It's a family bank and I run the Hong Kong branch. I came back for my sister Alexandra's wedding." He drank some whisky and Dana's high spirits faded; he would be going back to Hong Kong and that would be that. "Juliana was married two years ago," he added.

"I'm an only child," Dana said, feeling suddenly bereft. "How many of you are there?"

"I have three sisters, the third one's Jennifer."

"That's a heavy responsibility," she said, "but you don't seem bowed down by it." He was anything but careworn; there was a devil-may-care attitude about him—or maybe that would be true of any man who'd come through the war in one piece and was as smashing as he was. She had never met anyone quite like him. Most young men made her feel as superior as a dowager; he made her aware that she was young and very inexperienced. He must have had hundreds of women, she thought. I'm probably the first virgin he's talked to in years.

He laughed. "I'm not bowed down at all. Mother keeps the girls in order—and she's very strict, I can tell you. I don't envy them."

"I know," Dana said, "my mother's like that."

"I didn't get that impression," he said; the smile had vanished.

"Who keeps you in order?" Dana asked, sure he must be married to some chic, sinuous daughter of a regiment.

"No one, it's an impossible task."

Dinner was announced, and Lady Broadhurst directed that Dana be taken in by one of the marquesses. All through dinner—impatiently she counted six courses in a country still forced to ration itself!—she made conversation with her marquess, but she was aware that Drew's eyes turned as often in her direction as hers did toward him. She was grateful for glossy dark hair and huge gray eyes, for a good figure and a closetful of gorgeous clothes. I owe you one for that, Mother, she thought, and then, he's exactly what you always wanted for me—except that he's going back to Hong Kong.

He took her dancing after dinner. They made up a party with the attaché's daughter and her cousin and the two marquesses. He was a good dancer, but she had expected him to be; he would be good at everything he did. She had always admired people like that, people like her mother and father.

"When do you go back to Cambridge?" he asked her.

"In a week. When do you go back to Hong Kong?"

"I don't know yet. Are you free for dinner tomorrow night?"

"Yes," she said, "I'm free all week."

"Miss Ellis, you are utterly without feminine guile."

"I don't answer to Miss Ellis, call me Dana. And yes, I guess I am."

"How do you explain that?"

"I have no explanation. My mother despairs of me."

There was an interested gleam in his eyes. "Does she? Why?"

"She doesn't see any future for me digging up bones and bracelets and extrapolating the life of ancient civilizations from them."

"Do you see any future in it?"

Her mouth smiled, but her eyes were grave. "Up to now I've been more concerned about the past than the future."

They stopped talking and she leaned toward him, hoping he would draw her closer. There was a lovely flutter inside her when he did. Her cheek touched his and she caught the faint green aroma of vetiver in his cologne. Her arm lay decorously across his shoulder, but after a moment she put her hand on the nape of his neck. He moved away to look down at her and she colored, expecting him to comment on her obvious attraction to him with a look or even a smile, but he pulled her close again and they went on dancing.

At the huge door of Broadhurst's mansion she put out her gloved hand and he took it. "Tomorrow night at eight," he said when the footman opened the door for her. "I'll pick you up."

"No, I'd rather meet you." She wanted to keep this for herself. Broadhurst was always writing to her parents about her as it was.

They arranged a meeting place and she slipped inside and ran up the broad staircase to her room, startled by the force of her attraction to him. She had never even had a crush on a boy before. She either liked them as friends—Skip was special—or she didn't, but she had never yearned for any man like this. It was hard to believe she had met him only six hours ago.

It was two o'clock in the morning and that meant it was nine in the evening in New York. On impulse she picked up the telephone and put in a call to the Park Avenue apartment. Then she undressed, avoiding the sight of her naked body in the mirror, resisting the urge to touch herself, to feel how she would feel to him.

"Daddy?" she said breathlessly when the call came through fifteen minutes later.

"No, darling, it's Mother. He's in California. Are you all right?"

"Yes, I'm fine, just wonderful. I'm still at Lord Broadhurst's." Dana stopped for a second, then plunged on. "Maman, I think I'm in love."

"That's wonderful," Ema said doubtfully. "Tell me about him."

"No, not until he's in love too. I don't want to jinx it."

"Is he wonderful?"

"The most wonderful man in the world, handsome as a prince and clever too." She almost said that both her parents had met him, but her mother was so quick, she might guess. "I wore the Balenciaga tonight," Dana said, "the ruby one, and you were right, it's gorgeous."

"Please don't get carried away, Dana," Emanuelle said.

"Oh, Mother, stop worrying, you'll love him."

They talked for a while, then Dana hung up. She would not tell her mother who he was. In the first place, Ema wouldn't believe in nonsense like love at first sight. And Dana would probably never see him again after tomorrow night. Then, too, her parents had met him; it was as if they had a prior right to him. Dana was tired of the prior rights of parents, she wanted him to be hers alone for as long as she had him, even if it was only tomorrow night.

But she could tell Caro! She had always told Caro everything. She drummed her fingers impatiently while she waited for the call to go through.

"Hello, Mrs. Price, it's me."

"Hello, me. Are you having a happy holiday?"

"Better than that. Caro, I'm in love!"

"Who is he?"

"Drew Saxon—actually Sir Andrew. Julian Saxon's son. Remember him?"

"Oh, yes, he wasn't the sort of man you'd forget. How long have you known his son?"

Dana looked at the bedside clock. "Six hours and forty minutes." There was a silence on Caro's end of the line, and Dana laughed. "I know, it's not like me, it's absolutely crazy, but there it is. I love him."

"And he?"

"He's interested."

"Interested isn't enough."

"It's enough to start. I'll do whatever I have to do to make him love me. There's something about him so—I don't know, he needs someone, I just know it."

"But Dana! You're always making snap judgments and then you're too stubborn to change your mind. Your prince might turn into a frog—or a Henry Price."

For the first time that evening Dana frowned. "What's wrong with Henry?"

"Nothing—except that he's just Henry, not a prince at all. I can't blame him for that, can I?"

"Then it's the twins. Are they okay?"

"The twins are wonderful. I didn't mean to rain on your parade. Promise to tell me everything that happens."

"Whatever happens, don't tell my mother!"

"Of course not. Anyway, I never see her. Nothing goes on in Chicago that would interest her." Caro paused. "Are you sure you don't want her to know?"

"I'm positive! I want to do one thing in my life she hasn't orchestrated. Is that so terrible?"

"No, I know just what you mean. More power to you. Good luck with your baronet, Dana, you deserve it. I hope he deserves you."

"Oh, he does. The funny thing is, Mother would approve of him; he's just what she wanted for me—English, handsome, titled, rich. But we have a lot in common, he has a father he still can't live up to and I have a mother. Thanks for listening, Caro. Love you. Good night."

Dana hugged herself and smiled as she got into bed. She would say nothing to anyone until whatever was going to happen between them happened—or he went away and put an end to the delicious anticipation she had never felt before. She lay back naked on the pillows—she always slept nude—and tried to imagine him making love to her. She had read *Ideal Marriage* and knew how it was done, but she had no idea how it felt.

I must be in love, she thought, really in love.

# 83

Drew, dressing for dinner the next evening, knew he was attracted to Dana, but she was very young and he was more curious about Emanuelle Beranger. His father had lived half his life in a secret and powerful alliance with the woman, and he wanted to know more about her.

Whatever his shock in the *Star* office that day, Drew had admired Emanuelle Beranger for her courage in defending his father. He no longer judged his father—he, of all people, had no right to judge anyone—but he had suspected for a long time that his mother *had* known about the liaison. It explained Davina's venomous personality—with everyone, strangely enough, but his father, whom she worshipped as if he were not responsible for his iniquity.

She had been worse than ever in the thirteen years since his father's death, and now she was dying of leukemia. He stayed on in England, waiting for her to die without wanting her to. He found himself feeling sorry for her for the first time in his life.

Drew would never understand, though, why his mother turned most of her venom on him; nothing he did ever seemed to please her. At least she spared his sisters her sarcasm, although she ruled them like a sergeant major and gave them little affection.

He wondered what kind of woman her rival was, and he listened attentively to everything Dana said about Emanuelle Beranger that second evening. There was no need to draw her out; she talked a lot about her mother. She had a frankness that was decidedly un-English, and it was a refreshing change.

He found himself thinking about Dana after she had been back in Cambridge for several weeks, and he realized that he was interested in the girl herself, not only what she could tell him about his father's mistress.

He called her a few times, but another month passed and it was March before he went to Cambridge to spend a Saturday with her. He had felt vaguely uncomfortable about doing that: his father and her mother had been sexually involved, after all, something Dana obviously didn't know.

But that's nothing to do with me, he told himself on the drive up. It's time I stopped being such an insufferable prig about it!

His discomfort faded completely the moment he saw her. He liked her intelligence, her forthrightness, and her humor. She was very knowledgeable in her field and it fascinated him to hear her talk about ancient civilizations.

"This is my favorite church," she said when they went to explore St. Benet's. "It dates back to Saxon times. Do you suppose one of your ancestors came to worship here?"

"I have no idea," he said, looking down at her. She was wonderful to watch. She had the same unforgettable wide gray eyes as her mother and the same mouth, but unlike her mother's, her face was unguarded, mobile, and very expressive. It gave away whatever she felt. Her hair was dark and silky and her figure was lovely, slim but full-breasted. Quite suddenly, standing there in the church, he knew he wanted her.

"I prefer to think so," she said. "My friend Caro and I thought your father was straight out of Camelot when he came to lunch that day—and heroes seem to run in your family."

Drew shook his head. "My father was a real hero; he fought for his beliefs as long as he could, even when they became unpopular. I"—he shrugged—"I just did the going thing, what everyone wanted me to do."

"But you did it with panache," she said, and added, "I hate to do the going thing. I told you my mother despairs of me."

"What's the going thing for American girls?"

"The same as for English girls: marry well and have children."

"A fate worse than death?" he inquired, still looking at her.

"I used to think so," she said, gazing at him steadily—and he knew then that she was in love with him. It put him off; he was not interested in marriage, not anymore, and he had not sunk so low that he would seduce a young girl just because he wanted her. He was a man of thirty-two; at twenty-four she was still a girl and obviously inexperienced.

He thought about that after he left Cambridge and headed back to pay his weekly duty call on Davina. Apart from his mother's approval, he had always had everything he wanted—until Fenella Bayliss.

"The marriage announced between Miss Fenella Tremayne Bayliss and Sir Andrew James Julian Saxon, Bart., will not now take place," the announcement in *The Times* had said briefly. Fenella had said much more, but the sum of it was that he had changed too much, he was not the same man she met in 1940.

But damn it, five years of war would change any man! He had no intention of putting on the old school tie and finishing at Oxford, and he refused adamantly to settle down in a country house and start raising a family. He wanted to *live* for a while first, by God, to enjoy the surging life that by some miracle was still his; he wanted to celebrate every night and know he was not holding a potential wake.

And he wanted Fenella with a crazy hunger that offended her every time he kissed her. It was not only lust—he needed her love as much as he wanted her body—but she would not hear of sex before marriage and she would not marry during a war.

"You must not touch me there, Drew," was what she said most often during the war.

"For God's sake, darling, we're engaged, we're in love, don't stop me now."

But she had stopped him and he, depressed by her outdated codes, had taken other women to the flat in Mount Street—well named, that was—to ease the sexual tension that, piled on all the other tensions, was unbearable.

And of course he did not quiet down, as she had expected, when the war ended. By then his hunger for her had ended anyway. He had gambled with his life and he had won, but the world had changed; it was as restless and uncertain as he was. Danger was a drug, he could not withdraw from it abruptly and retreat to the calm, orderly domain his father and grandfather had loved so much.

He was responsible for his sisters and he would discharge his obligations, but his mother had no need of him, and by then he had admitted to himself that he disliked her as much as she had always disliked him. He felt he was truer to his inner self when the war ended. He still admired his father more than any other man he knew, but he was not of Julian's caliber and never would be. It was ridiculous to try.

His engagement broken, he had gone to run the Saxon, Vaillant branch in Hong Kong. He had craved something new and exotic to replace the daily duels with death, and the Far East supplied it. It was spiced with other ideas—strange food and drink and, occasionally, opium, although he indulged only at the beginning; Drew liked to feel what he was doing.

And there had been many women, of course, lovely, sophisticated, knowledgeable women who made love with skill and appetite, to provide all the excitement he craved for the past half-dozen years. Now, perhaps, he had had enough of that. He had come home for his sister's wedding and remained because his mother was dying, but now he thought of staying on in England even after she was gone.

He knew it was because of Dana. She was a mixture of innocence and wisdom that enchanted him. In the early weeks of spring he found himself telling her things he had never disclosed to anyone else—about Fenella, about his father, about the unspoken feud with his mother, and Davina's approaching death. Young as she was, she understood him.

Davina's illness dragged on into early spring and he went dutifully to Stridings to see her every Sunday, but almost as often he went joyfully to Cambridge to spend the Saturday with Dana.

"Will I interfere with early goddess worship if I arrive about ten o'clock this Saturday?" he asked her in May. Davina was sinking fast, but before he could deal with death, he wanted a few hours with Dana.

"That depends on which goddess you have in mind."

"Astarte."

"Then you must definitely come early; the fertility rites can't start without you."

"Fine, I'll be there by ten. Let's have a picnic."

He knew, driving up to Cambridge, that Dana gave him a kind of strength he had not tried to qualify. He dreaded his mother's death and his dread mystified him, for he did not love Davina. Yet he *should* love her, shouldn't he, she was his mother! But she was a cold woman, despite her passion for his father. No wonder his father had loved another woman more. And this afternoon he must go, the unloving son of an unloving father, twice-guilty, he, to send his mother off into that dark night he had faced so many times himself.

He shook his head deliberately. He would not think of Davina now, he would think of Dana, of Dana's sweet mouth that he had kissed so many times. It was a delight to kiss her, it would be a delight to make love to her, but he never had. There were so many women available to him for sex who were not as precious and as vulnerable as she was. She was as ardent as she was chaste; he knew she was ready to follow if he led her further, but he would not seduce her. It was not only gallantry; he was protecting himself too. He was not certain yet that he was fit to marry anyone, and if he made love to Dana, he must marry her or be unable to live with himself.

She waved from her window when he pulled into her street and his heart lifted.

"Isn't it glorious?" she said when they had found a place to picnic in the country. "There is no place as beautiful as England in the spring." She leaned back against the tree and stretched her arms up to the sky. "I have never felt this way before."

"What way?" he asked, smiling up at her.

"I can't describe it. Anyway, I think you know."

"Maybe I can remember if I try."

"Oh, Drew, stop pretending you're a jaded old party. You're as young as I am in a lot of ways." She eased herself down to lie next to him, looking up at the leafy tree.

"That's true, but how did you know it?"

"Because I know you. Maybe that sounds presumptuous, but I do. You are—familiar to me."

"I remind you of my father."

"No, I was with him for only an hour. It's something about the way you are. Defiant. It's how I am, too, but don't ask how I knew that from the first. I just did."

"You're much too good for a rake like me," he said. His attempt to say it lightly failed. He meant it.

"Ah, but I *am* a rake like you," she said.

She turned her head to look at him, her gray eyes shining with love, and he took her in his arms and kissed her. She moved to nestle close to him, and he felt the softness of her body.

He lay over her then, his hands tangled in her hair, his mouth pressed to the curve of her neck. She sighed with content when one hand caressed her breast, then moved down to the firm fullness of her thighs. He knew she would be warm and wet and open to his touch, and he knew that no one had ever made her quicken before, that he was the first. Tears of passion and tenderness came to his eyes, and the core of him was touched by more than her body, more than sex, more than his desire and this prelude to fulfillment.

"You're so sweet," he whispered against her mouth. "Sweet."

"Yes," she murmured, trembling. She heard him across a river of sensation and a forest of delight, wanting more, aching for it.

He wanted her, it would be like sinking into honey, but not here, not now, not today when he could not stay with her. He held her in his arms, basking for a while in the nearness of her before he moved to arrange her clothes and smooth down her skirt.

"Why did you stop, Drew? Was it me?"

"No, Dana, not you. But I have to go to Stridings. My mother is much worse."

"Oh, darling." She put her arms around him. "I'm so sorry."

"The doctor thinks she'll go today or tomorrow and the girls need me."

"Of course you must go." She looked at him curiously and he felt the question she did not ask.

"I just didn't want to talk about it with you, I wanted to forget it. Today I had to see you first, be near you. You . . . you help."

She held him close for a moment. "I'm glad you came." She began to gather the picnic things. "Try to call me tonight."

"I will if I can." They got into the car. "Dana?"

"Yes?"

"I think I'm falling in love with you."

"Why does that make you sad?"

He shook his head, inarticulate for the first time in his life with anyone besides Davina. "It's just . . . it's the wrong day, isn't it?"

She sat close beside him until they were back in Cambridge and he watched her go, feeling the warmth fade out of sight when she did. Before he was halfway to Stridings, he knew he would marry her.

# 84

"How is she?" Drew asked as soon as he walked into the small drawing room at Stridings where the eldest of his three sisters sat wearily on the couch, drinking tea.

"Still hanging on," Juliana said. "You know Mother."

He nodded, taking her hand. "Can I go up and see her?"

"Yes, she's been asking for you. Alex and Jenny are with her now. She looks so beautiful, but she's terribly weak. Have a cup of tea."

He refused it and went upstairs to his mother's bedroom, surprised that she would have asked for him. His sisters looked up from her bedside, their faces alight at the sight of him.

Davina, propped up on her silken pillows, opened her eyes. "Hail," she said, "the conquering hero comes." Her voice was faint, but still sarcastic.

Alexandra and Jennifer blushed painfully, as they often did when Davina was particularly nasty. Her illness had made her worse, even, than she had been after their father died. They had always been afraid of her, but they worshipped her, too, a goddess to be propitiated only by the sacrifice of themselves.

"How are you, Mother?" Drew asked, feeling foolish to ask such a question of the dying.

"As you see," she said. "Have you come to gloat?"

"Mother, for God's sake," Jenny whispered. She shook her head sadly at Drew.

"Go on downstairs, both of you," Davina ordered. "I want to talk to Drew alone."

The girls fled and Drew took Jenny's chair. Davina seemed to sleep for a few minutes and he sat there looking at her. She had always been a beautiful woman; she still was, but as a shadow, an attenuated reflection of herself, as in a defective mirror. Then she stirred again and her eyes, only slightly faded from that bright electric blue, opened. She gestured toward the door that led to Julian's old dressing room, now her nurse's bedroom, and after a moment he understood she wanted it closed. He complied and came back to the bedside.

"I have something to tell you," she whispered. "Something worthy of you at last." As always, she managed to convey her contempt for him.

He resented it, and the old feeling of helplessness it evoked. He wanted to tell her something that made him happy, something she would not be there to share. "And I have something to tell you. I'm going to be married."

"Indeed? I always said I'd rather die than be the Dowager Lady Davina, and it looks like I'll have my wish. Who is she?"

"You don't know her, Mother. She's American."

"How typical of you, Drew, you never did anything right."

"Dana's right, she's the best thing that ever happened to me."

Davina's emaciated hand paused in its attempt to bring a handkerchief to her mouth. "Dana?"

"Dana Ellis. Her father's the publisher, Harding Ellis, who did those broadcasts during the war. Father knew both her parents."

The hand holding the handkerchief dropped like a stone and then, incredibly, Davina laughed. It was a silent laugh, she had no strength to propel it out of her lungs and past her colorless lips, but she was undeniably laughing. It was terrible to see, and Drew rose from his chair to get the nurse, but his mother shook her head and with a movement of her fingers put him back in his place.

"I never thought of this," she said, and her voice was stronger than it had been in weeks. "I thought of so many things by way of retribution, but I never thought of this."

He sat in silence, sure her mind was wandering.

"You can't marry her," Davina said. She smiled and with an effort raised her head an inch from its mound of pillows. "It's part of what I wanted to tell you. You can't marry her because she's your sister."

"What?" Drew said stupidly. "What?"

"You're not my son, Drew, you're hers."

"Whose? What are you talking about? Of course I'm your son."

She told him in disjointed phrases who his mother was and how he had come to be raised at Stridings. "Your father never knew," she said maliciously. "He thought you were mine to the end. No one else knew except your grandfather and that harlot."

"I don't believe you," Drew said, turning his head away.

"Yes, you do. Or you will. I never lived at Glengowrie, where she stayed until you were born. I was in Edinburgh in a house your grandfather rented for me. I'll give you the address if you want it. She was at

Glengowrie, at Silvermoor Cottage. Mrs. Seaton, she was called, you can check in the records. She's your mother, that French whore, and your sister's mother. The apples didn't fall very far from the tree. Lovely story isn't it?" Davina let her head drop to the pillows and her eyes closed.

"My God," Drew said.

"I've had a lifetime of you and your bloody damned mother. Now you can live with it the way I've had to all these years." She almost spat the words out. "I did it to keep him. I don't even mind dying now that I've got it off my conscience." Her eyes opened again and she looked at him pitilessly. "You should be grateful to me; you won't add incest to the blots on your family escutcheon—or have you already done that?"

Drew kicked the chair over in his headlong plunge out of the room. He ran up the stairs to his own apartment, closed and bolted the door, and sat in the dark, breathing hard. In the space of one day he had found a love and lost himself. It was like tumbling through the sky before a chute opened, like slamming into the icy surface of the Channel and feeling the water close over his head. It was hard for him to breathe.

His face was wet and he realized that he had been crying, but he did not know whether it was for Dana—my sister, he whispered into the darkness, shuddering—or himself. His father hadn't known; Davina said so.

And his mother? Who was she, why had she given him away? What kind of woman would do that?

He sat there for two hours, his mind traveling up one path to a blank wall and down another. Then he moved stiffly. He got to his feet and went into his bathroom and washed his hands and face without turning on the lights. He had the eerie conviction that he would not see a familiar face in the mirror, not Sir Andrew Saxon's at any rate; he had no right to that title, he was a bastard. If his father had known, he would not have left him Stridings, either, or the banks. He had no right to any of it.

And Dana, he thought, his breath catching in his throat, he had no right to love her the way he did, to touch her the way he had. To the burden of illegitimacy he had almost added incest.

He unbolted his bedroom door, planning to get out of this house, away from Stridings and the dying woman who despised him. Juliana was coming up the stairs.

"She's gone, Drew," she said. "Mother died a few minutes ago." She came to him and put her arms around him and he held on to her because he needed to hold on to someone. "I'm glad you came in time." His sister looked at him with eyes as blue as Davina's, but they were loving eyes. The girls had always loved him; he could not have borne his father's death without them. "We're so grateful we have you to look after things, darling," Juliana said. With her handkerchief she dried the tears that had reappeared on his face.

With a heart like lead he accepted the responsibility. It was the least he could do for his sisters—no, his half-sisters, like Dana. When it was all over he would go away, back to Hong Kong, to determine what restitution of property he should make to his father's legitimate heirs. He would act like a man now, whatever else he was. He went downstairs to call the doctor and then Davina's solicitor. He never looked at Davina's face again, not even when she lay in the chapel in her coffin. Otherwise he played the part of a bereaved son.

He refused Dana's calls, making excuses through the butler: Sir Andrew was making arrangements for the funeral, he was receiving condolence calls from his family and friends, he had taken his sisters out for a breath of air.

Finally, when his "mother" had been buried at his father's side, when her will had been read and his omission from Davina's last bequests had shocked the relatives, when he was in London about to embark for Hong Kong, he called Dana from the pier.

"Why, Drew?" she demanded when he said he was going back to Hong Kong.

"It's business," he said stiffly, looking through the windows of the call box, trying to keep his voice steady. "Arising from my mother's death."

"And you'll have to stay for an indefinite time?" She took a deep breath. "You're saying good-bye to me, Drew, and I want to know why. Tell me the truth, please, whatever it is."

He almost put down the telephone, but in the end he told her part of the truth. "Dana, it was getting far too serious between us. I don't want to marry. Not you, not anyone, ever."

"I don't care, Drew, you don't have to marry me! I just want us to be together."

"No, you don't, not that way, you don't know what you're saying."

"I know that I love you! And you said you were falling in love with me."

"I was wrong. It was . . . it was attraction, excitement, but not love." It was hard to say it. "Not on my part, anyway."

There was a heavy silence for a moment before she spoke very softly. "That's honest, at least. But, oh, Drew, it was on mine." He knew she was crying, and it broke his heart.

"Not really," he said, "believe me, someday you'll know I'm right. Good-bye, Dana, I have to board my ship." He dropped the telephone into its cradle and rested his head against the cold door. "I'm sorry," he whispered, "my poor darling, I'm so very sorry."

"But what else could I do?" he pleaded. There was no answer. He pushed the door of the booth open, crossed the pier, and went up the gangway. There was little of youth left in his face.

* * *

Dana, in Cambridge, pleaded too. "What's wrong with me, what did I do?"

He loved her, she knew he did, but not enough to marry her, not even enough to be her lover. Why not? It had been bad enough before that sunny afternoon, but now she knew what it was like to respond to a beloved man. It was like being naked in the summer sun, like a warm waterfall, sheltering and powerful and, by its beauty, unforgettable. She still ached for it.

There was something about him that clutched at her heart, something she loved without any reason. She wondered if they had met in some other life, and then berated herself for such an antiquated fancy.

She had always had the things she wanted, her mother had seen to that, but Drew was not a commodity to be bought or provided because she wanted him. Drew had to be won, and she had failed to win him. She was not woman enough for such a man, but she wanted no other.

She had been looking forward to her parents' arrival, to telling them about Drew. Now she had nothing to tell, except that she had suffered the first and most abiding rejection of her life. The only thing she would share with them was that she had been offered a post as assistant custodian in the Museum of Natural History in New York and had accepted it. There was nothing to keep her in England.


But she could not live at home anymore. She rented an apartment in Gramercy Square and fell easily into the social round she had generally avoided before.

"It's diverting," she told Caro in that autumn of 1951 when they met for lunch at the Plaza. "Almost as good as dinosaurs for making a girl forget her mistakes."

The two young women, both dressed in suits, furs, and discreet but opulent jewelry, waited until the waiter served their lobster salads and departed. Caro had presence now. Her shy manner was gone, but in its place was an air of bitter disillusion.

"Not even a dinosaur could help me," Caro said. "I don't know which is worse, living with a mistake the way I do, or not being able to forget one, like you."

Dana looked at her friend intently. "I'm sorry, Caro, I didn't know it was that bad."

Caro shrugged. "Maybe it isn't, maybe all marriages are like mine. Henry and I get along as well as most of our married friends. That's how things are done: he has his affairs and I pretend not to know. The truth is I don't much care what he does, and that's the worst part of it."

Dana shook her head. "I'd care, all right! What a bastard! You ought to have a few affairs of your own, just to show him what it's like."

"That's no solution, is it? And my parents would disown me if I even mentioned divorce." Her hands shook as she lit a cigarette. "My parents have always ruled me; now they've taken over my daughters as well. The girls have been told I'm mean to Daddy—and I can't explain why to them, they're only four years old."

"That's infuriating!" Dana said, aghast. "Well, damn it, at least a lover would mean a little excitement, a few happy hours for you."

Caro didn't agree. "Your affairs haven't made you happy."

Dana pushed her almost untouched lunch away and lit a cigarette. "You're right, they don't, not even Skip Atwood. I've been trying to make it up to him—believe me, I know now how he felt when I told him . . . what Drew told me—but it's no good and we both know it." She rested her face between her hands. "And I want children, too, Caro, as much as you did. But Drew's children, no other man's. Lord, I wish I could forget everything that happened in England! I wish I'd never met him!"

"No, Dana, be glad you did," Caro said.

"Why, for God's sake?"

"Because you've been wildly in love at least once in your life, and it doesn't happen to everyone. I've never felt about Henry the way you did about Drew."

She should have said *The way I still do*, Dana thought when they had parted, Caro to return to her loveless marriage in Chicago and Dana to a pursuit of pleasure that was exciting only in that moment of sex when her body left her heart behind, not before and never after.

She was haunted by fantasies of what love would have been like with Drew, and she pursued a fulfillment that seemed within reach but was always just beyond her grasp. She never blamed Drew for having rejected her, she blamed herself. Drew would not have abandoned a real woman, a woman like her mother.

# 85

Emanuelle sat at her table in the cocktail lounge at Danielle's, finishing her second *café exprès* and relishing a Gaulois cigarette. From time to time people stopped to talk to her: a New York assemblyman, a senator from the Middle West, two ambassadors, and three society women who sat on the boards of New York's most powerful charities.

The political people wanted their names in the *Star* and the society women wanted the women's page to support their charities. The ambassadors were the most amusing, they just wanted to gossip.

She was making notes when Harding arrived. "What are you chuckling over?" he asked, bending to kiss her cheek.

"Something the Brazilian ambassador told me about Tom Blessing's latest amorous attempt in São Paolo."

"Tom Blessing is too old to hobble around São Paolo, much less make amorous attempts." He ordered a scotch and water from the waiter and Ema asked for a champagne cocktail. "Anything political?"

"The Middle West wants more farm support and New York wants more federal funds for blue-collar housing." Ema looked up to see a soberly dressed woman standing at her side. "I'm sorry, I didn't see you, would you like to speak to me?"

The woman hesitated and Harding got to his feet. "I'll be back in a moment." He held his chair for her. "Won't you sit down?"

The woman took his seat. Her severely tailored black suit and hat made a stark contrast to the gilt and ivory decor of the cocktail lounge. "My name is Frederika Riis," she said. "I'm a social worker. I hope you'll be able to help me."

"In what way?" Emanuelle asked, and waited for Miss Riis to explain. The woman's face was strong and scrubbed under her black felt hat, with a high-bridged prominent nose. She had heavy, sweeping brows and a wide, firm mouth. Her ring finger was bare, and she wore no jewelry, nail polish, or makeup. She makes me feel like a popinjay, Ema thought, conscious of her white-piped black wool suit and her small black hat veiled in starched white.

"I'm trying to raise money to buy a house, I don't care where, Long Island or New Jersey. I need it to shelter abused girls. I don't have a penny and I haven't been able to raise any public funds. People don't want to hear about this kind of thing."

"What kind of thing?"

"Incest."

Ema put down her champagne cocktail and looked at Miss Riis blankly. "Incest?"

The woman nodded. "The most prevalent form of child abuse, even though no one will admit it, least of all the victims."

Ema cleared her throat. "I didn't think it was so prevalent."

"It is. Fathers with their daughters, for the most part, but there are uncles and brothers, too, having relations with helpless girls sometimes as young as three years old. Yes, I know, it's incredible, but take my word, it's true." She leaned forward, her square face earnest. "Miss Beranger, I've raised money for divorced mothers and unwed mothers and women pregnant by rapists. I've campaigned for birth control and even legal abortion. All that was hard enough, but I can't raise a dime for this. It takes more courage than most people have even to admit the problem exists. You have a reputation for courage."

Ema said nothing. Her mind skittered around the subject and found it untouchable, like a sea urchin bristling with ugly black spines. Miss Riis watched her for a while, then gave a resigned nod and got up to go.

Ema touched her arm. "Please, Miss Riis, I can't talk about such a project here. We'll have to meet somewhere else. Where can I get in touch with you?"

A gleam of admiration lit up the woman's brown eyes. She opened her shabby handbag and produced an index card with her name, address, and telephone number written on it. "I'm out most of the day," she said, "but you can reach me after nine at night."

"I'll call you as soon as I can," Ema said.

"I hope so. I'm sorry to have bothered you here, but this was where I was sure to find you." Miss Riis looked around the cocktail lounge, obviously calculating its cost. She smiled. She had beautiful teeth. "I read your society column too. Good evening." She marched off. A few of the cocktail patrons looked at her with supercilious smiles that angered Ema. What right had they to patronize such a woman? She put the index card hastily into her handbag as Harding approached.

"Who was that? She has a marvelous face, right off Mount Rushmore."

"A social worker," Ema said. She finished her champagne quickly and held up her empty glass so the waiter would bring her another. She was upset, but she was still an expert at hiding it.

"Who needs money."

"Of course."

"Is it a good cause?"

"A woman like that always has a good cause," Ema said. "I'll have to find out more about it. Oh, there's Dana."

She's so beautiful, Ema thought, watching her daughter stop to speak to people she knew. I don't know why she sleeps around the way she does.

Dana's suit was gray broadcloth with a closely fitted jacket and a slim, straight skirt. Her blouse was gray silk. Opals shone from her earrings and the brooch on her lapel, and her makeup, under her gray velvet pancake hat, was expertly applied.

"That's the damnedest archaeologist I ever saw," Harding said proudly. He knew nothing of his daughter's high-class promiscuity and Ema hoped he never would. "She looks like she spends all day at Elizabeth Arden instead of in that dusty museum."

"A late bloomer," Ema said, keeping her worries to herself. "Remember what a time I had getting her out of dungarees?"

"Still no hope for Skip?"

"No, that's ancient history. Shhh, here she comes."

After Dana's affair with Skip two years ago, there had been two broken engagements followed by several brief affairs. She always brushed aside Ema's questions about the man she had met in England, dismissing it as a belated schoolgirl crush, but Ema was convinced he had been the cause of Dana's sudden interest in makeup, clothes, and sex.

She was hurt, Ema thought, and she's not over him, or she wouldn't be trying to prove herself with other men.

"Can you have dinner with us?" Harding asked her.

"No, Daddy, just a drink. I have to go home and dress. I'm going to the theater with Peter Higham."

"That playboy?" Harding exclaimed.

"He's fun," Dana said, "and very sophisticated." Her eyes met her mother's and glanced away.

"He should be, he's almost twice your age," Harding grumbled.

Sophisticated, *mon oeil*, Ema thought, the man's a mighty lover, by all reports. It was amazing to Emanuelle that Harding never noticed Dana's new ripeness, but fathers preferred to ignore a daughter's sexuality. Except *my* father, she thought suddenly, and her heart began to pound. No, she told herself severely, that was long ago, it's all forgotten. She regretted her promise to Miss Riis.

Dana left for her Gramercy Park apartment after one drink.

"She's beautiful," Harding said, "but apart from her work she isn't happy. I wish she'd find a real man and settle down."

"I told you she's a late bloomer. She's having all the fun she couldn't be bothered with in college."

"It's the men she's having it with that make my hair stand on end," Harding said.

"What shall we do this evening?"

"Let's have dinner here, it's the best French food in town."

"And I can watch the money roll in," Ema said, smiling. "Then we can go to the Embers and listen to Errol Garner for an hour." She didn't want to spend a quiet evening at home tonight.

But they were home and undressing for bed by midnight. They had been sleeping in separate bedrooms since Harding's return from the war eight years ago, but they still made love frequently in the comradely, satisfying fashion, she supposed, of most long-term marriages.

They had a great deal more in common than most couples; they liked the same people and the same things. They often worked late at the *Star* and then went out for steak to the Pen & Pencil or Christ Cella or Pietro's with their journalist friends.

And she knew what troubled him. The Korean War had depressed him; he could see no purpose worth more bloodshed. It was uncanny how he had come full circle to Julian's preoccupation with war, although he never spoke of that to her. But where Julian had sought to eradicate the concept from civilized minds, Harding was devoted to keeping the memories of war alive, all of them, from the Blitz to Auschwitz to Hiroshima. It was the only way, he believed, to prevent it all from happening again.

"I hope he confides in you," Ema said to Kenneth Conan the last time he was in New York. Kenny's war pictures had made him a celebrity; he was a free-lance photographer now. "He doesn't say much to me."

"He doesn't have to," Ken told her. "He's just sick at heart, he can't get the carnage out of his head. Neither can I, that's why I run around the world as if the devil were after me."

But Harding traveled less than ever, and so did Ema. It was the closest to a conventional marriage they had ever known. They were affectionate with each other and considerate in a way they had not been before, but the special fire of his devotion was gone and its absence left a hollow feeling deep within her. She had never appreciated before what he had offered her: approval for what she was—or as much as he knew of what she was.

She loved him as she had never loved him before, but she was afraid to say it, lest it stir memories of the past best left at rest.

But she had always had an appetite for rapture, quite apart from the sexual fulfillment they still had together, and there was no rapture without intense love, freely expressed.

Maybe I'm beyond rapture now, she told herself, getting into bed. But she didn't believe that, and she envied Dana her youth and the real passion she would find when she fell in love with someone who loved her.

Harding tapped on her door and put his head in. "Any room at the inn tonight?"

Why must he knock, why must he ask, protecting himself from refusal with a joke?

"Always," she said, turning back the covers for him. He got into bed beside her and took her in his arms and the melody of a French song that had haunted her lately drifted through her mind:

> *Plaisir d'amour ne dure qu'un instant;*
> *Chagrin d'amour dure toute la vie entière.*
> Love's pleasure lasts a moment;
> Love's sorrow lasts a lifetime through.

Then he kissed her, and she took the pleasure while she could and let the sorrow go.

# 86

Dana walked into Emanuelle's office at the *Star* and stopped in surprise. Tillie Blessing, swathed in black broadtail, sat at Ema's desk leafing through a sheaf of papers. Her elegantly shod feet rested on the desktop. Her legs were thin as sticks.

She looks more like a mummy every day, Dana thought. "Mrs. Blessing," she said brusquely, "what are you doing at my mother's desk?"

"Waiting for your mother," Tillie said. "We're doing a Christmas charity ball together. How did you manage to tear yourself away from your stuffed animals?"

"It's my day off," Dana said. "I came by to discuss something with Mother." Despite her dislike for Mrs. Blessing, Dana looked very pleased with herself.

Tillie extended her arms in feigned joy. "Let me guess. You're engaged at last."

Dana sat on the edge of the desk and lit a cigarette. "No."

"Then it's high time you were, my girl." Tillie flapped the papers against the desktop. "I don't mind telling you, you're getting a reputation."

Dana flushed, but made no reply.

"What are you now, twenty-six? You'll end up on the shelf if you're not careful."

"Mother didn't marry until she was twenty-six," Dana said, annoyed.

"The second time. But your mother had a reputation, too; I suppose it runs in the family."

"How dare you talk about my mother that way! And put down her papers." Dana made no attempt now to hide her dislike for the woman.

"Temper, temper," Tillie said, obviously pleased at having provoked

her. "They're only press bulletins, everyone will read them tomorrow."
She smiled thinly. "But there's one here I know will be of special interest
to Emanuelle." She handed a telex to Dana.

> Monte Carlo—The engagement was announced today
> of Sir Andrew James Julian Saxon, Bart., to the lady
> Carlotta Margharita de Roja y Albafuente, daughter of
> the Spanish grandee. The wedding will take place in
> June in the Cathedral of Monaco. Sir Andrew, once ex-
> pected to follow in his illustrious father's footsteps,
> abandoned banking a few years ago and is now con-
> sidered the leader of the international set—and the
> best-looking playboy around.

Dana walked over to the window to avoid Tillie's piercing black eyes.
She read the telex again, made an unsuccessful attempt to speak, then
cleared her throat and looked for something to say.

"It's just another press release. I don't think it'll be of special interest to
Mother."

"Ah, but it will. Your mother had a soft spot in, shall we say, her heart
for Sir Andrew's father. Not that I blame her, mind you, he was the best-
looking man I ever saw."

"I know," Dana said blankly, "I met him."

"Do tell. When?"

"When he was here, lecturing. Mother brought him to Silvermoor for
lunch." She was talking just to talk, but she was thinking of Drew's voice
on the telephone. I don't want to marry, not anyone, not ever. She had
accepted it—what else could she have done?—but she had come to believe
that was not all of it. His rejection of her festered still, a wound that would
not heal except in those perversely soothing moments when she gave her
body over to another man's hands and felt wanted, possessed, even
loved, however briefly, however spuriously.

It had been more than a decision not to marry. Something had sent him
away, something that had happened at Stridings when his mother died.
Dana had thought of all sorts of things: that Lady Davina's disease was
hereditary and Drew was afraid to have children; or his mother had told
him something, heaven knew what, that had made him decide never to
marry at all. A reason, any reason at all, was easier to bear than rejection.
And he *had* loved her; he had told her so.

But he was engaged to marry now! Whatever his mother told him could
have been only about her, Dana! But what? What had she done that was
so terrible?

Her expression turned from stricken to stubborn, what Ema called her

Harding face. She must see him again! She must make him tell her whatever it was and then she would put his fears to rest and maybe—her heart leapt—his wedding in June would be to Dana Katharine Beranger Ellis!

She came back to herself to hear Tillie Blessing's sly, insinuating voice. ". . . very discreet, of course, but I could tell he was in love with her."

Dana turned, thinking she meant Drew and his Spanish fiancée. "When did you see them together?"

"Often enough. In Venice, here in New York, once in Paris—and of course my husband saw them in Berlin."

Dana shook her head in perplexity. "In New York? When was he in New York?"

"When you met him, little goose!" Tillie said impatiently.

"Mrs. Blessing, are you talking about Sir Julian?"

"But of course, my child."

"And you want me to believe he and my mother . . . ?"

"Who and your mother?" Emanuelle said, walking briskly into the office. "Hello, darling, what good fortune brings you here? Sorry I'm late, Tillie, it couldn't be helped." She shooed Tillie away from her desk and dropped her briefcase on it. She picked up the press releases before she glanced at Dana's face and then at Tillie's. "What is it?" she asked peremptorily. "Tillie, what mischief have you been up to now?"

"Just having a little gossip," Tillie said, reaching hastily for her bag. "Ema, it's too late, I really can't stay, we'll talk about the ball some other time." With a last look from mother to daughter she left the office.

"Dana?"

"Mother, were you and Julian Saxon lovers?"

Ema sank into her chair. "Is that what she told you?"

"I want *you* to tell me—or I'll keep asking until I find out."

With a deep sigh Ema nodded.

"For how long?" Dana asked.

"Years, Dana, a long time."

"Did his wife know?"

"Yes."

Dana flushed deeply and went to sit opposite her mother. "I can't believe it," she said. "You did that to Daddy?"

"Dana, I knew Julian years before I met your father. I'd never have married Daddy if I'd known Julian was alive."

"But you went on with the affair after you were married." Dana's eyes were fixed on her mother's. "Did Daddy know?"

"He . . . not until the war started. Then Julian was killed."

Dana's eyes narrowed slightly, putting dates together. "No wonder you were so strange when you came back. You only left England because he was killed."

Ema shook her head. "I was coming back anyway, to be with you."

Dana's hands curled into fists on the desktop, one of them still clutching the telex. "You don't expect me to believe that, do you? You were never interested in me and Daddy, not really, you were only interested in your precious career—and your lover."

"Dana, you know I love you. Everything I did was for you, to make your life a better one than mine had been. As for Julian, that didn't concern you at all, it was between the two of us and your father. Harding and I are still together; he understood it, why can't you?"

Dana handed her the crumpled telex. Ema read it, glanced up quickly, then read it again. She waited.

"I love him," Dana said, too upset to notice Ema's sudden pallor. "And he loves me. He left me after his mother died and now I know why. She told him about his father and you. What a juicy scandal it would have made if his son and your daughter married! If Tillie knew about you, a lot of other people did. Drew wanted to protect his family and me too." Dana got to her feet. "No wonder he's nothing but a playboy now, no wonder he didn't want to be like his father after the way that man hurt his mother. Well, I don't care about scandal and I'm going to Monte Carlo to tell him so. I'm going to marry him if he'll have me." She thrust the chair back and got to her feet.

"Dana," Emanuelle said, and it was an admonition, sharp and commanding. "Sit down. You can't go to Monte Carlo. He won't marry you." She looked at Dana's defiant, stricken face, and her tone softened. "Darling, he didn't leave you because he was afraid of scandal, Drew wouldn't give a damn about scandal after the life he's led. And Davina didn't have to tell him about his father and me; he found that out in 1940."

"Then why?" Dana said, frantic now. "When he said he loved me!" Her head went down on the desk. "What is there about me that drove him away?"

Ema came around the desk. She knew all too well what that feeling of unworthiness could do. She bent over her daughter, trying to save her. "Listen to me, Dana, because this is very hard for me to say. Drew didn't marry you because he can't. He's your half-brother. That must be what Davina told him before she died."

Dana gasped and moved away from her, holding her stomach as if she had been hit. "Oh, no," she whispered, "oh, my God." She flinched from Ema's consoling hands. "No, don't touch me, leave me alone."

Ema went back to her chair and lit a cigarette with shaking hands. When Dana did look at her, the beautiful gray eyes were dull and dark as lead. "All right," she said, "you can tell me the rest now."

Talking, Ema had a suffocating sense of disaster. The last time she had told this story she had believed Drew was gone forever, and by the time she finished, she knew she had lost Dana too.

"Why didn't you tell me?" Dana asked. "I'd have understood when I was old enough."

"A child is never old enough to hear something like that from her mother."

"But I'm not a child anymore, I'm a woman. I've had a mind of my own for a long time, no matter how hard you tried to make me a carbon copy of yourself."

"That isn't true," Ema said, "I just wanted you to have—everything."

"An English home!" Dana said scornfully. "An English nanny, an English governess. An English education, an English aristocrat for a husband. It was what *you* wanted, Mother. I never did!"

"It was what Drew had. I gave him up so he could have it. I wanted you to have more."

Dana shook her head. "So you made me the rival of a brother"—she shivered at the word—"I didn't even know I had. Well, it didn't work, Mother, I'm still who I am, whatever that may be and even if I'm not what you wanted." She took a handkerchief from her purse and dried her eyes. "I can't stay in New York anymore, not now," she said. "I'm going away."

"Where?"

"To Israel, on a dig." She lifted her shoulders and let them drop. "I came here this morning to talk it over with you. I got more than I bargained for, didn't I?" She got up from the chair.

"When will you go?"

"Day after tomorrow. I'm a last-minute replacement and they can't wait." She looked at Ema coldly. "A replacement. That's how you thought of me, isn't it?"

"No, never. Children aren't like dining room chairs, one can never take another's place. I left him, yes, but what else could I have done?"

"You could have told me he existed!" Dana went to the door. "You could have trusted me."

"I trust you now! Isn't that enough?"

"Too little, Mother, and too late." She opened the door, then closed it again. "When will Daddy be back?"

"Next week."

"I'll leave him a note. Poor Daddy. Does he know about Drew?"

"No." Ema straightened in her chair. "And don't you dare threaten me."

Dana shook her head. "No one can threaten you, Mother, you're made of steel. I'm not going to tell Daddy, that's a pleasure only you deserve." She went out, closing the door behind her.

Emanuelle sat with the telex still in her hand, mechanically smoothing out the crumpled paper. We throw separate pebbles in the pond, Sir James had told her; the misfortune is that the ripples sometimes touch. This time their touching had destroyed all the carefully planned patterns of her life. Drew, who had once admired her, however grudgingly, must despise her now. In the two years since Drew had known she was his mother he had made no attempt to contact her, even to ask if Davina's truth was the only truth.

And Dana had put a distance between them far beyond the miles that would separate them now. She loved Dana unselfishly—or so she had believed until she was accused of forcing her daughter to live the life *she* wanted, of making one child the other's rival, of not trusting Dana.

How was it possible for love to become tyranny?

"Miss Beranger?" her secretary said. "Are you all right? I've been buzzing . . ." Behind her secretary loomed the square figure of Frederika Riis. From the midst of her misery Ema's gaze locked into those steady brown eyes that had seen so many horrors.

"Yes, I'm all right," Ema said, moistening her lips. "Come in, Miss Riis, sit down." She wanted to hear about the horrors, she wanted to hear how right she had been to protect both her children from them.

"Whatever happened," Miss Riis said, her shrewd glance noting Ema's pallor and her shaking hands, "you'd better tell someone about it."

"I will," Ema said, "but not today."

# 87

APRIL 1955

There are worse things, Ema said to herself at Dana's wedding in a garden in Jerusalem. It was her infallible formula for dealing with trouble, for putting it into perspective.

Today the trouble was not in watching Dana marry the professor of archaeology she had chosen. The trouble was Dana's unrelenting resentment of Ema. Her letters home during the past two years were always addressed to both her parents, but they were really written to Harding.

It was not difficult to hide their estrangement in the bustle of wedding preparations. In this sunny place they had been alone together only once, Dana made sure of that. Her anger at her mother was still virulent, like a fever that peaked and fell, but she swore she would not show it. "For Daddy's sake," she said.

There was always the hope that things might change, but Ema knew that could happen only if this marriage was a happy one. There was no way, under the circumstances, for Emanuelle to determine the exact nature of Dana's love for her new husband, but there was no doubt in Ema's mind that Dana did love him.

Calvin Lloyd Bannister was a tall, slender, quiet-spoken man of thirty-five with a gentle kind of humor. His thin, intelligent face was famous in his field, but he would never have more than the modest fortune he had come into when he was twenty-one, and he seemed to care as little about amassing money as Dana did. All very well, Ema reflected, when you've always had enough of it. His only passion, aside from Dana, was his work, and Emanuelle thought a shared interest was a good basis for marriage, sometimes a better one than love. At least it lasted.

But would there be rapture in this marriage? How old-fashioned that sounded nowadays, more suited to a perfume than to one of the heights of human experience! Perhaps Dana was better off never to have known it, she would not have to watch it fade away. Or would she always want it, as Ema had and still did, even though Dana knew it was out of reach?

Dana and Calvin were exchanging rings now, and Harding, standing at Ema's side, was misty-eyed. Only a few of the guests were fashionably dressed, although the garden was large and riotous with flowers and sweet-smelling vines. This was not the wedding Ema had always dreamed of for her daughter. She had visualized the lawn at Silvermoor under silver and white marquees, or a country church in England, with guests whose names were always in the news—except for Tillie Blessing. As far as the *Star*'s society column was concerned, Tillie and everyone connected with her had ceased to exist. It was petty vengeance on a nasty old woman, but it was better than none.

One thing I'll never be, Ema thought, is saintly. Even her feelings for Dana alternated between remorse and anger that Dana judged her so rigidly.

The simple ceremony ended and the company burst into a joyous chorus of congratulations. It had been a civil wedding, but Dana had told her parents it would turn into a typical Israeli party, and so it did. The marvelous music began, and the dances that delighted Ema. Dana, looking very young in the embroidered white lawn dress Ema had brought from Paris for her, smiled up at her new husband and Ema felt comforted.

Once the newlyweds had departed for a honeymoon in Japan, Ema and Harding took some time to explore Israel. They needed the change after Harding's battles during the McCarthy era in America, when people began accusing their neighbors as the Germans had under Hitler.

"There have been un-American activities committees before," Harding had written on the editorial page of the *Star* when the red-hunting senator was at his most virulent. "I remember Martin Dies, but Dies cannot be compared to the McCarthy menace. I had supposed the Bill of Rights eradicated political fear in America, but obviously it had only retreated to the dark caves, where such dangers to freedom always lurk." Harding had received a subpoena to appear two days later, but he was one of the few to emerge from that ordeal almost unscathed. There had been a long day of shame in America and many lives ruined before McCarthy was censured by the Senate and guilt by association retreated again.

"I can understand why Dana loves the past," Harding said when they were driving across the Galilee toward the Mediterranean coast to board a ship for London. "The dangers are all known; they don't wait like dragons behind every tree."

"You love danger," Ema said, "you thrive on it."

But he did not agree as he once would have. And of course it was no longer true, not since the war.

* * *

"All this self-indulgence," Harding said over a drink in the ship's lounge after they sailed from Haifa. "It could become a habit."

"Not for you. No one's been more active in supporting Israel than you have."

"Anyone who saw those camps before they were turned into green parks has to support Israel," Harding said. "Also anyone who isn't too dim to perceive her strategic importance as the only democracy in the Middle East."

"There, you see," Ema said, pleased at his show of spirit. "You're much too young to retire." She knew retirement would be bad for him, but he seemed tired. Ema always had to remind herself that he was on the far side of sixty.

"Not until you do," he said, "so I'm in for a long run and a busy one."

Work was still Ema's cure-all. Her association—it was now a friendship—with Freddy Riis had led to the purchase of a large frame house in New Jersey. Half the purchase money was discreetly raised through the women's charities Ema had fostered since the Depression, but the rest, and the monthly upkeep, came out of Ema's own pocket.

There had been no articles in the *Star* about the prevalence of incest and the effects on its victims. Ema had never even suggested such a series to Harding; for her it cut too close to the bone. She thought Freddy, sensitive and perceptive as she was, had guessed that Ema hadn't even the courage to try, just as Freddy knew she preferred to supply the monthly money herself rather than try to raise it openly. The subject was simply too hot to handle, in print or otherwise.

The house was in New Jersey, a rambling three-story yellow clapboard with white shutters and a screened veranda. It stood on a corner lot with a wide fringe of lawn around it, sadly in need of care when Emanuelle first saw it, but the girls themselves had worked wonders.

Ema had never seen any of Freddy's little girls, nor did she plan to. Some things were tolerable only at a distance.

"The weather's changing," Harding observed when they were halfway to England.

"I wonder if a newswomen's conference is a good enough reason to put up with English weather."

"Come on, Em, you know you wouldn't miss seeing all those newshens for the world."


It was gray and pouring with rain in London. Neither of them mentioned that this was her first visit in fifteen years. Ema had been to Paris for the collections, to the Riviera during the off season, to Italy and Greece and Scandinavia, but not to England and never to any place when Drew was likely to be there too. London had always been inimical to her, but she relaxed on the second evening when she and Mary Alice had dinner alone at the Savoy Grill.

"You're the only woman in the world I'd come to meet through such a downpour," Ema said.

"And you're the only woman in the world who looks soignée in a mackintosh," Mary Alice said.

"How's married life?" Mary Alice had married the man whose study was Ema's bedroom during the war.

"Nice and cozy by now, Darby and Joan. And yours?"

"The same," Ema said, but it wasn't really true. Darby and Joan had come down through the years together, faithful and true, hand in hand, confiding in each other. There was a vast terrain she and Harding never ventured upon, like no-man's-land in the first war; it was a place where their marriage might be destroyed.

"Speaking of marriage, I see young Saxon's divorced. That didn't last long. But then, he's not the man his father was, is he?"

"I don't know much about them," Ema said.

Mary Alice eyed her obliquely. "Come off it, Ema, I know Andrew Saxon was the squadron leader who went down in the Channel. And I guessed you and his father were that way about each other for years. Damn it, woman, we're old friends, I'm not going to print it!"

"All right, yes, we were—once—but it ended some time before the war began. What's his son like now, do you know?"

Mary Alice lit a cigarette before she settled in for a good gossip. "I saw him in Monte just a month ago. He's a real stunner, very sexy, it runs in the family, but he's different from his father. Julian Saxon was an honorable man and it showed, however misguided his principles were. His son's something else again. If he has principles, they aren't noticeable, and as for women, he's the kind who loves 'em and leaves 'em."

"Maybe he had an unhappy childhood," Ema said archly, by way of camouflage.

Mary Alice laughed. "Spoiled rotten, if you ask me. He got all the looks and charm in that family—the three sisters are pretty enough, but they're all pale pink English roses—and it went to his head, if you know what I mean. Young Saxon sowed some wild oats out in Hong Kong right after the war, which was the right and proper thing to do. Then he dropped out of the news for a while and seemed to be settling down in Saxon, Vaillant until his mother died. Then he started kicking up his heels again and never looked back. It helps when you own a bank to keep you in funds. He's shot down more women than he did Nazis."

"'How are the mighty fallen,'" Ema said sadly.

Mary Alice agreed. "I know it's horrible to say, but the war was the high point of our time; it brought out the best in people."

"Harding doesn't think so."

Mary Alice nodded. "So I gather from what he writes. There's a case to be made for both sides."

"I don't agree. I met an SS officer when I was doing that series on Nazi women. He wanted to make love to me. He attracted me in the way that absolute power attracts, as well as corrupts. It makes me shiver to think of it now. I always wonder how many children he murdered while the SS ran those death camps."

The two women sat in silence for a moment until Emanuelle gave herself a little shake. "But we were talking about Saxon. What do you suppose changed him?"

"Maybe he couldn't live up to a hero's image, his own or his father's. Anyway, he's the sort of man women of all ages dream about, but not the kind I'd like my daughter to marry, if I had a daughter. How's yours, by the way?"

"Just married to an archaeology prof, one Calvin Lloyd Bannister, Ph.D. They met on a dig and had the wedding in Jerusalem."

They talked until after ten and Ema was still unsettled by what she had heard when she got back to the Connaught. Harding was out with some war buddies and that meant a very late night for him, but she wasn't ready to go to bed. She poured some brandy and sat down with British *Vogue*, leafing through it without really seeing anything.

The telephone rang and she was astonished to hear Drew's voice when she picked it up.

"I want to see you," he said, "if you're alone." It was a demand, not a request.

"All right," she said, and her hands began to shake. "Please come up."

# 88

She had not seen him since that day at the *Star* and he had changed, but not only from youth to manhood. He still looked like his father, but he had lost that luster that had been Julian's until the day he died.

"Would you like a drink?"

He shook his head and remained standing when she sat down, his hands thrust into the pockets of his twill slacks, pushing back the open blazer that had been expertly tailored to his broad shoulders. "I've really come to look at you," he said at length. He said it vindictively, and she gathered herself against what was coming.

"Look at me?"

"I wanted to see what kind of woman could have done the things you did."

Ema straightened in her chair. "How can you possibly know what I've done, except from what Davina told you? She was not the most charitable of women, especially not to you."

"I can't blame her for not liking me. She did what she had to do!"

"And I?" Ema demanded angrily. "What did I do?"

"You abandoned me—sold me is more accurate—and simply forgot I was alive." He ran his fingers nervously through his short dark hair, then thrust his hands back into his pockets. "Do you know what you did to Dana? Do you even care how much she was hurt? My God, what if something had happened between us before we knew what we are to each other? But you didn't care any more for Dana than you did for me. I don't know why my father loved you, but he obviously didn't know you. You were too clever for him by half; women like you always are."

"That's enough." Ema got up, her eyes blazing. "You had better go."

"I'll go," he said cuttingly, "I've seen what I came to see, my *mother*, God help me." He started for the door, then turned back. His face was twisted by anger and confusion. "You're as much of a fraud and a fake as you've made of me. I have no legitimate right to my name or my title or my position. I keep them so I won't embarrass my sisters or dirty my father's memory, but I don't really belong anywhere. You did that, and I'll hate you for it till the day I die." He covered the space to the door in three strides and left the room, slamming it behind him.

She sank into the chair. She felt skewered to it by the bitterness he had vented on her. His contempt for her was pure Saxon, the same monumental contempt that had let them manipulate her with impunity, play God from the moment Julian was found alive. They had made a real Saxon of Drew, and she hated him as much as he hated her.

She burst into tears. It was how Harding found her, in a state of nervous collapse. She would tell him nothing of the reason for it, and he helped her to bed and called a doctor to give her a sedative. They were to have stayed in England a week, but she begged him to book passage on an earlier ship, and they sailed the next night on the *Queen Elizabeth*.

For two days she used the sedatives as an excuse to be alone, to pull herself together. She knew Harding believed that London, with its memories of the Blitz and Julian's death, had overwhelmed her. She could not deny it without telling him everything—and she had never told anyone everything.

Late on the third afternoon she got up to dress for dinner. Harding was ready first and watched her at her dressing table the way he liked to. Her hair was frosted with white now, the effect was regal and sophisticated, but she looked pale and tired. She tried to smile at his reflection in the mirror, but he was stricken by the mute misery in her eyes.

"Ema," he said impulsively, "don't you have any idea how much I love you?"

"I know, I know," she whispered, "but it isn't the same."

"That's true, it isn't, but you have to allow my old jealousies and my hurt pride as I allowed your need to do as you did."

"I do," she said, and her voice shook. "But you wouldn't love me at all if you really knew me. If people really knew each other, no one would be able to love."

"Ema, I know you better than anyone does. I know where you came from and what you did to get where you are. I know you're not the *grande dame* you pretend to be, that you prefer beer to champagne, that you can be honest to the point of brutality and more loyal than anyone I know. I know you, all right, and I love you for exactly what you are."

"Do you really?" she said, and her face was earnestly hopeful, like a child who has been promised a special gift. Her lips trembled, and she got up from the dressing table and stopped to touch his face tenderly, then left the bedroom and went to sit on the couch in the salon.

He followed and poured their drinks from an icy shaker on the buffet. He handed her a dry martini and sat down in the chair facing her, sipping his own.

Suddenly she thought of the day Julian first came to Saxon, Vaillant and assumed, finding her there, that she came from decent, if modest, circumstances. It had all begun and ended with pretense.

"I would like to have been loved just for myself," she said.

"You never trusted me to do that, Ema," he said.

Herself. Emalie Anne. For a moment she was back in the bedroom above the *épicerie*. She could smell him. She could feel the mattress under her and hear the springs creak while he destroyed her. She had tried all her life to forget the colossal humiliation he had forced upon her, to erase the assault on her womanhood.

She shook her head. "You have no idea what it was like."

"I don't care, Ema! You were poor, but that's no crime—and it didn't stop you. It doesn't matter where you start out, it's how you end up that counts! You had intelligence and drive and courage—everything that matters."

To her surprise, for she was not aware of crying, her face was wet.

"Ah, yes, I had everything!" she said. "Poverty and squalor, smells and shouts and lust."

He had not seen her like this since the night of the attempted abortion, at once desolate and furious, as though she craved comfort but would not accept it. He did not approach her but sat still in the chair facing hers.

"But you won, Ema," he said gently, made heartsick by her anguish, "you won. You got away from it."

She put down her glass and lay back on the couch, one arm across her face. "Because I had to! Because my father raped me when I was fourteen years old."

He felt suddenly old. "My God, Ema, my God! Why didn't you ever tell me?"

"I never told anyone," she said, still hiding her face. "It's not the kind of thing a woman tells. It made me feel unworthy, unfit to be who I was. I had to be someone else." She stopped for a moment, then went on in a torrent of words she could not control. "For years I was terrified he would force me again. I had to get away from him, from men like him. I thought other men, rich men, were different. They're not, most of them. But he was, my Julian was."

Her arm dropped and she turned her face to Harding, but she didn't really see him or the way he looked as she went on. "You knew him. Is it any wonder that I loved him, that beautiful man? He was the first I ever knew of tenderness, he made me feel that the—the other thing had never happened. We were both sure he would live if we stayed together, it was our talisman against death. When they told me he was dead, all the love I had ever known died with him. Even my baby had a better chance with his people than with me. I had nowhere to go and I felt dead too. I thought he was a girl. You see, they took him away from me the minute he was born. I never saw him until we met that night in the Ritz bar in London, but I thought my baby would be safer as a Saxon than as a bastard in a world that would have made him pay for what I did."

"Ema," he said, immobile in his shock. "Is Andrew Saxon your son?"

She nodded. "Julian never knew it until just before he was killed. Drew didn't know until Davina died. Davina told him. She probably called it an act of conscience." Her mouth twisted. "Conscience. It ruined him. And by then he had met Dana; they were in love with each other."

"But—he might have married Dana if she hadn't told him, for God's sake!"

She twisted her hands, her head bent. "I know," she said, "I know. At least Davina's malice spared them that. But Dana hates me for it. So does Drew, for that and because I left him in the first place." She lay back again, her eyes closed. "He said neither of us is what we pretend to be, we're both frauds. Like mother, like son. The other night he came to tell me how much he despises me."

"So that's what happened in London!" He whistled softly. "Doesn't he remember what you risked to save his father's reputation? Doesn't he understand why you gave him up?"

She shrugged. "He doesn't care. It didn't earn me any grace to have done that for Julian, not from him. And it lost me you," she said, too weary to cry now, "and I loved you, even though I didn't know how much until I lost you. Please don't look away, Harding, it's true, even if there was a part of me I couldn't give you. She was already gone, that girl I was before my father destroyed her, the girl I could pretend to be only with Julian because we lived all those old fantasies together."

They looked at each other. "If only you could believe me," she said. "I've lost Dana and I never had Drew, but I once had you and you are very dear to me. She could love you now, that girl, if she were still alive." She turned her face to the back of the sofa and lay there quietly.

The stateroom was still except for the sound a great ship makes riding the Atlantic. Ema might have been alone on the vast ocean. She thought she could not bear it if she were.

She heard him get out of his chair and her heart stopped. Then his hand stroked her hair. "Who is she," he asked, "that girl who loves me now?"

"Emalie," she said, turning to look at him eagerly. "Emalie Anne Bequier."

He sat down and took her in his arms. "Tell me about Emalie Anne," he
said. "Tell me all about yourself."

# 89

Ema stood at the window of her bedroom at Silvermoor and watched the long line of limousines close ranks along the drive while the stream of people who emerged from them crossed the lawn and disappeared around the house toward the river. The cars had been arriving since mid-morning, but Ema was waiting for her own Rolls to return from the airport before she went down.

She turned from the window to look at the room she had redecorated three years ago, after that harrowing, healing voyage back from England. She had chosen the soft neutral colors and rich fabrics she loved—pale gray silk, amber satin, and ivory brocade. But it was Harding's room, too, and the lines of the antique-white furniture and draperies were straight and simple.

They had embarked upon a different kind of marriage then, at last unshadowed by secrets. It was ironic that the emotional fulfillment that had eluded her all her life should have come when she was nearing sixty; and it was cruel to have found their paradise so late only to have it end so soon.

Dana heard her little son stirring in the second cabin of the Ellis Enterprises jet and the soft sounds of his nanny hushing him with promises of the lovely bottle being warmed for him.

Did such a little thing ever comfort me? Dana wondered, and remembered again the warmth of her father's arms and how long it had been since she had seen his smile and then that he was dead and she would never see him again.

Oh, Daddy, she told him, I'm so sorry, I'm so sorry. I should have come home more often, I shouldn't have let her keep me away from you.

But Ema didn't keep you away, her father's voice reprimanded her gently. She wanted you as much as I did.

But of course, Daddy didn't know why Dana and her mother would always be an affliction to each other. Harding didn't know about Drew. If he had, he wouldn't have been so much in love with Ema right up to the end.

Cal came to her side and put an arm around her. "Have you slept at all?"

Dana opened her tear-swollen eyes. "A little."

"Darling," Cal said, "you're only making it harder, blaming Ema for your father's death. She loved him as much as you did. I've never seen a couple more devoted to each other."

"That's because you didn't know her back when! My mother was never devoted to anyone but herself. And she never had a moment's remorse for what she did to Daddy." She knew Cal thought she meant only Ema's long affair with Julian Saxon. No one else knew the whole truth about Drew, not even Caro, and the end of confidence had meant the end of that friendship—another loss to lay at Ema's door. To her husband Dana had confided only her mother's adultery.

"It was your father's right to judge that, Dana, not yours," Cal reminded her. "She was *his* wife."

She turned sharply to her husband, ready to object, but he was looking at her the way her father used to when he was absolutely and incontrovertibly right. Cal reminded her of Harding in many ways. He had the same unshakable foundation, the same solid strength despite his mild-mannered exterior. Cal was a passionate man who did not make a display of passion except in private. She was grateful for him and she loved him very much, even though Drew still hovered on the edges of her life, the grand illusion, the one consummation she would never know.

She pressed her lips together and nodded at Cal, conceding that he was right. Then she put her arms around her husband and cried against him, glad she had him, missing her father, wanting so many things she could not even name, wanting to be so many things she could never be.

Ema heard the sound of wheels on the gravel and turned back to the window. She saw her son-in-law step out of the car carrying his six-month-old son and took a deep breath when Dana appeared after him. Ema crossed the bedroom quickly and was at the top of the stairs when the Bannisters entered the hall. She started down just as Dana started up, hoping desperately that it was symbolic, this meeting halfway.

Dana returned Ema's embrace, but the diffidence was still there like a wall between them, and Ema's hopes faded.

"Mother," Dana whispered. "Are you all right?"

Ema nodded. All right wasn't much, but it would get her through Harding's funeral.

The shock was over, but she knew the experience of loss was yet to come. She was well accustomed to losses, but this one was monumental. Still, she would not show her grief today. At least five hundred people were waiting at Ema's favorite place overlooking the Hudson to pay their last respects to Harding Ellis, but only the few Ema really loved had any right to her grief.

She clutched it as ferociously as she had held Harding when she woke to find him dead at her side. It was *her* grief, she had earned it by all she had done and left undone.

She walked down the stairs with Dana to welcome Calvin and take her grandson, Calvin Ellis Bannister, in her arms. It was sweet and strange to hold their child's child. She and Harding had been in Israel when the baby was born and were planning their second trip there when Harding died. He had always tried to make things easy for her, and he had died the same way, quietly, in his sleep, of a massive heart attack.

Standing there, her face pressed against their grandson's sweet warm little body, she knew she must put it out of her mind somehow, that wakening to find Harding so silent and so cold, and the sound of her own anguished screams of denial that brought the servants running while she rocked him, trying to warm him back to life, as if love alone had that power.

"Nanny will take Ellis up to the nursery, Mother," Dana said. "You can't hold him all through the service."

Ema shook her head. "Don't take him. I need him, I want him with me." She rocked the little body tenderly.

"He might cry, Ema," Calvin said.

"He won't be the only one who cries today."

Kate and Spencer joined Ema and the Bannisters in the hall. The three Atwood boys and their wives followed them, Skip pale and silent at the sight of Dana. Freddy Riis was there, too, and Ken Conan, red-eyed and looking oddly unappareled without his camera, and round little Monsieur Étienne. They went through the house and out onto the lawn. Ema carried Ellis, alive and warm, against her shoulder.

"It's ghoulish to read Daddy's will today," Dana said when the funeral was over and the mourners had gone. Her eyes were still swollen and heavy. "I don't care about Daddy's money." She glanced at her mother, but Ema, sitting on one side of the dining room table with Dana and Calvin, said nothing.

"It's better to get it over with, darling," Kate told Dana soothingly, leaning across the table to touch her hand.

Harding's elderly lawyer, Samuel Partridge, cleared his throat and picked up a thick sheaf of papers bound in blue; it seemed too heavy for his fragile old hands.

"This is Harding's will," he said. "He had many holdings, so there is a lot of legal jargon about stocks and shares and the people responsible for how it all runs. It can take several months to settle an estate of this size. I thought it would be easier if I told you the essentials today and left the details for another time." He looked at Ema over his glasses. "Is that acceptable?"

She nodded.

The lawyer cleared his throat again. "First, there's a long list of bequests to Harding's staff and friends. He had a lot of friends." His voice quavered and he paused a moment, then collected himself and peered over his glasses at Kate and Spencer. "He left one million to each of your sons—he looked upon them as nephews—and he wanted you, Mr. Atwood, to have his ivory chess set and Mrs. Atwood to have the house in Maine for her lifetime." He paused and Kate took off her glasses and put her head on Spencer's shoulder.

"He knew how much I loved that house," Kate said, her eyes streaming, "but Ema . . . ?"

"It'll be a comfort to me to know you're there with the children, Kate."

The lawyer consulted his notes and continued. There was a separate ten-million-dollar endowment for the baby and an equal amount for any other children Dana might have, to come out of the estate with Dana as trustee. Harding left five million dollars to his son-in-law and a five-million-dollar grant for archaeological research to any institution Cal and Dana designated.

Mr. Partridge paused again. "The balance of the estate, worth about one hundred million dollars, he divided equally between his wife and daughter during Ema's lifetime—it will go to Dana and her children afterward. The same is true of Silvermoor, although the land, of course, belongs to Ema. Ema and Dana are co-executors of the will with my law firm. They can either take over the chairmanship of his companies and run them—probably with the help of the people he placed in positions of authority—or liquidate them, in which case, of course, the money reverts to the estate to be divided equally as before. But his newspaper, the *Star-Tribune*, he left entirely to you, Ema." Partridge took off his glasses and looked at her. "He wanted you to be managing editor as well as publisher; it was very important to him." He wiped his glasses with a large white handkerchief and put them back on. "And that's it," he finished. "Now I'll leave you in peace. I'm available whenever you want me. Just call."

When he had gone Ema sat bemused, aware of the enormous wealth and power that had just descended on her—and the enormous responsibility it entailed. "I can run the *Star*," she said, "but utilities and airplanes and the rest are beyond me." She looked at Dana.

"I don't know anything about business," Dana said. "Anyway, what does it matter now?"

"It mattered to him, Dana," Ema said. "His success may not have won him a Nobel Prize or a page in the history books, but it was his monument. He built it all by himself, from nothing, and he wanted you and his grandson to have everything he worked for."

"And you," Dana said, and her manner was ambiguous.

"I don't think you ought to talk about it anymore tonight," Kate said, watching them. "I think it's time we all went to bed."

Ema nodded. "But we have to settle some things before Dana leaves."

"We plan to stay for a few days, Ema; there's plenty of time," Cal said, and Ema looked at Dana.

"I'm glad you're staying," she said. She had not really expected a reconciliation with Dana, but maybe they could find some way to share their lives, even at a safe distance.


She woke very early and lay in bed listening to the silence of the house. She was not indifferent to the great wealth she had always coveted; what remained to be seen was how she was to fill the hours of her life when the world and power slept. Her hand touched Harding's pillow. She pulled it close, inside the circle of her arms, and cried silently. His book and glasses were still on the night table, and she took those and held them, too, missing him as she could not have missed him before these last three years together.

At dawn she called the groom to saddle a horse for her. She needed to feel the wind in her hair and the fresh morning air on her face. She washed her face, pulled a comb through her hair, and dressed quickly. She went out through the sleeping house and walked down to the stables to mount her chestnut mare and set off toward the trees, avoiding the new grave on the slope above the river.

When she heard hoofs galloping after her she knew it was Dana. She reined in her horse and waited until Dana came alongside, and they let their horses amble through the sun-streaked trees.

"I'd forgotten how beautiful Silvermoor is," Dana said. "Israel has its own kind of stark beauty, but I miss the green."

"You should come and stay when your latest project is finished. It's a perfect place for a child."

"Maybe we will. We haven't even thought where we'll go next."

"Does the baby have everything he needs in the nursery?"

"Of course he does, Mother. When were you ever less than perfect?"

"Most of my life, according to you."

Dana stopped her mount and Ema reined in too. "Mother, please," Dana said earnestly, looking down at her gloved hands. "I have to say something to you. I know now it wasn't for me to judge what happened between you and Daddy—or anyone else—and I apologize for that."

"But you won't forgive me for Drew?"

"No, I can't."

"I'll tell you something, Dana. I don't seek your forgiveness for that because it wasn't malicious. It was a blunder of fate."

"Suppose we'd eloped, suppose the baby were his? Would you have told me then?"

"No, it would have been too late. I'm sorry if that shocks you, but there it is. But that's not what you can't forgive, Dana, it's that I wasn't the perfect mother and I didn't save you from heartache the way mothers are supposed to do. But it's an impossible task; if it hadn't been that particular sorrow, it would have been another one."

"Oh, of course, my punishment for not doing exactly what you wanted me to do! You had my life planned out for me before I was born!"

"And brought you up to be so strong that I didn't succeed."

"No, you didn't," Dana said triumphantly. "Cal certainly isn't the sort of husband you had in mind for me."

"Is that why you married him, to spite me? Is Cal someone else you can't forgive me for?"

Dana was quietly intent. "I don't know what you mean."

"I think you do. You don't love him the same way you loved Drew and it makes you feel guilty. It's far easier to blame me."

Dana gazed at her in silence.

"Oh, yes," Ema nodded. "I know what it's like to love two men and resent the one who deserves more than you can give him. It's how I felt about your father and it was unbearable; he was worth more than half a loaf."

"It took you long enough to find it out!"

"It took the time it took. There's no timetable for becoming an adult, some people never do. In the end he knew I loved him for himself. It had nothing to do with Julian."

"Did Daddy know about us?"

"He knew everything, all of it."

"About Drew? And me?" Dana reddened, wondering why Harding had never mentioned it. And then she almost wept again, appreciating her father's respect for her privacy, remorseful that she had never repaid it with total confidence.

"Yes," Ema said. "About you and Drew and about me, what I'm really like."

"And what are you, Mother, besides overwhelming and smart and beautiful and just too bloody much?"

"Frightened, a lot of the time, just like anyone else. And angry with myself for my monumental mistakes. That's a waste of time, though, you and Drew are angry enough."

"Drew? Have you seen him?" She was both curious and incredulous.

"In London, right after your wedding. It was not a pleasant encounter. He despises me—for your sake, of course, but I think more because I gave him to Davina Saxon—she was a fearful woman. I didn't really; I gave him to his grandfather, but he wouldn't let me tell him that. I just didn't want my child to be illegitimate—it was a terrible stigma then, much worse than it is now. But I had to live in my time, not yours, and I wanted my child to have its rightful place in the world. But that birth had no joy in it." She put a hand out, almost touching Dana's arm. "You were my joy. Maybe I was wrong about what I wanted for you, but not why I wanted it."

"Oh, Maman," Dana whispered, clutching at the horse's mane. Her fingers threaded through the coarse black hair.

"Listen to me just once more, Dana. You ought to write to Drew, even see him. I think he needs someone to tell him he doesn't have to destroy himself, someone who knows the truth and loves him anyway."

"Like you." Dana looked at her mother across a narrower distance than before.

"Yes, but he won't listen to me. And apart from helping Drew, it would let you love your Cal the way you really want to. Dana, you're like your father, but you're like me too. You'd never have married Cal unless you loved him; you'd never have had a baby by him. It would be better for you to discover that now, not after twenty-nine years of marriage, the way I did."

Dana nodded, promising nothing. She relaxed her fingers from the horse's mane. "What will you do about all Daddy's companies?" she asked after a while.

"Run them; it's what he wanted me to do. He wanted to keep me busy because he knew I'd be lonely. But half of them are yours; you must decide about those."

Dana shook her head. "I'd rather leave all that to you."

"Think it over, I might run them into the ground."

"Not you. Daddy knew what he was doing."

They chirruped to the horses and moved off, both of them too emotionally exhausted to know where this had led them.

In a few days the Bannisters left for Israel and Ema closed Silvermoor and went back to New York to assume responsibility for all of Ellis Enterprises.

# 90

---

The law offices of Partridge, Tobias, and Black were almost as impressive as the firm's clientele. Alan Black could always tell, from his vantage point behind the desk, whether prospective clients were old-rich or new-rich by the way they reacted to Chippendale and Persian carpets. But the woman sitting opposite him was a client of long standing. No furniture could overwhelm Emanuelle Beranger. Alan often wondered if anything could, or ever had.

"How are you today, Mr. Black?" She was removing her soft kid gloves gently, with the care fine things deserve. She never called him Alan although he was twenty years younger than she and had been a junior partner of the firm when he first met her.

"Flourishing, thank you, Madame Beranger."

The French form of address came automatically to him. She had been an American citizen for many years, but her manner and her bearing were undeniably European, and lately she used French phrases more than she had.

"You were very kind to fit me in," she said, coming directly to the point of her visit. "I would like to make an addition to my will."

He picked up a pen and a pad and waited.

"My daughter has had a second son in Manila." She smiled. "An outlandish place to have a baby, but they were on a research expedition in the Philippines."

"Congratulations," Alan said. "They're both well?"

"Very. My daughter was always unconventional." She seemed proud of that. "And little Harding is to have the same legacy as his brother."

He nodded. "Everything else remains the same."

"Of course."

"And there are no changes in the sealed bequest."

"Definitely not."

He had always wondered to whom she would have left such an odd bequest—a bulky manuscript—in the first place, much less under seal, but she was not a woman to be questioned as she so blithely questioned everyone else.

She closed her handbag and took up her gloves, smiling. "Well, that takes care of Harding Bannister. His grandfather would have been proud."

Harding had been dead for three years now, and old Partridge had turned the management of his estate over to Alan when he retired.

"I know how much you miss your husband," he said.

Ema thought a minute. "But you know, he's always with me. The strange thing about people you love is that you begin to be aware of their presence, not their absence." She sighed. "I wonder I'm not offered a table for six when I dine out alone; I travel with a host of ghosts about me."

He wanted to hug her. She was a very kind woman, although very few people knew it. Another of her secrets was the endowment of a school for girls. "Calling it a home would create legal problems," she had told him. "These girls have families, that's precisely the problem. A school makes it easier to let their fathers save face." It was hard for Alan to believe what she had told him about the little girls Freddy Riis rescued, but Emanuelle Beranger told it to a lot of people who could help do something about it. She had a long-established reputation for exposing what other people preferred to sweep under rugs.

He knew by now that her withering cynicism, the vitriolic observations her columns were famous for, were only a façade, that for some reason he would never know, she chose to hide her real nature from everyone but the few she trusted—Kate Atwood, who still ran RSVP, and Frederika Riis, the benevolent dragon who presided over the school. There was also the famous photographer, Ken Conan, and, unexpectedly, the doughty little chef at Danielle's. Her daughter, Dana, was rarely in America, but Madame Beranger spoke about her often in a way that touched Alan.

They walked together to the door of his office.

"How are you finding the single life?" She asked him because Drew had just divorced his second wife. Ema was not surprised. Drew had gone to hell right royally, and nothing would bring him back.

"Difficult," Alan replied.

"I wish I knew why so many young people divorce these days. We were expected to struggle on for the sake of children and reputation."

"It's the times," Alan said. "Everything is changing. It's hard to know where we stand with each other as men and women."

She studied his puzzled expression for a moment, then offered him her hand. He had a momentary impulse to kiss it. She was a regal old bird, with her silver-streaked hair, elegant clothes, and the gold-headed cane she carried purely for fashionable effect—she was tall and slender and always moved quickly. He was very fond of her. Since his divorce he'd thought seriously of taking her to dinner and the opera some evening.

Emanuelle went reluctantly to her next appointment. She was on her way to her doctor, a visit she had been putting off for weeks. She had been in need of the gold-headed cane too often of late.

"You can't keep up your schedule with a heart like that," Dr. Hargreave said when Ema had dressed and was in his office again. "You've got your own empire *and* the one Harding left you *and* the *Star*—*and* you rush around the country and stay at parties until all hours of the night. If you want to live out a respectable span, Ema, you'll have to slow down. If there were any chance of your doing it, I'd tell you to retire."

"I'll retire when I die, the way Harding did. I don't mind having a heart, if I've got to have something. It's a better way to go than some I've seen. No, I've no intention of retiring, Wallace. The empires, as you call them, pretty much run themselves, I just poke my nose in unexpectedly every now and then to make sure no one's hand is in the till. But the *Star*'s my pride and joy, as it was Harding's. At my age there isn't much left but politics and gossip."

"What about Dana and your grandchildren? If you were a normal woman, they'd be enough pride and joy for you."

"Wallace, we have never agreed on what is normal for a woman. Besides, the children live their own lives far away from me, as children should—and I didn't come to consult you about family relations. My affairs are all in order and I'm prepared to depart this vale of tears—prepared, but not eager. Just tell me what to do to extend my stay."

But as Ema left the doctor's office and got into her car she was thinking of Drew again. He was the only thing in her life that was not in order; he was unfinished business.

The Bentley drove her home to the sumptuous duplex on Park Avenue, and she went into the library, asking her housekeeper to cancel her engagement for the evening and bring her a light supper here instead. She sat by the library fire, wanting a cigarette and damning her traitor heart and the feeling of helplessness it had summoned back into her ordered, insulated life.

Of course it was the intimation of mortality that made her want to see Drew. He had returned to banking after the second divorce, and although he was still a member of international society, he was no longer its crown prince. She would have liked to think his wild years were over, and she wondered if time might have softened the edge of his disdain for her, but she had never even considered finding out. It would have meant going to him like a supplicant, and she was beyond that; she had had enough of Saxon pride that had never taken *her* pride into account.

She gave herself a little shake. It was something she did not really want to do; it was the fault of her heart—about which she would say nothing to Kate or Freddy or Dana.

But while she nibbled at her supper and drank the one glass of wine the doctor said she might have, she was still thinking about Drew. She scarcely noticed when Nedda took the tray away, clucking because Madame had barely touched her poulet poché en gelée, and she was roused from her reflections only by the blaring horns of a dozen cars below, symptom of an impatient era, Auden's age of anxiety. She walked to the window and drew the curtain to look down at the Christmas trees all along Park Avenue. She wondered how long ago her heart began to break—literally break down.

"Old fool," she said to herself, turning away from the window. "You may be threatened with sudden extinction, but it changes nothing. What's done is done. I did what I had to do"—she threw her arms into the air in a gesture of incredulity—"as he believes Davina did, of all people, and if he can't accept me, then to hell with him." She left the library and walked through the entrance hall, going slowly, too slowly, up the stairs.

When she reached the top she looked down the long graceful curve of the stairway, thinking what a luxury it had been to run up a flight of stairs, to drink coffee, to dance until the wee hours and then make love all night. She pressed her lips together and went into her bedroom to answer the telephone.

"Kate," she said, "you always know when I need you."

"What did the doctor say?"

"He said I was impossible."

"Tell me," Kate insisted.

"It's nothing, really, he just thinks I'm wearing myself out. He wants me to start acting my age and retire."

Kate laughed.

"I know," Ema said, "that was my reaction too."

"If that's all, why do you need me?"

She knows me so well, Emanuelle thought, glad there was someone left who did. "I always need you when I'm feeling rebellious. You're solid and sensible and I'm not."

They talked a while longer, arranged to lunch together the next day, and said good night. It was a daily exchange, no matter where Ema was—but she traveled far less now.

The bedroom seemed to hum with silence once the connection was cut. Ema nodded her head abruptly.

"Yes," she said. "I need someone." Then she added more resolutely, "Just someone to help with my work."

# 91

Alan Black glanced at his watch when he was shown to his table at Danielle's. He was five minutes early for his appointment and he smiled to himself. He had obviously been looking forward to it more than he thought.

On the surface it was a fully deductible business lunch: Emanuelle Beranger had asked him to find her an assistant. It was an unexpected request from a woman as fiercely possessive of her work and her privacy as she was, but as usual she had offered no explanation.

"As it happens, someone springs to mind," he had told her.

"Who?" she demanded.

"Madame Beranger, that would be indiscreet. Please be patient."

"Life once taught me exquisite patience, but I've long since lost the habit of it."

"I'll call you at the *Star* this afternoon, will that be soon enough?"

"Barely."

He saw Carolyn Price come in and got to his feet. She looked like a typical debutante, and nowhere near her thirty-four years. She had dark blond hair, hazel eyes, a slender figure, and perfect teeth. She was not wearing the very short skirt and beehive hairdo that was fashionable. She was dressed in a tweed skirt and a cashmere sweater—from London, he was certain—and what probably were Ferragamo shoes. Her coat, borne off by the captain after he seated her, was a mink-lined Lawrence of London silk raincoat. Alan's ex-wife had a coat like that.

But beyond that classic appearance, her resemblance to young society matrons ended. She was the most unaffected woman of her class Alan had ever met. She was devoid of coquetry, and he found that refreshing.

They ordered lunch and he asked if she would be interested in working for Emanuelle Beranger. "Given the circumstances of your divorce, I thought . . ."

"Yes," she said eagerly, "we both know I could use the money—and something to do. And I know her—or I did when I was a girl. Her daughter and I were at school together."

"Then you know she's something of a dragon."

Carolyn smiled. "I'm willing to have a go, all the same. I always admired her." She hesitated. "One thing, though. I prefer to use my maiden name, Carolyn George, for working purposes."

"That's entirely up to you. I'll call her right now to arrange an interview." He signaled the waiter for a telephone and called the *Star*. Miss Beranger had gone home, so he tried her apartment. Ema's housekeeper, Nedda, answered.

"Madame is out," Nedda said, "she will have to return the call."

He was surprised when the maid hung up so hastily, but he arranged to call Carolyn as soon as an appointment had been arranged, glad of a reason to speak to her again so soon.


Nedda put down the hall telephone and hurried back to Emanuelle's bedroom. Dr. Hargreave was there with her.

"I feel better already," Ema insisted.

"Angina is frightening, but it can be controlled," the doctor said, pointing to the bottle of pills he had given her.

"You mean it feels a lot worse than it is until it kills you," Ema said.

"I've given you a mild sedative and you must rest today, Ema. You can go out tomorrow. But carry those pills with you; they're no use at all if you're at the *Star* and they're here." He turned to Nedda and she nodded. She had been with Madame for many years, first as a maid, now as a housekeeper-companion.

When he had gone, Ema closed her eyes. Nedda took her mistress's hand and sat watching her anxiously, reaching quickly to answer the bedside telephone when it rang again.

"It's Mrs. Atwood," she said and, when Emanuelle nodded, handed her the receiver and went out to hover in the hall.

Kate listened quietly until Ema had finished. "Shall I call Drew?"

"*Mon Dieu, non*," Ema said with considerable vigor. "Do you want to kill me? I'll call him someday when I'm good and ready. If. You're not to worry, *ma chérie*, I'll be fine. I'll call you tonight. Yes, Nedda's right here."

Nedda came back, took the receiver, and replaced it. "You must rest now, Madame."

"Yes, I feel drowsy. Who was that on the telephone before?"

"Mr. Black. I told him you'd call as soon as you could." Nedda drew the curtains, filtering out the bright sun. "Have a nice nap now. I'll cancel your dinner engagement." She hurried away, as if expecting an objection.

Emanuelle, too frightened by the monster that had just assailed her heart, did not object. Call Drew? If she were honest with herself—and when had she ever been anything else?—it was what she wanted to do, just once. But what would she say to him?

No matter, she had written out everything he would not let her tell him. It was her bequest to him, and he would have it when she was dead, not a moment before.

She turned on her side and slept the whole night through, unaware of Nedda's frequent visits to make sure Madame was breathing, or of the disconnected bedside telephone and Nedda's considerate call to Kate Atwood that evening.

The next morning there were calls from Edison and Ken Conan, and visits from Freddy and Monsieur Étienne.

"What did Kate do, send out a message by jungle drums?" Ema exclaimed, but she was grateful to have such friends as these. Finally she returned Alan's call and accepted his invitation to go to the opera that night. "But what about my assistant?"

"I'm in a meeting; I'll tell you all about her this evening."

They had dinner in the Louis Sherry restaurant at the Metropolitan. "It's Carolyn Price, but she's resumed her maiden name," Alan told her. "She says she knew you when she was Carolyn George."

"Caro George?" Ema said. "Of course, that sweet, shy little girl. But what a disappointing divorce! It was the only potential scandal in a very dull season, and it was settled out of court."

"I'm glad you remember her so well," he said, laughing.

"Yes, she married Horrible Henry Price right out of school and faded from sight. But he was notorious enough for both of them, how could she possibly have matched him? I'm not sure I want to hire a society chit, divorced or not. They're all dilettantes."

"Not Caro, she's different and very clever. And she's had some experience on the society page of a suburban paper."

"I'm in no mood to comfort a grieving divorcée, either,"

"I saw no signs of grief. Now, stop being difficult, Madame Beranger, you know you want to talk to her, about your daughter's schooldays, if nothing else."

Emanuelle agreed to see Caro just as the lights dimmed and the curtain rose on the opera that meant so much to her, the story of a Parisian courtesan who loved a man she could not have.

She seemed entranced, as she always was at the opera, but this time she saw and heard nothing. She was years away, in Sir James's office in London. She was at Silvermoor Cottage in Glengowrie hearing an infant's cry. She was outside the opera, heavy with an unborn child, running after a limousine in the snow.

"Madame Beranger!" Alan's voice was urgent and anxious as he shook her gently. The house lights were up and the intermission bustle had begun, but she had stayed wrapped in her memories. "Are you all right?"

"I'm sorry, I seem to be very tired."

He insisted on taking her home. "You ought to see a doctor," he said in the car.

"I have seen a doctor."

"Are you seriously ill?"

"Not seriously," she said, "just terminally, like everyone else."

He took her to her apartment. "You'll have to take better care of yourself," he told her, too affectionately for her to take exception. "I'm going to make sure that you do. You need Caro's help, so try to be civil when she comes tomorrow." He smiled, relenting. "You already have a ferocious reputation; there's no need to improve on it."

When he had gone she sat on in the lamplit library, resting for the climb upstairs. She had been so successful, poring over the joys and sorrows of public people's private lives. She wondered if any of them was capable of the banked anger she had carried since that long-ago morning rushing through the park like a madwoman after she had heard part of the truth from Davina. Anger had shaped her life, made her the kind of person she became, single-minded, careful not to love too much, aloof until Harding found his way to her. Her anger had broken her heart—and now her protesting heart was having its revenge.

A giant hand began to squeeze her chest, and she reached for the bottle of tablets she had so quickly learned to keep nearby. She put one under her tongue and waited while it did its work. She felt not only frightened but lonely. She could have called any number of people, any of them would have come. She could have called Dana. She could have called Drew.

But after all that had happened he would not come and that would surely finish her.

She leaned back as the constriction in her chest loosened its grip. She opened her eyes and looked at the fire, feeling better. Her eyes turned to the Montmartre silhouettes among the photographs on the long table near the wall, seeking the comfort Julian had always given her, and a little smile curved her lips. "I mustn't," she told herself, "I have work to do. I can't sit here with my memories like a silly old woman."

But she knew it was hopeless. She poured herself a brandy and gave herself over to memory the way a woman gives herself to a lover.

"Julian," she said. "Julian." And the name was still magic.

The fire had burned low by the time Emanuelle roused herself, her face wet with tears and her hands crossed protectively over her breast as if it harbored only agony for that lost love, not the mundane pain it produced to plague her now, to stop her, finally, when nothing else ever had.

# 92

Emanuelle dressed carefully for her meeting with Carolyn George, wondering if she and Dana were still in touch with each other. Her own relationship with Dana was much improved, but it seemed as if her daughter must keep a distance between them for a little while longer to complete her metamorphosis to womanhood. Then Dana would come home, figuratively if not in fact.

Ema had to face the truth: from playing the part of one so long, she had become a forceful woman, and her daughter could not flourish in the shadow Ema cast. Dana had inherited Ema's forceful character along with her gray eyes, and there had been a running battle for control between them, but Dana had begun to mature only in another climate.

So they wrote long letters to each other, diaries of their lives past and present. Once they had talked together as mother and child on the couch right here in this library. Now they were redefining themselves as two individual women. The one thing Dana still lacked, Ema thought, was compassion.

Dana made judgments. People were good or bad, actions right or wrong, as if life were so simplistic and human beings as shallow as paper dolls.

And out of the past had come Caro George—is she the same way? Ema thought—friend of the child Dana, confidante of the young woman, with an emotional disaster of her own. Ema wondered if the ex Mrs. Price was really such a gay divorcée—no signs of woe, Alan had said. But what did men know of women's defenses against the world? There was manlove and there was womanlove and the two were worlds apart.

She would soon find out all she wanted to know about Carolyn George, and she smiled, realizing that she *had* become something of a dragon. She must try to be on her best behavior for Dana's friend, not ask impertinent questions as if for an item in the society column.

Voices in the hall now made her compose her face and straighten her back, but the telephone rang and she was speaking into it as Carolyn came in. It gave Emanuelle a chance to inspect her. She was far prettier as a woman than she had been as a child. She had the same smooth pale hair, wide-set amber eyes, and that graceful way of moving that had been such a contrast to Dana's deliberate slouch, but she appeared to have lost her shyness. She was simply, classically, and expensively dressed in the style Ema liked best for American women of her age.

Caro examined the large collection of celebrity photographs displayed on a long refectory table against the wall, aware that she was being studied by the formidable woman on the telephone.

Emanuelle continued talking rapidly while Caro, fascinated, studied the family pictures that made up the greater part of the collection. There were many of Dana—even one of Dana and Caro together—and Harding Ellis. There were pictures of Emanuelle's grandson, among other boys, including one particularly appealing dark-haired youngster with a smile like Ema's. He was dressed in old-fashioned knee socks and a cropped jacket with an Eton collar. There was a faded charcoal sketch of a young woman who looked like Dana, but judging from her hat and hairstyle must have been Emanuelle when she was young. There were two black cutout silhouettes—they were the same girl and a young man—of the kind Dana had seen once at a country fair in Maine. And there was a *Life* magazine cover of Sir Andrew Saxon, The Flying Baronet. No wonder Dana had been infatuated with him! Her letters had been full of him for months before they suddenly stopped coming and the two girls had drifted apart. But what was his picture doing here?

"My gallery pleases you?" Emanuelle asked, putting down the telephone.

Caro came to shake hands. "Hello, Mrs. Ellis. It's good to see you again." She gestured toward the collection. "Yes, very much, particularly the pictures of Dana."

"Will you tell her so when you write?"

"We haven't written in years."

Emanuelle smiled enigmatically. "I must tell you who some of them are. That is Kate Treadwell Atwood, my special angel, whose school I once worked in. She's a widow now, like me, but we own RSVP together and she runs it with two of her sons, the other is a doctor. The lady in the locket is the first friend I ever had—and the most demanding. Her name was Danielle Larchet. That one is Matilda Blessing, *la vieille Méduse;* I was once her social secretary. She was a terrible bitch, but she's dead now. God is sometimes merciful. And of course you knew my husband, a truly gentle man if ever there was one." She waved a hand. "The rest are either celebrated or personal. Now, tell me about yourself," she said.

Caro was politely evasive, as only the wellborn are trained to be, Ema thought; that means I'm not to ask personal questions. "My daughters are at school in England, and you already know the rest," Caro finished. "I prefer to be called Caro George. Since my divorce," she added with a Mona Lisa smile Ema liked, "I am happily Priceless. I'm a very organized sort of person and Alan said you wanted someone like that."

"Yes, I do." Ema's decision had been made. Caro was precisely the sort of polished young woman, obviously bred to wealth, that Emanuelle had always wanted to be, had wanted Dana to be. But for all Caro's breeding, there was something vulnerable about her, and it went straight to Ema's heart. There I go, she thought, always wanting someone to mother. "I think we'll do very well together," she said.

She began to show Caro the files she kept at home. "These are business files; I keep the society secrets at the *Star*—locked, of course. People would kill to get their hands on my files. We'll go to the *Star* this afternoon."

At the end of the day Caro called Alan Black. "I think she's lovely. She talks as if she'd ruin anyone to get a story, but I don't think she's such a tiger."

"Think again—she'd get it and print it too. There've been several lawsuits since her husband died. He kept her in check."

Caro laughed. "Not without a struggle, I'll bet! But I like her. She says what she thinks."

Alan suggested that they have dinner together. Before she met him, Caro called Emanuelle to see if there was anything she could do on her way over in the morning.

There was not, but Emanuelle, having dinner with Kate, was relieved that Caro would be there tomorrow. "She's sensitive," Ema said, "and vulnerable. I'll be good for her."

"Now, Ema, don't try to run her life until she asks you to."

The two old friends regarded each other lovingly, happy to be together, poignantly aware of time passing. Kate was almost seventy and Emanuelle saw it, no matter how she tried not to, just as Kate saw that Emanuelle was no longer merely slender. There was a new fragility about her that made Caro's arrival doubly welcome.

Caro quickly slipped into Ema's schedule. It included daily conference visits to the *Star* and RSVP when Ema was in New York, with letters and articles dictated into a tape recorder in the car en route between the offices or to dinner or the theater or a party. The work was parceled out by Caro to four secretaries. Ema held court almost every evening in the cocktail lounge of Danielle's and Caro, astonished by the hunger for publicity that gave so much power to the press, often sat with her. The rest of the time they traveled—to Paris and Rome, to the Kentucky Derby and the polo matches, to Palm Beach and Cape Canaveral. Ema loved rocketry and space.

Caro enjoyed the inner workings of RSVP as well, the way parties were planned with military precision but given with stunning glamour, the way food was prepared in RSVP's sparkling catering kitchens, the way favors were chosen from the eager suppliers of New York.

"You're like Marie Antoinette at her *levée,* choosing trinkets from the fortunate tradesmen allowed to wait upon her."

"I am, rather," Ema said with satisfaction. "I never thought of it that way."

But it was the *Star* that captivated Caro most of all. There was a sense of urgency as bulletins poured in from all over the world to be sifted, evaluated, and assigned to the staff of reporters. The power a newspaper could exercise was almost frightening. The women's page, on the other hand, was more fun. Caro loved to hear Ema and Edison Carter talking about high society—it was called the Jet Set now.

"Those wretched airplanes of dear Harding's have turned all the seasons upside down. *La grande semaine* is still Paris in July, but there's been a summer season on the Riviera ever since Grace married Rainier! The principality's a madhouse in August."

"Now, Edison," Ema said, "you know you love all those galas."

"True, but the place has changed. No more live pigeon shoots—Her Serene Highness disapproves of blood sports. And her interest in La Leche League—I ask you, Ema, is breastfeeding a topic for high society? What would dear Noël say if he knew?" He tilted his carefully barbered head and looked at Ema. "When are you coming to Monte again?"

"Not while the Jet Set's there, that's what I pay *you* for," Ema said. Monte Carlo was where Drew was most likely to be.

"I'm sure this lovely child is pining to go," Edison said, placing an avuncular hand on Caro's head.

"This lovely child can go wherever she likes—provided I can spare her." Caro smiled. "I'm willing to wait, Edison."

"You'll wait a long time, then." The little man smiled. "Ema loves to grind the faces of the rich."


Every June Ema held a weekend house party at Silvermoor for the presidents of Harding's companies. "They all chafe at taking orders from a woman," Ema said, "but money and stock options persuade them. My dear Caro," she sighed, "women are a long way from parity with men, and the ones I deal with park their dinosaurs at the door."

"It's still lovely being back at Silvermoor. When is Dana coming?"

"Soon, soon. Now, what's in the mail this morning?"

Dana's letters came regularly, but Caro soon stopped asking when she would arrive. Something had happened to keep Dana at a distance, very likely a deepening of the old anger and resentment Dana had so often confided when the two girls were close friends. Caro was not surprised; she had trouble enough with her own parents, who had refused to see her since her divorce disgraced them. They extended only one grudging invitation to Chicago each summer, but Caro preferred to fly to England to see her daughters during the school recesses.

Caro had fallen into a comfortable affair with Alan Black, but her hours with Ema were still the most exciting part of her life. She had discovered that Emanuelle Beranger was the kind of person one either loved or detested. Caro had joined the small circle of people who absolutely adored her.

# 93

DECEMBER 1962

Caro came into Ema's bedroom with a pile of invitations and announcements in one hand and her logbook and tape recorder in the other. Nedda had cleared away the breakfast tray, brought a fresh pot of herb tea, and placed Caro's chair and a small table near the bed.

In a year she's changed my whole schedule around, Emanuelle thought, half-annoyed, half-gratified. Somehow they had fallen into this pattern of late morning starts, unusual for a woman who had been an early riser all her life.

Emanuelle accepted anything that would make it possible for her to go on working indefinitely, even in a less active capacity. She had turned the running of Ellis Enterprises over to its individual company presidents long ago, and this year their supervision had become the responsibility of Saxon, Vaillant/New York in return for Ellis Enterprises' huge account with the bank. She had always sworn she would be a Saxon, Vaillant client one day, and *pardi*, now she was!

But she would not give up the *Star*. It would have been beyond her solitary strength to run the women's page, write a column, and be managing editor, too, but Caro made it possible. And since Caro had come, she thought less about Drew.

"It's a little like having Dana back," Ema had told Kate only last night.

"When are you going to see Dana and the new baby? He's a year old already."

"The Yucatan Peninsula is not the place to hold a family reunion. They'll be coming in the spring—and high time too. I can't have my grandson growing up a savage."

"Ema, that's wonderful!" But Kate remonstrated a minute later. "Remember, though, you swore not to interfere."

And she wouldn't, neither in Dana's life nor in Caro's. She had come to love Caro very much, for herself and her youth and her enthusiasm for the new ideas that were beginning to shape the 'sixties.

Ema's sins didn't seem so heinous in the second half of the twentieth century. Few young women today would understand why she had guarded her secrets so ferociously and paid such a colossal price for having done so.

You had to have been there, Ema thought, saying good morning to Caro.

"The Merrymans want you to come down for the Anderby Hunt in the spring," Caro said. It was her way, as it was Ema's, to skip unnecessary preliminaries beyond the first "good morning" of the day. She opened the logbook, turned on the tape recorder, and went on.

"Sally Chesterton is going to marry Prince Helmut and requests the pleasure on the tenth of June next at the Schwarzenhof in Vienna. The Sandy Josephs had a baby boy—Micah Steven, nine pounds, twelve ounces. Mrs. Harvey Bishop is having a fund-raiser ball for the Democratic party next April fifteenth." She paused, waiting for Emanuelle to reply.

"Yes to the Hunt, that's where they'll decide who the next Republican candidate is going to be, even though no one has a chance against Kennedy. No to Sally Chesterton—the man's a degenerate, royal pretender or not; send Edison, he loves Vienna. Five dozen yellow roses along with that English pram I ordered for the Josephs. With a Paddington bear inside for the baby—in thirty-five years that baby will be the Democratic presidential nominee." She stopped, then asked abruptly, "How are your children?"

"Very happy at school." Caro offered nothing more about her twin daughters. "And the ball?" she asked, pointing to the heavy cream vellum invitation.

"You go to Whissie Bishop's ball for me," Ema said. "Who knows, you might meet a degenerate prince of your own. Charge a magnificent gown to the working-clothes account at Bergdorf's. Next?"

They finished the invitations and decided which of the day's events each would cover, Caro taking the more strenuous ones, with no comment on either side.

"Tell me, Caro," Emanuelle said when Caro was preparing to leave, "do you really care about all these people?" She gestured toward the pile of invitations.

"Some of them," Caro said, "but not any more than you do."

"I still wonder why you came to work for me."

"It was all I was qualified to do—and you pay well." Caro smiled. "I needed the income."

"Didn't you get a decent settlement out of Horrible Henry?"

"No. I made him one."

"What?" Emanuelle was nonplussed for once.

Caro laughed at Ema's unaccustomed look of surprise. "It was the only way I could make him agree to a quiet divorce—he always needs money—and it would have been messy for the children otherwise. My parents were against me, and Henry didn't want me to divorce him, either. It was a bruise to his ego."

"After all his philandering? We heard about it all the way from Chicago! He does have the most peculiar taste in women." She was angry for Caro. "Considering all he did, how was your ego?"

"Not too healthy." Caro went toward the door. "But it wasn't so much what he did to me as what he couldn't do for me, what we never had together."

"And what was that, Caro?" Emanuelle's voice was gentle, caring.

Caro stopped near the bedroom door. "Rapture, passion, bliss." She paused to organize her thoughts, her head back in a way that was familiar to Emanuelle by now. "I was brought up with very modest expectations, really. To marry, do charity work, grow flowers, have children. Henry was a brilliant match at the time, but we were never really in love. We were just physically . . . agitated, enough to decide we had to get married. I never expected more. I don't think I even expected him to be faithful." She smiled ruefully. "Then I woke up to find I was thirty and a bit, wondering if that was all there was for me, if that's all love was about. It couldn't be love, I decided, if I didn't even care about Henry's women. So there was no point in being married to him no matter what my family said. They're still furious about the divorce; they think a lady ought to put up with anything rather than make a scandal. They talk to Henry, but they won't talk to me—and they've seen to it that the girls side with their father, just as they threatened they would if I persisted. The girls are still too young for me to explain things to them. Maybe someday they'll listen, when they're older." She shrugged. "And here I am. There's a certain satisfaction in freedom, although I don't think it'll ever replace romance." She went out the door. "I'll check in with you this afternoon."

Emanuelle sat fuming when she had gone. "*Merde!*" she muttered, preparing to get out of bed. What a lot of love went to waste on men like Henry Price, who never knew a good thing when they had it.

It hadn't taken her a year to know she and Caro were very much alike behind their respective veneers. She was far more aggressive than Caro would ever be—and no wonder, Caro wasn't born in a slum. But Caro's determination to get the most out of life was the same, never mind the reasons for it.

Their affection had sprung from a better climate than exists between most mothers and daughters. They had to behave politely to each other, they had to be considerate. She liked Caro's brains and breeding and her fey sense of humor, the way she dressed in tweed and cashmere and mink. If Caro had been her daughter, she would have saved her from a man like Henry. Whom Ema loved she wanted to protect and defend.

"I couldn't do without her now," Emanuelle realized, and comforted herself with the thought that there was no reason to do without her. Caro was not in love with Alan Black; in America it was ludicrous for women over thirty to fall in love at all. And a woman who had been married to an *imbécile* like Henry Price would never take that chance again.

Ema had learned long ago there were either good men or bad men; there was nothing in between. She had been privileged to have been loved by two good ones, but her son was of the other variety.

"Men!" Ema sniffed as she rang for Nedda to run her bath.

But it wasn't Nedda who came to answer her ring, it was Caro.

"I'm so sorry, Ema, but Skip Atwood just called. Kate has had a stroke."

Emanuelle blanched and sat back down on the bed. Caro handed her the nitro tablets, but she shook her head. "I'm all right," she said. "Just stay here for a few minutes."

When Ema had dressed, Caro ordered the car and they went downstairs together. They sat in the limousine saying nothing, holding hands.


Death has been given a bad press, Ema thought, and deservedly so. She sat by the bed watching Kate slip away and softly implored her not to go.

"Try, Katharine," she whispered, "please try, the way you always did for me." There were so many things she still wanted to tell Kate, so many talks they had never had time to finish.

They were happening too often, these partings that left such enormous voids. Pieces of Ema's life were being chipped away, and soon there would be nothing left of her, either.

Kate died an hour later, and there was no comforting indication that it was a spiritual transport or a transition from one state of being to another. It was simply the going out, the eclipse, the leaving of a woman who wanted to stay, a woman Emanuelle had cherished and loved devotedly for almost half a century. Nothing would ever be the same without her.

"She always defended me," Ema said to Caro in the car as they drove away, "that shy, frightened girl defended *me*, long before she became a strong, confident woman." Ema gazed out of the window. "I made her a red silk dress once, when we were both poor. But there was one thing I couldn't give her. She wanted to be movie-star pretty, just for a little while." Ema shook her head. "She was so much more. And we went back so far. There's no one I can talk to now about the old days in the Treadwell Female Academy." Or about Rupert, Ema thought, or Tillie and Julian and Drew and the myriad things, vital and inconsequential, that make up a life. That's what old friends were, a link between the beginnings and ends of you.

Now all Ema had was Caro. She knew she had come to love her too much, but I'm a born gambler, she told herself, and Caro's worth the risk.

"What about Alan?" Emanuelle asked her one evening at the *Star*. "Still no rapture?"

Caro shook her head, reluctant to admit it. "Maybe it doesn't exist for me. And now I must get to that opening. See you in the morning."

"What time is your plane to London?" Caro was going to spend two weeks with the twins.

"Not until eight in the evening. I'll have plenty of time to finish up."

Emanuelle watched her go, feeling bereft already, but she consoled herself that Caro would be back from London before Dana and Cal arrived with Ema's grandsons.

# 94

APRIL 1962

Harding must have been just like that as a little boy, Ema thought. She looked at her grandson as he stood beside her armchair in the library an hour after his arrival. Dana watched from Harding's chair on the other side of the fireplace.

Ellis was squarely built and crackling with energy, but he had his father's professorial air, comical in so small a boy.

"Grandma," he demanded, his sturdy little legs planted wide apart, "are you very old?"

"I'm sorry, Mother," Dana murmured, "he's at that age."

"Why do you ask?" Ema was as serious as Ellis.

"Daddy says you're a monument, and monuments are very old."

"Then I must be too," Ema said after brief reflection.

"Old enough to die?"

Ema considered carefully before she answered. "Not yet," she said firmly. "Not until you're all grown up."

"I'm very glad of that," Ellis said.

"So am I."

"Grandma, may I play with the toys now?"

"Of course, my love, I put them there for you."

He ran off to Dana's old playroom upstairs and Ema poured the tea Nedda had brought. It was a time of day, and a special room, from which she always drew a measure of calm. The silky buff leather of the chairs and the cream-colored velvet draperies had been renewed several times, but the room looked exactly as it had when she and Harding first moved into the apartment after their wedding thirty-five years ago, even to the lush groupings of plants near the windows and the cut-crystal vase of yellow roses that always stood on the desk. Memories, Ema felt, stayed fresh in a familiar setting.

"We always had tea here when you were very small," she said to Dana. "It was the nicest time of the day."

Dana nodded. "I remember it too. I suppose you have it here with Caro now." Caro, with her usual tact, had left on an extended round of errands soon after the Bannisters arrived. Cal was at Columbia University, discussing the next project he and Dana wanted to undertake.

Ema passed a cup to Dana. "I'm very fond of Caro."

"So I noticed," Dana said. "You seem very much at ease with her." There was a slight stress on the last word. Dana's manner was as bland and casual as her clothes, but there was a note in her voice that still betokened disapproval to Ema.

Ema glanced at her briefly, then poured another cup of tea. "You mustn't begrudge me Caro," she said. "She's all I have now, with Kate gone—and you so far away."

Dana blushed. She looked for something kinder to say. "It's terrible for her to be separated from her children."

"She and I have that in common."

Mother and daughter gazed at each other, on the brink of something. It was Dana who spoke first.

"Your letters have meant a lot to me, Maman," she said, ill at ease.

Ema waited, hoping for more.

"You're a fine writer," Dana went on.

Ema's shoulders sagged. "That isn't why I wrote them." Her voice was heavy with disappointment. The silence between them thickened, then was broken by the sound of Ellis's laughter floating down the stairs.

"It's good to hear a child's voice in this place," Ema said. "It feels like a home again."

"I just hope Ellis and the baby don't ruin your lovely things."

"You know they're more important to me than *things* could ever be," Ema said, more sharply than she had intended. She confronted Dana. "Why do we sit here talking carefully like strangers at a society tea?"

Dana put down her cup and saucer abruptly and the teaspoon clattered onto the polished surface of the table, spraying droplets of moisture. She rubbed at the spots with a pocket handkerchief, then stopped and stared at the table. "I shouldn't have come!" she said in a strangled voice. "Nothing's really changed, not even after all those letters! I hate feeling this way!" She stood and turned toward the fireplace, her back to Ema.

"What way?" It was all Ema dared to say.

"Self-conscious," Dana said angrily. "Embarrassed. I *won't* accept the blame for what happened to us, but do you think I like the way we are any more than you do?" The rigid lines of her body told almost as much as the words. "I miss this room," she said, and her voice shook. "I miss you. I want to feel the way I did when we sat here together, but I *can't*, I've lost the habit of it! We're not the same, we're different people now, and we'll never get that feeling back again." After a few moments she drew a deep breath and turned back to face her mother, speaking quietly. "But those letters did make me understand how you felt about Daddy and— everyone else."

"And how I feel about *you*?" Ema's voice pleaded and her hands were urgent, tightly clasped. "Until you were born I never dreamed I would love you so much. I've never stopped. Don't you want my love? Can't you believe in it, Dana, even now?"

Dana's head dropped to her hands. "Yes, of course I believe in it, Maman, it's just not the same. I can't be what I used to be, not after all these years." Her voice trailed off. A long minute passed before Ellis's laughter trilled down the stairs again.

"It's all right, Dana," Ema said gently. "We *have* made a start. I didn't really believe we'd fall into each other's arms."

Dana crossed the space between them in two steps. Balanced on Ema's chair, she put an arm around her mother, her head resting against Ema's. "Oh, yes, Maman," she said, "we've made a start."

They sat there wordlessly, afraid to endanger this first, fragile reunion by saying any more.

It's too soon to talk about Drew, Ema thought, looking at the gallery of photographs on the long table. She had put away the pictures of Drew, but maybe someday . . .

Ellis's voice sounded from the doorway. "You've been crying!" he accused in alarm.

"A little, darling," Dana said. "Because we're happy to be together again." She went back to her chair. "How are the toys?"

"*Remarkable*," Ellis said.

"He sounds like Cal exclaiming over a rare fossil," Ema said, turning to the little boy to relieve the tension.

"You must thank Grandma for all the new things," Dana told him.

Ellis approached, his eyes shining. "Thank you *very* much, Grandma. I like the red car best. I'll take Harding for a ride in it as soon as he wakes up from his nap."

"Come sit near me," Ema said, making room for him beside her. "Which did you like second best?" She listened to his excited description of the toys, and when it ended she hugged him and stroked his hair as he nestled contentedly against her. She whispered her love to him softly, in French, while Dana listened to the familiar litany, as warm as love itself, and was shattered anew by all she and her mother had lost.

"Maman," she said finally, "will you take the children next month while Cal and I are in the Congo?"

Ema looked up from her absorption in her grandson. "You'd trust them with me?" She seemed uncertain of herself, a feeling Dana had never before connected with her mother.

"There's no one I trust as much as you." Dana cleared her throat, determined to control herself for Ellis's sake. "And Nanny will keep them in order."

"I don't want them to be orderly, I want them to enjoy themselves!" Ema looked down at Ellis. "Do you like the idea of letting me spoil you for a little while?"

Ellis looked first at his mother for confirmation, then up at Ema and nodded emphatically. "I like the idea very much," he said.

The two women's eyes met over his head and they smiled at each other for the first time in years.

*Sainte Vierge,* Ema thought, holding Ellis, it's going to be all right!


"Alan wants to marry me," Caro confided several months later while they "designed" a society wedding.

The apartment still felt empty without the children, and Ema welcomed the work while she waited for Dana to come to New York again. Now that Kate was gone, Ema liked to supervise the really big affairs for RSVP with Caro's help. It was very relaxing, like playing paper dolls.

"Shall we have the wedding white and yellow?" Caro was saying. "Or white and green?"

If she's this casual about Alan's proposal, she can't be planning to accept him, Ema thought with relief. "Green is passé," Emanuelle said, "and yellow is insipid. Let's have it all white."

"*Quel scandale* that'll make," Caro said, writing it down in what she called her nuptial book. "Only the bride is supposed to wear white."

"This is not a royal wedding. Tell me about Alan."

Alan, not content with the random affair they were having, wanted to settle down. Caro was touched by the proposal, but she had doubts about accepting it.

"What I feel for him is sweet and comfortable. It's nothing like what our little bride is feeling, but I'd be crazy to let it go, wouldn't I? I don't want to spend my declining years alone."

"You mean like me?"

"No, if I were like you, I wouldn't think about declining years."

*Penses-tu?* Emanuelle said to herself. I think about them all the time.

"I think we need twelve tents for fifteen hundred guests, don't you?" Caro continued.

"Make it fifteen, it might rain," Emanuelle said, and added that they were going to do the summer season on the Riviera—the Grand Prix, the Red Cross Gala.

"I thought you hated the Riviera in August."

"I lied, that's the secret of my success," Ema said. "And distance makes the heart see clearly. You can delay giving Alan an answer until our return. By then you'll have come to your senses."

"What a sly boots you are, Ema."

On their private jet flight to Nice, Caro worried about Ema. She did not need her pills more often than usual, but Caro was sure something was disturbing her, even though the breach between her and Dana had been considerably narrowed.

"It may take a long time," Ema had told Caro after Dana was gone, "but one day it will happen for you and your daughters, too, I'm sure of it."

Caro was not so sure. Some things, once broken, were irreparable. Her friendship with Dana seemed to be one of them.

"You always admired her," Dana had observed the one time the two young women were alone.

"As you do," Caro said.

"Yes, all right, as I do."

"And I love her," Caro had persisted. "So do you, in your own strange way."

"Caro, don't interfere in something you can't possibly understand."

"I could say the same to you! I *do* love her." Caro had paused, wondering if she had the right to say it, deciding that she must. "She's not very strong, you know."

"Not strong? Emanuelle Beranger?"

"Not well, then. It's her heart."

Dana, suddenly collapsing into a chair, had shivered. "Oh, no, not now! Is it serious, Caro?"

"One day it will be, but there's no telling how soon."

And Dana, hugging herself for comfort, had whispered, "It's not fair, Caro, it's not fair. Why didn't she tell me?"

"That would make it real to her."

Dana, nodding, had put out her hand. "Forgive me, Caro. Thank God you're here to take care of her. I could never imagine anything getting the better of her! I never thought of this."

Even so, the atmosphere between the two young women was strained. Probably, Caro had concluded, because she knew too much about Dana: people often resented those to whom they confided their failures. And all that aside, Dana envied a surrogate daughter who could love Ema unreservedly.

For all Caro had lost along the way—her parents' approval, her children's trust, pride, marriage, money—she could not bear the prospect of losing the beautiful, imperious woman now seated at her side, whose capacity for love was enormous and who, for reasons Caro did not completely understand, gave so much of it to her.

Well, you won't ever be alone again, Caro promised silently. She looked at Ema; her skin was smooth and delicate against her silver-streaked hair. Ema's beautiful eyes were still luminous and changeable and she was always perfectly turned out. There was a fresh scent about her like rose petals, a powdery scent reminiscent of summer evenings and fresh linens on a closet shelf.

"Don't you want to undress and lie down?" There were two large bedrooms in the plane's midsection.

"Don't fuss over me," Emanuelle protested, "I was supposed to die a year ago and I'm still having a jolly good time. Besides, I'm only sixty-two." She took Caro's hand affectionately. "I'm really glad you fuss. I was thinking the other night that whenever things were really bad for me, it was a woman who said, 'Come on, Ema, it's time to get on with it.' First there was Sister Marie Angélique, who taught me English and manners. Then there was Danielle and after her a dour old Scotswoman. Then my darling Kate. And Freddy and Mary Alice, both of them women of few words but much heart. And, thank heaven, you. Women are a woman's truest friends; only they know what it's like to live in a man's world." She gave Caro's hand a little pat. "I think I'll have a doze right here."

She closed her eyes and tried to drift off, but she missed the whirring of the props. Jets were even more unnatural than propeller planes had been. No wonder those people were called the Jet Set.

Where is my Dana on that list of women friends, she thought, Dana, who had rectitude but not the grace of compassion? But a daughter was not a friend. A daughter—a child—was infinitely more and still less than a friend.

Drew would not be on the Riviera, Ema had made certain of that before she suggested this trip. He was off on a cruise to the Greek Islands that would keep him at sea for the entire month of August.

# 95

Caro sat alone on the terrace of the Carlton Hotel in Cannes, enjoying her breakfast. The beauty of the French Riviera was intoxicating, especially on a day like this, when the sea was cobalt blue and the sky soft and cloudless. There was a lovely breeze on the terrace and she savored the taste of her café au lait and the buttery flakiness of her croissant. Soon she would take the open car and drive into the back country.

Ema had gone on a yachting trip to Italy, but Caro had chosen to stay at the hotel. It was a good idea, Ema agreed, Caro needed some time to herself.

"You're hoping I'll have a little fling for myself," Caro said.

"Of course, it's time you diversified. It'll be easier without a duenna in tow."

Caro was unaware of the man who had been watching her from another table since she sat down for breakfast. Finally he approached her table.

"I beg your pardon," he said with an English accent, "but are you Carolyn George?"

It was a face she had seen many times before; she sat looking up at him, trying to place him. He was a handsome man in his forties, with the beginnings of gray at his temples and a Riviera tan that made his dark eyes look black. He was dressed in slacks and a sport shirt, but he had all the accoutrements of wealth—the alligator belt, the Cartier watch, the seal ring, even the jacket he carried by one finger, slung over his shoulder, and above all, the assurance.

"Yes, I am," she said, "and I'm sorry, but I don't remember where we met."

"We haven't met," he said. "I'm Drew Saxon, a friend of Dana's. She used to talk about you."

"Of course," Caro smiled. "I work for her mother." She was thinking of the *Life* cover on Ema's table. The Flying Baronet. That had been taken twenty years ago. He had acquired a different reputation since. "Would you like to sit down?"

He did, saying he had been on a cruise but had changed his plans at the last moment to fly back from Athens. "I've been here often enough, but I've never really seen the place properly, you know, just stopping here and there to look at it."

"Neither have I, that's my project for the week."

"All on your own?" He smiled. It was such a brilliant smile, vaguely reminiscent of someone, that she didn't mind the leading question at all.

"All on my own. Mrs. Ellis is yachting this week and I'm on vacation."

His smile faded slightly, but in the next minute he said, "I have a car, if you'd like a tour guide."

The car was a Maserati, and he was a very good driver, one of those men who seem one with a high-powered vehicle. They drove out of Cannes and headed toward Fréjus and the Esterel Massif. The hills, not as high as some of the Maritime Alps, had a lonely, brooding quality and the different tints of the porphyry rocks—yellow, red, blue, purple—were exquisite. It was an open car and they did not speak much while it rushed along the winding roads, but they turned to each other often to point to a special view and those silent exclamations of delight, oddly enough, brought them closer than polite conversation would have done.

They stopped once to walk along a wooded trail for a while and it seemed perfectly natural to Caro for him to take her hand. The touch of those warm, bronzed fingers on her skin excited her in a way her husband never had and, she knew now, Alan never would. For a second she felt like a fool, but then she said to herself, why should I, I've been waiting for it long enough.

Yet she was still a product of her generation. She had grown up at a time when women waited to be approached by men. Wearing panty girdles and gloves, she thought, with a ridiculous desire to laugh. She was wearing neither today. I wish he'd invite me to lie down under a tree, she thought. I want him to take off all my clothes and make love to me and all he's done is touch my hand.

No wonder Dana had fallen in love with Andrew Saxon the moment she met him! And been so devastated when nothing came of it. Caro wondered what had really happened; that was one thing Dana had never confided completely and the friendship had lapsed soon afterward. But this man, after all, was not the sort to take love as seriously as Dana had in those days—as Dana probably still did.

I don't feel in the least serious about love, Caro thought. I'm ready to float away on it.

They walked back to the car and drove on until they found a place to eat in a tiny village hooked to the mountainside. There was just one long table for anyone who wanted lunch, and the food was served family-style, passed around in large bowls. There were luscious red tomatoes marinated in olive oil and basil, then pâté de campagne and cold chicken with a salad of sweet and slightly bitter greens dressed in a mustard vinaigrette. The crusty bread and salted butter were superb, and the cheeses ripe and nutty. The wine was light and red and very heady, the coffee strong, and the plum brandy like hot velvet. It made Caro's mouth feel full and soft, ready to be kissed.

They saw more spectacular views on the drive back to Cannes, constantly altered by their vantage and by the changing light, and arranged to meet for dinner. Caro went to have a bath, basking in her immediate attraction to a man she had just met. It made life suddenly, incredibly, romantic and she had been persuaded she had lost her chance at that. She took a white piqué evening dress out of the closet and held it against her deep tan, amazed at how very young she looked and felt. She held the dress away and looked at her naked body in the mirror. She imagined him there with her and closed her eyes with a little sigh.


Drew was looking forward to the evening too. That surprised him because she was not like the women he had known since Dana, all those years ago. Furthermore, it was not attraction that had made him approach her in the first place, it was an attempt to see Emanuelle Beranger—his mother. He had flown back from Athens when he heard she was on the Riviera; Carolyn George was only a way to meet his mother, and his attraction to Caro was unexpected. Lately, though, Drew had begun to think he'd had enough of falling into bed with superficial women. Caro George was not superficial, he knew that because she was Dana's friend, but it was obvious no matter how little they had said to each other today.

It would all be over as soon as Emanuelle returned to Cannes, but for the moment he was eager to be with Caro. They drove to La Bonne Auberge on the sea road to Nice for dinner, and then on to a night club.

"How long will you stay in Cannes?" he asked her while they danced.

"As long as Ema wants to." She opened her eyes and looked up at him. "Have you ever met her?"

He was vague about it. "Once or twice, during the war."

"But not when you knew Dana?"

"No, why?"

"I just wondered. She's a remarkable woman, one of the best-hearted people I've ever known."

"Is she?"

"Oh, yes. Didn't Dana tell you?"

"Yes. She still writes about her fairly often."

Caro was surprised. "You and Dana correspond?"

He was offhand about it. "Yes, the way old friends do, the odd Christmas card, wedding announcements from me, birth announcements from her."

That wasn't true; their letters to each other had been serious and frequent for many months now and almost exclusively about Emanuelle. He smiled, that smile that reminded Caro of someone.

"Well, you'll meet Ema when she comes back. She fosters her reputation as a frosty lady, but she really isn't. If you like real people, you'll like her."

"What are real people?"

"Dana's one. I hope I'm one." She laughed. "I think maybe you are, but it's hard to tell."

"Why?"

"You're—overwhelming."

Coming from her, it embarrassed him. "Hardly."

"I had to be reminded to call you Sir."

"Oh, that. Baronets aren't all that splendid, you know, they're not lords. The title's hereditary, but for the rest we're like other people. Who reminded you?"

"The concierge. I asked if Mr. Saxon was in the bar and he said Sir Andrew was. He wasn't pleased with me at all, I can tell you. I could tell he was thinking, another of those American barbarians after a title. It's true in a way."

"Is it?" He laughed, delighted now. "Tell me about it."

"I met your father once, at Dana's house. We dreamed about him for months, we named all of our noble knights Julian, and we put him into all of the stories of Camelot."

"Yes, so did I. He was a very brave man."

What had Dana said on the telephone the night she met him? We have a lot in common; I have a mother and he has a father. But there was a great difference. Drew did not resent his father. The loss still seemed fresh to him and Caro longed to comfort him, but it seemed an intrusion. She leaned against him, dancing and dreaming. When they finally ended the evening and he took her back to her hotel room, he kissed her, and her mouth, longing for it all day, longed for more.

"Tomorrow?" he asked.

"Tomorrow," she said, wanting to say tonight. It was a long time before she slept. What would happen tomorrow? Would he make love to her?

* * *

Drew was wakeful, too, thinking over all that Dana had told him in the letters that had begun to arrive three years ago. Their effect had been to change his romantic memory of her into friendship first and, at last, brotherly affection. And their new relationship made him want to see his mother before it was too late. "Your mother loves you very much," his grandfather had said just before he died. It had taken all this time for Drew to understand what those words meant.

He was not sure Emanuelle would even speak to him after what he had said to her in London, but he had to try. Thanks to Dana, he knew he had been deaf to half the story—Emanuelle's half.

He was a sportsman with men and a lover with women, but he had never been just himself. "Just himself" had been hateful to the woman he'd thought of as his mother—and to his real mother, too, or so he had thought when he discovered she had abandoned him. He was only a scrap then, a cry was all he was, needing her.

But what had *she* felt? He had never stopped to consider that until the first letter came from Dana. Now he wanted to hear it from Emanuelle too. He wanted her to accept him, to trust him.

He had felt terribly alone lately, except for his sisters, Dana included, and they had families of their own, their own lives. He wanted a life of his own, not the jaded excuse for one that he led, and he had been making a real effort to do something worthwhile at Saxon, Vaillant. But he needed to know the stranger who was his mother before he could go much further with his evaluation of himself, to know this woman who had been his father's enduring love. She had to be an extraordinary woman for his father to have loved her so much, so long. She had left Drew for a good reason, according to Dana, but he wanted her to tell him herself.

He and Carolyn drove to Saint Tropez the next day and swam at a sandy little beach below the red cliffs. It was when they were lying side by side in the sun that the feeling between them expanded from strong physical attraction to include something more.

"Caro," he said, rising on his forearm to look down at her, "this may sound odd, but trust me, will you?"

"In what way?" She kept her eyes closed against the sun, against the nearness of his body.

"In every way, whatever you might hear about me."

She put up her arms by way of answer and he kissed her, gently at first, then passionately because she trusted him and no one had since his father and Dana. He was inexpressibly moved by that kiss, and he held her close to him, trembling like a boy, tasting the salt on her lips. The strip of swimsuit across her breasts slipped down, and his mouth brushed her nipples. They looked at each other.

"Let's go back," he said, and she nodded.

Soon they were alone together, naked and warm from sun and wine. They knew they were in love before they touched each other. The taste and shape and feel of love had started on the beach. Now she knew the taste and shape and feel of him as she had never known a man before. It was what she had been waiting for, a surge of passion beyond the physical, a desire for more of him than she could hold in her arms or touch with her mouth.

They had three more days and nights to confide in each other before Ema came back to Cannes, and by then he had told Caro who he was.

"Of course," she said once her astonishment subsided, "it's Ema's smile. I wonder why I didn't see it."

"I want her back, Caro, I know that now. I owe her a great deal."

"Yes, darling, you do. I'll help all I can."

So many other things about the enigmatic woman she had come to love were becoming clearer to Caro now, including the long estrangement between Ema and Dana. That was healing, but Caro's friendship with Dana, on thin ice before, was doomed now. Dana had loved Drew Saxon with all the pure passion of youth, and a part of her still did.

Caro said nothing to Emanuelle when she arrived late the next afternoon. This was too important for a hasty, blundering exchange.

"Was it a good trip?" Caro asked.

"Dull," Ema said. "Let's go to the casino tonight. I need some diversion. The best kind I know is to watch the privileged classes wallowing in privilege."

# 96

They met in the glossy precincts of the Palm Beach Casino, a meeting that shouted of conflict from the first moment. Ema, with Caro at her side, saw him across the crowded lounge and watched him make his way toward her.

"Good evening, Madame Beranger," Drew said when he approached. "I'm glad to see you again."

Emanuelle only nodded, straight as a ramrod in her chair. He was even more like Julian now. He seemed less broad than he had been in his glorious youth, and there was gray in his hair. His eyes had always been his father's.

"Will you and Miss George dine with me?" he asked.

"Thank you, we're dining elsewhere, with friends." She turned to go and Caro, with a shake of her head and a beseeching look at Drew, followed her.

"You were very rude to him," Caro said.

"I don't like him."

"I do, I spent a lot of time with him while you were away."

Ema's heart sank. "Is he the reason for the way you look?"

Caro nodded.

"Rapture?"

"Rapture."

Emanuelle sighed. "I hope that's all it is."

"No, it's a great deal more. He seems to have an equally strong effect on both of us."

"He has the same effect on all women; he's that sort of man."

Neither of them had any appetite; they went directly back to Ema's suite at the hotel.

"You know how I've come to feel about you," Ema said, sitting down near the high open windows to the balcony. Her gray eyes were dark with worry.

"Yes, Ema. I love you dearly too."

"Then please believe me. Andrew Saxon is not the man for you."

Caro shook her head. "I'm in love with him, Ema. I want to marry him."

"Oh, Caro, don't be fooled by that cruel charm of his. If you must marry someone, let it be Alan; at least he won't break your heart! Andrew's been divorced twice already, for years he's led an empty life, one of the useless people who fill my column. He was never the man his father was, God knows why, he had everything to make him be."

"I know," Caro said. "You made that possible."

Ema looked at her intently. "Of course, he would have told you." She was disdainful. "Typically Saxon. It was not his to tell."

"He didn't at first, he told me last night before he asked me to marry him. He told me about Dana too. They've been writing to each other, did you know that? He said it was your idea in the first place. He's here partly because of her."

Ema took a deep breath. Dana? The daughter she thought lacking in compassion? She was overcome, but at length she said softly, "Well, he might not have told you everything, so I will."

The two women sat in the light breeze from the Mediterranean, the elder now wistful, now earnest; the younger entranced, outraged, sometimes tearful. Ema told her about Julian and Davina, Sir James and Drew and Dana. But the worst of it she had shared only with Harding.

"I couldn't help Dana," Ema finished, "but I can help you." Her hands reached automatically for a cigarette, remembered there were none, and dropped, still empty, to her lap. "And I don't want to lose you. I could never see you if you married him. He didn't tell you that, did he?"

"Oh, Ema, why do you think he came to Cannes? Only because he heard you'd be here. He wants to know you, isn't that enough for a start?"

"Once I dreamed of it, but he's too much a Saxon, just as I wanted him to be. Ironic, isn't it?" She reached for Caro's hand. "Please listen to me, Caro," she pleaded. "He's the most charming man you'll ever meet, but he's not what he seems. He hasn't changed."

"There's a lot more to him than charm—and he gets that from you. His anger, his foolish attempt to strike back at you by the life he's been leading—none of that is admirable, but it's no more heartbreaking than Julian Saxon's sense of honor. Or Dana's, if it comes to that, making judgments from the lofty heights of right and wrong. Honor can be so cruel." Caro took Ema's hands in hers. "You love him, Ema, you just can't forgive yourself for giving him up."

"Nor can he!" Emanuelle said. "How could he possibly? He believes

Davina did only what she had to do. That colossal lie! What hope can there be with her between us? How can I suppose he'll understand me? No, Caro, I *must* leave the past alone, it has more pain than I can cope with now." She shook her head. "If I lose you, it'll have come full circle; he'll have evened the score."

They were still at an impasse when they went wearily to bed. Caro met Drew early the next morning at a café on the Croisette.

"She's refused, hasn't she?" he said as soon as he saw her face.

Caro nodded. "But you must keep trying, Drew. She isn't strong, it's her heart."

He shook his head in despair. "And I once accused her of having none at all. She's a very proud woman, Caro, she won't forgive the things I said to her."

"Maybe not, maybe you'll have to live with that. But you need each other. She's lived all of her life on the outside looking in at you. She did it for your sake as well as her own. Maybe she was wrong, but at least she *tried*. So must you. She never had the habit of trust, and you've lost it, but if you don't get past your pride, you'll lose each other forever."

"And you?" he asked her. "Would I lose you?"

Caro shook her head. "Not if you're willing to wait. I won't leave her while she needs me. I love her."

Emanuelle had come out to the terrace of the Carlton for breakfast. She sat there alone, a distinguished woman with a face much younger than her years. She wore a pale apricot linen dress and wine-dark coral jewelry while she drank camomile tea and longed for coffee. She was trying to examine her motives with as much objectivity as she could summon.

Before Caro entered her life, Emanuelle had welcomed age and solitude as twin centurions against the dangers of love. She had never expected her defenses to be breached by a trick, as the wooden horse had breached the walls of Troy. It was one thing to be tricked, another to fling wide the gates and invite disaster in, as she had opened her heart to Caro. It would be unbearable to lose yet another child to a Saxon.

She was alone, as she had been so many times before, but this decision was not hers to make. Caro wasn't hers, any more than any of the people she loved had been hers, except for a little while, the time it took to love them. Drew, above all, wasn't hers, had never been. She could not hope to repair a lifetime in the years she had left. She could not trust her impulse to try; impulse had misled her far too often.

She saw Caro and Drew come onto the terrace and knew that her battle was lost. If life had taught her anything, it was this: when a man and a woman decide they are meant for each other, nothing else matters, and if not honor, duty, loyalty like Julian's, then certainly not caution like hers.

And I'm not so old, she thought, that I don't remember how it is to be in love.

"Ema?" Caro said, anxious and loving.

"It's all right, Caro, don't look like that." Ema took her hand and looked past her at Drew, across an emotional desert. "I want to speak to you," she said to him. Then she rose and left the terrace and Drew, after a look at Caro, followed her upstairs. She sat down, aloof in her chair, until he had closed the door and she was alone with her son for the second time in their lives.

"Must you marry her?" she asked, and her stormy gray eyes looked up at him as if she could see inside him. *Bon Dieu*, he looks more like Julian every time I see him, she told herself, trembling with the effort to keep her dignity and her distance. "You are a much-married man."

He shook his head. "This is different. I'm different. I love her. I've never known a woman like her." He paused, then he said it, "Not since Dana. I've had bad luck since then."

"And you blame me for it, as Dana does."

"No, not anymore. Neither of us does. You couldn't have known we'd meet, you couldn't have known we'd fall in love. Dana's a lot like you. So is Caro."

Emanuelle was silent, unbearably touched by the very sight of him and the sound of his voice but still on her guard. If I were a young woman, she thought, I wouldn't care a damn how many mistakes you'd made.

They gazed at each other, knowing there was far more for them to talk about than his marriage to Caro George.

"*Eh bien*," she said finally, taking refuge in French, "*comment s'en sortir de cet embarras?* How do we get out of this quandary?"

Drew moved toward her. "We could try to forget the past and start from here."

"Oh, no!" Emanuelle said, so insistently that he stopped where he was. "I will never forget it. The past is all I have left of your father, what we had together, what we didn't have. I loved him so, even he never knew how much." Her eyes filled, and she stood and turned away from him, embarrassed to weep in front of this grown man who was also her infant son.

"And me?" he said it softly, but his face, which she could not see, had lost its look of deliberate calm. "Loving him so much, did you have nothing left for me?"

"You!" she said, unaware of his expression. "You are the one thing I have ever regretted." She heard what she had said and put out an apologetic hand, her face still hidden from him. "But not for conceiving you,

Andrew, never that. For leaving you. I have been remorseful all my life that I ever left you."

"But there was nothing else you could have done!" he said, moved to defend her from the profound grief he heard in her voice, saw in that outstretched hand. "You had no choice! Even Davina knew that." He went to her side, anxious, caring. "And what does it matter now if I once thought I had to defend her? Was it for me to choose between you and Davina? I only knew you'd left me; it was all I could think about, I couldn't bear it."

She turned to look at him, and then he put his arms around her, amazed at how frail she was because her will was so strong. After a moment she touched his face with a tenderness she had practiced in her dreams since the day he was born. "Oh, my darling, I never meant you to know it. I never meant you to know anything about me at all."

Suddenly he was mortally afraid to let her out of his sight a moment before she had to leave him forever. "Come home to Stridings with me," he said, "it's where you belong."

There was an unfathomable look on her face. Then she smiled and he knew what she had been like when she was very young and in love with his father. "Yes," she said, "I will."

"Come and sit down now," he said huskily. "Caro will have me on the carpet for tiring you."

"I'm not in the least tired," she lied. "I shall dance at your wedding." And he believed her. There was nothing she couldn't do.

They crossed the room and sat side by side on the couch. They began to talk and Caro, looking in, left them alone together.